EXTRA ... **ACCLAIM**
FOR ...
CAM ...

"Judd d...
opment. ...
—E...

—*Zane Grey's West*

"An impressive performance . . . a classically simple,
fast-paced tale. Marks Judd as a keen observer of the
human heart as well as a fine action writer."
—*Publishers Weekly* on **Timber Creek**

"Abundance of historical detail . . . a heartfelt attempt
to glimpse the soul of an American hero.
By any standard, Judd succeeds."
—*Booklist* on **Crockett of Tennessee**

**Other two-in-one Westerns from
Cameron Judd**

*Timber Creek
Renegade Lawmen*

*Snow Sky
Corrigan*

Available from St. Martin's Paperbacks

This is a work of fiction. All of the characters, organizations and events portrayed in this novel are either products of the author's imagination or are used fictitiously.

THE QUEST OF BRADY KENTON / KENTON'S CHALLENGE

The Quest of Brady Kenton copyright © 2001 by Cameron Judd.
Kenton's Challenge copyright © 2001 by Cameron Judd.

For information address St. Martin's Press, 175 Fifth Avenue, New York, NY 10010.

ISBN: 0-312-94435-7
EAN: 978-0-312-94435-3

Printed in the United States of America

The Quest of Brady Kenton St. Martin's Paperbacks edition / January 2001

Kenton's Challenge St. Martin's Paperbacks edition / November 2001

St. Martin's Paperbacks are published by St. Martin's Press, 175 Fifth Avenue, New York, NY 10010.

10 9 8 7 6 5 4 3 2 1

THE QUEST OF BRADY KENTON

CAMERON JUDD

St. Martin's Paperbacks

CHAPTER

1

ALEX Gunnison looked out over the crowd gathered before the platform erected in front of the grandiose Tabor Grand Hotel. On his face was a rather ghastly smile, put on for the assembled public and reflecting not at all his true feelings at the moment.

Not a soul smiled back.

Gunnison was seated at rear stage, beside Jack Dunaway, founder and editor of the *Leadville Guardian,* sponsor of this special town-wide celebration of Leadville's growth and heritage.

At front stage, standing at a podium, the mayor of Leadville was droning on in boring fashion, as mayors at podiums are obliged by tradition to do.

Gunnison leaned to the side and whispered to Dunaway.

"Look at them, Jack!" he said. "They hate me! You can see it in their faces!"

"They don't hate you," Dunaway whispered

back. "They just expected Kenton, that's all."

"No. They hate me."

Dunaway studied the group. "Well, if they do, they hate me more, because I'm the one who promised them Kenton—"

"Only to deliver Kenton's subordinate partner instead."

"Uh . . . yes. But when this is over, you at least get to leave. I have to stay and put up with the complaints."

"I'm sorry this has fallen out like it has, Jack. It's inexcusable on Kenton's part."

"Any chance that this is one of Kenton's stunts, and he'll show up at the last moment and surprise us?" Dunaway asked.

"Kenton is in Denver, Jack. He won't be here."

"I know he's your friend, Alex, but I could very nearly kill Kenton for leaving me in the lurch this way. A lot of these people came a long way to see him."

"Oh, don't go killing Kenton," Gunnison said. "That pleasure is to be mine alone."

"He does this kind of thing to you a lot, I hear."

"Not like this. Usually he just vanishes, and I don't know where he is. This time he at least had the decency to tell me he was about to stab me in the back before he sank the blade."

The mayor was at last reaching the end of his speech, so Gunnison began to pay attention. Waving his hand dramatically, the mayor declared, "Ladies and gentlemen, I give you now the editor of the

Guardian, Leadville's newest and, dare I say it, finest newspaper, the sponsoring business behind this special day. Mr. Jack Dunaway, please come to the podium and introduce our guest of the day."

Almost no one clapped as Dunaway, looking ashen, headed for the podium.

Somebody yelled, "Where's Brady Kenton?"

Dunaway, ignoring the shouter, shook the mayor's hand, then gripped the top of the podium.

"My friends," Dunaway said, "we're privileged to have with us today one of the journalists who, a few years ago, redoubled the fame of this town."

"We don't want that one!" a man shouted. "We want Brady Kenton!"

Gunnison, tense in his chair, closed his eyes and wished he were somewhere, anywhere, else.

"Brady Kenton was, unfortunately, unable to fulfill his pledge to be here today," Dunaway said, not fully masking a tone of bitterness. "But we are quite lucky to have his associate, Mr. Alex Gunnison, here in his stead. Mr. Gunnison was here with Kenton during the Briggs Garrett affair, as some of you surely recall. Why, he even found his wife in Leadville—so he's very nearly a Leadvillian himself!"

"Send him away! You promised us Kenton!"

Dunaway feebly raised his hand. "Ladies and gentlemen, Mr. Alex Gunnison!"

Six people, perhaps, applauded. A score actually booed. The rest stood silent. Gunnison rose, the smile on his face as fixed as a dead man's, and advanced to the dreaded podium.

Right now he truly hated Brady Kenton.

*   *   *

When it was finally, mercifully, over and nothing was left but the residual mental anguish, Dunaway very kindly bought Gunnison some supper and a couple of tall beers. Gunnison largely ignored the former and paid devoted attention to the latter. Neither had said more than a handful of words since the conclusion of Gunnison's speech.

"So, how's the wife?" Dunaway asked at length.

"Fine."

"Good. See her much?"

"Not enough. Like always, most of my time is spent away from home, trailing around after Kenton."

"Yeah. Well, I'm glad she's doing well, anyway." And there Dunaway's feeble attempt to start a conversation died pitifully.

After a few minutes of silence and another beer, Gunnison asked, "Did all that go as badly as I think it did?"

"You made history tonight, my friend. You just delivered the worst-received speech in the history of Leadville."

"Do I have the right to be as angry at Kenton as I am?"

"Oh, yeah."

"And was this evening a disaster for you, as its sponsor?"

"Yep." Dunaway drained half a glass of beer at a swallow.

"I'm sorry Kenton ditched you. And that I was so poor a substitute."

Dunaway hammered down his empty mug and wiped foam from his upper lip. "Kenton is a celebrated man. More so, frankly, than I can explain, him being the unreliable scoundrel he obviously is."

"It's his personality. His looks. His skill. People like him the first time they see him. And ever since he published the Gomorrah story, his celebrity is all the greater."

"I admit I've always liked Kenton myself. But not tonight. Tonight I despise him." Dunaway snapped his fingers for another beer. "I'll lose a few subscribers. But I suppose I'll get over the anger in a few days."

"You will. I always do. I've never been able to stay mad at Kenton. And the truth is, even though he's been more annoying than ever lately, I've been too worried about him to stay angry."

"Because of this crazy business about that serial novel?" Dunaway asked.

"Refresh my memory, Jack: how much did I tell you about all that?"

"Well . . . that Kenton has gotten the idea that some serialized novel in *American Popular Library* contains clues about how he can find his dead wife. Correct?"

"Essentially so, yes."

Dunaway's beer arrived. "But that's bizarre. I always heard his wife died years ago in a train accident."

"There is, actually, strong recent evidence that she survived. That doesn't mean she hasn't died since from some other cause, of course."

"But if she wasn't killed, why didn't she return to Kenton?"

"Good question. I can't answer it, and Kenton can't, either. Between you and me, I think he's afraid to find the answer. But he's still devoted to finding her, if that can be done. More than devoted. He's obsessed lately. And it grows worse by the day."

CHAPTER

2

DUNAWAY watched the bubbles in his beer rising and popping.

"How in the world could he have gotten such a strange notion about a novel in a magazine?" he asked.

"The idea was planted in his head by someone else. Do you know William Darian?"

"One of the editors of the *Popular Library,* I think?" The reference was to one of the day's most popular fiction magazines, which published serialized novels in six editions per year. Each edition would keep as many as ten novels running at a time, each one edited to make sure that each novel segment ended with the protagonists in some dreadful or unresolved situation.

"Yes, that's the man."

"I've only heard of him. Never met him."

"He's a fairly levelheaded fellow, apart from

having a drink or two too many sometimes, though Kenton says Darian believes he has that situation hidden. Or I always thought he was levelheaded, until he wrote Kenton and told him this novel might have something to do with Victoria. Maybe Darian drinks more than people think! Anyway, when Kenton heard that, so much for his Leadville obligations. He was off to Denver to meet Darian and I was left to come here in his place to be abused by the rabble."

"Have you read this novel?"

"Only three installments have been published so far. I've read those. I do admit that there are some remarkably coincidental similarities between the details of the novel and those of the actual train crash that involved Victoria and her sister."

Dunaway leaned forward, growing interested now.

"Coincidental, though, as you say. That's the key distinction here, right?"

"Yes, clearly so. There are plenty of train accidents, after all, so it's not all that remarkable that some novelist would create a fictional train-crash scenario that happened to resemble an authentic one somewhere. In fact, perhaps the crash that involved Victoria was used as the model for the one in the novel."

"What's the novel's title?"

"*The Grand Deception.* I can't recall the author's name. Probably a pen name, anyway. I remember that it struck me as sounding like a pen name."

"So Darian is the one we can thank for starting Kenton on this wild-goose chase. All because he happened to serialize some cheap novel."

"That's pretty much it. Except that Darian wasn't the acquiring editor for *The Grand Deception*. Someone else at the magazine is dealing with the author and the manuscript. It has Darian stirred up enough to make him think there was some kind of conspiracy and dark, hidden clues. It surprises me, really. Like I said, I always thought Darian was levelheaded."

"So what does *The Grand Deception* say happened to Victoria's counterpart character?"

"Candice. The noble, abused heroine. In the novel, she survives the crash, with injuries, and is carried away unseen by a physician who also survived the same crash. He'd been on the train, following her, because he'd grown obsessed with her. He takes her away to California, hides her from her family and friends, and allows the idea that she's dead to grow and become accepted. Meanwhile, he's working on healing her and transforming her into his own idealized notion of a lover and mate. That's as far as the story's gone."

"Alex, this is obviously some hack novelist who has read about the accident that involved Victoria, and probably knows about Kenton's quest to find her and all that. He's applied a little imagination and come up with a plot for a melodramatic novel."

"That's what I think, as well. And maybe, if he keeps his head, Kenton will draw the same conclusion. But these days he doesn't keep his head as well as he used to." Alex frowned, hesitated, then ventured into territory he hadn't intended to explore. "I'll tell you something, Jack, between you and me. Kenton is losing his touch very quickly: He's neglecting his work, drinking more again, and devoting himself more to this quest for Victoria than to his professional duties—today being an obvious case in point. He spends much of his time sketching Victoria rather than working. And my father is beginning to notice. In fact, he's come to wonder if Kenton is even worth keeping around anymore. It's been five months since Kenton has turned out a publishable new piece of work, Jack. Did you realize that? The Gomorrah story has been big enough to carry him for a while, but he's ridden that horse about as far as it can carry him. And recently he's missed two assignments, and did such a bad job on a third that the *Illustrated American* opted not to publish the finished product. First time ever that's happened. Kenton's never been rejected by his own employing publication before."

"Wow. How'd he take it?"

"He hardly seemed to care. And that, more than the rejection itself, makes me worry about him. He's letting this Victoria-quest of his take him over. And—for heaven's sake, don't repeat this—my father is very nearly ready to fire him. When he learns that Kenton failed to appear here today . . ."

"Whoa! Wait, wait. I'm mad at Kenton, sure enough, but I don't want to be the cause of him losing his job and his status. Maybe if we don't say anything, word will never reach your father that he failed to show up today."

"Word will get out. Your competing newspapers here will be sure to crow about your failure to deliver the great Kenton. But don't start getting a guilty conscience if something happens to Kenton. If he loses his job, you won't be the cause. Kenton is the one shooting himself in the foot. My father is sympathetic to Kenton wanting to find his wife, but he's tired of paying Kenton and getting no good work back in return."

Jack shook his head sadly and drank deeply from his glass of beer.

A man came by the table and looked sourly at Gunnison. "I was out there for your speech. You ain't no Brady Kenton, young man, and I suggest you no longer try to go filling his shoes. It was quite a disappointment, expecting to see Kenton and having somebody switch the goods at the last second."

Gunnison glared up at the fellow. Astonishing, how some folks would go out of their way to spread insult. "What do you expect me to say to you, sir? If you didn't like my talk, then ask this man here for a refund . . . oh, wait. It was free, wasn't it. So you've got nothing to whine about."

The man grunted bitterly and walked away.

"Sorry about that," Jack Dunaway said. "That's Charlie Lee. Local hardware-store man. Known for his rudeness."

"The world's full of Charlie Lees. Jack, I'm ready to vanish into my hotel room and wait for tomorrow to get here. I'm taking the first train out."

"I'll get your honorarium to you tonight, Alex. Thanks for helping me out today."

"I'll not accept an honorarium. The *Guardian* can pay my expenses here and back and we'll call it even. Kenton let you down, Jack, and I'll not see you pay for being misused. Kenton owes you an apology, and I intend to insist that he provide it to you."

"Are you going to Denver to join Kenton?"

"I don't think so. I think I'll go to my father and try to dissuade him from firing Brady Kenton. And I'm going to see my wife, and spend some time with her . . . and consider whether the time might have come that I need to break my partnership with Kenton. I've followed him around for a lot of years now, Jack. Always in his shadow. Always the one that no one is interested in seeing or hearing. Hang it all, I know I'm a lesser light in the journalistic world than Brady Kenton, but even a lesser light wants the opportunity to shine where it can be seen."

CHAPTER

3

ALEX Gunnison retreated into his hotel room, but not for long. A restlessness overtook him that he could not shake, and soon he took to the streets, walking and winding through the narrow, haphazard avenues of this famed mining town.

He recalled the first time he walked these streets, back in Leadville's less civilized days, when a man had best know how to watch his back, and his wallet, if he expected to survive unscathed.

The town had changed quite a lot since then. The rougher edges were wearing away. It was a town, not a mining camp. Sidewalks had become more uniform, streets better kept, buildings more permanent and beautified. Alex thought wryly, If a town can grow and become better, why can't I? Why am I still hardly any better off than I was the first time I was here?

He tried to argue back at himself. His future, he

told himself, was bright. His father was the owner and publisher of America's most successful general-interest magazine. Eventually he would inherit it all. He'd be a wealthy man, able to work as much or as little as he wished. He could make up many times over all the time he had missed with his wife while he was busy traveling the country with Brady Kenton.

And besides, despite the feelings he'd aired to Dunaway, was working as Kenton's partner really so bad? Many other journalist/illustrators would gladly leap at the opportunity to do what Gunnison did.

Gunnison put all the weights on the balance and let them settle, and came to a realization: he was deeply unhappy with his life, personally and professionally. A shadow hung over him, and nothing he could do could seem to dispel it.

The shadow was Brady Kenton. It was as he'd told Dunaway: as long as he was Kenton's partner, he would never be noticed. He would always be second best, the fill-in speaker rather than the first choice, the tail instead of the head.

He thought: I've got to get away. For my own sake, and for the sake of the family I'd like to have before I get much older.

But could he do it? To no longer be Brady Kenton's partner would change his life dramatically . . . a gain in most ways, but a loss in another. The truth was he was devoted to Kenton, angry as the man often made him.

And he was worried about Kenton. The man had done some strange things in his time, but it wasn't like him to shirk responsibility as he had lately. This running from an obligation firmly made to a friend, Jack Dunaway, was not at all typical of Kenton.

"Mr. Gunnison, sir."

Gunnison was surprised by the proximity of the unseen speaker, slightly behind and to the side of him. He turned quickly.

A smiling, friendly-looking man, tall and lean, was standing in the recessed doorway of a closed lawyer's office. "I'm afraid I startled you, Mr. Gunnison. I do apologize."

"Oh, no apology needed. I was just lost in thought."

The man stepped down from the doorstep and put out a powerful hand for Gunnison to shake. "James Serrals. Farrier, occasional blacksmith, and real estate speculator. Also at one time a prospective journalist and illustrator—it never worked out—and therefore an appreciative reader of the *Illustrated American,* and an admirer of your work. You're quite a talent, young Mr. Gunnison."

"Thank you . . ." Gunnison pumped the powerful hand, confused. He was accustomed to hearing readers talk about Kenton, not himself.

"Kenton's very good, probably the best. But I've taken note of your contributions, and I do believe you'll top him before long."

Gunnison couldn't hold back a smile. This was as refreshing as a drink of cold water on a hot day.

"Thank you indeed. Those are kind words."

"A little difficult, I'd say, having to put up with such a famous partner, when you yourself are very skilled."

"Oh, I consider it an honor to work with Kenton. My day will come. Meanwhile, I try to learn everything I can from him." Gunnison was playing it noble—the overlooked protégé humbly acknowledging the overbearing master.

"Well, you've got a good attitude. By the way, I enjoyed your talk today. Fine job, considering the audience was set on Kenton."

"I appreciate your saying that. It's been a humbling day, quite honestly."

"Be patient. The day will come when they'll be yelling for you, not at you. I've got no doubt about it. Buy you a drink?"

"Thank you, sir."

"Come on. The best watering hole in town is not two blocks from here."

When the warmth of the flattery wore off, Gunnison wondered why a stranger such as Serrals would be so friendly to him. He soon realized that Serrals was simply one of those rare people who were authentically friendly to those they found interesting. Serrals chatted amiably, openly curious about Gunnison's work, about the process of moving from concept to finished product, about the technology of producing and distributing a national publication.

As Gunnison talked, he forgot his resentments

toward Kenton, and even the pain of his earlier miserable public appearance. He ordered a sandwich, which Serrals insisted on paying for, and drank what he promised himself would be the final beer of the day.

He was in the midst of a discussion of recent improvements in printing-press technology when he cut off in mid-sentence, frowning as he looked over Serrals's shoulder.

Serrals, noticing, glanced behind him. "What is it?"

"At that window there . . . there was a woman. Looking in."

"Oh. Do you know her?"

"No . . . but she seemed to know me. She was looking right at me. Very intent. Then she glanced over her shoulder, back down the street, and darted away."

"Well, you did make a public appearance today. Perhaps she wants to meet you." Serrals grinned slyly. "Just keep in mind, Mr. Gunnison, that you are a married man."

"No worry there. I'm a faithful husband. But there was something . . . never mind. She's gone now, anyway." He paused. "She looked very sad. Or afraid. I wonder what made her run?"

"Sorry to say, Leadville still has plenty of rough edges. We've civilized ourselves quite a lot since the last time you were here, but there are still footpads, soiled doves, gangs, and the like. I don't know if you can really have it any different in a mining town, try though you may."

They talked on a while longer, then left the bar and headed for a cafe for coffee and cake, Serrals having declared himself in the mood for a little dessert. The hour grew late; the proprietor announced that closing time was at hand.

Gunnison thanked Serrals for the food and drink, the conversation and company, and took his leave to head for the hotel and his waiting bed. He was exhausted, eager for rest and looking forward to the next day, when he could leave Leadville.

As he walked along, he thought about the woman he'd seen in the window, and looked about for her.

He'd not seen her clearly or long enough to tell much about her. She'd appeared ragged, hair windblown, face somewhat drawn. His impression had been of a woman, not a girl, the age, though, hard to determine. Thirty or so, perhaps. She'd had a shawl over her shoulders, he thought, though this was more a suggestion of his memory than a settled recollection.

It was her look of fear and sadness that stuck with him most clearly. In the brief moment of eye contact he had maintained with her, he'd felt a sense of communication, perhaps of pleading.

She had been looking for him. She had a purpose in looking through that window . . .

He laughed at himself. He was more tired than he'd realized, and had drunk two or three too many beers! One chance glance at a woman through a cafe window, and he was spinning wild tales and fantasies, reading entire volumes into nothing more than a shared glance.

He reached the hotel, collected his key at the desk, and headed up to his room.

CHAPTER

SHE was in the hallway, waiting for him.

He froze when he saw her. She was seated in a chair at the end of the hall, and though she looked frail and pitiful and not at all dangerous, he reflexively reached for his coat pocket and the small pistol hidden there.

She came to her feet, caution in her eyes, lips slightly parted, trembling. Had she been less ragged, less weathered, Gunnison might have thought her attractive. And he might have felt a protective impulse, for clearly this was a woman in great fear.

"My name is Alex Gunnison. May I help you, ma'am?" Gunnison asked cautiously.

"Please, sir, I'm sorry to be bothering you," she said. "I mean you no harm, I assure you."

An English accent! That was a surprise.

"What do you want from me?"

"I saw you speaking today, sir. I came to Leadville because of the big celebration and the speech-making and all. But, sir, the truth is I came to find Mr. Brady Kenton."

Gunnison felt a slight burst of annoyance. Was this yet another case of some pitiful woman getting lovestruck over the handsome and famous Brady Kenton? Gunnison had seen it before. Kenton was too much a gentleman to take advantage of such female devotees—as far as Gunnison knew, any-way—but still it flattered his ego, and Kenton had always found ways to subtly remind Gunnison that it was Brady Kenton the ladies liked to meet, not his younger associate.

"If you were at the meeting today, you should have heard it announced that Brady Kenton isn't here. His plans changed and he didn't show up. I took his place."

"I know, sir. I did hear that, but even so, I was hoping maybe you could direct me as to how I might—"

She pulled back abruptly, as if trying to hide her-self in the shadows around her. Gunnison heard footsteps in the hallway behind him and turned. An-other hotel guest was coming up to his room.

The man glanced at the woman, but broke into a smile as he recognized Gunnison.

"Mr. Gunnison, sir! A pleasure to see you here! I want you to know I enjoyed your talk today . . . quite a good job."

Gunnison was so surprised to receive the eve-ning's second compliment that he wondered if he was being mocked. But the man seemed sincere.

"Thank you, sir. I have the impression, though, that most people hold a very different view of my performance."

"Bosh! It was a fine piece of work. Well, sir, good evening." The man peered into the shadows at the end of the hallway. "And to you, too, ma'am."

He fitted his key into the lock, turned it, entered, and was gone.

Gunnison turned to face her again. "You drew back when that man came up. Did he frighten you?"

"I thought he might be somebody else, sir. That's all. Please, Mr. Gunnison, can you tell me how I might find Mr. Kenton? It's so important that I meet him!"

"Mr. Kenton is in Denver."

"Denver . . . so I've come all the way here for nothing, with him on my heels . . ."

"Is this 'him' you refer to the man you thought had come up the stairs a moment ago?"

"Yes, sir."

"Are you in some sort of danger, ma'am?"

"I am, sir. I can't deny it."

"An estranged or violent husband?"

"Oh, no. No, sir. I'm not married." She withdrew again as someone else mounted the stairs. This new-comer proved to be a woman, heading for the floor above. She passed their level without even looking down the hall at them.

He turned back toward the Englishwoman again.

"Well, perhaps we should find . . . ma'am? Are you all right?"

She had staggered to the side, and would have fallen had she not caught herself against the wall. Her face had gone white as milk.

Gunnison went to her and helped steady her to an upright posture again.

"You're sick, miss?"

"No, no . . . hungry, that's all. I haven't eaten for a couple of days."

"Come with me. I'll find a cafe still open and buy you a meal."

"No, sir, I can't. He might find me there, you see. I know he's here . . . I've seen him this very day, sir. He's looking for me."

"Who are you talking about?"

She nearly fainted again.

This woman needed care. Though conscious of the social impropriety of taking a strange woman into his hotel room, Gunnison decided to place her in his bed for rest and find food to nourish her. And if she wasn't willing to go where food could be had, then he'd bring food to her.

He picked her up.

"Please, sir, you need not . . ."

"Nonsense. You're half-starved and exhausted, and I intend to see you fed. I'll take you to my room and let you rest. And don't worry—I'm a gentleman, and will treat you like a lady, with utter decency. Don't be afraid, and don't argue. You are in need of rest and food."

"Mr. Gunnison, you need not!" The protest, though, was not heartfelt. He knew she was hungry.

As she leaned on his arm, he led her to his door, opened it, and ushered her in. He was grateful that no one else had been in the hall. People loved to talk, and he would hate for some kind of rumor to make its way back to his wife.

"What's your name?" Gunnison asked her. She was lying on the bed, her left arm thrown across her brow. She seemed weak, and Gunnison suspected she was feverish. She'd felt warm against him as he'd helped her into the room.

"I am Rachel Frye," she said.

"From London?"

She looked at him in surprise. Her face was extraordinarily pale. "How did you know?"

"Your accent." Gunnison was secretly proud of his ability to differentiate between accents. He was best at it with Americans, but not bad at it with British folk and Scotsmen, either.

"I am indeed from London, sir." She closed her eyes and moaned involuntarily.

"I think I should bring you a doctor along with your supper," Gunnison said.

"No, sir, please don't. You're doing too much for me already."

"You're ill."

"No, just hungry, and tired. No doctor, please."

"Very well, but if you worsen, I'll not be dissuaded. I'm going now. I'll try not to be long. I'll lock the door from the outside. But you can open the lock just by turning this latch here, see?"

"I'll not open it for anyone, Mr. Gunnison. In case it's him, you see."

"You should be safe here. I'll go on now." He opened the door, paused, and looked back at her a last time. "By the way, why do you want to meet Brady Kenton?"

She had closed her eyes and did not open them as, in a very soft voice, she gave an answer that hit Gunnison like a hammer. "Well, sir, the honest truth is, I need to find him because he is my father."

Two minutes later, Gunnison was standing alone on the street, beside the now empty stage on which he'd made his miserable presentation. He was playing over and over in his mind the stunning thing he'd just heard.

It had astonished him so much that he'd not even replied to her. He'd just gaped at her a couple of moments, then closed and locked the door and walked on out to the street.

Kenton, her father? Impossible! Kenton had been married only to Victoria, and to Gunnison's knowledge had never fathered any children at all. If he had, Kenton would have made no secret of it, nor neglected them. He wasn't the kind to let public sensibilities stand in the way of duty.

Well, she's lying, then, for some self-serving reason, Gunnison thought.

He glanced back up at his window. He saw the

curtain move, as if maybe she had been standing there, looking out. Watching for her phantom pursuer?

Or watching Gunnison himself, maybe, waiting for him to get out of sight so she could rifle through his baggage, take his money and valuables . . .

The whole scenario suddenly fell together. She was simply a clever vagrant who had heard him speak today and had put together a scheme to get herself into his room, and him out of it, so she could rob him.

He'd not stand for it. He'd march back up there and confront her.

He turned back to the door, but stopped before entering, thinking again. If this is all an act on her part, he thought, then she's one of the finest actresses in America.

The fear she'd showed had been no fraud. And her fever had seemed real, too. The accent certainly was authentic, too; he had a good enough ear to know the real thing. Also, the accent didn't mesh well with her claim to be the daughter of an American journalist who, to Gunnison's knowledge, had never set foot in England. So, if she was a fraud, why would she intrude such an ill-fitting piece into the puzzle when she'd already achieved what she wanted: entrance into Gunnison's room?

Maybe she wasn't lying, at least not intentionally. Maybe she was not sane. Such people often wound up on the streets.

Insane . . . that was a frightening thought. Gunnison decided he'd fetch her food, give her a little time to rest, then get her out of his room as quickly as possible. Or, on the alternative, he'd let her stay, but check into a different room himself. Maybe a different hotel.

He turned and headed down the street.

When Gunnison vanished around the next corner, something moved in the darkness of an alley across the street from the hotel. A figure as dark as the shadows themselves stepped out and looked down the street in the direction Gunnison had gone, then up at the same window Gunnison had looked at.

The curtain moved again, as it had when Gunnison was still standing on the street. For a moment, silhouetted in the window's light, she was there.

The curtain fell. The man who had emerged from the alleyway moved forward, quickly, heading for the front door.

He had seen her, but was afraid she had seen him, as well.

He would have to move fast.

CHAPTER

5

ALEX Gunnison walked back up the dark street, bearing a tray and very conscious of the stranger following him.

The sense of déjà vu was strong. He'd been tracked almost like this right down this very street back in '79. Except that time it had been bright daylight, the streets crowded with people.

Now it was dark, the streets as close to empty as Leadville streets ever were. That only made the stalking figure seem all the more threatening.

Come closer, friend, Gunnison thought. Come closer and I'll put this tray into your face with one hand while I go for my pistol with the other.

"Sir, sir, pardon me, sir . . ."

Gunnison ignored the man.

"If you'll just let me ask you something . . ."

Gunnison readied himself to heave the tray. But when he turned, he didn't do it. The man appeared far more pitiful than threatening. He was old, ragged, and clearly had been down on his luck for many years. He approached Gunnison with a manner much like that of a dog that has been kicked ten too many times.

"Is there something I can do for you, sir?" Gunnison asked.

"Well, if you might, sir, I'm nigh starved, and I smelled your food . . ."

Gunnison felt a wave of deep pity. No question here that this man's need was real. It's a sad old world, Gunnison thought. So many people with so little.

"Are you hungry, sir?"

"Mighty hungry, son. I'm sorry to be bothering you . . ."

"Sir, I can't share this food here with you, but . . ."

A few moments later, the man was walking away, bubbling over with thanks, clutching the money Gunnison had given him. Gunnison watched to make sure he headed not for a saloon but for a cafe. He did.

Gunnison grinned and resumed his journey to the hotel.

Sometimes the best feeling a man could have was to help out his fellow man. Gunnison had double cause to feel good tonight, then. He'd helped first a lonely Englishwoman, and now a pitiful old vagrant.

Saint Gunnison. Brady Kenton would be proud.

* * *

He knew something was wrong as soon as he reached the landing on his floor. Pausing, he looked down the hall. It was dark down where his room was, but it looked as if the door might not be fully closed—and he'd left it locked.

Gunnison hesitated, then set the tray down in the hall, quietly, and reached beneath his jacket. No one else was in the hall; there was no noise from his room.

He drew his pistol and advanced slowly toward the door of his room.

It was open, slightly. Gunnison's heart began to hammer quite hard. He edged down the hall, pistol ready, paused near the door, then wheeled around, pushing the door open the rest of the way with his foot, the pistol held level and ready to fire.

She was gone. The bed was empty. He glanced around, used the mirror to see the parts of the room he couldn't see otherwise.

She wasn't hidden under the bed or behind the wardrobe. She had left entirely—and, interestingly, had not taken any of his possessions when she did.

Gunnison holstered his pistol, frowning, concerned.

Why had she fled? Especially considering that she was weak, sick, hungry . . . and food was on its way?

No way to know. Maybe she really was insane and had fled for no good reason. Maybe there really was a man pursuing her, and she'd been found and forced to run.

Gunnison examined the lock and latch. It was undamaged. Nobody had kicked this door open; she had opened it from the inside.

Gunnison went back out to the hallway and picked up the tray of food. He carried it back to the room and set it on the table. Maybe she would return momentarily.

But she didn't return. Gunnison eventually took the tray back outside, onto the street. It didn't take long to find a vagrant; there were plenty of them in Leadville.

"Here you go, friend. Enjoy your meal." The man was devouring the food with the vigor of a starved mongrel as Gunnison went back up to his room. He extinguished the light, undressed, and went to bed, feeling depressed and oddly worried about Rachel Frye, a virtual stranger to him, yet someone who had managed in mere moments to engage his sympathies. He hoped she was all right.

Gunnison fell asleep wondering if she really could be Brady Kenton's daughter.

CHAPTER

6

GUNNISON awakened early the next morning, eager to get up and away from Leadville. He couldn't stop thinking of his home and his wife.

But first there was breakfast to be had. He left the hotel and went toward the nearest restaurant, looking for flapjacks and coffee.

Gunnison was on his second cup when another man entered the cafe. He seemed familiar, but Gunnison couldn't immediately place him.

Ah, yes. It was the man who had spoken to him in the hallway of the hotel, while Rachel shrank back into the shadows. Gunnison smiled and nodded a greeting at him.

To his surprise, the man looked at him coldly and seated himself at his table so his back was turned to Gunnison. Gunnison frowned, sipping his coffee and wondering what he'd done to offend the man. It both troubled and annoyed him.

Gunnison paid his bill and was about to leave, but a burst of resolve came over him. He'd find out just what had caused this stranger to be so unfriendly all at once.

He turned and walked over to the man's table. By now the fellow was busy with ham and eggs, and glanced darkly up at Gunnison only once before focusing his attention on his plate again.

"Pardon me, sir," Gunnison said. "A word, if I may."

The man still didn't look up. "Suit yourself," he said.

"I've always been told that the gentlemanly thing to do is to look at those to whom you're speaking," Gunnison replied.

The man did look up, sharply. "I agree—if both parties in the conversation are gentlemen."

That made Gunnison angry, but more than that, perplexed. "That's quite an unexpected thing to say to a man you spoke to with seemingly the greatest respect only last night."

"That's because at the time I spoke to you, I wasn't aware of certain aspects of your behavior."

"I beg your pardon?"

The man glared at Gunnison. "I make no claim that I'm a candidate for canonization, Mr. Gunnison, but I do see myself as a moral man. One who believes in faithfulness within marriage."

"What are you driving at, sir?"

"Need you ask? You, Mr. Gunnison, are a married man. You said so yourself in your speech—

which, let me say now, I didn't enjoy nearly as much as I told you I did. I was simply trying to be polite to you because you'd been so ill-received and I felt sorry for you."

"I am a married man. And a faithful one."

"Faithful! Keep in mind, sir, that my room was next to yours. I heard the fighting and shouting, you and some female most certainly not your wife, shouting and cursing, going at it like cats and dogs—no doubt having gone at it like rabbits before that. Or perhaps she was a lady and refused you, and that was the reason for the row."

Gunnison could have justly struck the man across the face for those comments, but the content of what was said had caught his attention. "Wait a minute—there was fighting in my room?"

"Why, you know there was! I could hear you right in the middle of it!"

"No, sir. If you heard a man in my room, it wasn't me. If I may, sir, I'd like the opportunity to sit down here and clarify something that you have misperceived, quite honestly, I assume."

"Well, I don't . . . I'm not really sure I . . . oh, suit yourself."

Gunnison pulled back the chair opposite the man and sat down. "There was indeed a woman in my room last night, but not for what most would assume—as you have—were inappropriate reasons. She had come to me in hopes of finding out how to contact Brady Kenton, and I saw that she was hungry and ill. When she nearly fainted, I took her into the room to let her lie down, while I left to buy her food. When I came back, the door to the room had been opened, a couple of things were askew, and she was gone. But I knew nothing of a fight. I swear that to you, before God."

The frowning man fidgeted. "Pardon me for saying so, but your story sounds suspect, Mr. Gunnison, and I'd disbelieve it in most circumstances . . . but I did see that woman at the back of the hallway when I came up, and know that you are telling the truth when you say she seemed ill. In fact, I'd noticed the same woman in the crowd while you spoke. She was very ill at ease, looking around, almost distraught. She seemed to be afraid."

"She was afraid. She told me that there is a man who has been hounding her. She's been fleeing from him here, while trying to find Brady Kenton at the same time. That's her tale, anyway."

"I saw no man giving her any heed when she was listening to you speak."

"I never saw her from the stage. I was too busy suffering the woes of an unwelcome speaker to notice any particular person."

The man paused, thinking, then drew a deep breath and thrust his hand across the table. "Mr. Gunnison, I owe you an apology, and I hope that you'll shake my hand in acceptance of it. My name is Timothy Kempson; I'm a wholesaler of dry-goods supplies, from Cleveland."

Gunnison shook the hand. "I understand your misperception of the situation, Mr. Kempson. If I'd heard what you did, I'd have perceived it the same way. But all that's to the side now. At the moment I'm worried about this poor woman." Gunnison confided to Kempson his suspicion that she was delusional, running from a man who perhaps did not even exist.

"Well, the man I heard in that room, and out in the hallway immediately after, certainly did exist. I assumed it to be you, of course."

"A voice like mine, then? Someone about my age?"

"About your age, perhaps . . . but now that I listen to you more closely, in fact, the voice was quite different. More like her voice, in its way of speaking, anyway."

"An English accent, you mean, like hers?"

"Oh, is that it? Yes! I detected she had an odd way of speaking, but couldn't account for it exactly." Kempson actually blushed. "The truth is, Mr. Gunnison, I'm not a much traveled man. This Leadville trip is the first time I've been out of Cleveland in fifteen years. I'm embarrassed to tell you that I'd never heard an English accent before. Never met an Englishman or Englishwoman in my life, or if I did, I didn't know it."

"Did the man you heard have an accent just like hers, then?"

"Well, with the yelling and all, it's hard to tell much about accents . . . but yes. I'd say it was the same accent."

"Interesting," Gunnison said. "Then her phantom

pursuer—if that's who he was—is probably also from England."

"I wonder where she is now?" Kempson said. "She seemed to be very upset, to say the least. Lord, I feel a fool for making such a foul accusation against you. I can generally tell when a man is telling the truth and simply making excuses—and you're telling the truth."

"Yes, I am. And I wonder what became of her, too."

"Did she ever say who is after her?"

"No. I had little opportunity to have much conversation with her. When I came back and found her gone, I assumed she'd simply left. There were a couple of things knocked over, but I didn't consider the possibility of a fight. The door had been opened, not kicked in, and I'd left it locked. Why would she have opened it to a man she was scared to death of?"

"Maybe she thought it was you, returning with food."

"Maybe . . . or maybe she had detected he was coming, and had opened the door to let herself out so she could run. I did think I saw her looking out the window after I went out onto the street. Maybe she saw him out there, too, and decided to run, but got cut off by him in the hall before she could get out of the building."

"All I know is, there was a man and a woman, screeching and yelling and cursing at each other in the doorway and then in the hall. Well, the man was doing all the cursing."

"Might he have carried her off? Or did she get away from him?"

Kempson recollected a couple of moments. "Couldn't tell for sure . . . but it seems to me they both left on foot, running, her ahead of him. He could have caught her."

"You didn't look to see?"

"Yes, but it happened fast. By the time I got my head out the door, they were gone. A couple of others on the floor also took a look, but they were even later at it than me."

Gunnison felt quite disturbed. Maybe he, like Kempson, has misperceived a few things. Maybe Rachel Frye was neither criminal nor insane. Her male antagonist certainly didn't appear to be imaginary.

Maybe her claim to be Brady Kenton's daughter wasn't a figment, either.

"Mr. Kempson, sir, thank you for your information," Gunnison said, standing. "I intend to thank you by paying for your breakfast."

"Why, sir, there's no need for—"

But Gunnison was already at the counter, laying out money. He gave Kempson a wave and final nod, and headed out the door and back to the hotel.

CHAPTER

7

THE clerk was a different fellow than the one on duty during the night, and knew nothing. And no, the night clerk there before him hadn't seen any kind of chase. If he had, he'd have been talking about it when he left this morning, Gunnison was assured. The night clerk was like that—the kind to talk. Most likely, if anything of the sort had happened, the night clerk had been asleep on the job and missed it. He was like that, too—the kind to sleep on the job.

Gunnison had every intention of questioning each person who had been lodged on his floor the night before, but to his misfortune, all but one—an overweight woman of society with a snobbish attitude—had checked out.

He tried to question the woman about the ruckus of the night before, but she claimed to know nothing of it. Gunnison sensed two things: she had indeed heard it despite what she said today, and she, like Kempson initially, blamed him for it, assuming he was the male involved. Unlike Kempson, she was not willing to be persuaded otherwise.

Gunnison was left in a quandary. He'd been eager to abandon Leadville, but now he felt he couldn't. A woman might be in danger . . . a woman who claimed to be Brady Kenton's daughter.

It didn't seem a likely claim, but what if . . . what if?

Gunnison sat down on a chair on the porch and thought things over. He could put this behind him, go ahead and leave. He could remain in Leadville and try to find out what happened to Rachel Frye. Or he could take the best of both options, tell the local law about what had happened, and leave the matter of Rachel Frye and her phantom antagonist in hands other than his own.

The latter was the most appealing idea, because it let him shift the responsibility for Rachel Frye's welfare, thereby assuaging some of his guilty feelings over abandoning this town while she might be in trouble. Not all the guilty feelings, though. The vague chance that she really could be Kenton's daughter made Rachel Frye much more than one more troubled woman in one more western town.

Gunnison headed out to find a policeman.

The search took him in memory back to an earlier Leadville policeman he'd known. Old Clance Sullivan! He'd never known a fellow more thoroughly Irish. The memory of Sullivan and the adventure Gunnison and Kenton had shared in this sky-level town brought an unexpected burst of sentimentality to Gunnison . . . and a new round of worry about Brady Kenton and his recent personal deterioration.

Gunnison's earlier irritation with Kenton was beginning to fall away, though he hardly noticed.

Gunnison walked for ten minutes and saw no sign of a policeman. He wryly began to consider committing a public crime in hopes of drawing one out.

Tired of depending on chance, he headed for a nearby apothecary shop to ask where the nearest outpost of the town law might be.

The shop was cool, shadowy, pleasant, and was filled with the fragrance of coffee brewing on a little stove in the back. Gunnison paused simply to enjoy the place for a moment, then looked around for a clerk.

"Hello? Anybody here?"

No reply. He walked farther inside. "Looking for a clerk! Anyone around?"

A door into a back office and storage area stood open, and through it Gunnison saw another open door, leading to the area behind the store. He could see as well the corner of a privy. That explained it. The clerk had vacated the store momentarily for an outhouse visit.

Gunnison quickly moved through the office and out the back door. He loitered about the back lot, waiting for the man to emerge from the outhouse.

After a few minutes went by, he began to doubt the man was in the outhouse at all. He went to the outhouse door, knocked tentatively, and received no answer. He opened the door. Empty.

Why would anyone simply abandon an open store in midday, not even bothering to close the doors or hang a sign?

Gunnison's curiosity was mildly aroused, but this wasn't a matter that concerned him. He turned to head back up the alley to the street and continue his search for a policeman, but just as he did, someone called to him.

"Hello, sir!" a man's voice said. Gunnison saw a hefty fellow, very out of breath and sweaty, plodding toward him from behind the next store building. "Sorry . . . if you were looking for . . . me . . . in the store. Whew! I'm plain ole wore out! Not used . . . to running."

Gunnison eyed the man's red and dripping face. "Are you all right, sir?"

"Fine . . . fine. Just tired. Too fat, I am. My wife tells me . . . all the time I'm too fat . . . for my own good, and she's likely right. Certainly I'm too fat . . . to be chasing down a wife-beater . . . like I have been."

"A wife-beater?"

"Yeah, yeah . . . poor old gal! The old boy seemed to want to pound the very life out of her! I heard them out here in the back, and stuck my head out to see what the commotion was." The man paused a couple of moments to catch his breath.

"There they were, the woman cringing and the man with a big old stick in his hand. Now, I know there are them who say that a wife is a man's possession and that he has the right to discipline what's his, but I reckon I'm a little different in my thinking. I don't believe in beating your wife, no sir."

"Neither do I," Gunnison replied. "But how do you know it was his wife?"

"Well . . . I guess I don't. I just assumed it was."

"What did this woman look like?"

"Slender, sandy-haired, maybe thirty years old . . . hard to say how old she was. She looked like she'd been around the mill a few times, if you know what I mean."

"Did you hear her speak?"

"Heard her screech. Why are you asking?"

"I might know who it is . . . but if so, then she'd have a British accent."

"I don't think there are accents when it comes to screeching."

"What about the man? Did he have an accent?"

"He never said a word, other than calling me a damned fool for interfering. He might have talked with an accent, but I really couldn't say. It's hard to tell when somebody's shouting."

"Well, then, what color was the woman's dress?"

"Blue, I think. Yes, blue. Kind of on the lighter side."

Gunnison nodded. Rachel Frye's dirty and ragged dress had been light blue. "Did she get away from the man?"

"I think so . . . to be truthful, I couldn't tell for sure. She went one way and he went another. But after I left, I suppose he could have chased her down again. By that point I'd done all I could and came back here."

"Tell me where you saw them last."

"You aren't going looking for them, are you?"

"I am. Please tell me! It's important."

The man explained as best he could to a nonresident how to find the place where he'd finally abandoned his chase. Gunnison thanked him and headed off in that direction as fast as he could go.

But as he did, Gunnison wondered why he was doing this.

Although really he knew why: the idea of standing by while a woman was abused was something he would not tolerate. Especially one he knew, at least a little.

Even though Rachel had merely whisked in and out of his life like a cloud of dust on a breeze, he felt he knew her to some measure, and that she was therefore to a degree his special responsibility.

If some scoundrel was hurting Rachel, he'd have Alex Gunnison to face because of it.

He soon found the area the shopkeeper had described, and realized he'd been here during his previous Leadville sojourn. Not far from here had stood a billiard parlor that had burned. The area had changed a lot, but still had enough of its old landmarks to help him get his bearings.

But he didn't see Rachel or her pursuer. Probably they'd gone a long way from here by now. He hoped she'd gotten away from him.

Gunnison stood there helpless and out of breath. He looked all around, wondering where she had gone, then sighed and knew he had to give up.

He headed for the street, frustrated in his helplessness. He couldn't explain the mystery of Rachel Frye, but he instinctively felt a deep sympathy for her. He hoped it hadn't been she the shopkeeper saw being beaten. He hoped she escaped whoever was pursuing her.

Gunnison stopped, turning. He'd heard something . . .

It was unmistakable. A woman's outcries, a man's grunted curses, the sound of something brutally thudding on flesh . . .

Gunnison ran back the way he'd come, leaped a fence, dodged around an outbuilding, avoided the bite of a frightened dog whose sleep he interrupted by stepping on its tail, then vaulted another fence.

There she was in a little empty, weedy grove along a back street, kneeling with her arms over her head to protect herself from the blows being rained down upon her by a burly, dark-bearded man with a stick in his hand. He cursed her with each blow, and she let out cries of terror and pain at every impact.

CHAPTER

8

GUNNISON, furious, leaped straight at the man from behind. He bowled him over hard, landing atop him. The fellow was too surprised to fight back, and lost his grip on the stick he'd been using as a club.

Gunnison balled up his fists and began pounding the man around the head and neck, striking hard, irrational in his fury. It was the first time Gunnison had ever seen a woman being struck so brutally, and it stirred up an animalistic hunger for vengeance. He intended to beat this man until he was either dead or wishing he was.

Rachel began wailing and screaming; the sound simply drove Gunnison all the harder. Then he realized there was something odd about it, and turned just in time to see her coming at him with the same stick the man had lost . . .

It wasn't Rachel.

This woman was a stranger. Similar to Rachel in

height, build, and hair color, but with a face revealing many more years than Rachel's, and with an accent that was more southern Georgia than Britain.

In the wake of that surprise, an even bigger one presented itself. The woman began to hit Gunnison around the shoulders with the stick.

"Don't you hit my Freddie!" she screamed, her voice harsh. "You leave my Freddie alone!"

Gunnison couldn't believe it. He ceased his own attack and shifted to defense, throwing up his arms much as the woman herself had been doing only a minute before.

"Quit that!" he shouted at her. "What are you doing? I'm helping you, can't you see?"

"Don't you beat my Freddie!" she yelled again. "He's my sweet husband, my sweet husband!"

Gunnison fell off the man, literally pounded off him by the woman. The man helped, too, giving a big upward shove that bucked Gunnison off like he was a horseman on a wild mare.

As he hit the ground, Gunnison knew he was in trouble. He'd made a dreadful mistake, and it would cost him. This was obviously one of those couples who hate and abuse one another, but despite all the pain they generate will abide no outside interference in their private war.

The woman caught Gunnison a hard blow across the temple, stunning him. Gunnison fell to one side. The man kicked him, driving him the rest of the way down.

Stars exploded somewhere deep in Gunnison's skull. His vision went black, white, black, then dissolved into a sea of swirling colors. Another blow struck his head, jolting him farther toward senselessness, but leaving him still with just enough awareness to marvel that a woman he'd possibly saved from being beaten to death was now seemingly trying to inflict that avoided fate upon her very rescuer.

He felt a big hand dig under his jacket . . . no, no . . . the man was taking Gunnison's own pistol! And Gunnison was losing consciousness and couldn't stop him.

As Gunnison seemed to be turning and twisting into a deep pool of darkness, he found the strength to pray that he would not meet his end like this, shot to death in a Leadville back lot with a pistol stolen off his very person.

He collapsed facedown, eyes closing, the end surely near . . .

He was almost unconscious when he heard the blast of the gunshot, deafeningly loud.

Gunnison woke up on a bed, staring at an unfamiliar ceiling while two equally unfamiliar male figures loomed at his bedside. "Hello, young fellow," the smaller and older of the two said to him. "My name is Dr. Silas Jackson. You're in my office, and, I'm glad to say, still among the living."

Gunnison thought hard . . . it was difficult to do so with a brain still groggy. "I was . . . shot."

"You surely almost was," the second figure said, and as soon as he heard the voice say those four words, Gunnison was transported straight to Texas. The accent was Texan, top to bottom.

So was the man's look. Gunnison took in a lean, sun-browned face, whiskered; a pair of piercing black eyes beneath thick brows; a firm chin; and trail clothing that managed to hang neatly on his lean and muscular frame despite being rumpled and somewhat dirty. His hat, a rich brown that was not far from black, was still on his head and was the only fully clean item of clothing on him. Almost as meticulously kept was the leather gunbelt strapped around his waist, though Gunnison could see only a little of this because of the long black linen duster the man wore.

"The name's Best. Jessup Best. Former Texas Ranger, now a detective for private hire." Best put out his hand for Gunnison to shake, and Gunnison managed despite feeling very weak and sore. "Your name is Gunnison, I think."

"That's right."

"I seen you on the stage, talking."

"You should have had mercy—shot me then."

Best threw back his head and laughed heartily. "A man who can keep his humor about him even after being pounded on the noggin by a madwoman and the man who loves to beat her is a man I can admire. You from Texas, Mr. Gunnison?"

"No. Missouri."

"Oh, well. Can't win them all. Your partner Kenton is a Texas boy, ain't he?"

"That's right."

"I come to Leadville because of Kenton."

"So did a lot of people. And quite a few of them booed me when they found out Kenton wasn't here."

"Well, I had reason beyond just wanting to hear him speak to find Mr. Kenton." Best shifted his hat back on his head a little and turned to the doctor. "Doc, reckon me and Mr. Gunnison could have a private moment here? I need to talk to him a bit about some things best kept just between the two of us. No offense intended."

"No offense taken," the doctor said. "I've got rounds to make anyway. Just leave him lying down for now. I don't know how bad a head blow he took. Sometimes the effects take a while to show themselves."

The doctor exited, heading out the door and onto the street, taking his black bag with him.

Best sat down on a tall stool beside Gunnison's bed.

"Need to talk to you, sir. Tell you a few things and ask you a few questions, too."

"I've got one for you first. How is it I don't appear shot, when I heard the pistol going off?"

"That was my pistol you heard, sir. I heard the fighting and came upon the scene in time to see that sorry son of a gun just about to pop a cap right into your head with what I think was your own pistol. I drew and shot before he could. He took the slug through the arm. He'll get to keep his arm, but suffice it to say he won't be beating his woman with it for a few months."

"If you'd shot it completely off, I'd have no objections."

"Shot his head off would have been best. The world don't need the likes of him. There's laws about such things as murder though, so I let him live."

Best had a twinkle in his eye and an ever-present lightness of manner that Gunnison liked. Best was a man confident in himself, his perceptions, and his ability to handle what they told him, and it showed.

Gunnison found himself reminded of Kenton both because of Best's confidence and the Texan accent. Kenton had never lost his own drawl, no matter how far he'd traveled or how many governors and presidents he'd dined with.

But now Best grew somewhat more serious. "I told you I came here because of Kenton. But it ain't what you're probably thinking. I came because I knew Kenton being here would be likely to draw a certain somebody here . . . somebody I've been chasing now for quite a good while, under private hire."

"Who would that be?"

"Depends on what name she's using at any given time."

She? "Would the name she's using at the moment by any chance be Rachel Frye?"

"It would, Mr. Gunnison. It would. I take it you've run across her?"

"Yes. She came to my hotel room, looking for Kenton. And she said there was a man pursuing her."

"That would be me."

"If so, then I can tell you she's very terrified of you, sir, and talks about you like you're the devil himself."

"I don't doubt it. To her I am a devil. Because if I catch her, she'll wind up back in Texas facing a devil of a penalty for a devil of a crime."

"What crime?"

"Murder, Mr. Gunnison. The foulest and bloodiest murder seen in Texas for many a year."

CHAPTER

9

GUNNISON felt the hackles on the back of his neck rise. "Who did she murder?"

"The family who hired her as a maid. Fine people, finc as could be, name of Rawlings. They took in a poor little orphaned English girl, hired her, gave her boarding and food, made her like one of their own family. But one thing they didn't know about this gal: she'd come from her native land because she was fleeing the charge of murder. Murder of her own parents. Then, once here, she did it again. Murdered the Rawlings family, husband and wife and daughter. Cleaned out as much as she could in cash and jewels and fled."

"Are you sure? She didn't strike me as the kind to do something so wicked."

"Can't really judge folks that way, Mr. Gunnison. If there's one thing I've learned, both as a Ranger and after, it's that you can't tell from looking on the outside what there is down on the inside of a man . . . or a woman."

"You're no longer a Ranger . . . so you're chasing her as a hired gun, basically?"

" 'Hired gun'—don't know if I like that term. I'm not planning to shoot anybody, unless I have to."

"Just a way of speaking."

"The answer is yes, I'm hired. Relatives of the slain."

Gunnison was thinking. "How did you happen to be close by just when I was about to be shot?"

"I'd been following you. Figuring you'd be a lure for our lady friend."

"Why?"

"Because I know she came to Leadville looking for Brady Kenton. With Kenton winding up not being here, it made sense she would go to see you instead, to try and find out how to get to him."

"Mr. Best, someone came after Rachel Frye while she was in my hotel room. I was gone to find her food. There was a row of some kind. I had told that the man who fought with her had an English accent."

"It's no surprise. There's people of all kinds in Leadville."

"But if you are the man who has been chasing her, who would the Englishman who came up to my room have been?"

Best shrugged. "I can't say. If I had to guess, I'd peg it as someone who saw you leave your room and decided to take advantage of your absence to rob you. He probably didn't know he would find someone still in the room. And I can imagine how she would have reacted . . . she's a violent woman. Quite honestly, Mr. Gunnison, if she was in your room, you're lucky to not have been hurt, or worse, by her. It may be for the best that that intruder showed up and ran her off."

Gunnison thought that over. "She told me something very strange . . ."

"I can guess. She told you that Brady Kenton is her father."

"How did you know?"

"Because Rachel Bryan Smith Harrington Bailey Frye Jackson . . . I can't remember all the other names she's used . . . has claimed to be the daughter of everybody from Robert E. Lee to the man in the moon. Hell, she'd have claimed to be your daughter if you'd been a little older. But mostly she's claimed to be the daughter of Brady Kenton. And the purely queerish thing is, I think she believes it." Best pointed at his temple and made circles with his finger. "The woman is loco. And dangerous. And I intend to find her. Any notion as to where she is now?"

"No. But I thought that was her today, being attacked."

"No! Did you?"

"It was part of the reason I was so fast to jump in and try to help her."

"You believed she was being attacked by the

mysterious man who's been trailing her."

"That's right."

Best laughed again. "And it turned out to be nothing but a couple of married folks who make a habit of beating up on each other!"

Gunnison smiled, though it didn't seem that funny to him. It wasn't Best who'd almost had his head blown off with his own pistol. But he couldn't fault Best, whose fortuitous arrival, and quick gunman's skill, had probably saved his life.

"So about Kenton being her father . . . there's no chance of it being true?"

"Oh, no. Just a tale she tells. It opens doors for you if people think your father is somebody famous. But I do think she believes it's true when she says it. Where is Kenton?"

"Denver. Visiting an editor for the *American Popular Library.*"

"But she doesn't know that?"

"She knows he's in Denver. I told her that much." He wished now that he hadn't.

Best nodded, more serious again. "That's good information for me to have."

"You think she'll go looking for him there?"

"She might."

"Would she be dangerous to him?"

"She could be."

"Has she threatened him?"

"Not directly . . . but look at what she did in England, and in Texas. She's got murder in her soul, that woman does."

"I've got to warn Kenton," Gunnison said. "No . . . I've got to go join him, so I can watch for her. Kenton is approached by a lot of people . . . he wouldn't know her from anyone else, but I would." He started to sit up, but a sudden burst of wooziness made him halt.

"Whoa, partner," Best said. "I don't believe you're up to running around just yet. A blow to the noggin takes some getting over. The doc told me you might be laid up for a time."

Gunnison groaned and lay back down. This was unbelievable. If only he'd simply gotten up this morning, minded his own business, left the hotel, and let Rachel Frye go her own way! He'd not be lying here helpless with a throbbing head.

On the other hand, had he not gone looking for her, he'd not have met Best, either, and learned the truth about the woman.

"What will you do, Mr. Best?" Gunnison asked with eyes closed. "Go to Denver to find her?"

"Unless I find evidence she has remained here or gone elsewhere, that's the likely bet," Best drawled.

Gunnison opened his eyes and looked at Best. "How long has she been following Kenton?"

He cocked a brow, thinking. "I don't know exactly. I only learned in the last two, three months about her starting to claim to be his daughter. That was no grand thing, because she's made the same claim regarding several other celebrated types, but when I began to hear from folks who'd seen her that she'd been talking about trying to find Kenton, then I realized that a good thing had come about. All I had to do was track Brady Kenton, and she was bound to show up sooner or later."

"Why hasn't she been able to connect with Kenton already?"

"Why, Mr. Gunnison, you know better than anybody how busy he is. He moves around a lot, but mostly where he goes ain't known to the general public in advance. That was what made this scheduled appearance of his in Leadville so important: it was one of the few times people could know in advance where Kenton was going to show up. When I heard about it I knew she'd probably show up here—which she did, though Kenton didn't."

"She's probably still in town," Gunnison said. "There's been no train out, I don't think, since yesterday afternoon."

"There's no assurance she'd ride the train, but quite likely you're right. Her only other options besides stowing away in a freight car are walking or persuading somebody who's going to Denver to take her with them. If the former, she ain't gone far, and the latter ain't likely."

"So you may still be able to catch her right here in Leadville."

"I hope I can. That would be best for me, and for Kenton, too. We'd get her out of the way before she could go bothering or threatening him."

"It's still nearly impossible for me to imagine her doing what you say she did."

"Believe me, sir, she did it. You don't know

about that woman like I've come to know about her, following her across the country, talking to those she's talked to, and so on. She's a great deceiver, for certain."

A great deceiver. The phrase made Gunnison think of the title of the serial novel that had diverted Kenton to Denver. *"The Grand Deception,"* he muttered under his breath.

"What did you say?" Best asked.

"Oh, nothing. Just the name of a story. What you said made me think of it."

Best chuckled. "Name of a story. All righty." He stood and touched the brim of his hat, nodding. In typical Texan style, he'd kept the big hat on his head throughout the whole conversation. "I'll be leaving you now, Mr. Gunnison. I hope you recover nicely from getting beat up. By the way, your pistol and other things are stored for you in that box there in the corner."

"Thank you."

"The doc will be back in soon, I'm sure. Meantime, I think I'll go see if I can't find our fugitive woman. Wish me luck."

"I do."

"Take care of yourself, Mr. Gunnison."

"You do the same, Mr. Best."

CHAPTER

10

DENVER, COLORADO

AFTER the train came to a halt with a screech of brakes and bursts of steam, Gunnison stood, picking up his bag from the other seat. He realized he'd risen too quickly when a wave of instability made him almost stagger to the side, out into the aisle.

He steadied himself and took a deep breath. He had to remember that it was going to take a while to get over the head blow he'd received. The doctor had warned him that he'd go through a lot of dizziness and even some disorientation for a few days. The doctor, in fact, had been strongly against him leaving Leadville so quickly.

And Gunnison wouldn't have done so if not for the arrival of a very unexpected telegram. It had come from William Darian of the *American Popular Library,* sent in care of the Tabor Grand Hotel.

What it said had been short, direct, and enough to make Gunnison get back on his feet right away, no matter what the doctor advised, and catch the first train toward Denver.

COME AT ONCE WORRIED ABOUT KENTON
YOUR HELP NEEDED.

What could be so wrong with Kenton that Darian, who didn't know Gunnison all that well, would wire Gunnison? Was Kenton sick? Injured?

The train journey had seemed to last forever, increasing Gunnison's restless feeling and giving him lots of time to weave terrible scenarios about what might have happened to Kenton. He hardly noticed that now that Kenton was in trouble of some sort, he'd lost all desire to separate himself from him. All that mattered now was to find him and provide whatever help he needed. Now, with his bag swinging at his side, Gunnison was walking through Union Depot, dodging side to side in the crowd. Outside, he hailed a cab.

"The offices of the *American Popular Library*, on Broadway," Gunnison said to the cabby as he settled into the comfortable seat.

"I know the place," the cabby replied, clicking his tongue and snapping the leads. The horse trotted off, horseshoes clattering on the pavement.

Gunnison tried to forget his worries for the duration of the ride. He'd always loved Denver, considering it one of the most beautiful, healthful, and generally pleasant cities he'd ever visited.

He'd first visited Denver back in the seventies. At the time, it was a city trying hard to rebound from the difficult year of '73, and soon to face the "grasshopper years" of '75 and '76, when crops would be wiped out throughout Colorado and the economy would suffer greatly.

Those hard days were long past now. The city, populated by about 75,000 people, was a metropolis of the West, full of fine houses and thriving businesses, and watered by a series of irrigation channels that ran water pumped from the Platte all through the city. Cottonwoods and maples shaded lush yards; large gardens planted in sunny lots provided vegetables in abundance for the city's families, and every corner and porchside flower bed was abloom with color. Gunnison found himself fantasizing about someday bringing his wife, and the horde of children they still hoped to have, here to live in this city a mile above the level of the distant ocean.

The cab pulled to the curb directly outside the building whose lower and second levels housed the offices of the *American Popular Library*. Gunnison hopped out of the cab, paid the driver, and with bag in hand headed for the door.

It opened before he reached it, and William Darian, a somewhat plump and bookish-looking man with that distinctive slight bloat that comes of too much liquor, came out with hand extended and reading spectacles propped up on his high forehead.

Darian's receding hairline provided him with increasing expanses of brow every time Gunnison saw him.

"Alex, thank you so much for coming," Darian said, talking fast and seeming nervous. "I've felt just terribly about the turn Kenton has taken . . . I'm afraid it's my fault. I suppose the things I showed him must have pushed him over the edge."

"What's happened, William?"

"Come up to my office and I'll tell you."

"Is Kenton hurt?"

"No . . . hurting himself, though. Hurting himself. And it's surely my fault. But what else could I have done?"

Gunnison knew then what it was. Intuition and a thorough knowledge of Kenton's ways spoke to him in a single voice.

Kenton was drinking hard again. That was what Darian would tell him. Ironic that the news would come from a man whose own drinking Kenton himself had commented upon. Kenton had had drinking problems from time to time through the years, usually during times when he was brooding about his lost Victoria.

Gunnison followed Darian through a maze of halls, into a large room filled with rows of desks, then up two staircases into a new hallway, off which opened a short passage that led to a suite of three offices, the central one being Darian's.

A large three-sectioned window with an arched top afforded an excellent view of the busy street below, and far beyond, snow-capped mountains. Darian, accustomed to the scene and distracted by his worries, paid it no attention, but Gunnison was for a few moments fully captivated.

Denver for him and his family, one day. He vowed it to himself on the spot.

"Alex, I didn't know I would cause a problem. I only wanted to tell Kenton about what might be a clue to the mystery regarding his wife."

"This serial novel, you mean."

Darian was fumbling with a cigar he'd taken from his desk. "Yes. *The Grand Deception*, written by someone under the name of Horatio Brady. As soon as I read the opening chapters, I knew there was something very unusual here. Very unusual, indeed."

"An apparent connection to the disappearance of Victoria."

"Yes. Virtually an identical description of the incident, including the central female character vanishing from the scene, and a description of how it came about." Darian lit the cigar, a cheap one with a strong smell. He tossed the match aside; it landed, still flaming, on a piece of paper, which caught fire. Darian noticed it a moment later, slapped the fire out and brushed the paper onto the floor.

"What scenario does the novel present?"

"If you haven't read it for yourself, you should. The impact of the similarities will strike harder that way. To sum it up, though, in the novel, the character named Candice—Victoria's seeming counterpart—is injured in the train crash and carried away from the scene by a doctor who was on the same train—on the train because of her."

"In love with her, you see. Obsessed with her even though she is married to another man . . . who happens to be a writer, I should note." Darian flipped ashes at the laden ashtray. They all missed, but several sparks landed on scrap paper and burned holes in the papers before flashing out cold. Gunnison was a little taken aback. Darian with a lighted cigar, in a roomful of papers, was a dangerous fellow.

"It could be coincidental . . . or it could be that the story was inspired by Victoria's disappearance, but with the details supplied by the writer's imagination."

"That's very true, and something I've thought of from the outset. But there are times a man must listen to his instincts, Alex. And mine told me that there was something in that novel, something below the surface. So I contacted Kenton . . ."

"Just in time to cause Kenton to abandon his obligation to speak in Leadville, and leave me to fill in. It was a most unpopular choice among most of my listeners, I should note."

"I'm sorry. Also sorry that it cost Kenton as much as it has."

"What do you mean?"

"Alex, Kenton has been suspended by the *Illustrated American*."

CHAPTER

11

"SUSPENDED . . ."

"Yes. Your father sent him word by telegraph. Kenton is on a month's suspension, without pay. During that time he is to rewrite two stories that the *Illustrated American* has rejected. If he fails, or if he has any further problems in terms of performance, or any public difficulty of any kind, he'll be dismissed permanently, and publicly. Kenton read the telegram out loud to me. Didn't try to hide it at all."

"But how did my father learn that Kenton didn't make his Leadville appearance?"

"There were complaints wired from Leadville by some unhappy townsfolk, and others who had come a long way to hear Kenton speak."

Gunnison, stunned, stared silently at another hot cigar ash burning out on another wad of scrap paper. It didn't catch, but almost did.

Darian was berating himself. "If only I'd waited a little longer before telling Kenton about *The Grand Deception*. He would have made his Leadville appearance and all would be well."

"Not necessarily, William. What's happened to Kenton has been building up for some time. I knew that eventually my father would get around to imposing some discipline on him. Kenton has been performing very poorly lately—it's becoming a pattern. Even if he'd followed through at Leadville, Kenton would only have turned around and gotten himself into some other kind of trouble later on." Gunnison sighed. "So that's the problem with Kenton, then. I was on pins and needles all the way here, wondering. To be honest, I'm a little relieved. I'd dreamed up worse things that could have happened to him."

"It's not the only problem," Darian said. "His reaction to it was . . . bad."

"He's drinking again."

"That's right. He's rented a room in one of the worst parts of town and is going to seed there by himself."

Gunnison felt a knot in his stomach. Poor Kenton!

"What about the *Deception* novel? Does he believe what you told him?"

"It was hard to judge . . . but yes, I think so. When he read it, sitting right where you are, he went pale. I've never seen him do that. He took a pencil, started making notes in the margins, underlining portions . . . Here, I've still got it. It was odd. He just rose all at once, tossed it aside, and walked out. He didn't come back for a couple of hours, and by then the telegram from your father had arrived. He read it—laughed, believe it or not—left, and never asked for the copy of the magazine he'd marked up."

"May I see it?"

The magazine was in a wooden file cabinet. Darian didn't even have to dig for it.

Gunnison flipped through it until he found the beginning of *The Grand Deception*. There was nothing unusual about the presentation—the standard dramatic etching and stylized typography on the title and opening initial.

Gunnison looked at the markings Kenton had made. He'd underlined several lines describing the train crash, added a couple of exclamation marks in the margins at certain points that apparently struck him as significant, and in one place triple-underscored and circled a couple of sentences, adding three exclamation points beside them. Also one word in the margin: "Kevington." Exclamation marks after it.

Gunnison frowned. "Did Kenton happen to say who this Kevington is?"

"No. He said nothing, really. Just seemed very intense, very disturbed."

"Kevington . . . I can't recall I've ever heard Kenton say that name."

"Notice something, Alex: he's written it beside a paragraph in which the name of the kidnapping physician character is mentioned."

"You're right. 'Dr. Lanval.' So, could he be saying that this Kevington fellow is Dr. Lanval's real-life counterpart?"

"I have no idea." Gunnison stood. "William, are you free to leave at the moment?"

"Yes."

"Let's go to a restaurant somewhere. I'm starved. And I want to read this story, and learn everything I can from you before I go and find Kenton."

It was definitely not one of Denver's finer buildings.

Gunnison stood on a rough boardwalk, looking up at the ugly edifice of poorly painted lumber and wondered if he could possibly be at the right place. He rechecked the note Darian had scribbled out in the restaurant. Yes, this was it.

The door opened and a man staggered out, drunk, covered in his own dried vomit, and not seeming to care. He stumbled past Gunnison, reeking, mumbling under his breath. A window above opened and a harpylike woman leaned out, screeching at the departing man, waving her fist. The man staggered on, not looking back, reacting to her only by lifting his arm and waving dismissively.

Gunnison braced himself and headed for the door. Kenton supposedly was on the third floor of this sorry place. He walked in and mounted the creaking stairs, hoping the place wouldn't happen to catch fire while he was in it. This place would be a tinderbox, with no way out but to leap from a window.

Room 302. Gunnison checked the note yet again, just to be sure, before rapping on the door. No one replied. He rapped again, leaning close to the door, and saying, "Kenton?" Still no answer came back.

He jiggled the doorknob. Unexpectedly, the door moved away from him, not having been fully shut. It swung back into a dirty, poorly painted room. Gunnison stuck his head through the door, looking around. The place contained only a table, a couple of chairs, one of which was overturned . . . and Kenton's folding drawing table. On the table was a whiskey bottle, half-empty, and a dirty glass.

"Kenton! It's me . . . Alex."

Silence. Gunnison walked through the little room and to the only door in the place, which led to a tiny bedroom. The bed was narrow, unmade. Several empty beer bottles stood or lay on the floor beside it.

"Oh, Kenton," Gunnison whispered. "How far have you let yourself fall? And why? Why now?"

He walked back into the main room and over to Kenton's drawing table. Kenton had been busy, it seemed, with more than drinking. Several sketches lay there; Gunnison recognized them as related to the assignments Kenton had recently failed to adequately complete.

Gunnison stood looking at them, and began to feel sad. It was pitiful, seeing this evidence of Kenton struggling to rebound from the failures that suddenly had endangered his job. Gunnison could imagine that Kenton must have been taken aback by his suspension; the man did have an ego and a tendency to believe that his status and fame made him invulnerable.

But Kenton was failing. The sketches were very much below his usual standards. Even the inevitable, subtly hidden images of Victoria that Kenton incorporated into almost every drawing he made were substandard.

It was the alcohol. The one thing that sometimes proved itself stronger than Brady Kenton.

Gunnison wondered where Kenton was. Gone out for food, maybe. There didn't appear to be any food here.

A ragged, dirty curtain hung over a west-facing window. Gunnison went to it and glanced out, hoping to see Kenton approaching.

Only a moment after he looked out, a window shattered in a saloon across the street and a man tumbled out amid shards and splinters. He landed hard in a smear of mud caused by the just-finished urination of a horse. Stunned, he couldn't even get up.

Gunnison watched, aghast, as a second man came out the window. This one, however, came out on a leap, voluntarily, unlike the most involuntary exit of the first man.

Gunnison became even more aghast when he saw that the second man was Kenton. Kenton threw himself right atop the man, grabbing him by the collar, lifting him up and shaking him. He was yelling so loudly that Gunnison could hear him all the way up where he was, through the closed window. He couldn't quite understand the words.

Kenton's victim, recovering, began to swing his fists up at Kenton, connecting a couple of times. Kenton let go of his collar with his right hand and began pounding back, much more effectively.

Gunnison bolted out the door, down the stairs, and to the street, hoping to get to Kenton before he killed the man.

CHAPTER

12

KENTON was drunker than Gunnison had ever seen him, and for that Gunnison was actually glad, because the alcohol was making his blows a little less exact than they would have been otherwise.

"No!" Gunnison yelled, grabbing at his partner's shoulders. "Good lord, man, quit this! Let him go before you kill him!"

Kenton, roaring and angry, tried to shrug Gunnison away. He laid three more hard blows against the face of the supine man below him, effective blows that clearly stunned the man.

Gunnison rammed Kenton as hard as he could, knocking him off. Kenton yelled, swore, and came to his feet uncertainly. He pulled back his fist and clumsily lunged toward Gunnison.

He froze when he saw who it was, and his face broke into a foolish-looking grin. "Alex!" he said.

"Alex Gunnison, by gum and by golly! Who'd have thought I'd run into you here!"

"Right. Who'd have thought it."

Kenton's anger apparently had died upon the sight of Gunnison. He lumbered over and slipped an arm around Gunnison's shoulder. His breath stank of whiskey and his body smelled as if it had not been washed for days.

"Alex, I'm glad you've come to visit me in my time of distress." Kenton had a big grin on his face as he said this.

Gunnison shrugged away from him, unable to bear his presence the way he was. People had gathered around while the fight was going on, and it was terrible to see Kenton humiliating himself this way.

Gunnison glanced at the man Kenton had been beating. The fellow had risen and was heading in the opposite direction as fast as he could. Good. The fight, whatever it had been about, was now at an end.

"Let's go back to your room," Gunnison said.

"You know about my room? My new home? Why, Alex! You're just full of surprises!" Kenton wheeled about to face the crowd. "My friend Alex Gunnison, ladies and gentlemen! A round of applause for him, all right?" Kenton began to clap. Others did the same, but mockingly, finding Kenton absurd and funny.

Gunnison wanted to sink into the ground. He tugged at Kenton. "Come on! For heaven's sake, get away from here before you humiliate yourself any more!"

"Humiliate myself?" Kenton laughed. "Whatever do you mean?"

"Confound you, come on!" Gunnison pulled him so hard that Kenton almost fell over. Gunnison lowered his voice to a sharp whisper. "Do you want these people to recognize you while you're like this?"

Kenton seemed to wilt all at once. "What would it matter? I'm a man who no longer has a job, Alex. Did you know that? Your father has fired me. Cut me loose. Given me the sack."

"We'll talk about it out of public view. Besides, as I hear it, you aren't fired, only suspended."

A distant whistle caught Gunnison's ear. "That's the police, Kenton. They're going to want to know who broke the window out of that saloon. And who tried to beat that man to death. And I can't imagine why we've not already got the owner of the place screaming in our faces."

"Lead the way, Alex. I'll follow. I'm in your hands."

Gunnison took him by the arm and led him away as fast as Kenton could stagger.

In Kenton's stinking, filthy rented room, Gunnison took the half-full whiskey bottle and heaved it out the window, before Kenton's eyes. Kenton winced like a bee had stung him, then staggered to a chair and sat down, leaning on the table.

"I'm a ruined man, Alex," he said. "I've been dismissed, sent packing, and all while I'm on the verge of finding my Victoria."

"Kenton, as I hear it, you've only been suspended. All you need to do is improve your performance and you'll be welcomed back."

"There's the rub, Alex. There's the rub. I can't improve my performance. The ability is gone. Look at my efforts there on the drawing table . . . look at them." Kenton raised his hand. It trembled badly. "And look at this. I'm through, Alex. I'm through."

Gunnison walked over and stood looking sternly down at the seated Kenton. He pointedly handed him the emptied whiskey bottle. "There's the reason you've lost your skill. There's the reason your hand trembles. You've drunk yourself right past the point of control. No one can hope to do decent illustration when he's got as much whiskey as blood in his veins."

"You're like a scolding mother, Alex."

"You need a scolding mother. And tell me something: why in the devil did you heave that man through that window?"

"He insulted a woman in the cafe. A most lewd comment, and I can't abide that kind of behavior."

"That wasn't a cafe, that was a barroom."

"They sell sandwiches, Alex. That's close enough to a cafe for me."

"There's every chance they'll come looking for you to pay for that window. And the police may want to have a word with you."

"Let them come. Let them empty my pockets and throw me in the deepest prison. Nothing matters now."

"I can't believe this, Kenton. You've spent your professional life with your nose in the air, acting as if your job hardly mattered to you, that you could walk away from it at any moment . . . and now you fall to pieces just because you might lose it. What's happened to you?"

Kenton looked up, and Gunnison studied his face closely for the first time since this reunion. He was startled. Kenton was unshaven, pallid, red-eyed. The left side of his mouth as well as his right eyelid had a vague but perceptible twitch.

Gunnison had seen Kenton drunk before, and ill before . . . but never had he seen him so thoroughly broken down. From the inside out the man was a shell, a remnant. And in the watery eyes was fear.

"I don't know what's happened to me," Kenton said. "I don't understand it. It's as if . . . I think that maybe . . . I don't want to say it."

Gunnison lost any anger or disgust he'd felt toward Kenton. His voice soft, he said, "It's me, Kenton. You can trust me. You can tell me."

Kenton lowered his head and cried.

Gunnison waited, saying nothing.

After only a few moments, Kenton pulled himself out of his tears—the old, in-control Kenton just starting to reassert himself again—and Gunnison was relieved to see it. It was too unnerving to see a man who'd always been made of iron begin to turn to water.

Kenton lifted his sallow face and looked squarely at Gunnison. "I've discovered there is a weakness in me, Alex. One that is very unexpected. I've become convinced that I'm on the verge of discovering at last what happened to Victoria, and I find that I can't bear it. I can't face it." He swallowed hard. "God help me, Alex, I don't know that . . . if ever I found her . . . that I could even face her."

Gunnison knew better than to patronize Kenton with false declarations of understanding, or unsolicited advice. He merely nodded.

"I can't comprehend it, Alex. What William told me, what he had me read in *The Grand Deception,* was like a jolt of lightning to me. I knew, Alex. I knew. The secret is in there. I could feel it. Sometimes, you just . . . know."

"Kenton, I met with William today. I read the novel's opening chapters myself. I can see the similarities . . . but there may be explanations other than some sort of mystic connection between a cheap periodical serial and the actual disappearance of your wife."

"Yes. Rationally, I'd agree with you." Kenton, despite his drunkenness, was sounding more like his old self. "But there are things there . . . one thing in particular that you can't know. Because I've never told you." Kenton paused. "Did you notice that the author used the name Brady as part of his pseudonym?"

"I did."

"I think that means something."

"Kenton, I agree that there is an almost certain connection between Victoria's accident and the novel. I think that accident inspired the novel. But it's imagination beyond that."

Kenton shook his head. "David Kevington was not the product of anyone's imagination."

"Kevington . . . a name you wrote in the margin of the magazine."

"Yes. It's a name I hate to write at all, much less to speak. The name of a man I despise. One of the few men in the world whom I would have been glad to kill outright. Maybe the only man who ever lived whom I can honestly say I truly hated."

CHAPTER

13

GUNNISON was surprised. He'd rarely seen Kenton express dislike for another person with such a pure and venomous contempt. "Is Kevington the counterpart of the mysterious French doctor who kidnaps Victoria . . . Candice, I should say?"

"Yes. But Kevington wasn't French. He was an Englishman."

"Are you telling me there was a real counterpart to this kidnapper physician?"

"There was. And he was a physician himself. Just like in the story."

"Who was he? Why have you never mentioned him?"

"Because it's painful. Unpleasant. It's not something one likes to remember . . . knowing that a man was following your own wife, like a hunter stalking prey. And knowing that you let your guard down long enough to allow him to climb onto a train on which she was a passenger, with no one to protect her but her sister . . . and me nowhere near."

"How do you know he was on that train?"

"I know the name of every person on that train, Alex. I studied the passenger list, the crew manifest . . . I even learned the names of a couple of vagabonds who had stowed away in one of the back cars. So you see, I only learned that Dr. David Kevington was on that train after he and Victoria were both killed. But we know now that Victoria was not killed after all. Maybe Kevington wasn't, either." Kenton looked Gunnison in the eye. "I think they both survived, just like Candice and Dr. Lanval in the novel. And I think that Kevington took her away, just as Lanval took Candice off to California. And I think that whoever wrote that novel knows it firsthand, as a fact, and is revealing the truth in the form of fiction."

"Those are big jumps, Kenton."

"Yes. But sometimes a man knows."

"Or thinks he knows." It was hard to speak this forthrightly with Kenton, who even after all these years—and even in this pitiful, drunken state—managed to somewhat intimidate Gunnison.

Gunnison went to the window and looked down onto the street. A sizable crowd was gathered around the front of the saloon whose window Kenton had ruined. The injured man was talking to a fellow with a notepad. Gunnison shook his head. He knew a reporter when he saw one. Just like almost every person in the United States knew Brady

Kenton when they saw him, thanks to the excellent likeness of the man published in each edition of the *Illustrated American.*

Gunnison looked Kenton over out of the corner of his eye. At the moment he didn't look a lot like himself, thanks to his disheveled, unwashed, and unshaven state. With any luck, the people below did not realize that the big troublemaker who had thrown the man out the window was America's most famous journalist. He decided not to mention the reporter to Kenton. He'd also not mention the fact that a uniformed Denver policeman was approaching the scene, walking at the side of a tall fellow in a long coat . . .

Gunnison looked closely. Was that Jessup Best? Initially he thought so. When the man came a little closer, though, Gunnison saw that it was not Best. Just a fellow with a similar gait and manner of dress.

If fortune smiled, no one had paid attention when he and Kenton entered this rooming house. Maybe the policeman would never locate Kenton, and once Kenton was sober, he and Gunnison could slip out of Denver unnoticed. Then, as Gunnison foresaw matters, it would be off to the head offices of the *Illustrated American* for a meeting with the senior Gunnison. It was time to take care of this problem with Kenton's job status. Gunnison understood his father's dissatisfaction with Kenton's job performance, even his suspension of the man, but in the long run it was a rather absurd situation. The *Illus-*

trated American needed Kenton a lot more than
Kenton needed the *Illustrated American.* Bad recent
job performance or not, there were journals and
magazines and major newspapers all across the nation that would pay dearly to have Kenton for their
own. The man could make a living writing books
and lecturing, if he ever chose to do it.

Gunnison turned away from the window. Kenton
was seated now, leaning against the wall, looking
sick and weary. His heart went out to the man.

"Kenton, are you afraid of finding her?"

Kenton looked up at him. "My, my, Alex," he
said, sounding remarkably rational for a man very
much drunk. Kenton had always been quick to
shake off the effects of the alcohol that sometimes
ensnared him. "Sometimes you are quite insightful.
And a little too straightforward, diplomatically
speaking."

"Why would you be afraid, Kenton? It's what
you've wanted for so many years."

"I know. I know. I think that . . . I think that I'm
afraid I'll find that, in the end, she's no longer alive.
And I'll have missed my last chance to find her. Or,
I'll find that she is alive . . . and doesn't want me."

"I don't know what to say."

"That's the thing . . . there is nothing to say. I just
have to face the facts as they are."

"Do you want to keep looking?"

"Yes. I have to. I have to know. No matter what
the truth may be."

"Do you really believe that novel carries clues?

Or are you just clinging to a wild hope?"

"Both. I understand how unlikely it all seems," Kenton said. He rubbed his temples. "I'm beginning to not feel well."

"You should lie down."

"I think I will."

Gunnison had been ready to tell Kenton about Rachel Frye and Jessup Best. But it could wait. Either or both might be in Denver right now, but neither were likely to appear here. It could wait. Gunnison sat by the window, watching the crowd below disperse. The policeman and the long-coated man with him moved on, not approaching the boardinghouse.

Kenton had been lucky this time. Unless, of course, that newspaper reporter had determined who he was. That sort of publicity could be fatal to Kenton's career, if it got back to the *Illustrated American*.

Kenton was in bad shape when he woke up. He avoided the light and sat with his eyes hidden in his hands.

Gunnison had gone out for food, but Kenton was having none of it. He did, however, take occasional sips from the coffee Gunnison had poured for him.

"I need to tell you something," Gunnison said. "I met a woman in Leadville. English. She said her name is Rachel Frye . . . and she claimed to be your daughter."

Kenton looked up at that. "What did you say?"

"She claimed to be your daughter. She came to Leadville to find you. She'd seen the publicity."

"Daughter! Lord, what foolishness."

"So there's no chance it's true."

"Of course not." Kenton buried his eyes in his hands again. "I've got no children, American, English, Chinese, Canadian, French, Irish, or otherwise."

Gunnison was glad to hear it. "I didn't think it could be true."

"The woman is either a liar or insane."

"Also dangerous. I need to warn you about her. It's one of the reasons I came to Denver to find you."

Kenton looked weakly at his partner. "Warn me about what?"

"I met a Texas Ranger . . . well, a former Ranger . . . who is under the hire of a family in Texas, whose relatives she purportedly murdered. He told me she'd also committed murder in England."

"Must be one devil of a woman."

"I suppose so."

"I'll keep an eye out for murderous Englishwomen, then. Why did she want to find me?"

"Well, she thinks you're her father. I guess she plans to tell you she loves you. Or murder you."

"Whoever she is, she's not important. What's important is that I keep pursuing my quest."

"Last night you said you were afraid to find Victoria."

"And I'm also afraid not to, so one balances out the other. What tilts the scale is that I refuse to end my days without having tried, without having pursued every possible lead." Kenton sipped his coffee carefully, wincing at the effort of swallowing.

"No more liquor, Kenton. You've got to stop with it before it takes you over completely."

"I know."

"Then swear it: no more liquor."

"Oh, come on, now, Alex, what good is—"

"Swear it, Kenton!"

"Oh, hell's bells, Alex."

"Swear!"

Kenton stuck up his hand. "I swear. There. Swear on my mother's grave. Swear on my grandfather's pocket watch. Swear on my uncle Walter's dead mule. Whatever you want."

"Thank you."

Kenton drank more coffee. "I think I'll try to eat a little."

"Then what?" Gunnison had his eye on the sketching table and its surrounding heaps of poorly done drawings.

Kenton followed Gunnison's gaze. He stared at the failed attempts at his craft. "Well . . . not that. I won't be doing that."

Gunnison realized the potential significance of what he was hearing. "You mean you're not going to finish the assignments that the *Illustrated American* is waiting for?"

"That's what I mean."

CHAPTER

14

"THAT could be a . . . costly decision . . ."

"Then it will cost me. I'm willing to bear that cost. But look at me, Alex. I received a suspension and the threat of firing from your father, and what do I do? Like a fool I scramble and try to make up for lost time, worrying and struggling as if I were some newly hired neophyte artist who would go under if not for my precious job . . . bah! No disrespect meant to your father, Alex, but I'm not dependent upon the *Illustrated American*. If your father chooses to let me go because I opt to follow the strongest lead I've yet found regarding what happened to my wife, well, then let him fire me."

Gunnison, having already pondered Kenton's lack of dependence upon the *Illustrated American*, could not argue with his point.

"I'm going to devote myself to finding the truth about Victoria . . . and, if she proves to be alive, to finding her. Yes, I'm scared by the prospect of finding her, as I admitted, but a man must do what he must. I owe it to myself and to her to discover the truth."

Gunnison made himself ask the question: "Even if you find that she has been alive all this time, and stayed away from you by her own choice?"

Kenton looked as if he'd been kicked, but only for a moment. "Yes," he said quietly. "In fact, I'm expecting to find that to be the case, if she's alive. Because why else would she not have returned to me?"

"The *Deception* novel presents a kidnapping scenario," Gunnison said. "And the female character being spirited far away. If something like that happened to Victoria—"

"Even so, Victoria would have found a way back," Kenton said. "She was a strong and self-reliant woman. If she lived, but didn't return to me, it could only be because she chose not to, or is in such a terrible condition that she couldn't. Even then, though, I think she would have found a way to get word to me of where she was."

"It may not be possible to find out the answers to these questions, Kenton."

"It's my hope that the novel will provide the clues I need. And don't look at me that way, Alex. I know it's a long shot at best. But at the moment it's my only shot."

Gunnison nodded. "I understand. But regarding

the professional side of this . . . will you allow me to make a suggestion?"

"Go ahead."

"Don't throw aside your job and your good standing with my father. You have some jealous competitors, and they would make hay with that, if it got out—and it would. Let's try to preserve the situation and still concentrate on this quest." Gunnison noticed only after he'd finished the sentence that he'd spoken in the plural—himself and Kenton working cooperatively.

"I can't do two things at once." Kenton waved at the heaps of drawings. "You can see that I've tried to make up for my failures. All I did was generate more failures. My talents are failing me, Alex. I'm too overwhelmed by this business about Victoria to concentrate on my work." He paused, then said, "You know, sometimes I've found myself thinking it would have been easier if there never had been any question about whether she was alive or dead. If the matter could have been so clear-cut that there was no question she was gone, then my life ever since would have been easier in some ways."

"Yes, but you would have had no hope of seeing her again, and I know how important that hope has been to you."

Kenton said nothing for a few moments. He'd revealed more of his inner self just now than he typically did, and Gunnison could see him beginning to reflexively pull back. Kenton cleared his throat and shifted the subject back to Gunnison's earlier statement.

"So how do you propose we salvage my professional standing with your father?"

"I propose that we work together on these drawings. Let me help you, Kenton. I've learned over the years to imitate your style fairly well. I'm not as good, of course, but I can handle the basics. You do the main portions of the drawings, then let me do the finishing work. Under your supervision, and following your direction and style. Together you and I can get these drawings finished in a couple of days, and get them to the *Illustrated American*. You can have full credit for them; that's not important to me in this situation. You'll recover the ground you've lost and regain your good standing. Then, you and I can both take some time away from the job. We can both use the break. And you can devote the time to exploring these new leads regarding Victoria."

"And you?"

Gunnison wanted to say that he'd spend the time with his wife—maybe concentrating on trying to start the family he wanted. But he knew it wouldn't be. The decision had seemed to make itself for him. "I'll help you, Kenton. We'll figure this thing out together."

Kenton thought it over, then shook his head. "Alex, I can't ask you to devote your time to what is essentially my own cause. It wouldn't be fair to you, and could get you in hot water with your own father. And I can't ask you to do work on my behalf that you won't get proper credit for. Besides, does this work really matter? I can find plenty of opportunities other than the *Illustrated American*."

"Certainly you can. But that's been true for years, and you've stayed on with the *Illustrated American* anyway. Why? Because you're loyal. You don't work for the *Illustrated American*—you are the *Illustrated American*. You could walk away from it, but you don't want to. If you'd been willing to walk away, you wouldn't have rented this room and put in all the time you have trying to make up for your inadequate work."

Kenton didn't argue.

"Let's do this together, Kenton. Let's take on these drawings and work as a team, and get this out of the way."

Kenton smiled, very slightly, and reached out to grasp Gunnison's shoulder a moment. "Thank you," he said. "You're a fine partner, Alex. Loyal to me when I don't deserve it."

Amen to that, Gunnison thought. I don't know why I do it. So much for all my notions back in Leadville of walking away from you once and for all.

"Come on," said Gunnison. "We've got some work to get out of the way. How's the hangover coming?

"Improving.

"You can work?

"I can work."

*   *   *

As they labored, they talked.

Gunnison was honest with Kenton about his lack of optimism about the seeming leads in *The Grand Deception* actually having much real value. Regardless, he was ready to pursue them, and would treat them as potential clues, no matter how unlikely.

"It seems to me, Kenton, that we're at something of a loss until we see more of that novel. And with the thing scheduled to be published over the course of a year or more, that's not a good situation for us."

Kenton, frowning over his drawing pad, shook his head. "No, it's not, and I don't intend to tolerate it. I want to see that manuscript in its entirety as soon as possible."

"Ah, but will you be allowed to do so? Don't such magazines usually have policies against allowing advance outside reading of their serial novels?"

"They do. Darian already informed me."

"Can he do anything to skirt the rules a bit in your case?"

"He could if he were the editor handling *The Grand Deception*. But he's not, and the editor who is, is staunchly refusing to let anyone see the novel as a whole in advance. He told Darian that those were the terms under which the novel was purchased from the author, who is remaining strictly anonymous. Darian hasn't even been able to catch a glimpse of the contract to learn the author's real name."

"Then there's nothing to do but wait the novel out."

"Of course there is. It's called breaking and entering."

Gunnison gaped. "What?"

"I'm going to see that manuscript, Alex. Whatever it takes. And I'm not waiting a blasted year to do it."

"Surely you don't actually intend to break into the building!"

"If it is the only way—"

"You can't be serious! Listen, Kenton, I said I'd help you, but if you think I'm going to—"

Kenton waved him off. "Alex, don't attach such importance to everything I say. Do I look like somebody who would actually break into a building?"

"With you, I never know. Let me talk to Darian again, Kenton. Maybe I can persuade him to work a little harder on convincing the other editor to not be so persnickety."

Kenton shrugged. "If you insist. But if he fails, I'm not overly concerned. I'll talk to this editor myself, if I need to. I can be a persuasive man when I have to be."

Gunnison smiled slightly. He'd just heard in Kenton's last sentence a flicker of the self-confident Brady Kenton he knew so well.

CHAPTER

15

J. B. Haddockson nibbled at his plateful of fried chicken—the same fare he ate every Wednesday evening in this same restaurant. Eating out was natural for him. He had no wife to go home to, and probably never would, being a very homely man with an abrasive personality, chronic bad breath, and a devotion to his work that precluded his doing much of anything else. He was alone, he hated to cook, and therefore the restaurants of Denver knew the man well.

Haddockson was a reporter on the staff of the *Denver Signpost,* a newspaper founded by his brother, Mort, two years earlier. His brother, a nicer and more appealing man than he, handled the advertising and general publishing end of the business. J. B. handled the news, and did so in an aggressive, scandal-hungry fashion that sometimes worried Mort, but which had certainly worked out well in practical terms. It was J. B.'s belief that the public wanted scandal in its weekly reading material. His theory was consistently borne out by the sales of the newspaper on the days he'd published something to make people shake their heads and click their tongues and in general complain about the low level to which Denver journalism had sunk.

But oh, how they would buy those papers!

J. B. was excited tonight, too keyed up to eat, picking at his food. He had the best story he'd run across in months, one that would ultimately generate national attention.

The only problem would be persuading Mort to print the story. Mort held the title of publisher and editor in chief, though he exercised the latter role only rarely, and almost always with veto power over something controversial J. B. wanted to publish. And what J. B. wanted to publish now would be controversial, indeed.

He was ready to print a story that would declare that none other than nationally famous journalist Brady Pleasant Kenton had gone on a drunken rampage in a barroom, assaulted a man, and heaved him out a window.

The problem was that no one had been able to authoritatively identify the man as Brady Kenton. But the circumstantial evidence was strong. Though the man was rumpled, unshaven, and dirty, several who saw him swore that he looked like Kenton, whose image was known across the nation. That alone would account for little, except for two things:

the man had been removed from his rampage by a younger man he called Gunnison—surely Alex Gunnison, Brady Kenton's partner. Secondly, it was known that Kenton had been in Denver in past days, visiting an editor at *American Popular Library.*

Besides, there was J. B.'s gut instinct. It never failed him. He knew, just knew, that it was Brady Kenton who had created such a drunken spectacle at that saloon. He'd heard that Kenton had an occasional history with drink, and also that the man had gone half loco in recent years, looking for a dead wife as if she were still alive.

The best thing about it was that the local police hadn't located Kenton to charge him in connection with the altercation. If they had, the story would already be in the bigger newspapers. As it was, it appeared that J. B. Haddockson was on his way to an exclusive.

J. B. paid for his mostly uneaten meal and left, veering toward his favorite barroom to put a couple down before heading to the office, where he would write his story. He'd have to do a good job, and build a persuasive case that the window-smasher really was Brady Kenton. Otherwise Mort would nix the story.

Back in the cafe, a greasy-skinned boy in a ragged apron sauntered over to J. B.'s table, secretly pocketed a few cents of the tip that was supposed to go entirely to the waiter, and cleaned up J. B.'s dishes. He carried them back into the kitchen, where he dumped most of them, but the plate with the sizable remaining portion of chicken he took to the back door. He threw the chicken out into the back alley. Good food for a stray dog.

When the door was closed again, Rachel Frye emerged from the place she'd been huddled, out of sight in an alley. She scrambled over to the piece of chicken, picked it up, brushed the dirt from it with her hands, and wolfed it down, gnawing at the bone until every scrap was gone.

Then she went back to her hiding place and cried. Her station in life had never been high, but she'd never imagined that she'd fall so low as to be eating thrown-out scraps in a back alley.

She cried, and prayed, and finally slept. She'd traveled all the way from Leadville, and was weary. She'd almost been caught by a railroad detective, and very nearly molested by another freight-car stowaway. Now that she was here, she wasn't sure that Brady Kenton was even still in town, or if he was, how she could find him.

Her dreams had mercy on her, however, taking her back to a place far away, and to a mother whose affection and gentleness were gifts that no subsequent evils could ever take from her.

They worked late into the night, arose early the next morning, and worked most of the day through again. Gunnison fell into a rhythm of work that made the hours fly past, and stirred a deep enjoyment of the creative process.

He enjoyed even more watching Kenton become his old self again. The liquor wore away, the spark returned to his eye, and his skills seemed to hone themselves even as Gunnison watched. Gunnison's contributions to the work became steadily less important as the hours wore on, Kenton carrying more and more of the load, doing the kind of work that had made him famous in his field.

"I'm glad you came along, Alex," Kenton said. "I hate to admit it to you, but you've been good for me. I'm glad you insisted that I get out of these drunken doldrums I've been in."

"Glad to be of service."

"I'm also glad we're getting this work done. I believe in fulfilling my obligations . . . it hasn't rested easily with me that I've failed to do so lately. I've been the least effective employee of the *Illustrated American,* and I'm not used to that status. It isn't pleasant. I can't blame your father for being so unhappy with me."

"When he sees all these new illustrations, a multitude of sins will be covered."

"Yes. And I'll be free to concentrate on the matter of Victoria. While you, Alex, can get home to your own lovely lady."

"Get home? I thought I was going to help you!"

"Alex, I've spent a big part of a lifetime away from my own wife because of circumstances I couldn't control. Your wife, on the other hand, is there at home, waiting for you. You should spend more time with her, and less with me, and with your work." Precisely what Gunnison had preached to himself for years. But it was a surprise to hear it coming out of Kenton's mouth.

"I appreciate what you're saying, and I'll gladly take you up on it," Gunnison said. "But not now. I'd like to see how this thing falls out." What he didn't say to Kenton was that he didn't yet trust him to maintain his sobriety, or his common sense. Kenton merited watching a little while longer.

"Alex, I insist that you go."

"Are you trying to get rid of me?"

"I'm trying to keep you from having to spend your time and energy on a matter that is essentially someone else's affair."

"We've always looked out for one another, Kenton. Besides, what affects you is my business. Keep in mind that one reason I was originally assigned to be your partner was to help keep you safe, well, and under control. You're a piece of valuable merchandise."

Kenton laughed. "So valuable your father has suspended me."

"He's only trying to force you back into line."

"Very well, then. Stay on if you wish. If we're lucky, it won't take long to learn the truth."

They finished the artwork far more quickly than either would have expected. After packaging the finished products and composing a telegram to be sent to the *Illustrated American* in advance of the coming package, both Kenton and Gunnison were in a celebratory mood.

"A good meal, maybe a glass of wine—one glass, and that's all," Kenton said. "That's what we need."

"I don't know, Kenton. We were fortunate to walk away from that little incident at the saloon without your being recognized. The local law is probably on the lookout for a man of your description. I suggest that we have food brought in rather than going out."

"Nonsense. I've never been one to hide. As for that window, I'll pay for its repair."

"That's not the point," Gunnison replied. "The point is publicity. If it gets back to the head office that you assaulted a man in a drunken rampage, even the exemplary job of makeup work we've done here may not be enough to save your job."

"Then I'll lose the job. Hang it, Alex, a man makes mistakes at times. Those mistakes carry a price tag. If the price of my recent mistakes turns out to be my profession, then so be it."

"All right. If that's how you want it. Just don't count on the *Illustrated American* paying your bail should you wind up in jail."

CHAPTER

16

KENTON, to Gunnison's surprise, kept a low profile and the evening passed with both of them going unnoticed. They ate thick steaks at a fine restaurant and had three glasses of wine each, not the single glass Kenton had promised. But no harm came of it and the pair of them returned to the rented room, talking of finding better quarters for the remainder of their time in Denver.

For now, though, the squalid room was theirs. Gunnison had gone out earlier in the day long enough to purchase a cot, and as he stretched out upon it that night, he was glad for it. The floor was hard, rough, and incredibly dirty.

Before he drifted away to sleep, Gunnison said a prayer for his wife far away, for himself, and for Kenton. As his consciousness faded, the affairs of the present seemed to line themselves up rationally in his mind. Because of two days of hard teamwork,

Gunnison was certain that Kenton's job had been saved. There had been no legal repercussions so far for Kenton's assault in the saloon. Kenton seemed to have worked through his personal crisis over the quest for Victoria, and it now appeared likely that Kenton would soon finish exploring the improbable matter of the so-called clues in the serial novel, and all this nonsense would end.

Gunnison had such a sense of relief and peace about it all that before sleep fully took him, he consciously forgave Kenton for that fiasco in Leadville.

Kenton paused at the door of the office building that housed *American Popular Library*, and glanced in a dark window to check his appearance. He liked what he saw. The bleariness was almost gone from his eyes, the sallowness from his face. Few exterior signs remained of his bout with alcohol and self-doubt. The old Brady Kenton was returning.

He walked into the office building confident that he'd obtain the information he needed within the hour. He'd probably come out with a full copy of *The Grand Deception* in hand and the name and home address of the author.

The man at the front desk was slender, bespectacled, bookish, and possessed of a haughty expression and manner. He looked at Kenton with no trace of recognition or respect.

"May I help you?"

"No need to sound so reluctant, young man. Indeed you may help me. My name is Brady Kenton."

As Kenton expected, the fellow's expression changed dramatically when he learned who his visitor was. He adjusted his glasses, stared Kenton up and down, then reached under the desk and pulled a folded copy of a newspaper onto his lap. He glanced at something on the page, looked at Kenton again, and put the paper back under the desk again.

This reaction did not surprise Kenton. The business with the newspaper, however, was a little confusing. Never mind, though. He was here about a serial novel.

"What can I do for you, Mr. Kenton?" The fellow sounded oddly reticent.

"I'd like to meet Mr. Jason Bell," Kenton replied.

"Jason Bell, the editor?"

"What? You have more than one Jason Bell?"

"No . . . no. Uh, do you have an appointment, Mr. Kenton?"

An appointment? Kenton hadn't expected that one. People normally threw appointment calendars out the window when offered a chance to meet the famous Kenton.

"I have no appointment. But if you'll announce me, I'm sure Mr. Bell will be pleased to see me."

"Pardon me, sir. I'll go tell him. Don't go anywhere."

"I assure you, I'll stay put."

The skinny man rose and turned to go back into the building, but paused long enough to again retrieve the newspaper. He folded it under his arm and scurried off.

Kenton resettled his coat, feeling perplexed by the man's odd manner.

A few moments later, the man was back, minus the newspaper. He looked darkly at Kenton and said, curtly, "Come on back, sir. Mr. Bell has kindly agreed to adjust his schedule and see you."

"How kind of him."

Bell's office was a floor below Darian's, in a corner, and very dusty. Its only window looked out onto the brick wall of the building next door. Papers and books and magazines and manuscripts were piled about the office.

Bell was short, rumpled, and shaped like his name. He stood behind his overflowing desk and looked at Kenton the way a man looks at a carnival barker.

Kenton was beginning to feel a little off balance, as if everyone but himself were in on some piece of secret information.

"My name is Bell, Mr. Kenton. Have a seat."

Kenton slid into the only chair in the room not piled with papers. "Thank you, sir."

Bell eyed him with obvious suspicion. "What can I do for you?"

"I'd like to talk to you about a novel that, I believe, you recently began publishing."

"Which one? I've got two in publication currently."

"I'm speaking of *The Grand Deception*."

"Oh, yes. Written by Horatio Brady."

"A pen name, I assume."

"Some of our novels are written under pen names. Others are published under actual names."

"What about *The Grand Deception*?"

"I'm not free to say, Mr. Kenton. Our contracts provide the strictest privacy for our authors."

Kenton glanced at the desk, reached over, and picked up a copy of what was obviously a book contract, albeit not for the one that concerned him. "I see that your concern for privacy governs everything you do, Mr. Bell."

Bell, with obvious irritation, reached over and snatched the contract out of Kenton's hands. He turned, scooted a stack of books to one side, and began to manipulate the dial on a small shelf safe. Bell's wide body blocked most of Kenton's view, but Kenton saw enough of the inside of the safe to realize that he'd just spotted the depository for Bell's contracts.

Bell slammed the door shut again, twisted the dial, and turned to face Kenton again. "May I ask the grounds for your interest in this novel, sir?"

"It's a private matter."

"What do you want to know about it?"

"How it ends. Who wrote it. And the origins of its plot."

"Out of the question. Our novels are published in segments, and no one but the author and the editor have access to the full manuscript."

"But I'm sure, sir, that you make some exceptions."

"None."

"Come now . . . we're both professionals. You do know who I am, I presume?"

"I know you. I was reading about you only this morning, in fact."

Reading about him? "Well, then . . . you'll allow me a bit of discretion, bend the rules, perhaps . . ."

"Mr. Kenton, I must ask you to leave."

Kenton was shocked. "I beg your pardon?"

"I must ask you to leave, sir. And please, if you have any notions of throwing me out of the window as well, be aware that we have a security officer in this building who will respond at once to my first call."

Kenton blinked twice, something coming clear. "Mr. Bell, when you said you were reading about me this morning, what were you referring to?"

Bell reached into the pile on his desk and pulled out the same folded newspaper the receptionist had brought back to him. He tossed it to Kenton.

Kenton opened it and went pale. Beneath the by-line of one J. B. Haddockson was a lengthy story with a screaming headline:

FAMED JOURNALIST BRADY KENTON VISITS DENVER, GOES ON RAMPAGE OF ASSAULT AND WINDOW-SMASHING!

Beneath it was a smaller deck head:

DENVER POLICE HAVE QUESTIONS FOR VANDALIZING WORDSMITH.

CHAPTER

17

"Oн, dear Lord," Kenton said.

"Surely you're aware of this story, sir."

"I was not."

"I suggest you leave . . . if the police are in fact interested in talking to you, I might be interested in helping them meet you."

"You have a nasty disposition, Mr. Bell," Kenton said, standing.

"Just leave, sir. That would be best. Just leave, and I'll not call the police."

"Well. Aren't you a saint."

Kenton went to the door, then paused. Turning, he said, "We've quickly gotten off on the wrong foot, Mr. Bell. Perhaps it's my fault, and perhaps I was presumptuous to ask you to divulge private information. But you must understand that my reasons are compelling. I wouldn't ask if there was not a highly important reason."

"I simply can't help you, Mr. Kenton."

"It may be that this novel contains clues to a loved one I lost long ago, and who for years I was sure was dead."

Bell actually took a backward step, and Kenton knew he'd just come across as a man at least mildly insane. "Mr. Kenton, please go."

Kenton turned.

Bell said, "It's only a novel, Mr. Kenton. Really. Just a serial novel . . . not even among the best we've done."

One last try. "You'll not even tell me the author's name? Privately, between you and me?"

"I can't. I'm bound by the terms of our contract."

"May I at least have your copy of that newspaper?"

"Take it."

Kenton left the building as fast as he could, and walked down the street looking like a hunted man.

When he entered the rented room, Alex Gunnison was there with a copy of the same newspaper.

"Kenton, we've got a problem."

Kenton tossed his own copy onto the floor.

"Yes. We certainly do."

Night, clouds overhead, thunder rumbling off in the distance.

Alex Gunnison was on the streets, looking for Brady Kenton, barroom to barroom. No luck so far, and Gunnison was worried.

He was beginning to consider checking the police station.

Kenton had been in a state ever since he'd come back from the offices of the *American Popular Library*. Gunnison didn't blame him. Kenton was in trouble, and his trouble had the potential to spread beyond a simple local police problem. The story of Kenton's assault would spread, eventually to the *Illustrated American*. Kenton's job might be pulled away from him.

Kenton had vanished about sunset, without explanation. When he hadn't returned a couple of hours later, Gunnison had been left to theorize about what was going on. Maybe Kenton had gotten arrested. Maybe the insane Englishwoman Rachel Frye had found him and murdered him, as she'd murdered those folks in Texas. Maybe Kenton had headed back to the bottle again. Maybe he'd decided to break into the *Popular Library* office and try to steal what he'd been denied earlier . . .

. . . Might he really have done that?

Gunnison stopped in the middle of the street, suddenly more worried than ever.

He headed for the *American Popular Library* offices as fast as he could go.

The building was dark, locked up. No sign of a night watchman. Gunnison circled it, looking at the windows on each level, trying to make out any sign of interior light. He also quietly checked the side doors and lower-level windows to see if any had been left open, or perhaps pried open.

He rounded the rear of the building. It was extremely dark back here. Only one door.

Gunnison rattled the door . . . it swung open.

He stood there, not sure what to do. Maybe it had been accidentally left open at the end of the day. Maybe it was simply an entrance into a store-room, not really an access into the building.

On the other hand, maybe Brady Kenton had pried it open.

Gunnison whispered a quick prayer for the protection of fools, and entered.

He seemed to be in a hallway. It was so black, however, that he had to feel his way. He reached another wall, found another door, opened it.

He was in another hallway now. It was short, though, and ended with him facing another door. There Gunnison paused, trying to decide what to do. He could be in great trouble for having entered this building. What if there was a night watchman after all? How would he explain his trespassing?

The door before him was unlocked. He swung it open, wincing at the loud creak it made. He stepped onto the staircase and began to climb. Though he tried to walk softly, every footfall seemed to hammer and echo.

His eyes were adjusting to the darkness, however, and it was easier to move about. He was also feeling fairly sure that there was no night security here, meaning that if he didn't betray his presence by the careless showing of a light or the making of excess noise, he should be able to explore undetected.

The stairs came to an end and he faced another door. To his surprise, this one as well was unlocked. And there seemed to be something odd about the workings of the lock.

After looking around to make sure there were no windows immediately at hand, he pulled out matches and struck one. By its light he studied the lock and latchwork. It had been forced, the marks still visible.

He shook out the match, fast. But as he did so, he glanced down the hall, and let out a little yell of fright as he made out what he was nearly sure was the shape of a man standing there . . .

Gunnison advanced backward, eyes on the dark and unmoving figure.

"Kenton?" Gunnison whispered.

The answering voice came from directly behind him, and made him yell out loud and leap a good four feet straight ahead.

"Talking to hat strands, Alex?"

After his leap, Gunnison wheeled so fast that he stumbled and fell on his rump.

"Kenton! Are you trying to make my heart fail me?"

"I'm ashamed of you, Alex, breaking into a building after dark. Don't you know this is illegal?"

Gunnison rose. "Oh, that's a rich comment, coming from you. I've been looking for you ever since it got dark, Kenton. I was afraid you were dead, or arrested, or drunk . . . or doing this."

"I'm sure you disapprove."

"What's the point of my saying so? You're here. You've made your choice."

"So have you."

"Yes. But we both can leave."

"Or we could stay. Alex, I didn't make the decision to enter the building lightly. I stood outside that back door for two hours before I decided to do it.

"You told me not to take you seriously when you talked of breaking and entering."

"Well . . . I suppose that when I told you that, you shouldn't have taken me seriously."

"Kenton, if we get caught . . ."

"You can leave. You should leave. I can do this alone."

"You can't. If you're caught, your job and your reputation will be demolished."

"I'm far along that road already," Kenton replied. "I'm already known across Denver, and soon across the nation, as a drunk who heaves other folks through barroom windows."

"So don't make it worse by becoming a second-story man."

"There's always the alternative of not getting caught. I'm going through with this, Alex. You needn't."

Gunnison hesitated, then said, "I know. But what the devil. I'm here."

"You're willing to help me?"

"God help me, I think I am."

Kenton slapped him on the shoulder. "Good man, Alex. You always play the right hand when a lot is at stake. Let's get this done and get out of here."

CHAPTER

18

KENTON and Gunnison crept through the building, using what dim light was available to them. Though he was reasonably sure the building was empty except for himself and Kenton, Gunnison all but tiptoed along, and kept holding his breath despite himself.

"How are we going to get into the office?" Gunnison asked in a whisper. "He'll have locked his door, won't he?"

"Not necessarily," Kenton replied. "How many times does your father lock his office door at the *Illustrated American*?"

"Never."

"Right. People feel secure in their own office buildings. Right at the corner here . . . yes. That door. That's Bell's office. I'll bet you ten dollars the door is unlocked, and give you the privilege of trying the knob."

Gunnison did. "Locked."

"What? Really?"

"Afraid so. Ten dollars, Kenton. Right now. Then let's get out of here."

"We never shook hands on that bet, Alex."

"So the bet is off?"

"No handshake, no bet."

"Glad to hear it. Because I lied about the door being locked."

Gunnison turned the knob and pushed the door open.

"Alex, you're a scoundrel after my own heart."

Gunnison stepped inside. "Lord, Kenton, this place is a mess. How do you hope to find anything?"

"I'm counting on my ever-present good luck."

"With the kind of luck you've had, we'll both wind up in the Denver jail. Wait! Why are you striking a light? That will be seen from the outside!"

"Not if you'll adjust that curtain a bit, and we keep the light cranked low and at floor level."

Gunnison got the curtain fully closed just as Kenton struck a match. He lighted a small candle on Bell's desk, and lowered it below window level.

"Exactly what are we looking for, Kenton? The manuscript?"

"If we can find it. If not, maybe some fragments, notes, an outline, the contract, whatever. I want mostly to see the ending of the story. If not that, the name of the author."

"I'll start digging."

"Look for the manuscript. I know where I can probably find the contract."

Kenton went to the shelf that held the small safe into which Bell had placed the contract. Moving books and general clutter aside, he revealed the safe's front. Kneeling, wriggling his fingers, he held the candle near the dial and began to manipulate it.

"You know the combination?" Gunnison asked.

"I tried to catch as much of it as I could. Bell kept his fat self partly in the way, so I'm not certain . . ."

Gunnison realized he was holding his breath again.

"Blast!" Kenton exclaimed.

"It didn't work?"

"I'll try again."

Gunnison watched as Kenton twisted the dial once more. A tug on the handle, though, showed the safe was still locked.

"So much for that," Kenton said, standing. "I'm disappointed. I'd hoped I could find out the real name of the author. And maybe an address."

"That may all be on the manuscript," Gunnison said. "Let's take a look . . . but we need to be careful not to disturb anything."

Kenton nodded and moved back into place the materials he'd removed from the front of the safe.

Gunnison began looking through the stacks of papers on the desk. He found notes, scribblings, doodles, letters, and several manuscripts, but all of the latter were apparently rejected ones ready to be mailed back to their writers, and none of the letters pertained to *The Grand Deception*.

Kenton, meanwhile, was digging about, as well, his frustration obviously growing.

"That idiot Bell obviously keeps his manuscripts under publication with him, or locked up some-where we can't find them," Kenton said.

"Then maybe he's not an idiot," Gunnison re-plied.

Kenton swore and slammed a stack of papers off the edge of the desk.

"Kenton! Good lord, man, do you want someone to hear us?"

"I've seen no evidence of a night watchman."

"We don't know that there isn't one. And look what you've done there. We'll never get those pa-pers back in the order they were! Bell will know somebody's been here!"

Kenton swore again, being unable to deny Gun-nison's point. He squatted and began picking up the papers he'd scattered, looking through them, trying to figure out if there had been any order to them.

Gunnison froze. "Kenton, did you hear that?"

"Hear what?"

"I think there's somebody else in this building."

Kenton looked worried, and cocked his head slightly, turning his ear toward the open door. "I don't hear anything."

"I did. On the floor above. I think maybe there's a watchman after all."

"Blast!" Kenton began piling the papers back on

the desk in a mad rush. He'd heard it, too, this time.

"Get behind that desk, Alex," Kenton ordered. He threw the last of the papers back onto the desk and snuffed out the candle.

"Behind the desk? How about out the door!"

"Hush! Hide . . . we might be able to get away with this yet."

One floor up, a red-eyed William Darian groaned and looked around his dark office.

What was he doing here? Why was it dark? Where had everybody gone?

He rubbed the back of his neck and looked at his desktop. On it sat a half-empty whiskey bottle, an overturned glass.

Oh, no, he thought. I've done it again.

He knew he drank too much, knew he was a fool to keep a bottle hidden in his desk, and a greater fool yet to sometimes take a nip or two at the end of the day. He'd lock his door, of course, keep it all hidden and secret . . . but one day he'd get caught.

He finger-combed his hair and chuckled. If he got caught, it wouldn't be tonight. He'd had a few too many and had fallen asleep right at his desk. The place had emptied out around him.

Lucky he didn't have a window in his door.

Darian stumbled back to his chair, not feeling very steady yet. His heavy heels clunked loudly on the wooden floor. But he didn't worry. Few people in this place worked late, and this was traditionally the night off for Joe Keen, the night watchman. So he could afford to be a little careless.

He sat back down, groaning, wishing his house weren't so far away from the office. He was drunk and would have to walk home, trying to avoid being seen by a policeman. His drinking was a great secret, and he lived in dread of ever having it revealed. He could imagine the humiliation of being arrested for public drunkenness, having people learn about it . . .

He shook his head, determined to clear it before he left the building. Maybe a cigar would help.

Darian dug through his ashtray, looking for a butt with some smoking distance left on it. Nothing. He opened a box on his desk and pulled out a fresh one. He bit off the end, clumsily, and spat it onto the floor. His hands were shaking, fingers numb. He dropped the cigar twice, then managed to get it into his mouth, and searched for his matches. It took three tries to light the cigar.

Darian sat there puffing, blowing smoke into the dark, and wishing he hadn't drunk so much.

He felt sick all at once. Maybe something was wrong with him besides the excess of whiskey.

He laid his head on the desk, cigar still in his mouth. A moment later he lifted his head, frowning.

What had he just heard? Somebody on the floor below?

It had been just a faint bump below. But he had

the most distinct feeling that it had been made by a human being, not one of the occasional big rats to which this building was home.

He sat frowning, puffing, listening.

CHAPTER

19

GUNNISON looked over at Kenton, whom he could barely see now that the candle was out.

"There's no question there's somebody up there . . . but I don't think he's coming down."

Kenton whispered back, "I suspect it's somebody working late. Which means we can probably finish our work and get out of here without drawing attention. I knew we were wise not to panic and run like you were ready to do! You'd probably have gotten us caught, Alex."

"Kenton, you insufferable, arrogant, reckless fool! Have you no mind at all? We should get out of here now!"

"Not until I at least find out who wrote that novel."

"Kenton, we're inside a building illegally. We're rifling through an editor's office. If we get caught, you can imagine the consequences."

"We'll be quiet about it. I'll look . . . you stand by the door and listen. If anyone starts descending the stairs, we'll be out the door."

"Kenton, this is insane!"

"We'll not have another chance like this. It'll take only a few minutes."

Gunnison knew he should walk out and leave Kenton to his own troubles.

He also knew he wouldn't. As always, he'd follow Kenton's lead, take any number of risks.

Obediently, he stood by the door, listening to the empty hall, waiting for the sound of a footfall on the stairwell.

Kenton began digging through papers again, searching, shuffling, making far too much noise to suit Gunnison.

Above, William Darian opened his eyes again, not having realized he'd even closed them. After his first awakening, he'd drifted off into a sort of semi-isleep state, but something had just awakened him once more. More noise, he thought, from the floor below.

Half-unconsciously, he picked up his smoldering cigar and puffed it back to life again, meanwhile listening hard. Oh, yes, no question about it. Somebody was downstairs, moving about. Not noisily, really, more like someone trying to keep his motions quiet.

Darian grew frightened, on several levels. If whoever was down there was a coworker, or, God forbid, one of his superiors, he'd have a real problem if he were caught drinking.

If it was an intruder, looking for money, he could have trouble of a whole different sort. People got killed in situations like that.

He tossed the cigar aside and swept the bottle and glass into his drawer, too quickly. It made a loud crashing sound.

Darian winced. That sound was so loud it had surely been audible all through the building.

Darian got up and headed for the door, panicked. He would get down the stairs and out as quickly as he could.

He tripped over his own chair, falling hard, striking his head on the corner of a shelf. He landed noisily, blacking out at once.

Across the room, the cigar he'd carelessly tossed away lay smoldering on the floor, inches away from a garbage pail overflowing with paper. Its flaring tip was beginning to dim already, but a breeze struck the drafty window and entered the room, blowing across Darian's unconscious form and also against the cigar, causing it to flare up again.

A scrap of paper, stirred by the same breeze, fell from the garbage pail and drifted directly toward the cigar burning on the floor.

"Kenton, let's go!"

Gunnison's order was unnecessary. Kenton had heard the crash upstairs and was suddenly ready to abandon this place.

Gunnison had slipped into the hall. Kenton was fighting panic, more concerned about this turn of events than his pride would allow him to reveal. If they were caught here it would probably result in arrest, and being the celebrity he was, arrest would bring publicity. There would be no chance of the *Illustrated American* lifting his suspension . . . probably he would be fired. Public scandal, public disgrace . . .

Public ridicule, too, if it was ever learned that the reason he was breaking into a magazine publishing firm was to read a manuscript that was mysteriously supposed to lead him to his lost wife.

Brady Kenton had to get out of this building, and fast.

He scrambled to the door, ready to follow Gunnison out. Gunnison, meanwhile, was well down the hall and almost to the stairs. This time he wasn't waiting for Brady Kenton.

Kenton's luck in leaving was about as bad as that of William Darian upstairs. His foot fell on a loose sheet of paper, which slid. He went down hard on his back, knocking the breath from his lungs so thoroughly that he simply had to lie there.

He heard footfalls on the steps, descending.

Kenton forced himself up, still without breath, and made it to the door. But once there, he faced a dark, looming figure with an arm extended, a heavy pistol at its end.

Kenton froze.

"Good move, good move," the armed man said.

"You just hold still as a statue, my friend, or I'll shoot you dead."

Kenton had no intention of moving an inch. He slowly raised his hands. Cutting his eyes quickly to the left, he saw that the hall was empty. Gunnison had made it out, apparently unnoticed.

"A night watchman, I presume," Kenton said.

"That's right. Didn't expect to see me, did you, sir! Bet you'd learned this was my usual night off. Well, surprise, surprise! Now, you just head back there and sit down in that chair."

"It took you long enough to detect me. Were you having a good nap?"

In fact, this was true. The crash in Darian's office had awakened him with a jolt. He'd known he'd heard something, but he wasn't sure from what direction it had come. When he'd heard the sounds of Kenton and Gunnison below, he'd pegged that as the source of the noise.

"Shut up, mister. Sit down in that chair like I told you."

Kenton went to Bell's chair and plopped down, disgusted and discouraged. He would maintain his demeanor around his captor, even try to retain a little of his famous cockiness, but inside he was despairing. This was a terrible turn of events, embarrassing, and ultimately harmful. His professional life and public reputation would suffer a major blow, no question about it.

"What's your name?" the watchman asked, still aiming the pistol at Kenton.

"Abraham Lincoln."

"Oh, you're the clever one, ain't you!" The watchman backed away, and without ever letting go of his pistol, managed to strike a match and light the gaslight near the door. He turned up the light and studied Kenton. The guard was a simple-looking fellow, overfed and right now a little over-eager. Kenton guessed the man had never actually nabbed anyone intruding in this building before tonight, so this was a big event for him.

"You look familiar . . . I've seen you before," the guard said.

Brady Kenton looked familiar to anyone who'd read the *Illustrated American*. "I don't think we've met, sir. And I wish we hadn't met tonight."

"You and me need to take a walk downtown."

Kenton was in no hurry to leave. The longer he could delay being turned over to the police, the more time he'd have to come up with some possible means of escape.

"How did you happen to be working tonight, if that's not your usual schedule?"

"Why do you care about that? You've got worries enough of your own. What were you after, money?"

"No. And I really don't care to discuss any of this with you."

Kenton's eye fell on a piece of paper beneath the desk, one he'd not seen during the search because the candlelight had been so much dimmer than the gaslight that now illuminated the room. He squinted, looking at the writing on the paper, then scooted his foot over and covered it, pulling it back toward himself. He deliberately knocked a pencil stub off the desk with his other hand, and reached down to retrieve it.

"Uh-uh!" the guard said, waving the pistol he'd probably never fired. "Hands above the desk!"

"Sorry." Kenton pulled his head up again, the paper now wadded in his left hand. He managed to slip it into the pocket of his vest.

"Why are we sitting here?" Kenton asked. "If you plan to take me to the police, why don't you do so?"

"I'm still trying to figure out who you are . . . I know your face is familiar."

"Would it make a difference if you knew me?"

The guard stared at him, narrowed one eye, and said, "Maybe it would. I admit that I might be inclined to go easier on a friend. Human nature, you know."

"Yes, indeed. And what is required to make a man your friend?" Kenton reached up as if to scratch his arm, but his hand paused on the way to gently pat his coat at the place where an inner pocket held his wallet.

The guard glanced around, as if fearing others were, impossibly, in the room to see him accept an offered bribe.

"Don't know. I'd have to think on it."

"Take your time. I'm in no hurry to meet the police."

CHAPTER

20

THE guard, nervous now, narrowed his eye again. "If I put my pistol away to roll a smoke, you won't run?"

"I don't think it would be necessary for me to run," Kenton said. "I think we've perhaps reached an understanding, you and me."

"Perhaps." The watchman slowly put his pistol away, slipping it into a backwards holster riding high on his left hip. He then removed papers and tobacco and rolled a cigarette. He was nervous and handled the job poorly, spilling tobacco all over. At length he had a smokable cigarette, which he put onto his lip as he reached for matches. As he fired up the cigarette, he eyed Kenton through the rising smoke.

"I know who you are," he said. "You're Brady Kenton, I believe."

Kenton considered lying, but rejected it. He was too easily identifiable. "I am, indeed."

"A successful man, you are. A man of some means."

"I'm not wealthy by most standards. Successful, yes."

"I want a hundred dollars. That's the price of my friendship."

Kenton actually felt relieved. He'd expected to have to pay a much more costly bribe than that. He frowned, though, as if he'd just been deeply gouged. "You're an expensive friend, sir. May I reach for my wallet without you reaching for your pistol?"

"You may."

Kenton produced his wallet, hoping he had the needed amount of cash. He did, with only a couple of dollars to spare. He handed the money to the watchman, who snatched it eagerly and stuffed it into his pocket.

"Thank you . . . friend. I think you can go now."

Kenton frowned. "I smell smoke."

The other laughed, a little contemptuously now that he had, in his own mind, gotten the best of the famous Brady Kenton. "Of course you do. I'm smoking a cigarette."

"What I smell isn't tobacco smoke."

The watchman dropped his cigarette and crushed it beneath his boot. He stepped out into the hall.

"Fire . . . there's fire upstairs! Smoke blowing down the stairwell . . ."

Kenton was up and past the watchman in a moment. He ran toward the stairs, pausing a moment to assess the amount of smoke, then pounded up them.

The watchman followed, not as speedily or bravely. He was wondering how all this was going to look for him. How the devil had a fire started? Would he be blamed? He hadn't even been on that floor—but he couldn't tell them that, because he was supposed to patrol every floor during his shift. Would they figure out he'd been sleeping in the basement most of the night? What about Brady Kenton's presence? Would that become known, and the fact he'd just taken a bribe from Kenton?

The smoke was thick in the upper hallway, and it thickened the farther the guard progressed. Kenton had already vanished into the roiling darkness ahead. The only light here came from the fire itself, the exact location of which the watchman hadn't yet pinpointed.

"Hey!" he yelled. "Where are you!" Then he couldn't yell at all, for hot smoke had filled his throat. He gagged and coughed and choked, and knew he had to turn back. He turned and advanced, and ran into the wall where it seemed to him the wall shouldn't be. Confused, he turned the other way, and ran into the wall again.

Panic set in. He felt he was lost in a box that was steadily filling with choking smoke. He slammed the wall again, turned, and could no longer tell at all which way he was moving.

Heart hammering, lungs filled with something

like airborne acid, he felt his consciousness begin to fade and his legs lose their strength. He sank to the floor and closed his eyes.

Alex Gunnison came to a stop in a dark Denver back street and leaned against a telegraph pole, panting and sweating.

He wasn't sure how far he'd run or even exactly in what direction. He'd deliberately taken odd turns and twists, cutting up driveways and through alleys, and even across a couple of dark yards, in an attempt to elude anyone who might have pursued him out of that office building.

As he caught his breath and shook off his panic, he began to realize that the effort had probably been overdone. No one had pursued him, apparently. All he'd managed to do was to get himself lost, and separate himself from Kenton.

A dog in a nearby yard began to bark at him. He ignored it, leaning against the pole, resting, beginning to worry about Kenton. Had Kenton gotten away, or been caught? Gunnison hadn't lingered to see if Kenton came out of the building after him. He'd assumed that he had, and that they'd reconnect back at Kenton's rented dive, but now he wasn't sure.

The dog's barking stirred someone in one of the nearby houses to come to a back door and yell at Gunnison: "Get away from here, you sorry drunk! Go lean on somebody else's pole!"

Gunnison waved contemptuously in the direction

of the unseen shouter. He'd been heckled enough in Leadville; he'd not abide more of it here in Denver. But he also straightened up and began to walk away, hoping to find his bearings once he reached a main thoroughfare.

It took longer than he'd expected, but finally he located a street he recognized and began walking in the direction of Kenton's room.

He was alone on the street except for the occasional pedestrian or passing horseman. Most of these either ignored him or gave a casual tip of the hat. A friendly city, Denver. And a place where a man could walk the streets after dark and feel safe.

Not that Gunnison himself felt particularly safe at the moment. Being nearly discovered breaking into a publishing office had given him the willies, and every shadow seemed like a pursuer.

He passed the cafe whose window Kenton had shattered, and winced at the memory. The place was still under repair, and Gunnison considered that Kenton was surely taking a great risk in staying in Denver after pulling such a foolish stunt—especially while living in a rented room within view of the very place whose window he'd demolished. Maybe this evening's experience would rid him of his obsession with that ridiculous manuscript.

Gunnison headed up the stairs to Kenton's quarters, hopeful of finding Kenton waiting for him there. He certainly hoped Kenton had gotten out of that publishing office . . . heaven forbid he'd been caught!

Gunnison reached the top of the stairs and turned the corner, then stopped, aware suddenly of another human presence near the door.

"Kenton, is that you?"

The figure advanced, and Gunnison knew right away it wasn't Kenton. He backed away, reaching beneath his coat for his pistol.

CHAPTER

21

RACHEL Frye advanced slowly, coming toward him from the end of the hall. For Gunnison the experience was almost eerily repetitive of his hallway encounter with this woman in Leadville, and she seemed almost ghostlike to him.

"You again!" Gunnison said, backing away farther yet and bringing out the pistol.

"You aren't going to shoot me, sir, are you?" she said. "Don't you remember me?"

"I remember you, oh yes."

"Why do you have that gun out, Mr. Gunnison? You're frightening me!"

Gunnison might have admitted that she was frightening him, too. Everything that Jessup Best had told him about this young woman flew through his mind, filling him with caution.

"Why are you here?" he asked.

"Because I need to find Brady Kenton, sir."

"So you followed me from Leadville!"

"I didn't follow you, sir. I came all on my own because you'd told me my father was here."

He's not your father, Gunnison thought. "How'd you come?"

"I rode in a freight car on a railroad train, sir, most of the way. But then a man got on that car and threw me off. So the rest of the way I walked, and once I rode some miles with a man in a wagon. I've almost exhausted myself getting here, sir . . . and he's still after me. I've seen him."

So Jessup Best was here, too. Still continuing his search for the English murderess. Gunnison wished he'd caught her already. He wouldn't be in this predicament. As unhappy as he was to see Rachel and as wary as he was about her based on what Best had told him, he still felt this instinctive urge to protect her. She seemed vulnerable and weak, not threatening.

"Have you knocked on the door?" Gunnison asked her.

"No . . . I didn't know which door was the right one."

"How did you know Kenton has rented a room in this building?"

"I asked a man on the street. He said that he'd seen Kenton come in and out of this building. But he didn't know the room." She paused, then added, "I wish I hadn't asked the man. He wasn't a good man . . . he took it wrong that I had spoken to him on the street. He thought me a different kind of woman than I am."

"The life you lead is dangerous, Rachel. Why do you run like you do?" Gunnison already figured he knew why, but was curious as to what she would say.

"I've told you, sir. You know I'm being pursued . . . Mr. Gunnison, I hate to ask you, but might you have food I could eat? I haven't eaten for a long time."

Gunnison still didn't fully trust her, but as before in Leadville, he couldn't help but trust her somewhat. She had an openness and sincerity about her that he couldn't believe was the mask of a murderess. Yet he'd found Jessup Best just as believable. Gunnison was confused by his own instincts, not sure which to follow.

But he couldn't just send her away hungry.

"There's food inside," he said. "I'll let you in and give you some."

"Oh, thank you, sir. Is my father . . . is Brady Kenton inside?"

"I don't think so. I was, uh, with him elsewhere earlier, and we became separated. He may not have arrived back here yet."

Indeed he hadn't. The room was empty. Gunnison wondered if Kenton had been caught. He hoped not. The publicity of another encounter with the law, particularly one involving breaking and entering, would surely be fatal to his career.

Rachel Frye looked about the trashy, decrepit

room as if it were the finest of dwellings. Gunnison wondered how long it had been since she'd had a real home.

"I feel safe in here," she said. "This is where my father lives!"

Gunnison was not in a mood to play along with foolishness.

"I told Brady Kenton about your claim to be his daughter," he said. "He tells me he has no daughters, no children at all, certainly no English ones."

"He wouldn't know about me, sir. There's no way he could."

Gunnison knew he should pursue the issue, but he was distracted just now, worried about Kenton.

"Sit down," Gunnison snapped. "I'll get you some bread and butter. It's the best I can offer you right now."

"Bless you, Mr. Gunnison." She seated herself at the rough little table, and examined Kenton's sketching paraphernalia with interest, touching none of it, though.

Gunnison brought her food, and a cup of water. He'd reholstered his pistol upon entering the room, but kept it on him.

She ate ravenously, finishing the food within two minutes. She picked at the crumbs, then thanked him yet again for his kindness.

"I'll get you some more," he said, bringing her the remainder of the loaf. He had purchased it at a nearby bakery the day before.

She ate again, a little more slowly this time. Gunnison watched her, and also occasionally looked out the window, hoping to see Kenton approaching. He wondered how Kenton would react to finding Rachel here, and what she would say to him.

But Kenton just didn't appear. Gunnison worried more.

"Did my father buy the bread I just ate?" she asked.

"I wouldn't be calling him your father just yet, Rachel," he said. "I don't think he'd agree to the title. And no, he didn't buy it. I did." He was finding her remarkably irritating right now.

"I do thank you for it, sir."

Her cloying, deferential politeness did not sit well with him. He didn't want her here right now, didn't want to be having to watch her with one eye while spying for the returning Kenton with the other. Hard though it was to believe she could really be the murderess Jessup Best claimed, he had to be cautious. Maybe it was her very meekness that made it possible for her to position herself where she could do the most harm. She was very likely insane, very likely living in a world of delusion and planning to murder Brady Kenton as a deserting father.

Yet she didn't seem insane.

Gunnison thought back on his first meeting with her in Leadville. Here was an opportunity to find the answers to some questions. Who had she fought with in the hall after Gunnison had left to buy her food? How had she escaped him? Why had her attacker had an English accent—might he be a pursuing husband, despite her claim to be unmarried?

But he didn't ask these questions just now. He was growing more worried by the moment about Kenton's absence. Something was wrong.

She crossed her arms on the table and laid her head on them.

"Tired?" he asked.

"Very tired."

"Go lie down on that cot there. Sleep, if you want." If she really was a murderess, he'd much rather have her unconscious than otherwise.

"May I?"

"I invited you to, didn't I? Go on . . . lie down." He chided himself for talking in such a rude tone. She might remember it later during a murder frenzy and pump him full of bullets.

The idea almost made him laugh. It was just too impossible to conceive. She just couldn't be a killer.

She fell asleep almost at once. Gunnison watched her, wondering who and what she was, and how much he needed to worry about her.

There was a shout on the street outside. Gunnison looked out the window. A man was shouting at another, waving for him to follow. Both of them ran up the street together. Then a wave of other people, six or seven of them, and a couple of horsemen. All going in the same direction.

Gunnison sniffed the air, frowning. He opened the window and thrust his head out.

He smelled smoke, fairly strong. He looked up

the street in the direction people were moving, but saw no flames or billows. He pulled his head back inside.

She was still sleeping, breathing deeply. Clearly this was an exhausted woman.

More people ran up the street. Still no sign of Kenton.

Gunnison stood undecided, then headed for the door. She wouldn't wake up for a long time. He'd find out what was drawing all the public attention, at the very least. And if Kenton didn't show up soon, he'd go looking for him.

Taking care to make little noise, Gunnison slipped out and into the hall. He didn't bother to lock the door.

CHAPTER

22

DOWNSTAIRS and on the street, he almost ran into a large, darkly clothed fellow with a wide face. The man put out two arms like small logs and held Gunnison back.

"Well!" the man laughed. "Slow down, my friend!"

"I beg your pardon," Gunnison said. "I was rushing out to see what the excitement was." He gestured toward the people moving up the street.

"There's a fire, I hear," the stranger said. "Someone was saying the office of that magazine on Broadway caught fire."

"Magazine? Not the *American Popular Library*?"

"That's the one."

Gunnison's heart nearly stopped. He gaped at the man, unable to speak.

The fellow laughed again. "What is it, young fellow? Have I sprouted devil horns on my brow all of a sudden?"

"What? No . . . no . . . dear Lord . . ."

Gunnison, forgetting all about the woman upstairs, turned and ran in the direction of the *Popular Library* office building.

The big man whom Gunnison had run into watched him run away, and chuckled. Odd that he should have encountered this fellow in particular. He had observed this fellow and the famous Brady Kenton coming and going from the building, since he lived nearby. A rented room, no doubt. He couldn't quite account for someone as famous and presumably well off as Brady Kenton renting quarters in such a squalid place as this, but he had the evidence of his own observations.

He watched Gunnison run until he was out of sight, chuckled again, and headed into the building. He'd seen Kenton leave the room much earlier in the day, and not return. With the younger one gone, the place should be empty. Maybe something worth having was lying around in there, waiting to be taken. It was worth a look, anyway. A quick visit in, a poke around, and he might come away with jingling pockets, at little risk.

He began to climb the stairs, hoping he'd find the room unlocked.

Gunnison joined the crowd gathered at the *Popular Library* building, looking wildly about for Kenton.

He was glad to see no flames, no sign that the building was significantly damaged, and that the crowd was dispersing rather than growing.

Gunnison collared a nearby man. "What's happened here?"

"A fire . . . well, there was one, but it's out now. It put out smoke, let me tell you, but not a lot of flame."

"How did it start?"

"I heard one of the firemen saying it began on the third floor. Probably a dropped cigar. Some fellow working late in his office."

The third floor . . . Gunnison and Kenton had been on the second. Gunnison felt intensely relieved. At least the fire hadn't begun because of something he and Kenton had done.

"Was anyone hurt?"

"A couple were. The man whose office the fire started in, and a security guard; both were knocked out by the smoke. But Brady Kenton was in there, Brady Kenton himself! He dragged them out. If not for him, they'd surely be dead."

So there had been not one, but two other people in that building while Kenton and Gunnison were pilfering through Bell's office! Gunnison was surprised to learn this. "Is Kenton all right?" he asked.

"Yep. But the police hauled him off to talk to him. I suppose about the fire, and maybe about that window the newspaper said he busted in a barroom here recently."

Gunnison frowned. Kenton was in the hands of

the police? Might he be arrested, either for the broken window incident or for his unjustified presence in a burning building, or both?

"Where did the police take him?"

The man gave directions to the station, and Gunnison, having only barely caught his breath from his last run, set off running again, determined to find Kenton.

A block later, Gunnison stopped abruptly. He'd just seen someone he thought he recognized—a figure striding in the same direction he was going, lean and tall. Walking, though, on the boardwalk on the opposite side of the street, and slightly ahead of Gunnison.

He paused long enough to catch his breath to a degree, then crossed the street.

"Jessup Best?" he said, approaching the duster-clad figure.

The man turned, and Gunnison stopped. "I beg your pardon," he said. "I took you to be someone else."

"Think nothing of it, amigo," the man said.

I'll be! thought Gunnison. He not only looks like Jessup Best, but sounds just as Texan.

Gunnison nodded politely at the stranger and headed back to his own side of the street. He moved along quickly toward the police station. He was embarrassed at having misidentified the man . . . yet even disregarding the fact that he'd confused the man with Jessup Best, he was sure he had seen him before. Where?

He remembered as he rounded the next corner. He'd seen that man walking alongside the policeman who had come to investigate Kenton's breaking of that barroom window. Even then he'd noticed a similarity to Jessup Best.

The tall Texan across the street watched Gunnison, scratching at his whiskers and looking thoughtful, until Gunnison was out of sight. "What name did he call me?" he muttered to himself.

Glancing up and down the street, he stepped off the boardwalk and fell in behind Gunnison, following at a distance.

Brady Kenton was struggling hard to keep his temper. As he sat in a very uncomfortable, straight-backed chair in a back room of the Denver Police Station, watching his interrogator pace back and forth before him, he was reciting to himself every reason he could think of why a man shouldn't assault a police officer.

The more time went by and the more smart-mouthed questions he received from Henry Turner, the man interrogating him, the less convincing his list of reasons became.

Turner strode back and forth like a strutting rooster, chewing on an unlit cigar and seeming quite pleased to have a celebrity such as Brady Kenton at his mercy.

"So let me get this straight," he said, clipping the spit-sodden cigar between his first two fingers and removing it from his lips. "You just happened to be walking by this building after dark, looked up, and saw smoke coming out a window."

"That's what I said. Congratulations on grasping such a difficult concept."

"Why, thank you, Mr. Kenton. I consider being congratulated by such a great man as you to be a true honor."

"If you're trying to be subtle with your sarcasm, you're failing miserably," Kenton replied.

Turner smirked at Kenton in a way that made Kenton want to strike him down. "Just following your lead, Mr. Kenton. Let's think about this situation we're talking about. Smoke coming out a window. Now, what does a man do when he sees smoke coming out a window of a closed-up building, with no lights on, after work hours at night?"

"Gosh, I don't know. Why don't you tell me and break all the suspense?"

"It seems to me that what a man does is go find the nearest policeman, or ring the nearest fire bell, or otherwise try to give some kind of alert to the proper authorities." Turner stopped pacing and wheeled to face Kenton. "What it seems to me he don't do is break inside the building and go poking around to see what's going on, all on his lonesome."

CHAPTER

23

KENTON could see where this was going, and didn't like it. The truth was that Turner had a point, and Kenton was beginning to realize he might not have been wise to have lied to the man about how he'd come to be inside the building. But he certainly couldn't have told him the truth! *Why, yes, Officer Turner, I did break into that building. I was looking for a manuscript, you see, or a copy of a book contract, rifling without permission through the private property of an editor who would have had heart failure if he knew I was in his office.*

Unfortunately, the lie didn't seem to be working out much better than the truth would have. And it had already come to Kenton's mind that he'd probably be in trouble when the security guard, now being treated at a local hospital for having breathed too much smoke, got around to giving his own version of the story to Turner. His tale wasn't likely to match Kenton's.

"I don't know what you expect me to say," Kenton said.

"The truth would be helpful. You broke into that building, Mr. Kenton. I wouldn't have expected it of a man of your fame and reputation, but then I wouldn't expect a man of your fame and reputation to go around heaving other men through barroom windows, either. But you did that, in front of many witnesses."

Kenton sighed. He knew it would come around to that before long. Turner had already mentioned that he was the officer who had investigated that window-breaking incident, a fact Kenton knew already from having read J. B. Haddockson's sensational story in *The Denver Signpost*. Even if he managed to talk his way out of the immediate situation, he still had that unresolved matter hanging over him. And it was obvious that Turner had it in for him. It was part of the price of fame, Kenton had learned: some people take pleasure in bringing down the proud and admired.

"I broke into that building because I was afraid someone was up there, overcome by the smoke," Kenton said. "And it's a good thing I did, too, because two men are alive right now who probably wouldn't be if not for me."

"Oh, I don't dispute that," Turner said. "It all turned out for the best, and that will certainly play in your favor. But when my gut tells me I'm being lied to, I get a little uppity."

"Why would I lie, sir? I listened to my own gut, and it told me to get into that building because people might be in danger there." Kenton hoped against hope that he'd talk his way out of this and be released before any version to the contrary of his own came from the security guard. He wasn't particularly worried about being contradicted by William Darian, who was unconscious when Kenton had found him in his burning office and dragged him out just in time. Kenton had fallen over the security guard's prostrate body in that smoky hallway as he was pulling Darian to safety. The end result was that he'd saved the lives of both men—but at the cost of having his presence in the building betrayed. At least Gunnison had gotten away undetected.

Turner leaned over, hands on his knees, face inches from Kenton's. "I'm going to get you, Kenton. I'm going to bring you down like a falling star. You've come to this city and assaulted a man in a barroom, staggered around drunk in public, broken out a window, and now you've been found inside a building without authorization. A building that caught fire for reasons we don't yet fully know. You're at the very least a curse and a jinx, Mister Great American Journalist, and maybe worse than that. Maybe a common second-story man. I'm going to find you out and expose you, and let *you* explain it to your admiring public."

Kenton smirked at him. "I'm glad to see I'm in

the hands of an unbiased lawman. And since you're so close to me, pardon the smoky smell of my clothing, Mr. Turner. I've been busy rescuing men from a smoky building. Saving lives. What have *you* been doing?"

"You think you're truly something fine, don't you, Brady Kenton! You think you hung the moon in the sky! Well, let me tell you what you are to me: you're a damned blue-belly Yank who betrayed his own to spy for the Lincolnites, and I've resented you ever since I heard my own dear, late father tell how you betrayed the Confederate cause, then went around wallowing in your fame thereafter. I'm going to see you jailed, Brady Kenton. I'm going to see you prosecuted for breaking and entering, arson, and theft, if I can find anything that you took from that publishing office."

Brady Kenton had taken only one thing: that stray sheet of paper he'd found under Darian's desk. It was now wadded into the toe of his shoe. If it was found and taken from him, it didn't much matter: he knew what it said, and that what it said was more than significant in his search for Victoria.

"If this is to be your attitude, sir, then I have nothing more to say to you outside the presence of my lawyer."

"And where might your lawyer be?"

"St. Louis."

"Bah! You think I'm going to wait on you to haul in some lawyer all the way from Missouri before I deal with you?"

"I do expect that. But be aware he might be delayed . . . he's involved in suing the trousers off ignorant policemen across America who think they can make up the law as they go along."

Someone knocked on the door. Without breaking his stare from Kenton's, Turner yelled, "What is it?"

"Joe Keen is here. They let him out of the hospital."

Kenton hated to hear it. Keen—the watchman at the *Popular Library* building—would no doubt reveal Kenton's alibi for the improvisation it was. And Turner would then have a good basis for locking up Brady Kenton.

Turner grinned wickedly at his prey. "Let's see what Mr. Keen has to say about the evening's events," he said.

Kenton smiled back. "Let's do. Shall I leave first?"

"Uh-uh. You stay put. Don't think of leaving this room. Me and you got more talking to do."

"Am I under arrest?"

"You will be."

Kenton paced the room a few minutes, wondering what Keen was saying to Turner.

Kenton wanted a cigar, a drink, a breath of fresh air, a nap, a walk—anything but this sitting and waiting in this closed-up room. But he could go nowhere.

He glanced at the door. It had been left open.

Couldn't go anywhere with permission, anyway. He could, however, just walk out . . .

Normally, Kenton would even consider such a thing, but one factor made the idea unusually tempting this time, that being the remarkable thing he'd learned from the scrap of paper he'd found on Jason Bell's floor. He longed to get out and away from here, so he could begin trying to make some use of this new lead. He wasn't sure just how to use it, but he sure as blazes could not make any use of it sitting here.

He actually thought about running. There was a fair amount of activity in this station tonight, several arrests having been made at a time the police force was depleted, three officers home with a fever. Kenton had heard the officer at the desk complaining about it when he'd been brought in.

Kenton meandered idly to the door and looked out. No one was paying attention to him. A look to the right showed him a door leading right out onto a side street. It was propped open to let a breeze blow through. He could be out that door in moments . . .

But then what? They'd come after him. He'd be a fugitive. Running would be seen as some sort of silent admission he had something to run from. Henry Turner had made it obvious that he intended to pin the blame for the fire on Kenton if he could . . . and probably that wouldn't be too hard, under the circumstances.

Ironic, Kenton thought. If he'd not broken into

that building, he'd not be under questioning regarding an unexplained fire. But he'd also not know the name of the author of *The Grand Deception*.

"Thinking about making a run for it?"

Kenton jerked his head around. A smiling man with a notepad in his hand was approaching. The fellow glanced from side to side in a way that let Kenton know that this contact was being made without permission.

CHAPTER

24

"J. B. Haddockson," the man said, sticking out his hand. *"The Denver Signpost."*

"Ah, yes. I'm fond of your paper. It works very well in the outhouse—the ink doesn't even smear!"

Haddockson forced a chuckle and dropped the hand. "Not all that witty, I have to say, Mr. Kenton. I thought you were renowned for your fast wit."

"Even more so for my disdain for sensationalized journalism. You're the one who wrote the story about me breaking out the barroom window, if I'm not mistaken."

"A factual story."

"Partly."

"Journalist to journalist, I hope you won't hold any exaggerations or missteps in that story against me. I did what I could with what I had."

"I believe in printing the truth."

"It helps to *have* the truth if you're expected to

print it." Haddockson glanced back; from his angle of view he could see Henry Turner interviewing a rather wobbly-looking Joe Keen. From the looks of things, Turner was not pleased to hear what Keen was telling him. Haddockson looked back at Kenton, who could not see Turner and Keen from his angle of view. "Can we step back inside a moment, have a little talk? Maybe you can give me the truth about that fire, and what you had to do with it."

"I had nothing to do with it beyond keeping it from killing two men."

"That's a story in itself. Want to share it? Save your reputation from the tarnishing it took the last time you graced our pages?"

"Aren't you thoughtful! Does Turner know you're in here?"

"Nope. So talking fast would be advisable."

"I have no desire to talk with you at any speed."

"Why were you in that building?"

"I've got nothing to say."

"Then respond to our first story. Why have you avoided the police? I know they've been wanting to question you about that assault and the broken window."

"I've been busy. And I've already told Turner that the damage will be paid for."

"Why didn't you say that before?"

"I wasn't eager to visit with good Policeman Turner. I didn't need the interference with the things I'm up to."

"Smart thinking. Turner intends to have you

locked up. I heard him bellowing that very salient fact to Joe Keen when I walked past."

Kenton pictured himself in jail and found the image intolerable. He'd not sit in some jail cell, falsely accused of arson, unable to act on his newly acquired information.

"What else did you hear Turner say?" Kenton asked Haddockson.

"You want to interview me, maybe you should agree to let me interview you."

"Fine, then. Just hurry."

"Tell me the details. Of the barroom incident, and of the fire."

Kenton spat it out as quickly as he could. Of the barroom matter he simply told the truth: he'd made the mistake of drinking too much, had let himself get out of control, and that was that. He was sorry and would make all the necessary restitution. As for the fire, he quickly repeated the same story he'd given to Turner.

All the while, his heart was racing and his conscience was screaming at him. How far had Brady Kenton fallen? Public drunkenness, assault, lying to the police, and now lying to the press. Too late to back out now, though. He told his story as convincingly as he could, and secretly admired the speed with which Haddockson could take notes.

"Your turn now," Kenton said. "What did you hear Turner say?"

"He was complaining. Apparently the editor you dragged out of there has come around, and is saying he thinks he may have left a cigar burning in his office. Further, I've talked to the firemen, and they confirm that the fire started on the third floor, apparently in the editor's office."

"Then Turner has no grounds to hold me."

"Oh, but he will. I know Turner. He's a corrupt lawman, Mr. Kenton. When he takes a dislike to someone, truth doesn't matter. He'll hound someone until he makes them wish they'd never been born. And he's got it in for you, Mr. Kenton. Others here tell me he's been out to get you ever since the barroom incident."

"Don't take this wrong, Mr. Haddockson, but why should I take your word for this? It seems to me you'd be quite glad for me to walk out of here. Your story would be that much better if I make a jailbreak."

"I won't deny that. But I can tell you that isn't my motive. I'm telling you the truth. Turner is out to get you."

"If I leave, I make the front page of your newspaper as an escapee."

"It's my job to report the news. You understand."

"Then I'll stay. I'll endure whatever Turner has in store for me."

Haddockson looked disappointed; his story had just become less interesting. "I'll make you a bargain, Mr. Kenton. I'll help you get away from here, keep it out of the newspaper, help hide you, if you'll do one thing for me."

"What's that?"

"Let me in on the bigger story. Your search for your lost wife."

Kenton stared at him. "Do you believe every rumor you hear, Mr. Haddockson?"

"Come now, Mr. Kenton. Everyone knows about your quest. People find it romantic and tragic. Women cry over such things."

"I think you should leave, Mr. Haddockson."

"You're taking offense? Why?"

"My private life is my own. It is not your business."

"You're a public man. You've exposed plenty of people to the public eye yourself. You understand the way the game is played."

"This is no game."

"It is for Turner. And he intends to see you lose."

"You'll lose if he finds you here. I'll tell him you attempted to persuade me to a crime to tell a more interesting story for the sake of your newspaper. I'll tell him you called him corrupt and tried to encourage my escape. I'll tell him you set the fire yourself. I'll tell him you are the real murderer of Abe Lincoln. I'll tell him whatever it takes to make things hot for you."

"He'd not believe a word."

"Get out."

"You're making a mistake. You help me out and I can do a lot for reputation repair. I hear a rumor, by the way, that you were suspended by the *Illustrated American*. True?"

"Out. Our conversation is through."

"And I thought we were getting along so well."

"Turner's on his way back. Get out or I'll tell him more lies about you than you could print in three editions of your rag."

Haddockson glanced out the door. "You're telling lies already. He's still questioning the security guard."

"Get out anyway."

"There's more than one way to get a story, Mr. Kenton. I can write about you with or without your cooperation."

Turner's voice boomed from the door. "Haddockson! Who the hell let you in here?"

Haddockson turned. "Well, Turner! How goes the world for you? What did the guard have to say about the fire?"

"Out of here, Haddockson. I ought to arrest you for interfering with a prisoner."

"So he's been officially charged?"

"Not yet."

"But he will be?"

"You don't know when to quit, do you, Haddockson? Get out of here."

"What will the charge be? Arson?"

Turner grabbed Haddockson by the collar and shoved him out the door. Haddockson glanced back at Kenton. "See you in print!" he called.

CHAPTER

25

TURNER slammed the door shut behind Haddockson and wheeled to face Kenton. "What did he talk to you about?"

"He tried to sell me a subscription."

"Answer me!"

"He told me that the firemen say the fire started on the third floor. And that a cigar might have been involved. And that I had nothing to do with it. What does the security guard say?" Kenton braced for the answer. The odds were the guard had implicated him for breaking and entering at the least.

Turner looked hatefully at Kenton. "He says you came in after the fire started. He says you saved his life."

Kenton was overjoyed, but tried to hide it. What a stroke of luck! Why would the guard have lied on his behalf?

It made sense all at once: the guard would hardly

have implicated Kenton. Not after Kenton saved his life—and paid him a bribe. Out of both gratitude and a desire to save his own skin, he'd paint Kenton as a full innocent in the matter.

"I'll leave now, then," Kenton said.

"Oh, no. Not yet. I'm locking you up, Mr. Kenton. I don't believe we've gotten to the bottom of this even yet."

"Lock me up? On what charge?"

"Assault. Destruction of property. Public drunkenness. You remember we've got more than one case involving you, don't you?"

"I demand my attorney."

"You can demand from a jail cell."

Another policeman came to the door. "Henry, need you here a minute."

Turner smiled wickedly at Kenton. "You stay put. I'll be right back."

He walked out again.

Kenton walked out right after him. It was not a move anyone would expect, and therefore he got away with it. He strode out almost on Turner's heels, cut to the right, and headed out that propped-open door. He headed for the rear alley, and would wind his way through a mazelike route before getting back to his rented quarters, where he hoped Gunnison would be waiting for him.

He was not going to spend the night in jail. He was not going to be delayed by a fool like Turner or intimidated by a ratty journalist like Haddockson. This escapade probably had ended any hope of his retaining his position with the *Illustrated American,* but Kenton found he hardly cared. He was ready to devote himself fully to seeking the truth about Victoria. No more halfway commitment, no more trying to mix his quest with a full work schedule.

It was time to go, time to get out of Denver, as fast as he could. And then to figure out what to do with the information now stuffed into the toe of his boot.

Five minutes later, Alex Gunnison walked up to the front door of the police station. He was irritated with himself, having gotten lost twice on the way here. Directions were something he had trouble with sometimes.

Kenton was somewhere inside, he supposed. Being pumped about the fire. Would they let him talk to him? Was he under arrest? If what Gunnison had heard at the fire scene regarding a cigar as the cause of the fire was true, surely they'd have no grounds for holding Kenton.

Gunnison was almost at the door when it burst open. Two officers rushed out, looking around wildly. One of them swore. The other faced Gunnison, grabbing him by the shoulders.

"You! Have you seen a man walking away from here, big fellow, beard, salt-and-pepper kind of hair?"

That sounded like a description of Brady Kenton. "No, I've not."

The officer swore and rushed away after the other one.

Gunnison entered the door. The desk officer had a dour look.

"Pardon me, sir, but I'm told that Brady Kenton might be here."

The officer rolled the stubby cigar on his lip from one side of his mouth to the other. "Brady Kenton, eh? We'd like to see him ourselves."

"What do you mean? He's not already here?"

"He was. Then he walked out the door while he was still under questioning. But they'll drag his rump back here and then he'll have plenty of music to face."

"Kenton escaped?"

"What do you know about him, young man? Just who are you?"

"Good evening, Officer," Gunnison said. He turned and was out the door in a flash.

The streets of Denver were dark and forbidding. Every shadow, every alley, every dark corner, potentially held a searching policeman, and the end of Brady Kenton's freedom.

Kenton found a place to hide across the street from the building that housed his rented room. So far he'd seen no sign the room was watched, and realized that the local police apparently never had detected that he was staying here. Taking a deep breath, he headed across the street and to the door of the building.

No one stopped him, no one called his name. He slipped in the door, and began climbing the stairs. He paused at the landing and looked up into the dark hallway that led to the door of his room. He detected no evidence of anyone hiding there. Proceeding, he went toward the door, then froze in place.

The door was ajar. There was no light inside.

"Gunnison?" Kenton said softly. "Are you here?"

No one replied. And Kenton, wishing he had his gun, pushed the door the rest of the way open and slipped inside.

"Gunnison?" Still no answer.

Kenton pulled matches from his pocket, struck one of them. Lighting a lamp, he looked about the empty room, checking for signs of burglary.

He quickly found some. His drawing table was turned over, his art-supply bag dumped out onto the floor. Over near the window, a chair that had been intact when Kenton left was now broken and lying on its side.

It appeared that there had been a struggle of some sort in this room.

Kenton began to worry. Had Gunnison been assaulted?

Taking the lamp in hand, Kenton began exploring. In seconds he halted, looking down at the floor.

Blood. There was blood on the floor.

Kenton instantly forgot his own danger. He cranked the lamp up brighter and began following the rather copious trail of blood. It led him back out the door into the hallway, and down the stairs.

Whoever had left this trail had probably been shot or stabbed, and judging from the rate of blood loss, was in severe need of medical help.

CHAPTER

26

KENTON exited the door onto the street. He noted a policeman going around a nearby corner, but the policeman did not see him. Kenton realized how conspicuous he was walking on a dark street carrying a lighted lamp. But it didn't matter now. Gunnison might be in danger and that was much more important than whether he himself was caught.

He actually almost hailed the policeman, but cut off at the last moment. No policeman would listen to him right now. He'd simply be hauled summarily back to the station and jailed, the matter of Gunnison ignored.

The blood led Kenton into an alley. He traveled down it, expecting to encounter a fallen body at any moment.

Around the rear of the building, Kenton did find a body, lying crumpled on the ground. He saw right away that it was not Gunnison, though, and felt great relief.

But since this was not Gunnison, it must surely be the burglar. And it must have been Gunnison who had injured him.

Kenton knelt and examined the man. He was still breathing, but weakly.

"Mister, can you hear me?"

The man made no reply, only moaned softly.

Kenton gently rolled him over. The man groaned again. The front of his shirt was drenched in blood. His face was wide and fleshy, his eyes pinched shut. By the light of the lamp, Kenton could see that the man was very pale. In his day Kenton had seen enough men die to realize that this man was barely hanging on.

"I'll try to get help," Kenton said. "Hold on, hold on as hard as you can, and maybe we can still save you."

But even as he finished speaking, Kenton saw something change in the man's face. The fellow let out a weak, faltering breath, and grew still. Kenton sighed and stood. There was nothing to be done for this man now.

So once again the sole issue became Alex Gunnison. Where was he? If he had stabbed this man and fled the room, had he done so simply because he had panicked, or because he himself was injured and seeking assistance?

Kenton stepped across the body and advanced farther up the alley. He heard something in the vicinity of a storage building that was surrounded by stacks of empty boxes, casks, and assorted rubbish.

"Gunnison? Is it you?"

Something stirred, something too big to be a dog or a rat.

Kenton watched as a figure rose before him. Someone had been hiding behind the rubbish.

"Ma'am?" Kenton said to the woman standing before him. "Are you all right?"

The burning lamp still sat back in the alley near the fallen body, but it cast enough light even at this distance to let Kenton vaguely make out the woman's features. The light played over his own face as well, and as so often happened, he found himself recognized.

"Mr. Kenton, sir?" she said, stepping forward.

She advanced, and he saw her clearly for the first time. As the lamplight revealed her face, Kenton gasped and stepped back, actually feeling faint.

He was looking into a face that was the very image of his lost Victoria.

Alex Gunnison couldn't guess what would happen now. Kenton had done some crazy things in his time, but never anything like walking out of a police station.

The ramifications of this occurrence were many-layered. All the work he and Kenton had done in making up the missed assignments was certainly for nothing now. Gunnison knew his father too well to believe he would put up with having Kenton publicly embarrass the *Illustrated American* in this manner. It was one thing to be a little eccentric, a very different thing to be a fugitive and accused criminal. Gunnison could only hope that Kenton had a very good reason for pulling a stunt like this.

The question was, where had Brady Kenton gone? Denver wasn't Kenton's city. He didn't know its every hiding place and back alley. Gunnison could only guess that Kenton had headed back to the rented room.

The room! Gunnison had forgotten for the moment that Rachel Frye was there! If Kenton did go back to the room, he would stumble upon her without a clue as to who she was or why she was there. Gunnison couldn't guess how she would react to encountering Kenton, the man she had searched for over so many miles. Would she know him? What if she really was dangerous, and attacked Kenton?

Gunnison turned to go back to the room.

"Pardon me, sir."

Gunnison wheeled very quickly, startled. Approaching him was the same man he had mistaken for Jessup Best a few minutes earlier. The fellow obviously had followed him.

Gunnison noticed for the first time the man slightly favored his right leg. He also noted the fellow had the look of a lawman about him. He'd always been able to spot them. This was worrisome, under the circumstances.

"Sorry to be calling you down, friend," the man said as he strode up. "I almost didn't do it, but if you don't mind, there's a question I need to ask you."

"What's that?"

"When we spoke earlier on the street, you called me Mr. Best."

"Yes, sir. You bear a strong resemblance to a man by that name whom I met in Leadville," Gunnison replied.

"Well, in that case, I pity the poor devil," the man said, grinning. "I regret that anybody else has had these looks inflicted upon them."

Gunnison gave the obligatory chuckle, but he was in a hurry and had no time for idle talk. "Is there anything else you need to ask me?"

"Yes, sir, there is. Would you tell me the first name of the Best fellow you knew?"

"Jessup. Jessup Best."

The stranger raised his thick eyebrows. "I *thought* that was the name you called. You knew Jessup Best?"

"I met him once, and had some conversation with him. He told me he might come to Denver, so when I saw you, I thought maybe he had shown up. You resemble him."

This all seemed rather straightforward stuff to Gunnison, but the stranger was looking at him as if it were all very confusing.

"When did you meet this man?"

"A few days ago, in Leadville."

"Tell me something about what he looked like, if you don't mind."

"Why are you asking? And who are you?"

"I ask your pardon, sir," the ever-polite stranger said, touching his hat. "My name is Turner, Frank Turner. And the reason I'm asking these questions is that I knew Jessup Best very well. But the one you met can't be the same man."

"Why is that?"

"Because the Jessup Best I knew has been dead for nearly a year."

Fine. So there was a coincidence of names. It happened all the time. There seemed to be no other reason to continue the conversation, and Gunnison was eager to get about his own rather urgent business. He started to turn and walk away, adding one last comment: "The Jessup Best I met is a Texas Ranger."

"What?"

Gunnison stopped and repeated what he had said.

"Well, Mr. . . ."

"Gunnison. Alex Gunnison."

"We've got quite a mystery on our hands, Mr. Gunnison. There's only been one Jessup Best in the Texas Rangers, and that's the man I knew. He's dead, Mr. Gunnison. I know it for a fact. I was there. I took a bullet through the leg on the same occasion."

"There *has* to be another Jessup Best in the Rangers. I met him days ago, and he certainly wasn't dead."

"I'm a Texas Ranger myself, sir. I tell you beyond any question that there's only been one Jessup

Best among the Rangers, and he's dead and gone. The man you met was an imposter. How did he persuade you that he was a Ranger?"

"I had no reason to doubt him."

"He must have looked a lot like me, else you wouldn't have mistaken me for him."

"He did. The way you walk, dress, talk . . . it's all the same." Gunnison paused, then asked, "Mr. Turner, come to think of it, how can I know that *you* are actually a Texas Ranger?"

Turner pulled back his duster and revealed a badge pinned to his shirt. Gunnison leaned over to examine it. Straightening, he said, "You're some distance out of your normal jurisdiction, Ranger Turner."

"That's a fact. Let's go have a drink together and let me talk to you about that, and a few other matters. I think it may be very important, maybe even providential, that we've run into one another. I have a notion I might know who this 'Jessup Best' you met really is."

Gunnison was intrigued, but under the circumstances he couldn't accept the invitation, not right away. "There's something that I have to do right now," he said. "Maybe I can meet you later?"

"Fine. I'll be at the police station."

"The police station . . . are you on special assignment with the Denver police, or something?"

"No. I'm separated from the Rangers for the time being. Kind of a forced vacation. But I've got a cousin, Henry Turner, up here on the local police force. I came to visit him, just to get away from Texas for a spell. I spend a lot of time at the station with him. Lack of anything better to do."

Gunnison wasn't eager to go back to the police station. Someone there might figure out he was Kenton's partner and try to hold him. "Can we meet somewhere else?" He hoped Turner wouldn't ask him why.

"There's a bar on the next corner. Jericho Tavern. I'll head that way in an hour or so. If you show up, I'll see you."

"Fair enough. I do want to talk to you, if the circumstances will allow it."

"I'll see you there."

Frank Turner touched the brim of his hat again, nodding, and turned and limped off toward the police station. Gunnison watched him go for a moment, then headed in the opposite direction.

CHAPTER

27

KENTON had no doubt that the young lady before him was, if not his own daughter, at least that of Victoria. Her face was the image of Victoria's as it had been when he married her.

"You're Rachel Frye?"

"Yes."

For a few moments, Kenton could only stare at her. Then he said, "Alex told me that you say you . . . are my daughter."

"Yes," she said. "I am sure that I am."

Kenton could hardly get out the next question. "Your mother's name is Victoria?"

"Yes. My real mother . . . not the mother who raised me."

"Is Victoria still alive?"

"She is still alive."

A great wave of emotion came over Kenton, and he stumbled to the nearest wall, leaned against it, and wept like a child. He had just learned the answer to a question that had haunted him most of his adult life. He didn't yet know the details, but the mere news that Victoria still lived was all by itself too overwhelming to take.

He regained control of his emotions with a great effort, and turned to face Rachel. "I'm sorry," he said.

"Oh, don't be sorry. I understand," she said. She smiled at him. "I was hoping you would be a tender man."

Kenton had a million questions for Rachel, but could not ask them now. Both of them were in a dire situation. Kenton nodded toward the body on the ground. "Did you kill him?"

"I had to. He attacked me. I didn't want to kill him, only to make him leave me alone."

"You were in my room?"

"Yes . . . Mr. Gunnison had let me in. I had gone to sleep. This man came in, and awakened me, but when he saw me, he came toward me. I don't know where Mr. Gunnison was . . . he was gone. I could tell that the man who had come in was going to . . ." She shuddered and was unable to finish the sentence. "I found a knife, and I defended myself with it. I cut him many times, but he kept on coming at me. I ran away, out of the building, but he followed me . . . he followed me with blood running all down him."

Some of Gunnison's warnings about this woman returned to Kenton's mind, causing a moment of wariness. He didn't really know her, after all. This story of attack and self-defense could be a contrivance; perhaps she had murdered this man cold-bloodedly, as she had supposedly killed the family in Texas.

But caution could not live long in the light of that astonishing similarity to his lost Victoria. He could not see her as dangerous even when he tried.

"We have a problem," Kenton said. "There are policemen crawling all over this town right now, looking for me. If they find me with you, there'll be questions, and maybe trouble. Especially when they find this body."

Tears flooded her eyes and she was trembling. "I've never caused the death of anyone before," she said. "I feel bad about it . . . I feel guilty. He was going to hurt me, but I still feel so guilty."

She certainly didn't sound to Kenton like the hardened killer Gunnison had warned him she was. "You did what you had to do. Now, though, we need to find a place to hide, and a way out of Denver as quickly as possible," Kenton said her.

"I'm accustomed to hiding," she replied. "And to running."

"Good," Kenton said.

He cocked his head at the sound of a train whistle in the distance. A late run was arriving at the Denver station.

"Have you ever ridden the rails—without a ticket?" he asked her.

"More than once."

"Are you up to doing it tonight?"

"I'll do whatever I need to do, whenever I must."

Kenton smiled at her. "I like that spirit," he said. "It's the spirit of a survivor."

She smiled back, and he felt a sudden deepening affection for her. It truly was like looking at the face of Victoria again, a face he had seen in his dreams, and subtly drawn into his artwork, for more years than he could count.

"We must make our way to the train station," he told her. "And we have to do it without being seen."

"I'm ready."

Kenton nodded. Right now he wanted to flee this city and come to know this young Englishwoman's story.

But what about Gunnison? How could he let him know what had happened and where he was going? He didn't even know where Gunnison was at the moment.

He thought of a way to get word to Gunnison . . . not a certain way, but the best he could come up with just now.

He knelt and without explanation picked up a stone, dropping it into his pocket.

They heard the sound of movement up on the street. Kenton quickly extinguished the light, took her by the arm and pulled her back in the opposite direction.

"Let's go," he said. "We're literally a stone's throw from fleeing Denver. There's very, very much I want to talk to you about."

They moved along the rear of a row of buildings, vanishing into the darkness.

The rail station was dark and substantially empty. It spread across the broad, flat area, with a high fence built around it. Kenton and Rachel hid behind a small shed at the edge of the rail yard, looking across the expanse.

"We're safe for now," Kenton said. "But I don't see any trains that would be good to stow away upon."

"I don't think I much care what happens now," she said. "I'm satisfied just to have been able to find you, my own father."

"Rachel, I must speak frankly. I don't see how it is possible that I could be your father," Kenton said. "Victoria was not with child when we last parted. I see her image in your face, but surely your father must be another man."

Rachel shook her head firmly. "No. She *was* with child when you last saw her. But she didn't know it herself."

"There's so much I have to learn from you," Kenton said.

"I'm eager to tell you," she replied. "I can tell you now, if you want."

"Tell me how she survived the train crash. Was she taken away by David Kevington?"

"Yes. He was on the train with her during the crash, but he lived. So did Victoria, and her sister, as well, as I understand it. Dr. Kevington took Victoria away in the midst of the confusion. The fire was so bad, the bodies so badly destroyed, that everyone presumed she was among the dead. That, at least, is what I was told."

"Who told you this?"

"Molly Frye. The woman who raised me. The woman I always believed was my mother."

"So Victoria didn't raise you?"

"No. I was raised by a scullery maid."

Kenton looked across the rail yard. A black man was sweeping the long, roofed porch of a nearby building. Other figures moved among the train cars and in and out of the various buildings. Now was not the time to enter one of the freight cars.

"Tell me what you can of your story," Kenton said. "I think we'll be here a while."

"It's a long tale," she said. "You must understand that it's something I've learned only because others have told me. There are some things I don't fully know myself. Some things I've had to guess at, the best I can."

Kenton said, "At least you've known something. I've known nothing all. All these years I've had to wonder and pose questions, with no one to give me answers."

She took a deep breath, and began to speak. Though her voice carried the inflections of working-class London, she was easy to understand and spoke in a voice that was pleasant to Kenton's ear. It, like her face, reminded him of Victoria.

"I've lived most of my life as Rachel Frye," she

said. "To my knowledge, I was nothing more than the daughter of Jack and Molly Frye, servants in the household of Dr. David Kevington, a skilled and moneyed English surgeon. I always stood in awe of Dr. Kevington, partly because he had about him a manner that seemed superior and beyond anything I could ever be. And partly because I knew he had lived for many years in the United States, studying in this country's best medical schools, and teaching there, as well.

"It made me jealous of him. I'd always felt a strong fascination with the United States, you see, which was something I couldn't quite account for, and which, oddly, seemed to upset my mother. She didn't like it when I would talk about wanting to visit America someday. She told me I had no place in America, that my home and my heritage was England. Now I see that I have an attraction to this country because my true origins are here. By blood I am an American, certainly on the side of my mother, and almost certainly on that of my father."

"By which you mean me," Kenton said.

"Yes. Please be patient with me—I will try to make it as clear as I can, as quickly as I can." She cleared her throat. "Life on the Kevington estate was sometimes difficult for us, but all in all, I was happy. The people I knew as my parents were good people, both of them, and raised me well. My father, Jack Frye, was an honest man, and simple. He loved my mother and myself dearly, and was loved in return.

"I had no brothers or sisters, and on the estate I seldom had playmates of my own age. There were on occasion other children, the offspring of other servants in the household, but these seldom stayed for long. Dr. Kevington was a difficult man to work for, often harsh and sometimes cruel. He loved liquor, and when he had had too much of it, could treat his servants with the greatest disdain. As a child I found him frightening, and tried to keep my distance from him. There were times I saw him watching me as I played or worked on the grounds, though, staring at me from behind the tall glass window of his study, with the oddest and most hateful of expressions. I felt he had an unaccountable loathing for me, and I sometimes dreamed of him at night, awakening in a fright.

"As fearful of Dr. Kevington as I was, though, I held a deep and unshakable interest in his wife, who was seldom seen. She stayed mostly in her chamber, a room I never saw, apart from its great, wide windows that looked down onto the gardens of the estate. I could see it from a window of my own room, in a cottage that we lived in on the southern edge of the estate. Sometimes she would be in the window, looking out. When the light was right, I could see her well enough to gain an impression of how she looked. What I couldn't make out with my eyes I would fill in with my imagination.

"She was a beautiful woman, with pale skin, and long, dark hair. Sometimes she stood at the window, but usually she sat. Often she wore a white gown.

My mother would scold me when I watched her. She would tell me that Dr. Kevington was jealous of his wife, and treated her as his own private treasure, and so I shouldn't look at her or Dr. Kevington might become angry.

"I couldn't really understand why that should be. Why would Dr. Kevington care if a servant girl watched his wife sometimes as she sat by her window? But my mother was adamant about this. She told me that it was important that I always stay far away from Mrs. Kevington.

"This, of course, only made Mrs. Kevington more mysterious and intriguing to me. I wanted to see her up close, maybe even talk to her. Somehow I had the notion that she was interested in me—that sometimes she was watching me while I watched her. I told this to my father once, and he laughed, and told me that I was a foolish little girl spinning silly dreams. But when he told my mother what I had said, she grew angry, and told me again I was never to have anything to do with Mrs. Kevington, and that Mrs. Kevington was very sick, and did not want to be bothered with silly servant girls. And so I never saw Dr. Kevington's wife up close through all my girlhood.

"But I did see her son. Paul Kevington was about a year younger than I. Though he was expected to stay away from the servants, when he was a boy he slipped away sometimes and would come and play with me and some of the other few servant children on the estate.

"In those days, I liked Paul, because he was fine-looking, and rich, and part of the world inside the house that I seldom was allowed to enter except to labor over the dishes in the kitchen washroom. I wanted to ask him about his mother, but I was always afraid to do it.

"As Paul grew older, his feelings began to change. He became unwilling to associate with the servants on any level but that of superior to underling. He stopped slipping away to play with me and other servant children, and began growing cold and rude whenever I did chance to see him. He was becoming more like his father, and less like the kind and loving person I imagined his mother to be.

"As the years passed, other changes came. Mrs. Kevington disappeared from her window. My mother told me that her health was improving. She was moving around the house now, and speaking for the first time in years. I was glad to note this, because I still felt a natural affection for Mrs. Kevington, even though I had yet to meet her.

"Paul Kevington began to come around again. He was interested in me once more, but his interest was different. I began to think that he was in love with me, though with Paul it was difficult to tell where love left off and lust began. I was an innocent girl, not accustomed to the ways of a worldly young man. But eventually, I was affected by his attentions, and began to feel what I thought was love toward him.

"Paul was physically forward with me, but I had

been raised well and refused what he would have me do. It was at those times that I wondered if he truly loved me, because he would grow furiously angry, and accuse me of being false-hearted. As time passed I found my resolve beginning to weaken. He vowed to me that he wished to marry me, and that there was no sin in what he wished me to do. You will pardon me, Mr. Kenton, for speaking so openly with you about such private things."

"I understand," Kenton said.

"Ultimately, however, I found I simply couldn't yield. I made the decision to tell him this, though I dreaded what I expected would be an angry reaction. To my surprise, I found him much changed the next time I spoke to him. He told me that he no longer wished my company, or my hand in marriage.

"I was shocked by this, unable to understand his change of heart. He seemed angry with me, repelled by me, but he wouldn't tell me why. When I asked him if there was hope that we might yet reconcile with one other, he simply laughed, very coldly.

"My mother, who had always been able to read my feelings, saw that something was amiss with me. For two days I hardly ate, cried often, and withdrew from the fellowship of my family. She asked me to tell her what was wrong, and at last I did. I confessed to her the romance that I had carried on with Paul Kevington, and told her as well about his sudden change in manner toward me.

"As soon as I had told her the name of the man

I loved, she went pale, and seemed ill. I knew right away that there were aspects to this matter that I did not yet know. She called me aside, into a private place, and told me information that changed my life and broke my heart.

"She told me that I could never love Paul Kevington, or have any relationship with him of the sort I had intended. Paul Kevington, she told me, was my brother. I was stunned, and asked her how this could be. Surely there was a mistake. But she was insistent: Paul Kevington was my brother by blood, sharing not the same father but the same mother. My mother, she told me, was the mysterious Mrs. Kevington, the same woman I had watched for so many years through the tall window. Though my mind rejected this information at first, my heart knew straightaway that it was true. I had had an innate awareness of some special link to the woman behind the window. Now I understood what it was.

"I demanded of my mother—or, I should say, the woman who for all those years I had believed was my mother—an explanation of how I had come to be raised as a servant if in fact I was the child of the lady of the house.

"She told me the story that she had never expected to tell, and which, in fact, both she and her husband, my surrogate father, had vowed never to reveal to me. Despite that vow, she chose to tell me the full truth, because my feelings for Paul Kevington gave me a right to know. And so she told me the story of the woman behind the window, your Victoria."

CHAPTER

28

RACHEL paused a moment, clearing her throat again. Even that brief delay was agonizing to Kenton.

"Please go on! What did she tell you?" Kenton urged.

"Mrs. David Kevington, she said, was not the first wife of Dr. Kevington. His original wife had died many years before, shortly before Dr. Kevington journeyed to the United States. The circumstances of her death, she told me, were mysterious. The marriage between the pair had been troubled, and some whispered that Dr. Kevington had poisoned his first wife.

"While Dr. Kevington was in the United States, she said, he became enamored of a beautiful, dark-haired woman who was the wife of a traveling American journalist. She told me the journalist's name was Brady Kenton. Though she didn't know all the details herself, she told me that Dr. Keving-ton had returned to England after the crash of a train in which both he and Mrs. Kenton had been passengers. She had been severely hurt, left senseless and unable to awaken, and he had brought her home with him to care for her to nurse her back to health.

"Dr. Kevington said they had been married in the United States, after she had divorced her journalist husband. The new Mrs. Kevington, as she was perceived, remained in her coma for month on month. Dr. Kevington tended her devotedly, but her prospects appeared uncertain at best.

"Complicating the matter was a fact that became evident only after time: the new Mrs. Kevington was with child. This fact created much consternation on Dr. Kevington's part, my surrogate mother observed. The child was not his, but that of his wife's first husband. This child, he said, would never be raised in his household.

"When her time came, Mrs. Kevington, still in a coma, gave birth to a daughter . . . to me. Immediately, I was taken from my natural mother and given to Jack and Molly Frye, who were told to raise me as their own, replacing the child stillborn to them shortly before. Thus I became Rachel Frye, the daughter of servants in the Kevington household, and my true mother, who gave birth to me with no knowledge of it, never even saw me in circumstances to let her know who I was.

"My surrogate parents, though they were paid by Dr. Kevington to take me as their own, were not mercenary in their motives. The loss of their blood child had left a great vacancy in their hearts, one that I filled. Jack Frye in particular seemed devoted to making my life better than the one he and his wife lived, and took pains to make sure I received as much education as possible. Though he himself was scarcely literate, he bought books for me, and had his wife teach me to read. Through the years he maintained a library for me, encouraging me to teach myself as much as I could, and to become well-spoken and articulate.

"I think he did this because he knew that my birthright and true station in life was being denied to me. I did what he asked, and as a result was able to provide myself with a formal education that I believe equaled or bettered the formal educations of many in better circumstances."

"Your articulateness verifies that," Kenton said. "You're a very well spoken young lady." As he spoke he was looking out across the rail yard, watching a train being pulled around into the rail yard, ready for departure.

"After my birth, Mrs. Kevington began to emerge from her coma. At times, I'm told, she would awaken, though never fully. She was initially unable to speak, though as time passed she began to be able to converse to a limited degree. The injuries she had suffered in the railroad accident had left her in a dire condition, though with Dr. Kevington's care she was beginning to improve, and there was hope that someday she would be fully restored.

"But there was a dark side. Molly Frye told me that Dr. Kevington took advantage of the limited understanding of his wife to persuade her that he truly was her husband, and that you, Mr. Kenton, were dead. He wanted her fully for himself, with no devotion left in her for you or anyone else from her former life.

"In her weakened state, it's likely that she accepted what he told her. My surrogate mother sometimes tended to her; she described her as a sad, quiet woman, a shadow of a person . . . but a shadow that was becoming fuller and richer with each passing month. But those months stretched into years, as you know, and at length the woman who had been Mrs. Brady Kenton became in her own mind wife of Dr. David Kevington.

"Shortly after my birth, Mrs. Kevington was again with child, this time fathered by Dr. Kevington. Just over a year after I was born, Paul Kevington came into the world. I have already told you some of his history and manner, and how I came to fall in love with him, not knowing we shared the same mother. My surrogate mother, who was quite perceptive where Paul Kevington was concerned, pointed out something to me that I had missed myself: Paul's suddenly harsh manner toward me was surely an indication that his own father had told him the same story that my surrogate mother had told me. He had learned our true kinship, and that we never could have a relationship other than that of brother and sister.

"I later learned that he had indeed been told the truth, by his own father. The circumstances had been much like my own: Dr. Kevington had learned that Paul loved me, and was forced to tell him that I was in truth his half sister.

"Paul Kevington, oddly, seemed to hold the circumstances of our births against me, as if my parentage were my own fault. He seemed to resent me because of this twisted hand that fate had dealt us.

"Paul Kevington and I parted with me brokenhearted and him full of anger. At the time I thought our situation was the most ironic and sorrowful turn of events that could have come. Soon, though, I began to learn more of the true nature of Paul Kevington, and to realize that it was my good fortune that he and I could have no part of one another.

"Let me tell you about Paul. He is a most remarkable young man, very talented in many ways. He is a skilled actor, capable of taking over a stage and playing virtually any role to perfection. He is equally skilled as an artist and writer. All in all, the man should have been able to make a good showing for himself in almost any area he might choose. But one quality he lacks: he possesses no evident human sense of morality. Paul Kevington is a man completely without sense of right and wrong, devoted only to his own well-being and pleasure. I am ashamed, in fact, that I share a blood kinship with such a man.

"After our relationship was finished, Paul turned his attentions to another young woman who lived in poor quarters within a mile of the Kevington estate. Her name was Jenny; she was a common and uneducated girl, but one of extraordinary beauty. It was clear to me what Paul's intentions toward her were. I was beginning to comprehend that he lacked the ability to truly love a woman. His interests were entirely for his own physical gratification.

"Jenny, though, was unable to see this, though I spoke to her more than once and warned her. She was flattered by the attention given her by a handsome and wealthy young man, who was known for his talents as well as his fine looks.

"I knew his intention was to take advantage of her, and I was correct. She came to me one evening, crying, telling me she was carrying Paul's child, and that Paul refused even to speak to her about it. Her father was a hard man, stern in his morality, and she knew she faced the most severe consequences for what she had done. Feeling pity for her, I told her I would find a way to help her. I spoke to a priest I knew, a man of good heart and forgiving nature, and made arrangements to meet her at a hidden place to help her escape from both her father and from Paul. She was afraid of Paul; some of the things he had said had made her fear he might seek to hurt her or even kill her in order to keep the child from being born.

"Before I could go to her, though, my surrogate father became ill. His heart simply failed him. I went to his side, and stayed with him for nearly a day until, very quietly, he died. I held his hand and wept.

"Then I remembered the meeting I had missed. I left, and went to look for her in the place we had said we would meet.

"I found the priest's corpse lying on a woodland trail before I got there. He had been stabbed. Terrified, I wanted to run away, but I worried about what had happened to Jenny. I moved ahead, and came upon her just in time to see her dying as Paul Kevington stabbed her again and again. I ran; he saw me, and chased me. I knew that he would kill me, no matter what.

"I hid for two days, afraid to reveal my presence to anyone. I stole food, lived in a barn loft, starting at every sound and shadow. Paul Kevington did not find me, but I soon realized that if he couldn't find me, he could still find my family. I ran home, and found my mother stabbed to death in her own bed.

"She had already been found by a neighbor. Because I had been absent it was feared at first that I was dead, as well, or that I was guilty of the killing. I learned these things from a neighbor who knew me well, and discovered that my surrogate mother had told her enough of my situation that she understood what was happening. She told me that there was no hope for me; Paul Kevington and his father would be believed, no matter what they said, whereas I, as a common servant girl, would not be. Paul Kevington could not afford to leave me alive, not after I had witnessed him committing murder. I had to flee the country. Otherwise he would find me and kill me.

"I had done research and discovered that Brady Kenton was not dead. I determined to find you, because I wanted to know the man who truly was my father. I took money that my surrogate father had saved for many years, which he kept buried in a jar at the rear of our house beneath an oak tree. With that money and the help of friends, I was able to secretly obtain passage on a ship and come to the United States.

"Once here, I quickly found that Brady Kenton was a far more famous man in this country than I had realized. I studied the *Illustrated American,* reading every story of yours that I could find. I studied your pictures, and was shocked to find that in many of them I could detect a subtle image of the same face I had seen through the glass of that high window in the Kevington house."

"Yes," Kenton said. "It's been my habit to include her image in my work as a tribute to her. Most people, though, are not perceptive enough to spot the images."

She took this as a compliment and smiled at him; to Kenton it was again like seeing his long-lost wife, and melted something inside of him. He was finding all of this almost too much to take in. After years of not knowing the truth, it was almost impossible to believe he was finally learning it.

Rachel continued her story. "I began trying to track you down. I had thought I could go to the headquarters of the *Illustrated American* and simply find you there, but soon learned that you're a man without a home, constantly traveling. To make matters more difficult, I discovered that you tended not to follow your schedules very closely. Not even the *Illustrated American* knew where you were . . . or if they did, they would not reveal it.

Kenton said, "If I had known you were trying to find me, I would have made it easier for you."

She smiled at him again. "I finally was able to trace you to Texas, where you had gone to work on a story. When I got there, I had no more money, no food. Since coming to the United States I have worked when I could, and where I could, to keep myself alive. I thought sometimes about actually advertising to hear from you, but still feared Paul Kevington. He had the means to travel to this country very easily, and given that I knew him to be a murderer, he had the motive to do so, as well. So I kept myself hidden.

"In Texas I worked in the household of a wealthy rancher. It was good work, and I was tired of traveling and hiding, and stayed longer than I intended. Meanwhile I continued to read the *Illustrated American,* and to attempt to find a pattern in your movements. I had grown more confident that Paul Kevington had not followed me from England after all, and that I was safe from him.

"And then, one day, he was there. He was mounted on a horse, on a hillside, watching the ranch.

"I panicked. I realized how determined he was to find me, how great a threat I was to his very existence as long as I remained alive. At first I couldn't guess how he had managed to track me to such an obscure place. Then I realized he had simply used the same logic I had. He knew that I would seek to find my real father, and so he tracked the famous Brady Kenton to Texas, knowing I would not be far behind.

"The very day after I saw Paul on that hillside, I heard that there had been trouble of some sort near the Mexican border. Some Texas Rangers had gotten involved in a fight with someone who was described as an Englishman. I knew it had to be Paul. A Ranger was killed in the fight, shot in the back. Another was wounded.

"My fear of Paul only increased. He was a madman! I had to leave right away. I took my little bit of money, my few possessions, and fled, not really sure where I was going. For quite some time, I remained on the move, taking jobs here and there to survive, sometimes, I admit, resorting to theft when I was hungry. I lost track of you, couldn't follow you. This was probably good, because it made it virtually impossible for Paul to track me in turn. I began to hope again that I had escaped him.

"Then, I read in the *Illustrated American* about your great adventure in Montana involving the fireball that fell from the sky. Suddenly, everywhere I went, I heard people talking about that story, and about you. And I heard someone say that you were seeking a wife whom everyone said was dead, but who you believed was still alive.

"When I heard that, I had all the more reason to find you, knowing I could give you the answers you wanted. I began tracking you again, hoping that Paul had given up and gone back to England."

CHAPTER

29

RACHEL continued her narrative. "This time, though, it proved even harder to track you. I would hear that you were at one place, working on a story, only to find when I arrived there that you had unexpectedly moved on." She hesitated, then continued: "I hope you forgive me, Mr. Kenton, but people were saying unflattering things about you in some of these places, saying you were distracted, haphazard, uncaring about your work. Some attributed it to bad habits . . . overdrinking, if I may say it straight out . . . while others said you were distracted by your quest for your wife."

"Both evaluations are true," Kenton said with brutal honesty. "My professional behavior over the past year has been anything but exemplary, as Alex Gunnison would certainly confirm to you. I have been obsessed with looking for Victoria, and I have been too quick to seek comfort in a bottle. I'm a far from perfect man, Rachel."

"I would expect nothing different, Mr. Kenton. As it has been taught to me, only one perfect man has ever walked this earth."

Kenton smiled. "Indeed."

She went on. "Suddenly, I found your clearest track yet: an announcement that you were to be a speaker at a special celebration in Leadville, Colorado. I was thrilled, but also frightened. The announcement was widely published. Paul Kevington would surely see it, too. By then, I had picked up evidence he was following me once more. Knowing he would go to Leadville was almost enough to make me stay away, but in the end the chance to find you was too irresistible. I went to Leadville, hoping that I could find you before Paul found me.

"But when I reached Leadville, you were not there. Your partner, Mr. Gunnison, was speaking in your place. And indeed Paul had followed me. Scared, desperate, nearly starved, I sought out Mr. Gunnison in hopes that he could protect me and take me to you. He hardly knew what to make of me, but he was very kind, and gave me shelter and food. Then, while he was away briefly from his hotel room, Paul found me. He attacked me in the hotel hallway. I fought him, and managed to escape. I hid, then slipped onto a train and escaped Leadville. Mr. Gunnison had told me that you had come to Denver. So I came here to find you . . . and now I have."

Kenton reached out and gently touched her hand.

"Indeed you have. And I'm glad. I believe your story. Gunnison told me things about you, things that had been told to him by a man I am now sure was Paul Kevington in the guise of a Texas Ranger. He said you had committed murder in England and killed a family in Texas, and that you would kill me if you got the chance. But I don't believe that. There is no falsehood in what you have said to me. I'm sure of it."

"I have told you the full and absolute truth," she replied firmly. "I am no murderer. The only murderer is Paul Kevington himself. He is the man who murdered my mother in England. And there was no murder in Texas except his killing of the Ranger."

Kenton suddenly turned his head and raised his hand, signaling for silence. He had heard a noise around the back of the shed. Rachel heard it, as well. Kenton felt her surge of fear like an electrification of the atmosphere around him.

"Who could it be?" she whispered.

Kenton again signaled for her to be quiet. He rose silently, and crept back toward the source of the sound . . .

An explosion of activity ensued. Someone scrambled wildly away, making abundant noise. Kenton scrambled, as well, but not in time to catch whoever it had been. He caught a faint glimpse of someone vanishing into the night.

Rachel was on her feet. "Was it him? Was it Paul?" Her voice was tight with terror.

"No, I don't think it was," Kenton replied. "Kevington wouldn't run. Kevington, I think, would take this opportunity to deal with the problem you—and now I—pose to him."

"Then who?"

"Probably just a vagrant. Such types tend to hang about rail yards."

"Did he hear my story? Why did he run? What will he do?"

Kenton shrugged. "I don't know, and it probably doesn't matter. The thing for us now is to get on a train. Look there. I think I see an opportunity for us."

He pointed toward a train that had slowly circled into the station yard during the latter part of Rachel's narrative. One of the sliding cargo doors on one of the freight cars was slightly ajar. And at the moment no one was positioned in the rail yard to allow them to see that side of the train. If Kenton and Rachel could move swiftly enough, and if they could avoid drawing the attention of anyone in the locomotive or on the caboose, they could get aboard and hide themselves.

"Now?" Rachel asked.

"Now," Kenton replied.

They left their hiding place, and advanced swiftly across the dark rail yard toward the open door of the freight car.

Gunnison had never been so worried about Brady Kenton, and that was saying a lot, because over the years he had grown expert in worrying about the man. This time he felt a sense of guilt, as well. He had left Rachel Frye, a woman about whose murderous tendencies he had been clearly warned, alone in Kenton's room. Now she and Kenton were both gone, and there was blood everywhere in the room.

Maybe she had stabbed him and dragged off his body. Maybe he had staggered off on his own, badly wounded and bleeding. In either case the thing to do now was to find help, even from the very police Kenton had fled. Kenton's life might depend on it.

Out of breath from running, Gunnison finally arrived at the police station. There was still much activity going on about it, the search for Kenton still under way. Gunnison rushed toward the door.

The door opened when he was within a few feet of it. He jerked to a halt as Frank Turner emerged, slapping his big hat onto his head with a vigor that suggested he was not in a good mood.

He seemed surprised to see Gunnison. "Back so soon?" he asked. "I was just headed for that barroom to wait for you, and get out of this sorry place." He thumbed over his shoulder toward the station interior behind him.

"Mr. Turner, let me pass," Gunnison said. "I need to see a policeman. I think Brady Kenton may be badly hurt, or worse."

"Hurt? How so?"

Though he considered shoving past Frank Turner to go inside, Gunnison quickly related what happened: the dark and empty room, the blood on the floor.

"Wait," Turner said. "Let *me* go with you. I can be of more help to you than any man you'll find on this police force here, and that's not bragging, just telling the truth."

"No offense, Ranger Turner," Gunnison said, "but I think I need an official policeman for this one."

"If you want help from someone who's more concerned about doing things right than harrassing folks he don't like, then I'm your man, not anybody inside that building." Frank Turner said this so forcefully that the words bore weight. He looked Gunnison squarely in the eye. "Take me to this room. If there's tracking to be done, I can outtrack any man within the bounds of the city, and once again it's not bragging, just telling the facts as they are."

Gunnison hesitated, stammering something vague.

"Listen to me," Turner pressed. "My cousin in there cares not a whit about Brady Kenton, about you, or about anything but using the law to his own ends and for his own satisfaction. He's been ranting and going on about all the trouble he intends to bring on Kenton, whom he hates as a 'Lincolnite.' The great war never ended for my cousin, you see. If you allow Henry Turner to search for your friend, you're not likely to see him found alive."

That was enough to persuade Gunnison. "Let's go," he said.

He and Frank Turner headed back in the direction Gunnison had come, Gunnison all but running, Turner doing his best to keep up on his limping leg.

CHAPTER

30

In a dirty, dank-smelling hotel room, Paul Kevington, dressed as a Texas Ranger, strode back and forth.

He was a worried man. He had come here from Leadville, certain that he must finally lay his hands on Rachel Frye, or perhaps lose his chance forever. He had come so close in Leadville! She had been literally within his grasp there in the hallway outside Alex Gunnison's hotel room, and yet she had gotten away. He still couldn't believe she had managed to do so. It was infuriating, and downright embarrassing.

Now that he was in Denver, he wasn't so sure he was going to find her at all. This was a sizable city, full of places a clever person could hide, and Rachel Frye was clever. He had to admit that much. It was no small feat that she had managed to evade him this long. The mere act of fleeing to the United

States had shown her savvy; had she stayed in England he would long ago have tracked her down and taken care of her.

Sometimes he wondered if she was more clever than he. He had an aggravating history of making mistakes where she was concerned. The first had been to fall in love with her, back before he knew their true relation to one another. What a twisted joke of fate that had been! It made him angry. And even though he knew it was illogical, he blamed her for it.

He also blamed her for having caught him in the act of murder. That one incident had sealed her fate. She had to die; he could not afford to leave alive a witness to his crime.

The murder of the meddlesome priest and the pregnant servant girl had not been his first killing. The first had occurred when he was only fifteen years old. The victim had been a vagrant, an annoying, drunken, bad-smelling, trespassing vagabond who had made a mistake of stumbling across Paul Gunnison as he rode on a remote portion of his father's estate on an unusually boring afternoon. In those days Paul had been enamored of archery; he had with him his bow and arrow. The idea of using a human being as a target had come to him in a rush, not anything he had planned, not anything he had fantasized about. But the power of the idea, once arisen, had been compelling, and after the vagabond managed to insult and annoy him, he carried it out without hesitation.

It had fascinated him to watch the old man die. Hiding the body, aware that any error on his part could destroy him, had given him a heady feeling like he'd never before experienced.

He had known when the act was finished that he had to do it again. In a life full of luxury but without challenges, where nothing he desired was withheld from him, it was fulfilling beyond description to have found a game worth playing, one in which the stakes were high, and real.

So he had killed again, then again, before he ever even touched the priest and the servant girl. He had not committed those killings merely for a thrill, of course. The priest had died for what he knew, and for being meddlesome; Jenny had died because Paul Kevington had no desire to be a father, and he had to be rid of both her and the unwanted life in her.

If only Rachel Frye hadn't seen him kill her! It wouldn't have been necessary to destroy her mother for fear Rachel had told her what she'd seen. It would not have been necessary to launch this great transcontinental chase.

Not that the chase didn't have its own inherent rewards. He found it gratifying and darkly empowering to realize that another human lived in terror of him, and watched for him as a sleepless child in a dark room watches for ghosts that can appear without warning. It was also fulfilling to pursue this chase on his own steam. His father, suspicious of his crimes, had cut him off financially. Paul Kevington had had to provide his own means of support as he chased Rachel Frye. The means by which he'd done it, he thought, were quite clever. His own creative skills had provided him the means to support himself while he continued the chase.

But what if she had managed to escape him for good? What if she returned to England, and revealed what he had done? What if she found Brady Kenton, and Kenton exposed him through his journalism?

Paul Kevington needed a drink. Time to hit the streets, get hold of a bottle, and calm his nerves a bit.

A sudden rapping on his door startled him, causing him to reach for his pistol.

"Who's there?" he said, taking care to speak in that perfect imitation of a Texas accent that had helped disguise his British origins here in America.

"It's me . . . Crane."

"Don't believe I know a Crane."

"You remember! I'm the man from the rail yard."

Kevington did remember. Crane was a local no-good who lived in a shack within view of most of the rail yard. Kevington had stumbled across him by chance right after he arrived in Denver, and had offered him money to report to him if he should cross the path of a vagrant Englishwoman. The rail yard had seemed a likely place for Rachel Frye to make an appearance; he knew she traveled by train sometimes.

Kevington reholstered his pistol and opened the door. He wrinkled his nose as Crane's earthy and unwashed pungency preceded him into the room.

"You've seen her?" Kevington asked in perfect faux Texan.

"Yes, sir. Not more than fifteen minutes ago. But if you want to catch her you'll have to hurry, because I believe she and the man with her are getting ready to slip out of the city."

"Who is the man with her?"

Crane arched one brow and looked sideways at Kevington, saying nothing. The message was clear.

Kevington dug bills from beneath his vest and stuffed them into Crane's hand.

Crane smiled haughtily. "Pleasure doing business with you, Mr. Best."

"Tell me what you saw, damn you!" Kevington snapped. For a moment, he forgot to maintain his Texan accent, and Crane looked surprised as he heard the English inflections in Kevington's voice. Kevington noticed that look, and if Crane's fate hadn't been determined until now, it was as of that moment.

"I don't know who the man is. He's a tall fellow, strong kind of build, fine-looking sort of gent. Grayish kind of beard and hair. I didn't know him, but he looked kind of familiar."

Kevington swore beneath his breath. He knew who it was: a man whose visage seemed familiar to almost every American because it was present in each edition of America's most popular magazine.

Rachel, that miserable cow, had found Brady Kenton.

CHAPTER

31

KENTON and Rachel stood inside the dark freight car long enough to let their eyes adjust to the diminished light. The car was about three-quarters full of assorted boxes, crates, and burlap sacks filled with grain or feed of some sort.

"I was thrown out of a railroad car like this back in Texas," Rachel said. "Do you know if the railroad detectives in Denver are very vigilant?"

"No, and therefore we must presume they will be," Kenton said. "I think the best plan for us is to get over in that corner there." He pointed toward the back of the car. "You can hide back there with minimal chance of being caught. I don't think many railroad detectives would bother to crawl over that many crates on the slim chance some vagabond has made a nest in a corner."

Kenton boosted Rachel onto the stack of crates. She crawled across the top, and looked over into the space Kenton proposed as their hiding place. "The space is fairly small."

"Go ahead and take that spot," Kenton said. "I'll hide out here where I can keep an eye on the rail yard through the door. That way, if anyone is caught, it will be me alone."

"Don't talk about getting caught. After searching this long for you, I don't want to be separated from you again."

"My sentiments are the same. But the crucial thing now is to make sure you get away from Denver and break Paul Kevington's trail. You are the one most in danger."

Rachel dropped over into the hiding space. He heard her move about a little, settling there. He was sure she was cramped and uncomfortable, but she did not complain. Kenton supposed she was accustomed to discomfort after so much time on the road.

Kenton found a recess of his own in which to hide, but from which he could also gain quick access to the door. The door remained open, something he expected would be noticed by the railroad crew before this train pulled out. So he had to be ready to make a run for it and draw the railroad men away from the car, if neccessary, and give Rachel a chance to get away even if he didn't.

He hoped it would not come to that. He already felt a strong bond with this young woman, whom he had now accepted as his own daughter. Yet it would take time to grow fully accustomed to thinking of himself as a father.

Kenton settled down as best he could and waited for the train to begin moving. He heard noise elsewhere along the line of cars, cargo being loaded into another freight car. He hoped nothing was to be added to this one.

Paul Kevington, out of breath, sweating, and thoroughly tense, paused at the edge of the rail yard. He had just pulled off what he considered a rather amazing feat. He had passed through Denver, at a time its streets were filled with searching policemen, and had not been stopped, not even noticed, as best he could tell. Not just anyone could have done it so well.

Even so, he was not in a self-congratulatory mood. He knew he had done a foolish thing back at his hotel room to stab that vagabond and leave him there. Another murder added to his record! And further, one that would easily be traced to him, once the body was found. The only solace he could find was that he was registered in that hotel under the name of Jessup Best rather than his real name.

He vowed to himself that he would become less impulsive, and keep his temper in check from now on. Impulsive actions could destroy him.

He scanned the rail yard, wondering where they were. No train had left Denver in the last several minutes; he had been listening and had heard no whistles or chugging locomotives. So his prey should still be close by, though no doubt hidden.

He looked at the lone train sitting in the yard,

obviously almost ready to depart. If Rachel and Kenton had come to the rail yard looking for a way of escape, that train was the only immediate possibility.

The locomotive came to life, belching smoke and sound. The railroad crew swung aboard. The train was about to pull out.

Uncertainty struck. Rachel Frye and Brady Kenton were probably aboard that train. In minutes it would be out of his reach. They would get away from him. They could abandon that train anywhere along the line and go in any direction. Brady Kenton could provide protection for Rachel, and resources that would allow her to disappear.

Kevington thought, If she escapes me tonight, I may never have another opportunity to catch her.

He had to think fast, and logically. He did not, and could not, know whether they were on that train, but under the circumstances, that was the best presumption. Thus he had to find a way onto that train before it was out of reach.

And there he faced a problem. Between him and the rail yard was a tall fence, one he was looking through even now. It was too high to vault and offered no handholds to allow him to climb.

He would have to board that train, somehow, as it left the fenced portion of the rail yard. But that would be risky. By the time the train passed the fence, it would be moving fast. He might not be able to swing himself aboard, or even worse, he might fall off and go beneath the wheels.

He would just have to take the risk. If Rachel escaped, especially in the company of a man with the American press at his fingertips, he was destroyed.

He watched the train slowly roll toward the edge of the rail yard. He spotted the place where the tracks exited the rear yard, and where he felt he would have the best opportunity to connect with the train, assuming it was not moving too swiftly by that time.

Kevington headed for that spot in a dead run, watching the train all the while. He noticed that one of the freight-car doors was slightly ajar. The railroad crew must have overlooked that one. Maybe, if he moved just right, he could throw himself directly into that opening as the car moved past.

He positioned himself, legs bent, every muscle tense as he locked his eye onto that opening, knowing the timing had to be just right, or . . .

But the train was moving much faster now. Too fast, he realized. To leap for that opening would only get him killed in a most horrible way. He watched his opportunity pass. The train, picking up momentum by the moment, was almost completely past him when he saw his only other opportunity. Fighting back the impulse to yell, he sprang forward, toward the moving train. He did not allow himself time to ponder the fact that he was a moment away either from a remarkable athletic success, or death beneath the wheels of the rolling train.

CHAPTER

32

BRADY Kenton was standing again in the center of
the freight car, looking out to the open door. The
dark landscape outside moved past at an ever-
accelerating speed.

He felt tremendously relieved. Fate had been
kind. No railroad detective had searched this freight
car, and no crewman had come along even to shut
the door. So it looked as though he and Rachel had
made it out of Denver. He had escaped arrest and
jail, and Rachel had gotten away from Paul Kevington one more time. Kenton vowed to himself that
she would not have to flee Kevington again. He
would protect her.

Kenton reflected on all that had happened during
his brief stay in Denver, and suddenly laughed
aloud as he was struck by the oddness of it all. He
had assaulted a man, smashed a barroom window,
made a drunken fool of himself in public, broken

into a magazine publishing house, made an enemy of the local police, sacrificed his reputation and probably his career, had a stranger fatally stabbed in his rented room, and now topped all that off by hopping a freight train like a common vagabond.

And all he had come to Denver to do was try to find some information about a mediocre serial novel published in a fairly nondescript pulp magazine!

The funny thing was, he really didn't care now about how all these things might damage him. Let his job go, let his reputation decline, let even his beloved fame vanish! None of it mattered now. He had finally learned the truth about Victoria, and discovered that he had a daughter to boot. His life had made a radical turn, but he regretted nothing about it.

Kenton climbed up on a stack of crates. "Rachel! You can come out now. We're moving, and nobody's going to be entering this car while we're in motion."

"Good . . . can you help me out?"

Kenton crawled across the top of the crates. He lit a match for light, holding it in his left hand as he reached down with his right to help her out. She smiled at him as he pulled her up, and for Kenton it was as if he had known her all his life, not just one evening.

They climbed down from the crates and into the open center area of the car.

"I like it better out here," she said. "I don't like closed-in places." She sniffed the air. "You smell like smoke. And it's not the match or the train's smokestack—I noticed the smell on you earlier."

"I was in a burning building earlier tonight," Kenton said.

"Really? How did that happen?"

"It's a long story. But suffice it to say, I learned something important when I was in that building. Have you ever heard of a magazine called *American Popular Library?*"

"No, I don't think so."

"It's a magazine based in Denver that publishes novels in serialized form. I was contacted recently by an editor at the *Popular Library* who knew about my search for Victoria. He had noticed a novel, edited by another editor at the same magazine, with a plot that had remarkable parallels to the parts of Victoria's story that we already knew. Now that I've heard what you have to say, I realize the parallels in the novel run even deeper. That would mystify me if not for the fact that when I was inside the building today, the one that caught fire, I found a scrap of paper that told me the name of the author of the novel in question."

"Paul Kevington."

Kenton was surprised. "How did you know?"

"It is an easy guess. Paul is a very skilled writer, with several publication credits in England."

"Well, now he has one in America. As best I can speculate, he sold the novel to the *Popular Library* to help finance his travels in this country. Though I wouldn't have thought that a man of his means would require the money."

"Paul Kevington and his father did not always see eye to eye. Dr. Kevington was always threatening to cut off his money, or so the servants whispered among themselves. Maybe he finally did so. Maybe he found out about his son's crimes."

"Dr. Kevington has crimes of his own to answer for. His son could hardly be worse than he is."

"He's a wicked man, indeed. I can't believe that at one time I was in love with him."

"He takes after his father," Kenton said bitterly. "Evil but charming."

"He's more wicked than his father," Rachel said. "Dr. Kevington at least took great care of your wife after the train accident."

"No greater care than I would have provided for her," Kenton replied. "It was I who should have had the opportunity to nurse her back to health. She was . . . *is* . . . my wife, stolen from me by a man who had no right to her. I have spent most of my adult life missing her, aching for her, hoping against hope that she could somehow still be alive, even during those times I felt I knew she had died. Don't ask me to find anything praiseworthy in Dr. David Kevington. I despise the man."

It was too dark for her to see his face, but she could feel the intensity of his bitterness. "What will you do now that you know where she is?" she asked.

"I'll go and take her back," he said without hesitation.

"Dr. Kevington will not allow it. He'll die before he lets her go."

"Then die he will. I'll be happy to oblige him."

She said nothing more. Kenton realized that his harsh and angry words had darkened her spirits. He wished he hadn't spoken.

"Let's put such grim talk aside for now," Kenton said, smiling even though he knew she couldn't really see him. "Now is the time to simply be glad that we're safe, and that we've been brought together. I would not want to end my life never knowing that I and Victoria had a daughter."

"Thank you, Mr. Kenton," she said softly.

"Please . . . Not *Mister* Kenton. A daughter shouldn't call her father 'mister.' "

"What would you like me to call you?"

"Just call me Kenton, if you'd like. Everyone else does."

"People call you only by your last name?"

"Most do."

"I don't want to call you what everyone else calls you. May I call you Brady?"

"You may. Victoria called me that. Hearing you say the name is like hearing her say it."

"I'm glad . . . Brady." She paused and gripped her stomach, which had just rumbled. "Excuse me! I'm hungry, too."

"So am I. But we have nothing to eat."

"Then let's rest instead. I've found that when

you're hungry and can't get food, you can sleep and not feel it so much."

They sat down on the floor, feeling the lulling rumble of the train beneath them. Rachel leaned against Kenton, relaxing, and fell asleep with remarkable ease.

Kenton initially felt tense having her so close, for this was all very new to him and she was still virtually a stranger, but at last he too relaxed. But he did not sleep. Instead he simply let himself experience the closeness of his own flesh and blood. It was unfair that he had not known her before now. It was unfair that she had been stolen from him just as Victoria had.

The balances had been uneven for a long time. Soon Brady Kenton would level them. He promised it to the darkness around him.

CHAPTER

33

ALEX Gunnison and Frank Turner, both out of breath and sweating, stopped and looked at one another as they heard the sound of the train departing Denver. They were nearly to the train yard, but now it seemed they might be too late.

"Kenton is on that train," Gunnison said between gasps. "I would bet on it."

Turner nodded. He was equally out of breath, and obviously in pain. He was favoring his bad leg despite efforts to hide it.

Gunnison ventured, "Would you like me to go on alone and let you rest your leg?"

"I can keep going as long as you do."

"Then let's move on. Maybe we'll get lucky and find them still at the rail yard."

When they reached the rail yard, they arrived at the same spot that, unknown to them, Paul Kevington had stood not long before. They both looked across the now-empty yard. "Not a sign of them," Turner said. "They're on that train, sure as the world."

Gunnison sighed loudly. "Maybe it's for the best. He would only be arrested if he were found still in Denver. At least we know from the note he left that the blood in the room isn't his, or hers."

"Let's take a better look around. Maybe they're just hiding."

They began walking the perimeter of the rail yard, still outside of the surrounding fence. At last, though, they came nearer the shed beside which Kenton and Rachel had hidden, though they had no way to know this.

"I can't believe what Kenton has done," Gunnison mused, growing angry in his frustration. "Running from the police! Breaking into buildings! He's thrown away a career that he spent years in building. My father will fire him for this, and Kenton deserves it."

"A man, just like a cat, can get his tail caught under the rocker sometimes," Turner said. "I've done it myself. Hey, who is that coming there?"

Gunnison had just spotted the same fellow. "I don't know, but he looks hurt."

Indeed, the man staggering and stumbling in their direction did appear to be injured. Or very drunk. When he was close enough, they noticed his shirt was crimson with blood.

Gunnison and Turner moved as one toward the

heavyset man, who appeared ready to collapse at any moment.

"Hey, now, friend," Turner said. "Have you hurt yourself in some way?"

"I've been stabbed," the man replied weakly, in a tone that indicated he could scarcely believe it.

"Stabbed? Where?"

The man gestured at his chest. He staggered to the left. Gunnison reached out, and steadied him.

"I think you should sit down," Gunnison said.

It was an unnecessary suggestion. The man was growing so weak he could do nothing else. He slumped heavily to the ground.

Gunnison and Turner knelt beside him.

"He said he would pay me," the man mumbled. "He gave me the money, but he took it back."

"Have you been drinking this evening, amigo?" Turner asked.

"No. Not drinking. I just told him what I saw, like he wanted, and then he . . ." The man's voice was growing softer. He was obviously on the verge of fainting.

"He's losing consciousness," Gunnison said to Turner. "We've got to find this man some help."

"Not exactly the best timing," Turner observed.

"Certainly not." Gunnison looked around helplessly. "How are we going to locate a doctor at this time of night? And what about Kenton?"

"Kenton probably has already moved on," Turner said. "Unless we find him soon we can only assume he hopped the train."

"Hopped the train," the injured man repeated, mumbling. "Hopped the train, yes. I *told* him they were going to hop the train. I told him he needed to hurry if he was going to catch them. Then he stabbed me and took back the money."

Gunnison was inclined to ignore this apparent babble as nothing more than that, but Turner narrowed one eye and looked closely at the man. "Are you telling me you saw somebody hop a train tonight?"

"Didn't see them hop the train . . . but they were waiting for it. I know they were going to hop it. I told him that, and he stabbed me. He shouldn't have stabbed me."

"No, he shouldn't have. Who did you see about to hop the train?"

"That man, that woman."

"I think I'd best run find a doctor," Gunnison said.

"Wait. Wait just a moment." Turner leaned even closer to the man. "You saw a man and a woman here at the rail yard, waiting for a train?"

Gunnison suddenly grasped where Turner was leading and was embarrassed he hadn't caught on more quickly. The man's seeming babble suddenly became much more interesting.

"Yes. I saw them. There, near my shed."

Turner asked, "Did you hear the woman speak?"

"Yes. She talked a lot. She was . . . was . . ."

"Foreign? British, maybe?"

"Yes. British. Talked different . . . kind of funny."

Gunnison asked, "Where are the man and the woman now?"

The man was unable to answer. He slumped to the side, eyes closing.

"We'll get no more from him," Turner said. "But he's verified for us that Kenton and the woman were here."

A harsh screeching pierced the darkness, followed by the appearance of a broad, feminine form moving fast in their direction. Gunnison was so startled he almost yelled. Something about the situation made him flash back to that incident in Leadville in which his attempt to save a battered woman had only resulted in his being battered himself.

"Oh, my poor Josh! What have they done to you, Josh?" The woman spoke in the same screeching tone in which she had screamed.

She dropped to her knees, gliding to the side of the wounded man. She struck Turner's legs in the process, bowling him over. He fell to the ground with a grunt.

She wrapped her arms around the wounded man. "Oh, Josh! Are you dead, Josh? Are you dead?"

Gunnison, tense as he was, had to fight away the impulse to laugh at Turner, who was struggling to get back on his feet. His fall had been most undignified.

To the woman, Gunnison said, "He isn't dead,

ma'am. He has been stabbed, but we don't know how badly. Are you his wife?"

She glared at Gunnison. "In the eyes of the common law we are! Don't you go judging!"

"I'm not trying to judge, ma'am," Gunnison replied. "I'm simply trying to find out if you are able to help us get care for him."

"Why did you stab him?" the woman demanded.

Frank Turner got back on his feet. "We didn't," he said. "Somebody else did. We're just trying to help him."

"From the amount of blood he's lost, I fear for him," Gunnison said.

Abruptly, the woman ripped open the man's shirt. Buttons flew. "Somebody got a match?" she said.

Frank Turner struck a match, and held it close to the wounded man's chest.

The woman examined the wound, and quickly declared, "It ain't so bad." She jammed a finger against the cut, making the man howl. "Josh always does bleed like a pig. Don't you, Josh."

"Bad wound or not, this man needs a doctor," Gunnison said.

"I'll get my brother to tend him," she said. "He sews up cut horses and such all the time. I reckon a man sews up the same as a horse."

"That's a fact," Turner said. "I've been sewed up by horse doctors many a time."

"But he could bleed to death!" Gunnison protested.

"Don't think so," Turner said, striking another match. He knelt and looked even closer at the wound. "She's right about his wound. You can see the blood starting to congeal there. And look how the wound goes. He was stabbed more or less with a sideways motion. It cut him under the skin, but it didn't go deep. That kind of wound bleeds a lot, but it's not that serious. I was cut in just same way myself one time, by a drunk Mexican. I bled a bucketful, but I was fine."

The wounded man, hearing this, revived a bit. He looked at the woman. "I'm going to live?"

Suddenly the woman was all emotion again. "Oh, yes, Josh, you'll live! You'll live to avenge yourself! Who did this to you?"

"The Texan fellow, the one who told us he'd pay us if we ever saw the Englishwoman. But he's not really Texan . . . he's English hisself," he said.

Gunnison and Turner glanced at one another. Paul Kevington! Who else could he be talking about?

"You're loco, Josh. Out of your head. I heard the man talk, and that's Texas talk if ever there was Texas talk."

"His talking changed . . . he talked like an Englisher. I swear it."

"He's telling the truth, ma'am," Turner said. "We know who stabbed him. It was an Englishman named Paul Kevington, who poses as a Texas Ranger. He's good at faking accents, it appears."

"He said he'd pay me if I found him the woman,

but he stabbed me instead," Crane said to the woman.

"I'll kill him," she said. "I'll hop on the next train and go right up that track and kill him!"

"He ain't up the track, Ruby. He's here in town."

She firmly shook her head. "He is not. Not any longer. I seen him myself, this very evening," she said. "He leaped onto the last train to pull out of here. I watched him do it, standing right over there. He leaped and hung on, and he's gone up the track on that train."

Gunnison went pale. Kenton and Rachel were probably on that train . . . and now Kevington was, as well. Did Kenton even know? Not unless he had been positioned to see Kevington make the leap.

"We've got to stop that train," Turner said to Gunnison.

"I know."

"The main office is over there, and the telegraph wire. We can wire ahead to the next station, have the train searched."

Turner's suggestion was sensible. It might result in Kenton being arrested and hauled back here into the clutches of Turner's corrupt lawman cousin, but it might also save his life.

Gunnison reached into his pocket and handed money to Ruby. "Take him to see a *real* doctor, not just some horse doctor. All right?"

She took the money with wide eyes, and nodded.

Gunnison ran toward the station office, leaving

the limping Turner behind, and Ruby the screecher
still kneeling on the ground, tending to Josh Crane,
a man Paul Kevington had stabbed and left for dead,
but who had lived to divulge his crime.

CHAPTER

34

THE man behind the counter in the station house was tired, irritable, and none too interested in what Gunnison and Turner had to say.

"So there's somebody stowed away on the train," he said snidely. "It's against the rules, sure enough, but it happens all the time. And I'm sure as hell not inclined to wire ahead to tell them to delay a running train just to find a couple of stowaway freight-car riders."

"You don't understand," Gunnison said. "There's not just a couple of riders, but three of them, and one is a great danger to the other two."

" 'Tain't my problem."

Turner stepped forward and flashed his badge quickly, then covered it up again. "I'm telling you in the name of the law to wire to the next stop and have that train stopped and searched."

"Let me see that badge again."

Turner reluctantly complied.

"Sorry, mister. But I don't think the Texas Rangers bear much authority in Colorado."

"Listen to me, compadre," Turner said, his voice going icy as he launched into a mix of truths, lies, and exaggerations that sounded very convincing. "I'm on special assignment with the Denver police force, and I bear their full authority when I give you an order. I'm on the trail of a murderer out of Texas, an Englishman named Paul Kevington. He is one of the three on the train. The other is an Englishwoman whom Kevington is intent on killing because she is the sole witness to murders he committed. The other man is Brady Kenton, the famous journalist. He'll be killed, too, if Kevington gets to him."

"Why would Brady Kenton be riding the rails like some tramp?" the man asked skeptically.

"Have you not been reading the papers, man? Don't you know that Kenton has gone off track lately? He heaved a man out a barroom window just days ago, and ran from the police this very evening when they were questioning him about breaking into a building that just happened to catch fire while he was in it. The man's loco, and the law wants him. That's one more reason for you to do what I tell you. You'll be quite the hero if you cooperate and help lead to the capture of both Kenton and Kevington." Frank Turner paused and went on in a much more grim tone: "And you'll be in one mess of trouble if your lack of cooperation results in them getting away . . . especially if someone ends up getting killed. I'll see you answer for it, I vow to you."

The man looked at Turner's stony face, swallowed visibly, and nodded.

"I'll get the message wired right away."

"There's a good man," Turner said, friendly now.

"And when you're done," Gunnison said, "tell us where a man might rent a good trail horse nearby."

Turner looked at Gunnison. "Why do you want to rent a horse?"

"I'm going to follow that train," he said. "I don't know if I'll catch up to it, but if they stop it, maybe there's a chance. At the very least I can go that train station and find out firsthand the results of that search."

"I'll be right beside you," Turner said.

The telegraph line began its chatter. Gunnison closed his eyes and prayed for the safety of Brady Kenton and Rachel Frye.

Kenton couldn't quite understand why he felt so relaxed. He was a fugitive from the law, a man who had just buried his career . . . but he felt peaceful just now despite it all. Rachel leaned against him, sleeping, and he had his arm around her. His daughter. A piece of himself he'd never known even existed. But now she was near, the darkness was all-enveloping and soothing, and all was well. The rest of the world could fall apart right now and he wouldn't care.

Kenton heard a thump above that broke him out

of his reverie. What was that? It sounded like someone atop the car . . .

He tensed, then relaxed again. Probably there was indeed someone up there: the brakeman. Those fellows could move along the top of a rolling train with the grace and stability of mountain goats on rocky crags.

But there was another thump above, heavy and leaden, the sound of something slipping and rolling . . . then yet another thump, this time on the side of the car.

Kenton glanced down. Rachel still slept heavily. He gently eased her over in the other direction, letting her rest against some of the cargo around them. She did not waken. He rose.

The train began a slow curve, making Kenton stumble slightly as he walked toward the still-open door.

More thumping on the side of the railroad car, like someone kicking . . . but that could only be the case if the person was literally hanging from the top edge of the car.

Kenton hesitated. If in fact the brakeman had fallen and was hanging on the side of the car, Kenton couldn't help him without revealing his presence, and ultimately, Rachel's. On the other hand, Kenton couldn't rightly let a man be endangered, maybe even killed, just to avoid being discovered as a stowaway.

He edged to the open door, through which a stout

wind whipped. He glanced around the edge, hoping to see without being seen in turn.

Sure enough, a man hung there, flailing a little in the wind, clinging to the top of the car desperately.

Kenton instantly forgot his own need to stay hidden. A human life was in danger.

"Hang on, Mr. Brakeman!" Kenton called out to the man. "I'll help you!"

The man twisted his head and looked in Kenton's direction. "Bless you, sir!" he said in a voice thick with the inflections of southern Alabama. "I'm about to fall!"

"Don't let go!" Kenton said. "I think I can reach you . . . and if you can hook the toe of your boot over the edge of that door latch there . . . yes, that's it . . ."

Kenton strained and stretched toward the brakeman, not sure he could quite reach him without sacrificing his own secure grip on the edge of the door. But he did reach him. The brakeman gripped Kenton's arm with one hand, shifted some of his weight onto his foot, which rested on the door latch, and thus relieved some of the strain on the fingers of his other hand.

"What now?" the brakeman asked in a tone mixing desperation and hope.

"I'm going to keep hold of you, and you're going to have to try to scoot yourself a little closer to the opening here," Kenton instructed. "Be careful . . .

just inch along. When you're in front of the door, I can pull you in as you let go."

"Are you sure?" the man asked. "I'm afraid I'll fall!"

"You will indeed fall if you stay as you are. You can't hold your weight forever. It's your only chance if you try to do as I say!"

Behind Kenton, Rachel was awakened by the noise. She sat up and looked around in the darkness. Kenton was visible to her, limned against the dim light of the nighttime sky. She couldn't tell what he was doing.

"Brady?" she asked. "What's happening?"

He heard her but could not at the moment respond, busy as he was. He gripped the brakeman as hard as he could, and with his other hand gripped the door equally hard. The wind tugged at him and also at the dangling brakeman, but despite it, progress was being made, however slowly.

"Easy, careful . . . there! Almost there . . . just another half-foot or so . . ."

The brakeman pulled himself up, let go for half a second, and grabbed hold again, this time a little closer to the opening.

"One more time!" Kenton urged. He wondered if the brakeman had yet thought about the fact that his benefactor was a stowaway. Maybe he would be so grateful for the help that he would not care, maybe would even preserve the secret. Kenton would certainly ask that of him. He wasn't about to be hauled back to Denver to be harassed and jailed by Henry

Turner. Not with a daughter just come into his life. Not with Victoria still alive, waiting to be found again.

"All right," Kenton said. "The timing has to be right . . . I'll count to three, and on three, you let go and swing in, and I'll pull at the same time."

Rachel was on her feet, watching breathlessly. "Who is he?" she asked in a frightened tone.

"The brakeman!" Kenton called back to her. "He slid off the top, managed to catch himself on the side . . . now, sir, together . . . one, two, *three*!"

CHAPTER

35

WITH a cry of exertion and aided by Kenton's sharp pull, the man fell forward into the car. Kenton was knocked back, almost bowling over Rachel. The brakeman lay facedown on the dirty floor of the boxcar, breathing loudly, letting relief wash over him.

Kenton rose and dusted himself off. He winked at Rachel, trying to reassure her, then realized it was too dark for her to see him.

The brakeman sat up, his breathing slowing. "I do thank you, sir," he drawled. "I've never done that before, after all my years in this trade. Thank God you were in here . . . whoever you are. Is that a woman standing there beside you? It's too dark to see well."

"It is. I'll not lie to you, sir. We're stowed away here, having had a mutual need to get away from Denver in secret, and swiftly. I assure you that our flight is purely innocent, and ask that you repay my aid to you just now by keeping secret our presence here."

The brakeman hesitated only a moment before saying, "Under the circumstances, I'm inclined to go along with that. I owe you deep gratitude. Thank you for saving my life."

"Glad to be of service."

"May I ask your name, sir?"

Kenton paused. "Do you mind if I don't say?"

"I'll make no demands. Thank you again for saving me. Lord! I thought I was dead for sure!"

Kenton said, "I've not told you my name, but do you object to saying yours?" As he did, he reached over and placed his hand on Rachel's arm, an unplanned gesture. When he touched her, though, he felt the tension of her muscles. She was rigid as a post, staring directly at the brakeman, who was invisible in the darkness except for his general outline.

The brakeman stood. Kenton heard the sound of metal against leather and knew a pistol had been drawn from beneath the brakeman's jacket.

But he wasn't a brakeman at all. Kenton knew it now, and knew who he was even before he spoke.

"Well, Mr. Kenton," he said, the Alabama drawl gone, his inflections now the precise ones of upper-crust British society. "I didn't fancy we would meet in this way, and certainly I didn't think that I would be placed in the situation of owing you my life."

Rachel leaned against Kenton, her body even

more tense. She made a small, strange noise somewhere deep in her throat and Kenton could almost
smell her terror.

"You do owe me your life, Mr. Kevington. And
I hope that you will let that fact affect your next
actions. Leave us be. Put that gun away."

"Ah, sorry, old man, but I can't do that. Your
daughter there, sorry to say, saw something she
shouldn't. I can't allow her to go on being a threat
to me."

"She's no threat. Your crime occurred in England, and this is the United States. No one here is
looking for you."

"Not entirely true . . . Texas has quite an interest
in me. That's been one of the things that has made
it interestingly ironic to go around portraying a
Texan, as I have. And I'm afraid I'll soon have a
bit of a problem in Denver, as well, once they discover a certain body in the hotel room I'd rented."

"Why are you telling us these things? They only
incriminate you. Let us go. Forget about us, and
don't add to your problems by harming us."

"My responses to that are related. First, I don't
intend to harm you at all. I intend to kill you. And
therefore there's no reason to be all that careful
about what I say to you. You'll never have the opportunity to repeat it to anyone."

Kenton's brain was running at full speed as he
searched for some way to stretch this situation out,
buy more time. Kevington was only a couple of

trigger-squeezes away from killing them on the spot.

"Then do me the favor of answering some questions for me before you do me in," Kenton said. "Why did you kill the man in Texas?"

"Oh, that. It wasn't planned. Unfortunate, really. Texas Rangers, I discovered, have an aversion to bank robbery, and I'd pulled off one of those, you see. They made the mistake of pursuing me. I killed one of them. The name Jessup Best was scratched into the leather of his gunbelt. I read it myself. Even borrowed the name as my alias in my later travels. I enjoy irony, you see."

"It wasn't by bank robbery alone that you've paid for your travels in this country," Kenton said. "You've turned author, as well."

Kevington laughed. "Ah, yes! *The Grand Deception*. Not the best piece of work, admittedly, but not bad. The storyline is one that I'm sure is of special interest to you, eh, Mr. Kenton?"

"It was that storyline that drew me to Denver, to try to find the ending of the story in advance of its publication. A savvy editor at the *Popular Library* noted the parallels to my Victoria's story, and alerted me. I came right away."

"Really? And did you read the end of the novel?"

"No. But I did discover the author's identity."

"Bah! That's no great achievement. It's the plot that matters! By the way, the novel ends with the death of Candice. Death by murder . . . killed by her own son. Quite a tragedy!"

Kenton felt weak suddenly. Had this devil murdered Victoria? If not, did he plan to do so? Or might he simply be toying with him like a cat toys with a mouse before killing it?

Whatever, Kevington clearly was enjoying himself. "By the way, Mr. Kenton, what was that phrase you just used? 'My Victoria'? Sorry to bear this bad news to you, but she hasn't been 'your' Victoria for upward of two decades. My mother loves my father, the man who saved her life. She no longer thinks of you, much less cares about you. She is far from being your Victoria."

Kenton could not reply to that. He knew his fury would be betrayed in his voice, and that was one satisfaction he would not give to Paul Kevington.

"My father hates you, by the way. I've never heard him mention you without cursing you. He says you were once rivals for my mother's affections. I guess you could say he won."

"Your father is a wicked man. He won nothing. He stole Victoria away. He gained her affection only because her injuries left her senseless for years, only because he lied to her, telling her I was dead. Only because he took advantage of geographic distance, and forced isolation, and an injured woman's weakened emotional and mental state, to force himself into her life. Had he not chanced to be on that train with Victoria, he would not have been privileged to steal her away before her fate could be known, and I could reach her. None of this would have happened . . . and you would not even exist."

Kevington laughed again. "He didn't 'chance' to be on that train, Mr. Kenton. He was there at Victoria's invitation. She loved him even then, not you. She was going to leave you. She was disgusted that she carried in her a life you had planted there. The same miserable life that now stands beside you. A life that won't be a life much longer. Hello, Rachel. How pleasant to encounter you at last!"

Rachel said nothing. She seemed frozen at Kenton's side.

"You're a damned liar," Kenton said. "You may be able to foist some lies on me, but you will not persuade me that Victoria did not love me. That is something about which there is no doubt. I lived with that woman. I loved her and was loved in turn. We were devoted to one another, more than to anything else in the world. She did not love your father. She feared and despised him, and hated him for pursuing her. These are facts about which there is no question, because I, sir, was there. I *know*."

"You are a fool, Kenton. Soon to be a dead fool. But let me talk to dear Rachel a moment, before we deal with . . . *final* matters. Rachel, my darling! How could you have been so thoughtless as to embroil Mr. Kenton in your problems? If you had been strong enough to resist the temptation to find your real father, you could have vanished so thoroughly I could never have tracked you. As it was, all I had to do was track Brady Kenton to find you. And now, thanks to your selfishness, you're going to get not only yourself killed, but Mr. Kenton, as well! What do you think of that? Doesn't it make you just burn with guilt?" He laughed.

"I hate you!" she said, her voice so tight and tremulous it could barely be heard. "You are a murderer and a devil, and I hate you!"

"Ta, ta, Rachel! It's not good to die with hatred in your heart. Sends you straight to hell, they say. Let's see if that's true."

He raised the pistol.

CHAPTER

36

THE train made another turn, the track circling to the right around the base of a bluff. Kevington stumbled slightly, losing his aim.

Kenton reacted to the opportunity. He shoved Rachel down. "Hide!" he ordered her. "Take cover!" Then he leaped straight at Kevington.

Kevington fired his pistol, sending the slug harmlessly into a cargo crate. Kenton was on him in a moment, knocking him down, struggling with him. The pistol fired again, the bullet going through the roof. Still the struggle went on.

Rachel was paralyzed with terror. She lay on the floor of the boxcar, hearing more than seeing the struggle going on mere feet away from her.

Hide, Kenton had said. Hide. But she couldn't even move.

Somehow she found the strength to force herself

up. She could think of no place to hide other than the niche in which Kenton had had her place herself earlier. Almost mechanically she moved in that direction.

The train curved again, throwing her off balance. She slipped toward the door, and lost her footing.

The pistol fired again, illuminating for a moment the fierce struggle going on between Kenton and the cursing Paul Kevington. Numb with fright, she felt faint all at once. Stumbling again, she fell out the door, and groped to find a handhold.

Somehow she caught herself. She was hanging out of the railroad car, legs swinging, nearly touching the grade, feet far too close to the metal wheels. She was hanging on to the edge of the door, her fingertips barely hooked over it.

"Rachel!" she heard Kenton shout. Somehow, in the midst of his fight, he had detected what had happened. "Don't let go!"

The pistol blasted. The slug passed through the door and sang past her face, missing her by an inch or less.

It was more than she could take. Her fingers lost their grip and she fell.

"No!" Kenton screamed. "Rachel!"

Kevington slammed the pistol against the side of Kenton's face. He raised it, clicked back the hammer for the fifth shot . . .

Kenton somehow managed to knock his arm away. The shot went through the far side of the car.

Kenton locked his arms around Kevington and the fight went on.

Above, and far down the length of the train, the true brakeman stood rooted in place, looking back along the car tops. He'd heard gunfire. At first he'd been unsure, but that last shot had echoed loudly off the side of the bluff by which the train was passing. There was no question that it was truly a gunshot.

Someone was firing off a pistol in one of the boxcars. Maybe a drunk vagabond in some kind of mindless celebration, or maybe a pair of stowaways at battle.

He turned and began running the car tops toward the tender and engine ahead. He would give word that the train should be halted and searched. Gunfire on a moving train was not to be abided.

Inside the boxcar, Kenton was growing weary. Kevington had only one shot left, and knew it, and the knowledge must have doubled his determination to make that shot effective, for he was fighting harder than ever. And Kenton was losing strength.

And he was distracted. Rachel had fallen from the moving car. She might have tumbled under the wheels or been killed rolling down the grade. Or perhaps she lay hurt back there in the darkness. His daughter . . . hurt and alone . . .

Kenton let out a roar and heightened his efforts. He would not let Paul Kevington kill him.

Or if he did, he would not die alone.

Kenton saw the open door beside him. In their struggle they had rolled near to it. With the right kind of effort he could—

Kevington got the pistol into position. Kenton saw the end of it inches from his face, aimed roughly at the center of his forehead. "This is it, Kenton!" Kevington shouted into his face. "One Kevington took your wife, and now another takes your life!"

The brakeman was nearly to the tender when he heard the sound of the sixth shot. "Hey!" he shouted. "Gunfire on the train! Gunfire on the train!"

They didn't hear him. The train rolled on. Swearing, he continued forward.

CHAPTER

37

WHEN Brady Kenton came to, it was daylight. But not a normal kind of daylight—it was a misty, green, organic light, soft and filtered, and with it a smell equally organic. The scent of fresh earth, something like that of a freshly dug cellar.

He groaned and tried to take a deep breath, but couldn't. His nose was shoved into the soil on which he lay. He was surrounded by greenery; a leaf tickled the back of his neck, making it itch.

Kenton moved his head a little, and the deep breath came. He groaned again, then pushed himself up, through the leaves that surrounded him.

He blinked in the broad morning daylight. For a time he couldn't figure out where he was or how he had gotten here. His memory was a muddle.

It hit him suddenly, and he looked around, wondering where Kevington was. No sign of him. Kenton stood, wary, and looked again. He was at the base of a steep trackside grade, down from the rails a good twenty feet, and he'd rolled into a natural recess in the slope, a crevice about the size of a large coffin, and covered over with brush. The brush had given way and let him fall into the crevice, then had covered him like a lid, hiding him.

Kevington had been with him when they'd fallen from the train. He remembered it now. They'd rolled and tumbled and suddenly had gone out the door, pounding down the grade and breaking away from one another. Obviously Kevington had rolled off somewhere else, and Kenton had dropped into the natural hiding place.

He wondered how long he'd lain there, knocked senseless. It must have been hours.

Kenton looked around, thinking maybe Kevington had been killed in the fall. If so, he couldn't be far away. But he saw no body.

On the other hand, Kevington might have lived. In the darkness he might have sought Kenton and been unable to find him. Even in the daylight he would have been unlikely to find Kenton in the hidden niche that had caught him. So maybe Kevington had wandered off eventually, assuming Kenton must have lived and headed back down the track . . .

To find Rachel. Kenton tensed at the realization. Rachel had fallen from the train farther back; to reach her he would have to walk back in the direction of Denver. What if Kevington was already doing that? He might find Rachel . . . maybe he already had.

Kenton had no weapon. Kevington had a pistol, unless he'd lost it in his tumble. Kenton looked around, hoping to spot it, but didn't.

No more time to waste. Whatever the odds, he had to go back down the track and find Rachel. He prayed that Kevington hadn't gotten to her already. If he had, it was already too late.

He examined himself to make sure there were no unnoticed injuries, and saw that his left arm was cut and quite bloody. But the blood was crusted now, and the arm didn't hurt much. He'd cut it somehow in the tumbling fight in the dark with Kevington.

It would take more than that to stop him. He climbed up to the tracks and set out walking as fast as he could back down toward Denver, keeping his eyes peeled for Kevington and Rachel, as well, hoping he would find the former dead, and the latter alive and well.

The station was nothing more than a watering stop, with a log station house and a tiny cafe that sold sandwiches, tea, and coffee. Normally trains stopped there for only minutes, but that had changed last night. A wire had come from Denver saying that the train now at the station should be stopped and searched.

The train, though, had been late in arriving, and when at last it did, the stationmaster learned that the delay had happened because the train had already been searched even before it got to his station.

At the moment, he was scratching on a pad of

paper with a pencil, taking down a report of what had happened. He'd learned long ago that when something went askew, the railroad loved words on paper. Document, record, and document some more. And make sure that any blame that came down, came down somewhere else.

"All right, slow down a minute," he said to the brakeman, scribbling as fast as he could. "You heard shots and had the train stopped and searched. And you found . . ."

"We found nobody. A boxcar with an open door and some blood on the floor, and a few bulletholes in it. Whoever it was fell out, or jumped, with the train still moving."

"No bodies found?"

"Not yet. There'll be a search now that it's daylight, I'm sure."

The scribbler nodded, chewing on his tongue in concentration, and finished his writing. He lowered the pad and looked at the other man.

"I don't know what happened here, but you and me have both done our duty. You searched the train once and I've searched it again, and there's nothing more to be found here. I'm going to send this report back down to the central office, and as far as I'm concerned, you fellows can roll that train on and get it out of here."

"I wonder who it was?" the brakeman said, looking again at the bloodstain on the floor.

"Some tramps, most likely. They'll probably be found dead somewhere back down the track. When folks fall off a train moving as fast as this one must have been, folks tend to die."

Rachel Frye hadn't died. She'd fallen screaming from the train and hit the ground hard, rolling like a log, abraded quite badly. Her dress was torn and filthy, hardly more than a rag now, and her arms were scratched and bruised.

But she was alive. And without any injury except a rib that was very badly bruised and maybe cracked, for it hurt her to walk and to breathe. She kept on walking and breathing anyway, heading up the track. She'd debated whether she should go back down toward Denver, or on up, and had decided on the latter. Denver was far away; the next train station was probably closer. And there she might find out the outcome of the fight between Kenton and Paul Kevington. She prayed that Kenton had prevailed.

She'd been walking since just after dawn, but had no idea how far she'd come. It felt like miles, but given her condition and the fact she was climbing in thin mountain air, she couldn't really guess how much distance she'd covered. The thing was to keep on going.

But suddenly she stopped. Up ahead, coming down toward her, was a man, on foot. He was at the moment too far away to make out clearly, but she saw that he was looking right at her, and knew it was too late to avoid being seen.

The man paused, then came on again, faster. He broke into a trot.

Her heart nearly failed her. It was Paul Kevington.

Rachel stood where she was, a rabbit hypnotized by the stare of a snake about to strike it, a deer frozen in the headlight of an oncoming train. She snapped herself out of it, and looked for a way of escape.

Off to her left, and down the slope, she saw something unexpected: a jumble of old train wreckage, including a locomotive. It was rusted and splintered and ugly, overtaken with vegetation. She supposed the railroad must have chosen to leave the wreck where it was because its location would make it nearly impossible to pull out again.

Right now it seemed her only hope. If she could hide there, maybe find something to use as a weapon . . .

She ran down toward the wreckage as Paul Kevington continued down the track toward her. He shouted her name, and it scared her to death even to hear his voice.

CHAPTER

38

PAUL Kevington felt a grim sense of satisfaction. He had her now. He'd seen her clearly as she ran down the slope, and watched her disappear into the tangled wood and metal of the aging train wreckage.

She was trying to hide from him. What a fool she was! Did she think he would pursue her from one continent to another, and across a vast frontier, only to let her evade him in such a childish way? He could be patient. Let her hide . . . he'd take pleasure in finding her. He'd enjoy what followed that, the final victory, even more.

He'd loved her once, back when he thought she could be his. Now that he knew she never could be, he despised her.

He stood at the side of the tangled wreckage, looking it over with a smile on his face. His pistol had been lost sometime during the tumble out of the train, and in the darkness he hadn't found it. He'd not been able to find Brady Kenton, either, but had decided not to worry about that for now. He'd deal with Rachel first, then find Kenton. Mostly likely the old word-scribbler had been killed in the fall from the train anyway, and he'd just not been able to find his body in the dark. He hoped Kenton had gone under the wheels.

"Rachel!" Kevington called. "Rachel, darling, why are you being so stubborn? Don't you know by now you'll never escape me? I'll follow you right to the gates of hell, my dear, and push you in! Show yourself, *sister*." He gave an ironic, harsh emphasis to that word. "Let's get this done with quickly and mercifully. Let's end this chase once and for all."

He glanced down and grinned as he saw a piece of rusted metal, fragmented and sharp on one end. He picked it up. This would do the job nicely.

"Come out, sister! Come out and let's you and I talk! Maybe we can find a better alternative than disposing of you! Maybe there's some way we can reach terms . . . maybe you can live through this!"

He didn't expect her to believe him. She knew he couldn't afford to leave her alive. But the chatter would have the effect of making her more unsettled, he hoped. Maybe she would make a sound and betray herself.

He continued his search, shouting, taunting, shoving aside pieces of wreckage. He'd find her soon, and the piece of sharp metal in his hand would settle his account with Rachel Frye once and for all.

*   *   *

Almost an hour after he began his walk down the track, Brady Kenton stopped and listened to the wind.

He'd just heard a man's shout.

Listening harder, he heard it again.

"Kevington!" he whispered sharply.

The shouting came from farther down the track. He set off in that direction on a run, as well as his sore muscles would let him.

It wasn't a good time to realize that age was catching up to him. Not with Rachel still to be saved—if it wasn't too late.

And maybe it wasn't. Why else would Kevington be yelling, if not in some attempt to find her?

Kenton ran on, grateful he was traveling downhill rather than up.

He rounded a bend in the tracks and stopped. He saw Kevington below, clambering about on the wreckage of a train. Kenton remembered reading about this train crash a couple of years earlier, and how the railroad had chosen simply to leave the whole mess where it was.

Rachel had to be down there, hiding. Why else would Kevington be searching two-year-old train wreckage?

Kenton's suspicions were confirmed a moment later by Kevington's next words.

"Ah, Rachel! I do believe I see you! I knew I'd find you! Why not come on out, and let's you and I talk!"

Kenton let out a yell. "Don't do it, Rachel! Stay where you are!"

Kevington wheeled, stared up at Kenton. Kenton heard him curse.

"Thought you were through with me, Kevington? Did you think I was dead?" Kenton began walking down toward Kevington, looking meanwhile for something he could use as a weapon. That metal fragment looked fearsome. "It'll take a lot more than a tumble from a train to do me in!"

Kevington seemed to have lost his banter. "Stay the hell away!" he shouted up at Kenton. "I'll kill her!"

"You don't even have her!"

Kevington responded to that with action. He clambered over a pile of twisted metal and reached what had been the cab of the locomotive. He vanished for a moment; Kenton heard Rachel's scream, and stopped. He glanced down and noticed a fragment of metal, much like the one Kevington had, and picked it up. If Kevington had just killed Rachel, Kenton would drive this metal through the man's heart, even if he had to die himself in the process.

Kevington rose with Rachel in his grip, the piece of metal at her throat.

"I'll kill her if you come a step closer, Kenton! I swear I will!"

Kenton decided to call his bluff. "No you won't. If you do you'll have nothing left to use to hold me back, and you know it. You can't afford to kill her!"

He took a few steps forward, ready to stop if Kevington appeared to actually be about to harm Rachel.

"I'm warning you!" Kevington yelled. "I'll kill her!"

"You won't do it."

Kevington sliced at her neck with the metal; Kenton saw blood flow out as Rachel screamed.

He stopped and lifted his hands, still holding the metal shard in his right one. "All right! All right! I've stopped! Don't cut her more!" He felt furious at himself, realizing that his bluff-calling had actually gotten her hurt.

Kevington laughed, back in control now. "Very good, Kenton. Very good. Now you know where we stand. And don't throw me any more of that nonsense—you know I will kill her. And even if you got to me and killed me in turn, what would it matter? She would still be dead! So you stay where you are, and do what I say!"

"I'm listening."

Kevington chuckled. "Let's see . . . what should I have you do? Oh, I've got an idea. Tell me, Kenton: what do you know of the land of Japan? Do you know that there are men there who, when dishonored, will actually disembowel themselves ritually? Have you heard of that?"

"I've heard."

"Good, good. Then let's see how honorable you are. If you want to save your daughter's life, then take that piece of metal in your hand and thrust it through yourself." Kevington laughed, but it was not the same laugh as before. This was a high, nervous giggle.

"I'll do nothing like that," Kenton said.

"Then I'll kill her!" And he cut her again.

"No!" Kenton yelled. "No . . . leave her alone."

"Do it!" Kevington screamed. "Show us that Brady Kenton courage! Are you man enough to save your own daughter? Are you?"

Kenton looked at the piece of metal in his hand. Dear God, could he actually . . .

He knew it would not save her. Kevington would kill her anyway.

But even so, he couldn't simply stand by and watch him do it. Kevington had Kenton in an impossible spot . . . and the intolerable might be the only way out.

"Do it, Kenton! Now!"

Kenton closed his eyes, said a prayer. He opened them again, then raised the metal fragment, pressed it slowly against his middle . . .

"No!" Rachel screamed. "No!"

She moved, pulling away from Kevington. The move was so fast he was taken by surprise. She yanked free of his grasp, tried to run, but he went after her.

The crack of the pistol was unexpected by all. Kevington spasmed and yelled. Another shot and he jerked, suddenly, head pierced by a bullet.

He lay on the ground a few moments, moving and making noise, but then went silent and still.

Kenton dropped the metal fragment and sighed in relief. He turned and saw Alex Gunnison running down toward him. Behind Gunnison, Frank Turner was rising, smoking pistol in his hand. He'd fired from a kneeling position, and it was surely the best long shooting with a pistol that Kenton had ever witnessed.

Rachel ran to Kenton and threw her arms around him. He closed his eyes and embraced her, never wanting to let her go.

CHAPTER

39

"THANK God we got here when we did," Gunnison said. "What he was about to have you do, Kenton . . ."

"I would have done it, for Rachel," Kenton said. "But it wouldn't have saved her. He would have killed her no matter what."

"It's a good thing that Ranger Turner is the skilled gunman he is," Gunnison said.

"It was a satisfying thing to avenge Jessup Best and save a couple of lives at the same time," Turner said. "Makes this trip to Colorado worthwhile, especially considering how disillusioned I've been with my sorry cousin in Denver."

"I owe you my life," Kenton said to Turner. "Thank you for handing it to me."

"My pleasure, sir. Tell me, are you going to write one of your stories about this?"

Kenton looked serious. "There's something I

want to ask of all of you," he said. "I want to ask you all to let me die."

Gunnison frowned. "What?"

"Listen to me," Kenton said. "I've done some foolish things recently. I've gotten myself into trouble I shouldn't have. I'm a fugitive from the law in Denver. I've lost my reputation through my own recklessness. By now, J. B. Haddockson has probably written a story accusing me of being associated with the fire at the publishing house, and recounting my flight from the police. My career is through, and I'm in for Lord only knows how many legal entanglements and so on . . . all at a time when the only thing I want to do is go find Victoria."

Gunnison said, "So you want to be . . . dead."

"In the eyes of the world, yes. Because then I can quit being Brady Kenton, writer and illustrator, and concentrate my attention on the only two things that really matter to me now: getting to know my daughter, and finding my wife."

"You'll go to England, then," Turner said.

"Yes. I have to go find her."

Gunnison paced about. "Kenton, you're asking me to lie to my own father, to the *Illustrated American* . . . to the people of this nation. How can I do that?"

"Simple. You just do it. And when it's over, and I've found Victoria and brought her home, then I'll reappear, and deal with all these old entanglements. All I'm asking is that, for now, you allow me to be officially gone. At peace. Free."

"Until you go to England, where will you go? What will you do?" Gunnison asked.

"I'll figure that out as I need to . . . no. *We'll* figure it out. Rachel and me."

Gunnison said, "Kenton, you promise me that someday you'll set this all straight, publicly? And explain to my father why I lied to him?"

"I promise."

Gunnison sighed. "Well, then, fool that I am, I guess I'll go along with it."

"I'm mourning Mr. Kenton's death already," Turner said, picking at his teeth with a twig.

Kenton smiled, then looked solemn. "I thank you all. Sincerely."

Rachel hugged him.

Turner tossed away the twig and stretched. "Should we bury the departed Mr. Kevington?"

"But for the fact he is Victoria's son, I would say no," Kenton said. "As it is, I would like to ask that you and Alex convey his body back to Denver. We'll create a story explaining my 'death' and why my body isn't available. Then, Rachel and I will go on, in secret, and find some place to stay where I won't be recognized. I'll shave my beard, dye my hair. And I'll get to know my daughter, and plan how I'll find my wife." Kenton paused. "Kevington implied that Victoria had died . . . but I don't believe him. I think he was toying with me."

"Only one way to know," Gunnison said. "You got to go see for yourself."

"Yes. And go I will. Maybe Rachel will go with me. I'm ready, Alex. Ready to find Victoria at last."

EXTRAORDINARY ACCLAIM
FOR THE WORKS OF
CAMERON JUDD

"Judd does his usual exquisite job of character development. This book will restore your faith in westerns."
—*El Paso Herald Post* on **Jerusalem Camp**

"Gripping and entertaining."
—*Virginian Tennessean* on **The Overmountain Men**

"Judd writes a mean story."
—*Zane Grey's West*

"An impressive performance . . . a classically simple, fast-paced tale. Marks Judd as a keen observer of the human heart as well as a fine action writer."
—*Publishers Weekly* on **Timber Creek**

"Abundance of historical detail . . . a heartfelt attempt to glimpse the soul of an American hero.
By any standard, Judd succeeds."
—*Booklist* on **Crockett of Tennessee**

KENTON'S CHALLENGE

CAMERON JUDD

St. Martin's Paperbacks

This is a work of fiction. All of the characters, organizations and events portrayed in this novel are either products of the author's imagination or are used fictitiously.

THE QUEST OF BRADY KENTON / KENTON'S CHALLENGE

The Quest of Brady Kenton copyright © 2001 by Cameron Judd.
Kenton's Challenge copyright © 2001 by Cameron Judd.

All rights reserved.

For information address St. Martin's Press, 175 Fifth Avenue, New York, NY 10010.

ISBN: 0-312-94435-7
EAN: 978-0-312-94435-3

Printed in the United States of America

The Quest of Brady Kenton St. Martin's Paperbacks edition / January 2001

Kenton's Challenge St. Martin's Paperbacks edition / November 2001

St. Martin's Paperbacks are published by St. Martin's Press, 175 Fifth Avenue, New York, NY 10010.

10 9 8 7 6 5 4 3 2 1

*In order to fulfill one of her life goals,
this book is dedicated to Lauren Burns.*

KENTON'S CHALLENGE

CHAPTER

1

ST. LOUIS, MISSOURI

THE SUN SANK WESTWARD, A WARM AFTERNOON GIV-
ing way to a chill that hurried the footsteps of under-
protected pedestrians rushing homeward to supper
tables and firesides.

Among the wind-nipped horde, Alex Gunnison,
newly named associate publisher of *Gunnison's Illustrated American,* the nation's most popular general-
interest magazine, walked without a shiver. In the
warmth of the afternoon he had regretted the woolen
suit he had chosen in the cold of morning, but now
he was glad for it. Comfort removed the necessity of
hurrying to reach his home and begin an evening that
loomed before him like an empty wasteland. With his
wife off in Colorado, the house he usually couldn't
wait to reach held little appeal for him tonight.

So he trudged while others hurried, his hands deep
in his pockets and his hat turned low to deflect the
wind. His house was four blocks ahead, the dog

awàited feeding in its pen, and the two cats were no doubt in their usual evening spots in the big side window, watching for his arrival.

He stopped and sighed. Let the cats wait. Tonight he felt too melancholy to go home. He'd go to Barrigan's instead and eat a leisurely supper, read the newspaper, maybe drink a few extra cups of coffee over dessert. Better that than languishing at home.

Speeding his pace, he headed for the next corner, made a left turn, and walked to Barrigan's, a favorite restaurant. He was greeted warmly at the door and conveyed to his usual table. Comments were made about the absence of his wife. "She's visiting relations in Colorado," he replied, "and I anticipate her return within the week."

Gunnison, who had eaten lightly through the day, was hungry and ordered a dinner built around pork chops and gravy. He sipped coffee while he waited and stared at the empty chair across from him where Roxanne normally sat. He and his wife ate at Barrigan's frequently, and it didn't feel quite right to be here without her. Better here alone than home alone, though.

He'd just received his plate when he noticed a heavyset man of about sixty approaching him from across the room, wearing rumpled clothing and the vaguely uneasy expression of one about to intrude into another's privacy. Gunnison sighed inwardly, anticipating being forced to talk to this man while his food went cold and uneaten on his plate before him.

"Beg your pardon, sir," the man said in a soft tone,

"but aren't you Mr. Alexander Gunnison?"

Gunnison hadn't been called Alexander in years. "I'm Alex Gunnison, yes."

"I thought you were, sure as the world! A man changes when he puts his boyhood behind, but there's always something of the boy remaining to mark him. In your case, it's the eyes."

Gunnison smiled with his lips and frowned with his eyes. "I'm afraid I'm at a loss, sir. . . . I think you must know me, but I have to admit I don't know you."

The man did what Gunnison had hoped he wouldn't: he scooted back the empty chair at Gunnison's table for two and sat down heavily. With elbows on the table and a warm smile on his face, he said, "I wouldn't expect you to recollect me, Mr. Gunnison . . . or can I call you Alexander, like I used to?"

"I go by Alex now."

"Well, Alex, you'd not be expected to recall me, as I said, but I sure do remember you as a boy, running all around your father's house and nigh knocking me off the ladder more than once. Oh, how your father would scold you! 'Let the men work, and be off with you,' he'd say. But I'd always stick up for you. I've enjoyed the presence of lively children all my days, ever since I raised my own brood."

"So you worked at my father's house when I was just a little boy."

"That's right. . . . My name's Bill Garry. You might remember me, eh?"

"I'm sorry, but I admit I don't." Garry had reached across the table to shake Gunnison's hand, and Gunnison clasped the hand, noting how callused and dirty it was. He'd find an excuse to slip to the washroom in a moment and scrub his hand clean before he ate.

"I was a carpenter in them days, back before I took a spill and hurt my back so I couldn't work no more. You remember when your father had that office room added onto the side of your house?"

"Yes, I think I do."

"I built them shelves that covered the two walls." Garry said it with pride.

"Really! Well, you'll be glad to know they're still standing, with not a sag in them."

"Oh, of course. What I build, I build to last. And how is your father?"

"He's well. But moving into retirement. He's made me associate publisher of the magazine." Gunnison wondered why he was volunteering information; all he was doing was assuring that the conversation would go on that much longer.

"Oh, I know all about it. I'm a faithful reader of the *Illustrated American*. Have been for years. I was proud to read of your advancement."

"Thank you."

Garry's smile faded as he went on: "But I was sad indeed to read of Mr. Kenton's passing away."

Gunnison nodded. "Yes."

"What a tragedy! For such a talent to be lost in so sad a way . . . I've missed him ever since. There's no one whose work compares to Brady Kenton's, and so I've always said. You've come close, Alex, but as you know, there'll never be another Brady Kenton."

"He was a remarkable man."

"I can't name another artist who became more famous doing what Kenton did."

"Kenton wasn't an artist. He was an illustrator," Gunnison clarified, then felt petty for saying it.

"Whatever you call what he did, I liked it. So did all of America, and hats off to your father's magazine for bringing Kenton to us." The man sounded almost emotional. Gunnison had run across this kind of Kenton devotion before. It made him more jealous than he wanted to admit. "Hard to believe that Kenton's dead."

He's not, Gunnison said in his mind, because for now that was the only way he could say it.

"People see him around, you know," Garry said.

"I hardly see how that's possible," Gunnison said, smiling tightly.

"Oh, lots of folks don't believe he's dead. He was always sort of a trickster, you know."

If only you knew, Gunnison thought.

Garry continued, "My brother Cordell, for example, who swears, absolutely swears, that he saw Brady Kenton himself not a week ago, in Colorado. It was a little mining town—for the life of me I can't recall the name of it. Cordell got back from Colorado two days ago and told me about it this very morning."

"He must have seen someone who resembled Kenton, that's all," Gunnison said.

"Perhaps, but Cordell met Kenton once, back in Chicago, and says he knows for a fact this was none other than the man."

"And you believe him?"

"I'd like to. I don't want to believe Kenton is gone."

"I understand. But I can assure you, Kenton is no longer here." Gunnison's wording was carefully chosen. He did not like to lie and tried to avoid it.

"And all the more sorrow to us for it. Well, anyway, I'll hope Cordell is right, and you are wrong."

"So do I."

Garry hesitated noticeably, then became quite serious in manner. "I hope you don't think me foolish for saying this . . . but I think you should investigate the possibility that Cordell *is* right. He was very sure he'd seen the authentic item in Colorado. Very sure."

Now there was no alternative but an outright lie. "I was there when he died, Mr. Garry. I saw his body. I'm afraid your brother can't possibly be right."

"All I can say is, he was mighty certain about it." Garry at last stood. "Well, I'll leave you to your meal. Sorry to have interrupted you."

"Not at all."

"Give my best to your father. Ask if he remembers me."

"I'll do that, Mr. Garry."

CHAPTER

2

GUNNISON STARED AT HIS PLATE A MOMENT BEFORE he began to eat. What Garry had just told him had unsettled him even though he had not let it show.

Kenton seen in Denver. Garry was the third person in just under two weeks to report such a sighting to Gunnison. The first two reports Gunnison had discounted, the second less easily than the first. But now a third. . . . What was he to think?

Gunnison picked up his fork and knife and sliced off a bite of pork. He ate but tasted it only slightly, his mind preoccupied.

It was possible Kenton was in fact in Colorado, at least theoretically. The news of Kenton's death, reported as fact in the *Illustrated American* and picked up subsequently by every major newspaper in the nation, was a fabrication, a fact known by only a handful of people, Gunnison chief among them. It was he who had written Kenton's obituary and who had eulogized his old partner movingly, standing beside a mahogany coffin weighted with old copies of the *Illustrated American.*

Gunnison still wondered if that deception, once revealed to the world, would cost him his position at the *Illustrated American,* a position greatly advanced since Kenton's supposed death. With Kenton thought to be gone forever, Gunnison's father, founder and publisher of the magazine, had at last advanced his son upward in rank, aiming him ultimately for the publisher's office. But once it was learned that Gunnison had cooperated with Kenton in foisting one of the greatest hoaxes in journalistic history upon the world—using the sacred *Illustrated American* to do it—Gunnison feared his own father would fire him. The senior Gunnison took his magazine and his conceptions of journalistic duty dead seriously. He would not abide deliberate deception, not from his own son, not from Brady Kenton, not from anyone.

It didn't matter. Gunnison would have carried out the hoax at almost any price, because Brady Kenton had asked him to. By becoming "dead" in the eyes of the world, Kenton had gained the opportunity to travel to England to seek his lost wife, Victoria, who for many years had been in the hands of the obsessed Dr. David Kevington. Kenton had taken with him his daughter, Rachel Frye.

But that had been nearly a year ago. Gunnison had received a single item of news from Kenton at the beginning, a letter sent to him at the *Illustrated American* office under a preagreed code name. The letter informed him that Kenton and Rachel had safely made their voyage and were preparing to begin the journey to the Kevington estate. Kenton promised another letter would soon follow . . . but none had ever come.

Gunnison had waited, waited, and waited more . . . but nothing.

He was worried. What if Kenton and Rachel had been captured by Kevington, or worse? The man had demonstrated his willingness to do extreme actions long ago when he'd taken the badly injured Victoria Kenton away from a train accident and spirited her off to his English estate. There he had slowly led her back to health again, though not before she had given birth to the daughter of Brady Kenton, conceived shortly before her accident. Victoria had never known of the birth; she was in a coma when Rachel Kenton was born and still in a coma when Rachel was given away to a servant family named Frye, to raise as their own.

Rachel had learned the secret of her true heritage many years later and had come to the United States and found Brady Kenton, her real father.

Now Kenton and Rachel were gone off to England . . . or perhaps off the face of the earth, for all Gunnison knew.

He worried almost constantly about the lack of news from Kenton and already was secretly planning a voyage of his own to England to find out what had happened to his friend.

But what if Kenton wasn't in England at all? Could he really be in Colorado?

If so, why hadn't he contacted Gunnison? And where were Rachel and Victoria?

Gunnison stared at his plate, lost in thought.

"Is something unsatisfactory, Mr. Gunnison?" a waiter asked.

"Hmm? Oh . . . no. Everything is fine. I've just been thinking about something."

"Can I bring you anything?"

"No. Not at the moment."

"Very good, sir."

Gunnison ate the rest of his meal without interruption, paid his bill, and walked back to his lonely house with his collar turned up and his hands thrust deep into his pockets.

Kenton . . . in Colorado.

Gunnison rolled the possibility over in his mind again and again and found it simply didn't fit. Kenton would not return without contacting him.

Not unless he was in trouble, major trouble, and didn't want to embroil his old friend and partner in it. Kenton was like that.

Nearly to his house, Gunnison stopped, sighed, and turned on his heel. His mind was churning; no point in going home just yet, because he couldn't relax if he did.

It was several blocks to the building full of renovated offices into which the *Illustrated American* had moved its operation only eight months before, but Gunnison walked them speedily despite his heavy supper. By the time he got to the office he'd worked off most of his tension.

He turned the key and entered the empty building. Not even a janitor around just now; Tuesday evenings the offices were empty except for the occasional late worker. The absence of lights in any windows indicated no one had stayed late tonight.

Gunnison didn't bother to light the hallway, walking it blindly by familiarity. He passed the little office that had been Kenton's. The door was slightly ajar, the room vaguely illuminated by the relatively brighter light outside. The desk was empty, the shelves still untouched and all Kenton's books in place despite the fact everyone believed him dead and the stuff should have been gone through long ago. Funny how nobody wanted to do it. Everybody liked having Kenton's office like it was. . . . It made it seem possible that he could reappear and come boisterously striding in like he always had. People around the office still talked in sentimental tones about this, like mourners at a funeral discussing how good the corpse looks.

Gunnison went to his office, lit and cranked up the light, and took a second look through the stack of mail he had received in the morning. He knew there was no letter from Charles Matthias, the pseudonym Kenton had chosen for his letters to Gunnison, but he looked anyway, just to be sure. Then he went to his father's office, the door of which always stood open, and examined his father's mail on the chance that a letter might have been delivered to the wrong Gunnison. Again, nothing.

Gunnison returned to his office and flopped down in his chair. He was tired, missed his wife, and was worried about Kenton. It had just been too long. He should have heard something by now.

The prospect of a journey to England seemed realer by the moment. But also daunting, especially as tired as he felt right now.

Gunnison leaned across his desk, resting his chin on the back of his crossed hands, then turned his head and rested his cheek instead. He closed his eyes.

CHAPTER

3

THE JAIL WAS SMALL, DIRTY, STINKING OF OLD COF-
fee and older cigar smoke. The town marshal who ran
the place had bleary eyes and the look of too much
liquor about him and eyed the Stetson-wearing Kenton with suspicion and Gunnison, who was clad in a
business suit, with something approaching disdain.

"Why should I let you see my prisoner?" the marshal said to Kenton. "What business is he of yours?"

"None at all, sir," Kenton replied with a smile. "But
he is a man who just robbed ten banks in succession
and killed five officers of the law in the process, and
it would be of tremendous interest to my readers if I
could sketch this scoundrel before he disappears into
the bowels of the courts and then on to the gallows."

"Ain't no concern of mine."

"Perhaps this is," Kenton said, reaching into his
pocket and pulling out a roll of bills. He tossed it onto
the desk in front of the marshal.

The marshal eyed it without words.

"I could arrest you for trying to bribe an officer."

"And I could report you to the town fathers for drinking on the job."

"Hell, they know I do it already."

"Take the money, Marshal. Give me fifteen minutes with the prisoner. That's all I ask."

The marshal reached over and took the money, pocketing it. He gestured with a toss of his head toward the big door leading into the rear cellblock.

Kenton and Gunnison followed the slightly staggering lawman through the door. The prisoner who was Kenton's target was in a cell on the left side of the cellblock; another prisoner, apparently drunk, was in the other.

"Who the hell is this?" growled the bank robber.

"His name's Brady Kenton. He's with the *Illustrated American*. This other fellow with him is his son."

"I'm not his son," Gunnison quickly corrected.

The marshal said nothing, just backed away from the cell and let Kenton go nearer to it. The bank robber was spread out across his bunk, staring at Kenton with a hateful gaze that it seemed to Gunnison was a little less authentic than it had been before he found out who Kenton was.

"I've heard of you, Kenton," he said. "I got no use for scribblers like you."

"America wants to know you, my friend," Kenton said, already beginning to sketch. "America is like that, you know. Crime and criminals intrigue us in the land of the free."

"I didn't give you no permission to sketch me."

Kenton just smiled and kept on sketching, and it was obvious that the man really didn't mind. It was an honor to be the subject of a sketch by the famous Brady Kenton.

It happened fast. The marshal made a strange, grunting sound. Gunnison turned and saw that the drunk in the cell behind him had put an arm through the bars and grabbed the marshal by the neck. His other hand was even then pulling free the Colt in the lawman's holster.

The lawman wrenched himself free, but the pistol remained in the prisoner's hand.

"What the—"

The pistol boomed, incredibly loud in the small space, the stench of expended gunpowder instantly burning Gunnison's nose. The marshal screeched as the bullet entered his thigh, dropping him to the floor at once.

Kenton had wheeled, letting his pad fall, and was making for the prisoner with the pistol before the man could withdraw too far back into the cell to be reached and before he could finish off the marshal with a second shot.

"No, Kenton!" Gunnison shouted.

But it was too late. The pistol went up, booming again, the bullet passing through Kenton's forehead and exiting the back of his head. . . .

Gunnison sat up with a grunt of alarm and stared wide-eyed across his desk.

A few moments later he was able to breathe again.

A dream. Thank God it had only been a dream!

But the events in the dream were based on a memory; they had been real, for the most part. The drunken and bribed marshal, the bank robber lounging on his cell bunk, the drunkard in the cell grabbing the pistol . . . all this had happened several years before, much as Gunnison had dreamed it.

But in the real-life version, Kenton had been able to grab the pistol away even before the prisoner could wound the marshal.

Gunnison closed his eyes and shuddered, unable to shake off the dream image of Kenton's head being shattered by that bullet.

Why would he dream such a thing?

He knew why. Because he was worried about Kenton. That maybe this time Kenton had run across a situation that he couldn't get the best of and it had gotten the best of him instead.

Gunnison rose, left the office building, and walked the lonely and dark way to his house, where he climbed into his cold bed and longed for his wife's return.

Gunnison arrived late at the office the following morning and was relieved that his father was not there to see it. Thank God for business travel!

But James Brooney, his father's unpleasant and nit-picking personal assistant, was there and stared at Gunnison with his usual cold arrogance. Word of this would get back to Gunnison's father. Brooney would make sure of it.

"Good morning, James," Gunnison said brightly as he passed the man who had become his in-office nemesis. He'd long since quit trying to win James over; clearly James viewed him as an heir unworthy to the throne he was soon to receive, and nothing Gunnison could do would change that. So now he just enjoyed what fun he could with James.

"Got something I want you to do for me today, James," he said in dead serious tones. "I want you to arrange to have the name of the magazine changed before the next edition."

"Change the . . . What do you mean?"

Gunnison paused at the door of his office and frowned at James as if he couldn't believe how dense the man was. "I said I want the name of the magazine changed. Right away."

"Sir, you can't change the name of the magazine without your father's permission!"

"Who says I can't? I'm going to be the publisher soon enough. . . . Can't I call it what I want?"

"You aren't the publisher yet, sir."

"Maybe I am. Maybe I got a letter from my father telling me that now I'm the man in charge."

"May I see this letter?"

"Who are you to make demands on me, James? I'm the one in charge here! And I want to name my magazine . . . Let me see. . . . How about . . . *The Flatulent's Friend*? That'll do. Go have a nameplate designed right away."

James, who had absolutely no sense of humor and was extremely prudish, reddened nearly to the shade of a tomato. "Sir . . . I can't do such a thing! It's atrocious. . . . Your father will . . . Sir, you can't mean it!"

"Of course I can't mean it, James. I'm just joking with you. When are you going to learn to laugh a little?" Gunnison swept into his office and closed the door, smiling to himself.

CHAPTER

4

THE EXCHANGE HAD BEEN OVERHEARD AND MADE the rounds of office gossip, causing much sneaking laughter at James's expense.

Gunnison, though, didn't much enjoy the levity, because he was immersed in worry again about what had happened to Kenton. It was terribly hard to know that Kenton had faked his death and not be able to tell anyone . . . especially now that he was worried. There was no one in whom he could confide, no one from whom he could seek advice. Kenton had made him vow not to tell anyone, even his wife. He'd kept his promise . . . mostly. Roxanne did not know Kenton still lived.

But Gunnison had told one other person. It had simply been impossible not to do so, for the sake of his own mental health.

Perhaps there were steps he could take toward finding his answers without further compromising the promise he had made. He thought hard, then stood and went to the shelf for his notepad. He sat down and put his feet upon his desk and began to write, balancing the pad on his crossed legs.

Fifteen minutes later, James lowered the temperature of the room simply by entering the door.

"You're working, I presume, on the introductory piece for the next edition?"

"It'll get done, James."

"It was due, you are aware, three days ago."

"It'll get done."

"Your father entrusted the job to you . . . a job on which he never ran late."

"It'll get done."

"So that is what you're working on?"

"No. I'm writing your dismissal letter. It's very satisfying work."

"You . . . my . . . uh, are you joking with me again, sir?"

"Go ponder on it awhile. Close the door as you leave."

James turned and walked away, chin up and steps a little too fast. He closed the door . . . hard. Gunnison shook his head. Poor James! He'd be glad to be friendlier to him if only he would quit being so blasted uppity.

James was right that Gunnison was behind on his work, and no doubt he would hear about it when his father returned from his travels. But just now Gunnison didn't care. He was writing a letter to Scotland Yard, inquiring about Kenton. . . .

But as he wrote, his enthusiasm faded. A letter would take a long time to reach England and a longer time again to be answered, if ever it was. This was merely an exercise in activity for the sake of feeling better, and that was all.

Gunnison ripped the paper off the pad, wadded it, and threw it across the room into the rubbish bin, just as the office door opened again and Billy Connery stuck his head in.

"You know, Alex, I've been thinking of coming up with some sort of game in which the object would be throwing a ball into a basket of some sort."

"Nobody would be interested, Billy."

Billy Connery, Irish-born illustrator who was five years Gunnison's junior and an employee of the *Illustrated American* since mere days after Kenton's supposed death. It hadn't taken long for him to become Gunnison's closest friend . . . and not much longer to become the one living person to whom Gunnison had betrayed the truth about Kenton's "death."

Connery entered the office and closed the door behind him. "Having trouble finishing that introductory column, are you?"

"I've not started it."

"What? But it was due days ago!"

"I know that, Billy."

"Sorry . . . it's not my place to point out deadlines to my own boss."

"That's not why I'm irritable. I'm just worried."

"About your wife?"

"No . . . although I do miss her, very badly."

Connery lowered his volume significantly. "About Kenton, then."

"Yes. It's been too long, Billy. I should have heard from him by now."

Connery looked at him seriously. "You should tell your father."

"I can't. Kenton made me promise firmly. He was very specific that my father in particular was not to know he's alive."

"Why?"

"I don't know. He has a strong sense of duty to my father. . . . Maybe having Father believe he is dead gives him a sense of freedom from that duty, so he can concentrate all his attention on finding Victoria. Whatever the reason, I made a promise to him."

"You already broke it once, when you told me."

"I know. I don't claim to be consistent. I just don't know what to do, Billy."

"You're going to have to go after him, I believe."

"I've been thinking that."

"You could probably find a professional pretext for going, so that no one would know the true reason for it. And you could take your Irish illustrator friend with you."

"You'd want to come?"

"It would be a welcome trip for me. And I'm the only person around who can help you, because I'm the only other one besides you who knows."

"I heard something last night that surprised me," Kenton said. "I was told that Kenton has been seen in Colorado, in some little mining town I don't know the name of."

"It's not surprising. As famous as Kenton's face is,

there's bound to be people thinking they see him. They say everyone has someone else who looks like them."

"Maybe that's all it is. But I'd heard something similar from someone else earlier."

"But it's impossible. Kenton would have contacted you had he returned to the United States."

"Yes . . . unless something was very wrong. Unless he had to hide so thoroughly that he couldn't. Unless things had gone so badly that he cut himself off from everyone he knew before."

"These are some substantial suppositions to be making on the basis of some rumors, Alex."

"I realize that. But I've got a bad feeling, Billy. Something is wrong . . . and somehow I've got to find out what it is."

"It does seem something should have been heard by now, I do confess."

"I think maybe I really will have to go to England."

"If you do, I truly would like to go with you."

"We'll see. I don't think I'll make any big decisions. Not until Roxanne gets home."

"You'll be glad to see her, eh?" Connery smiled brightly and winked.

"I will. And not just for the reasons you're obviously thinking about."

CHAPTER

5

THE TRAIN CAME TO A HALT WITH AN EAR-BUFFETING metallic screech and the piercing hiss of steaming brakes. Alex Gunnison stood on the platform so excited he was hardly able to restrain himself from dancing.

She descended, wearing her beauty like a robe, and he went to her nearly on a run, throwing his arms around her and kissing her right there in the midst of the crowd.

"Welcome back, Roxanne!" he said. "You don't know how I've missed you!"

She squeezed him until he couldn't breathe. "Of course I know. You think I didn't miss you just as badly?"

"Then you should have come home sooner."

"I couldn't cut the visit short. It had been too long since the last one for me to do that."

"I know. But I can't help but be selfish. I want you all to myself."

She gave him the kind of smile that could still melt

him despite their several years together. "I'm glad. Now tell me: how are the cats?"

"Fine. I'll bet you thought about them more than about me."

"Nonsense! Did you water the plants every day?"

"Of course."

"Oh, Alex, can we go to Barrigan's tonight? I'd love to sit back and relax and enjoy a good meal and just have the chance to look at you for a while."

"A marvelous idea. I'd already thought of doing that even before you mentioned it. I ate there while you were gone. . . . The place isn't the same without you."

He carried her bags in one hand and held her arm in the other, happy to be with her again. He put aside thoughts of Brady Kenton and decided, almost unconsciously, not to mention tonight his upcoming trip to England. There would be time for that later.

Brady Kenton had intruded into the life of the Gunnisons for years. Tonight he would not.

But as Gunnison and his wife were finishing their meal, lingering over dessert and coffee, Brady Kenton did intrude.

"Oh, I just remembered . . ." Roxanne said suddenly. "The strangest thing . . . Wait a moment. . . ." She began digging in her bag.

"What are you up to?" Gunnison asked.

"Wait. . . . Ah, yes, here it is." She pulled a ragged envelope from her bag and laid it on the table in front of her husband's plate.

Gunnison picked it up. "It appears to be an envelope addressed to the Buckeye Cafe in Culvertown, Colorado."

"Look on the back."

Gunnison flipped it over and stared in silence.

"Whose work would you say that was, Alex?"

Gunnison was gazing at a casual pencil study of a man in a vest and sleeve garters, carrying a food-laden tray.

"This looks like Kenton's work."

"Yes."

"Where did you get it?"

"I found it in that cafe, the Buckeye."

"What were you doing in Culvertown?"

"It was a side trip. I went with one of Aunt Karen's friends to visit her brother there. We ate at this cafe, and I found the envelope on the table."

"It's astonishing! I've never seen such a good imitation of his work. Or maybe it isn't an imitation at all. Maybe this is some old sketch done by Kenton years ago."

"The man in the sketch is a waiter in the cafe . . . the same waiter who waited on our table."

"Well, so he's worked there several years."

"He was wearing the same clothes as you see in the drawing."

"So the cafe has a uniform code of dress for its employees."

"Look at the postmark date, Alex."

Gunnison flipped it over. The postmark was only days old.

To his mind came the words of the man who had approached him in Barrigan's: *My brother Cordell swears, absolutely swears, that he saw Brady Kenton himself not a week ago, in Colorado . . . says he knows for a fact this was none other than the man.*

Gunnison was now almost sure that Brady Kenton really was back in the United States, in Colorado . . . yet he had made no contact.

Roxanne looked closely at her husband. "Alex . . . should I not have showed you that sketch? You look upset."

"It's just that . . . it's a bit of a shock, seeing what appears to be an authentic Kenton drawing, but which couldn't be."

"I know," she replied. "It's impossible. I inquired of the proprietor about the sketch, wondering if he knew who had left it. He didn't, but a waiter gave a description of a man who sounded remarkably like Kenton himself. He said the man had dined alone and seemed melancholy."

Kenton . . . dining alone. Perhaps he had failed in his quest to bring back Victoria and had been so depressed he had gone into hiding in a remote Colorado mining town. It wouldn't be the first time Kenton had gone off to hide and lick his wounds.

Gunnison wondered if Kenton was drinking again. And where was Rachel Frye, his daughter? She'd gone with him to England. Had she not returned?

Questions abounded, demanding answers, and Gunnison sat staring off into the dark corner of the restaurant, feeling frustration and restlessness rise because just now those answers could not be found.

"Alex, did you hear what I said?"

"Of course I did. You were talking about this sketch."

"No . . . I was telling you how eager I am to get you home and alone."

He smiled. "Intriguing, I must say. How could I have missed that?"

Gunnison folded the envelope and put it in his pocket, determined to forget about Kenton for the rest of the evening.

He doubted he would succeed. The questions were just too big to be forgotten.

When Alex Gunnison left the house to go to work the next morning, Roxanne stood in the doorway and waved him away with a bright smile on her face.

As soon as he was out of sight, though, the smile vanished, and she closed the door with her heart heavy and her brow creased by a frown.

Something was wrong with Alex. Something was so on his mind that it was pushing her out of his attention.

She wondered desperately what it could be and why he would not tell her about it.

That sketch on the envelope, maybe. Perhaps that had disturbed him in some way. She wished she hadn't shown it to him.

Returning to the bedroom, she looked on the bureau where Alex had placed the envelope last night. The envelope was gone. He'd taken it with him to the office.

CHAPTER

6

BILLY CONNERY STOOD BY THE WINDOW, LOOKING at the sketch where the light was brightest.

"Amazing indeed," he said. "You know Brady Kenton's work better than any man alive, Alex, but if I was asked to judge, I would have to say that this is indeed his sketching."

"You're right on both scores: I do know his work better than anyone does, and I can vouch for that as an authentic Kenton sketch."

"Which means the man is indeed back in the country and apparently spending his time in Colorado."

"Yes, but in hiding, it would seem. If not in hiding, at least cutting himself off from his friends."

"Why would he do such a thing?"

"He would do it only if something was very wrong. He's hiding because he must."

"Or because he wants to. Because he is in some sort of despair," Connery said.

"Yes. That could be. So what now?"

"Well, if it's my advice you're asking, I say throw

aside my earlier encouragement for you to go to England and replace it with encouragement to go to Colorado."

"My thoughts exactly. Colorado it is."

"We can perhaps come up with some pretext . . . a story we are to do about something or another. The shepherds of the Colorado mountains, perhaps."

"Already did it, back in '79."

"We'll think of something."

"I gather you're planning to go as well."

"Of course! Who else can help you more? And if we're to make the pretense of going to produce a story and art, it would be expected that I would go along anyway."

"That's true."

"And as I noted earlier, there's no one else you could go with who wouldn't become a millstone around your neck, because there's no one else but me who knows Kenton is still alive."

"Maybe I should take Roxanne. Maybe it's time I told her the truth."

"Kenton told you not to."

"Yes. But Kenton has always thought he could run every aspect of my life for me. I'm getting tired of having to keep a secret from my own wife just because he wanted me to, for some inexplicable reason."

"That's your judgment to make, Alex. You've already taken me into your confidence on the matter. If you want to tell your wife as well, that's your choice."

Gunnison did want to tell her yet also didn't. He knew Roxanne. She would be very displeased that he'd kept the secret from her as long as he had and would let him know it. She'd also never be able to keep it quiet, he feared. Willingly or unwillingly, she'd let it slip. And she would resent that he'd told Billy Connery before he told her.

"I think I'll hold quiet for now," he said. "But she'll think it strange that I've gone to Colorado right in the wake of her just getting back from there. She'll know it's because of the envelope."

"Then perhaps you shouldn't keep quiet."

But Gunnison was thinking hard all at once. "I'll tell her I'm going to find the man who did the sketch in hopes of hiring him because of his obvious skills."

"In other words, that you're looking for someone to replace yours truly."

"Don't get sensitive on me, Billy. We both know it's just a cover story."

"Shall I begin to make the arrangements?"

"Don't take this wrong, Billy, but if I'm going to Colorado ostensibly to find another artist, it wouldn't make sense for me to be taking you along."

Connery was crestfallen. "I don't want to be left out of this one, Alex. I'm as intrigued by this as you are."

"I understand. But I think it's going to be just me this time around."

Connery returned the envelope to Gunnison's desk with a sigh. "Very well, boss and governor. If you want Billy staying behind, Billy stays behind."

"Don't be peeved at me, Billy."

"Peeved? Don't know the meaning of the word,"

Connery said tightly, leaving the room without another glance at Gunnison.

The task of sorting and distributing the heap of mail that came almost daily to the offices of the *Illustrated American* was the prized and much-protected duty of Joe Stamps. Stamps was a somber man in his forties who looked fifteen years older than he was and whose mind had never developed beyond that of a boy. Gunnison's father happened to be a tenderhearted and progressive man who held the unusual view that society was obliged by common decency to provide a place and livelihood for those whose mental situations made it pretty much impossible for them to do so on their own.

He had hired Stamps shortly after the *Illustrated American* had moved to its current office building. Stamps had initially roused concerns among the less progressive-minded staff members, but time had proven him to be a good and reliable man with a strong sense of duty.

Stamps took his job very seriously, and on the rare occasion he made a mistake, distress almost overwhelmed him. When he entered Alex Gunnison's office, Gunnison knew at once that something had gone wrong.

"What is it, Joe?" Gunnison asked.

"I've made a mistake," Stamps replied, his voice tight. "I know how important it is for letters to reach you fast, and I try my best to make sure they do. But sometimes things fall off the table in the mailroom.

Sometimes even when I look, I'll miss them if they fall in behind something. I'm sorry."

"So you've found a letter that had fallen behind a table?"

"Yes, sir. It should have come to you a week ago. I'm sorry that it's wrinkled and dirty."

Stamps extended a crumpled envelope, smudged with grime.

"Thank you, Joe."

"I'll try not to let it happen again, Mr. Gunnison. Please don't take away my job."

"No one is going to take away your job over one lost letter."

"Thank you, sir. I really do appreciate it."

"Fine. You're welcome."

"I only wish I had looked sooner behind that table. Then maybe it wouldn't have been lost at all. From now on I'm going to look behind the table every day. No, twice a day."

"Good."

Gunnison was studying the return address of the envelope in his hand. It was that of a hospital in New York. He'd hoped it would be the identifying code name and address he and Kenton had worked out.

"Thank you again for not taking away my job, Mr. Gunnison."

"Fine. You can go about your work now, Joe."

Joe thanked Gunnison yet again as he headed out the door.

Gunnison tore the envelope open. The letter was written in a nearly illegible hand, clearly the product of someone working in a hurry. He had to read slowly just to make out what it said.

Once he was through reading it, he laid the letter on the desk and stared at it a moment. Then he picked it up, folded it and placed it in his pocket, and set out at once to find Billy Connery.

CHAPTER

7

BILLY CONNERY LOWERED THE LETTER AND frowned thoughtfully. "This Rachel Frye, that's Brady Kenton's daughter, right?"

"Yes."

"And she went to England with Kenton."

"She did."

"Then how has she come to end up in a hospital in New York?"

"A good question."

"Perhaps we can wire the hospital and find out."

"I intend to do that. I expect we'll find she's still there. It's a charity-based hospital, the letterhead indicates, so I doubt they'd throw her into the streets."

"I wonder if Kenton knows she's there?"

"I can't believe he would. He would never stand by while his flesh and blood was in some kind of medical crisis."

"This seems to be a common refrain."

"What do you mean?"

"This thing of 'Kenton would never' do this or do

that. Kenton would never come back to the United States without letting you know. But obviously he has. Kenton would never let his own daughter languish alone in a hospital far from him. But again, it appears he has."

"I can assure you, there has to be a reason for whatever he's doing. I've known Kenton a long time. I know the man he is."

"Unless the man he is now isn't the man you've known. Something might have happened to change him."

Gunnison couldn't deny this possibility. Kenton had a history of occasional lapses into despair and drinking, and at such times he would become different than he was in better times. Kenton's bad periods were inevitably triggered by negative events—severe disappointments, failures, personal crises of one kind or another.

Gunnison was fairly sure now that Kenton's quest to find his wife in England had failed. This blow, which would be the worst of his life, might have driven him further than ever before into drinking and self-isolation.

He had to find Kenton and help him, or Kenton might not be around much longer to be found at all.

"What will you do now?" Connery asked, handing the letter back to Gunnison.

"Go to New York."

"I'd like to go with you."

"No. I have another job for you. I want you to go to Colorado in my place."

"Really? To look for Kenton?"

"Yes. I need to go to both Colorado and New York, and clearly I can't pull that one off."

"You know that I've never met Kenton."

"No, but you've seen more than enough pictures of him. Besides, it might be good to have someone looking for him whom he's never met. If he saw me before I saw him and if he didn't want me to find him, he'd simply disappear. You'll be able to find him without rousing suspicion . . . I hope."

Connery, beaming, pumped Gunnison's hand. "Thank you, Alex. I'll not let you down. If he's there to be found, I'll find him."

"You'll have to be careful how you proceed. Kenton is clever, and if he's trying to hide, he'll not be easy to locate."

"It doesn't appear to me that he's been particularly clever," Connery replied. "He did a sketch and simply left it in a cafe to be found."

"I admit that does seem careless, if he's trying to stay in hiding. But maybe it was a simple oversight on his part."

"I will be careful. And if Kenton is in some sort of bad situation, I'll do all I can to help him."

"Watch out for yourself as well. Kenton may be hiding because he's in danger. If you find him, you could be in danger, too."

"What kind of danger?"

"I don't know. All I know is that Dr. David Kevington is a determined and dangerous man, willing to do whatever it takes to gain and keep what he wants.

He kidnapped Kenton's wife years ago and hid her away like his personal treasure. If Kenton managed to get her away from him, Kevington would probably know no limits in how he'd react, trying to get her back."

Connery pondered this a moment. "Kenton could be hiding from Dr. Kevington, then."

"Maybe. We can't know until we find him. But, Billy . . . if you do find Kenton, please be sure that you don't accidentally help somebody else find him, too."

Connery took this in thoughtfully, then nodded. "I will indeed proceed with great caution. And you do the same."

"I will." Gunnison shook the letter. "I wish this told me the reason that Rachel is hospitalized."

"Whatever it is, it must be no small thing, to keep her nearly unconscious for weeks."

"It doesn't even tell us whether it was illness or injury. This is a hurriedly written letter."

"Probably written by a physician with more work than he can handle. Can you imagine how mystifying, and frustrating, it must have been to have a patient who for weeks was unable to reveal who she was or who to contact about her?"

"I wonder if Kenton knows where she is?"

"Well, if he doesn't, you can tell him when you find him. I doubt he knows."

"How will you explain your New York journey to Roxanne?"

"I think maybe the time has come to do something radical."

"Tell her the truth?"

"Exactly."

Connery's living quarters were small, cheap, second-story, and within easy walking distance of the *Illustrated American.* Typical of an unmarried young male, he lived amid his own mess, clothing strewn all about and the remnants of three-day-old meals still lingering on molding plates in dusty corners.

He usually was oblivious to the clutter, but at the moment it was a problem because he was trying to pack, which involved having to do some serious digging amid the smutty heaps. With every atrocity he uncovered he grew more disgusted at his own slovenly ways.

One of these days he'd do better, he vowed to himself. Especially when he had a woman to impress. At the moment, there was none. Connery's romantic efforts of late had been faltering failures. But maybe, someday, there'd be a knock on his door, he'd open it, find some lovely creature on the other side, needing directions or help carrying something or to borrow a cup of flour, and a great romance would be born. It was a common fantasy for Billy Connery, though so far nothing remotely like it had happened.

There was a knock on the door. "I'll be!" Connery muttered. "Wouldn't you know she'd show up right when I'm about to leave for Colorado!"

But it wasn't the girl of his dreams. It was exactly

who he knew it would be: J. R. Randwick, who lived in the rooms across the hall. He played a dual role in Connery's life: friend and annoyer.

"Come in, J. R. What brings you over this evening?"

"Hearing you bumping around. What are you doing?"

"What does it look like? I'm packing."

"Getting ready to travel, eh?"

"You know, you ought to go into detective work, J. R. You're wasted back in the bowels of that bakery."

"Where are you going?"

"West. Colorado. Some isolated mining town called Culvertown."

"Big story, huh?"

"You might say."

"Alex Gunnison going with you?"

"No. This one's on my own."

"What? You're writing the story, too, not just drawing?"

"No, I'm not writing."

"So you'll just be publishing pictures, no story?"

"Questions, questions. You're full of them, J. R."

J. R. wandered over to Connery's table and tore a hunk from a loaf of bread there. Connery glowered at him. "Don't you have food of your own?"

"Sure. I just like this bread you've got."

"You should. You baked it yesterday."

"That's why it's so good. Hey, let me go with you to Colorado."

"What? You've got to work, my friend."

"Nope. The bakery is closed for two weeks. They're rebuilding the whole inside of it while the boss is off taking care of his sick father. I've got free time, and plenty of money saved up. I'm going with you."

"You can't, J. R."

"Why? Will I break your concentration while you scribble your pictures?"

"This is a different kind of a trip. I'm not going to be drawing."

"Then what?"

"None of your business, but I'll be looking for someone." There was a moment of inner warning: *You're about to say too much.* But what did it really matter? J. R. was harmless, and if he didn't give him solid explanations about why he couldn't tag along on his journey, J. R. would push and push and push some more.

"Who you looking for?"

"A man. A missing fellow. Somebody that Mr. Gunnison wants to find."

"Why not just hire a detective?"

"There's reasons."

"Aha! Secrecy. Something sneaky and covert. Now I know I've got to go with you."

"J. R., you can't. I'm serious about that. I've been given an assignment to carry out for Alex Gunnison, and I have to keep it quiet. This is a very important thing."

Connery noticed the way J. R. was looking at him,

intrigue mixed with jealousy. Despite himself, Connery felt a boyish surging of his ego and added an extra detail he would later wish he hadn't: "You might say I'm going to see if we can't bring a man back from the dead."

"What?"

"Never mind."

"No. You tell me what that means. You can't throw out something like that and not tell me what you're talking about."

"I can't say any more. I wish I could."

"You're looking for somebody who's dead?"

"No."

"Somebody who people think is dead, then."

Connery said nothing.

"That's it! You're looking to find somebody who people think is dead. Maybe somebody pretending to be dead."

"You better go, J. R."

"I've figured it out! Who is it? Tell me!"

Connery would not tell, though J. R. prodded and probed until Connery could hardly stand it. When J. R. left, he was angry and frustrated.

Connery finished packing and knew he'd made a mistake. Probably nothing would come of it, but he'd be sure not to let Alex Gunnison know what he'd just done.

He'd be much more careful from here on out.

It took some time for her to grasp what he told her, and when she did, her reaction made Gunnison wonder if he'd done the right thing in opening his mouth.

"Let me understand this," she said, a little icily. "All this time, Brady Kenton has been alive. The *Illustrated American* published a big story that was . . . a lie. Memorial tributes poured in from everyone from your father through the vice president of the United States . . . all for a man who really wasn't dead at all."

"That's pretty much it."

"All because he asked you to."

"Roxanne, you have to look at it from Kenton's side, and from mine. You know how important his quest for Victoria was to him. Most people scoffed at it and thought him a fool for believing his wife might still be alive . . . but he was right. By letting the world think he was dead, he had the freedom to go to England and seriously look for her. I had to agree to his request, Roxanne."

"But you lied to me, along with everyone else."

"He made me promise. He didn't want me to tell anyone at all. Only Rachel Frye, a Texas Ranger named Frank Turner, and I knew Kenton was still alive. He wanted to keep it that way. . . . Even to tell just one person opened the door to the truth getting out."

"But I'm your wife, Alex! We're not supposed to have secrets between one another."

"I'm sorry. I didn't know you'd react so strongly."

"It's just that the vows we made to each other when we were married were more important than the vow you made to Kenton."

"Oh, come now, Roxanne. . . . Are you trying to

tell me that there's nothing you know that I don't know? That you've never kept anything secret from me?"

"That's exactly what I'm telling you."

"That's hard to believe."

She was obviously offended. "It makes me wonder what else you're keeping from me."

"What?"

"I've wondered at times . . . I'm sorry to say this, Alex . . . but I did sometimes wonder if it was really Brady Kenton who kept you away from me for so much time over all those years. I wondered if you were away from me because you wanted to be."

"Roxanne!"

"And I wondered if there were . . . other women."

Gunnison wished now he'd not told her the truth about Kenton. He'd not had any notion that it would be such a catalyst for all this anger.

"There were never other women. Never. I've been forever faithful to you."

She stared at him, eyes beginning to fill.

"Roxanne, what can I say to you? Do you not believe me?"

Her lip trembled.

"Roxanne, I love you. I would die before I would be unfaithful to you."

Tears came. She went to him and put her arms around him. "I know. I know."

"Did you really doubt me?"

"No. I'm sorry. I was just angry that you'd keep such a secret from me."

"I hope you can understand why I felt that I had to."

"I do."

"And in the end, I did tell you. I broke my vow to Kenton today. Just like I broke it when I told Billy Connery." Gunnison decided not to reveal to her that he'd told Connery the truth months ago. Given her reactions so far, it was best to let her think he'd told Connery only today. He'd be sure to tell Connery not to say anything around Roxanne that would indicate otherwise.

"Yes," she said. "I'm sorry I acted like I did."

"Forget all about it." He hugged her. "You are glad to know that Kenton didn't really die, aren't you?"

"Of course . . . but I hope it doesn't mean that he'll come back and take you off on the road with him again."

"That won't happen. My days apart from you are finished. But I do have to go away one more time, just this once. I've got to go to New York."

"Because of the letter . . . Rachel Frye."

"That's right."

"Yes, you must go. But not alone. I'm going with you."

"With me? Roxanne . . . there's a chance, just a chance, that there may be some danger involved. Kenton may be hiding because someone is after him, or maybe Victoria. If so, they might be after Rachel as well."

"If there's danger, that's all the more reason for me to go. I want to look out for you."

"I'd rather have you safe at home."

"Has it crossed your mind, Husband, that if someone is trying to find Kenton, it won't take them long to come looking around Kenton's workplace, and his friends?"

Gunnison hadn't thought about that. It made sense, and scared him.

"They might watch this very house, Alex, thinking that Kenton might show up here."

Gunnison nodded. "I think you may have a point, Roxanne."

"I'm going with you to New York."

"Yes. You are."

"Will Billy be safe going to Colorado alone?"

"I hope so. . . . I'll talk to him again before he leaves and tell him to watch out. He's excited about his assignment and already packing even though his train won't leave until day after tomorrow."

"When will we leave?"

"Tomorrow morning. I want to get to Rachel Frye as quickly as possible."

CHAPTER

8

BY THE TIME THE TRAIN CARRYING BILLY CONNERY toward Colorado had left Missouri, the excitement of travel and adventure had given way to worry.

Connery sat by the window, staring out at the passing landscape, trying to figure out just how he'd go about locating Brady Kenton. His destination was Culvertown, one of the many Colorado mountain communities that had made the transition from mining camp to town. Though Connery had never been to Culvertown itself, he'd traveled once before in the Rockies and knew what to expect: a rough-and-ready town with a narrow main street, a few good brick edifices mixed with plenty of structures made of lumber, and with the mountains all around scarred from mining and covered over with rough miners' huts like pox scabs on a sick patient. And since Culvertown was still an active mining center, the population probably would be large and fluid, people coming and going literally by the day.

How would he start to locate Brady Kenton in such

a place? And come to think of it, how would he manage to make inquiries without looking like he was a candidate for an asylum? *Pardon me, sir, but I'm looking for the celebrity journalist Brady Kenton. . . . Yes, I know you read all about his death. . . . Yes, it was a sad thing. You haven't by chance seen the late Mr. Kenton on the streets recently, have you?*

Oh, well. He'd figure out a way. He pulled the envelope from his pocket and studied the drawing on the back of it. As an illustrator himself, he found it impossible not to be both admiring and envious of Kenton's skill. With only a few strokes of a pencil he could capture depth, character, the play of light and shadow. *Someday I'll be as good as that,* Connery promised himself.

As nervous as this whole undertaking made him, there was one aspect of it that he looked forward to very much: he would get to actually meet Brady Kenton, the man whose work had inspired him to become an illustrator himself. He'd wept when he learned of Kenton's "death," it having been a goal of his to someday meet the man.

Now he'd get to fulfill that goal . . . if he could find Kenton.

He could only hope that his reception would not be hostile. Having gone into hiding, Kenton would probably not be pleased to be found.

Connery was asleep when the train finally pulled into the station where he was to disembark. He lifted his head, tipped back the bowler hat he'd pulled low across his brows, and blinked a few times until his vision cleared. He'd been sleeping soundly, dreaming about Ireland, reliving a boyhood conversation he'd had with his grandfather, who was now laid away these several years beneath the green Irish sod.

Connery adjusted his hat, picked up his bag, and secretly patted his pocket to make sure the roll of bills he'd been provided by Alex Gunnison was still there. Alex had funded this assignment informally, avoiding an official expense report and simply forwarding Connery cash from one of the *Illustrated American* accounts. Gunnison was not about to go on record as having assigned someone to go search for a dead man.

Connery departed the train and took a deep breath of fresh mountain air . . . as fresh, anyway, as the air can be beside a smoking train in a mining town rich with belching chimneys. After having resided on a train since St. Louis, it felt tremendously good to stretch his legs and move about.

The first order of business was food, and he found this in the nearest restaurant. Eating at a table by a window, he watched people pass and tried to spot a place where he could obtain a horse. He was not yet at Culvertown. It lay high in the mountains, not yet touched by a railroad spur, though one was even now being constructed.

To reach Culvertown, Connery would have to either catch a coach or rent a horse and saddle. Gunnison had suggested the latter, in that having a horse would give Connery freedom of movement in and around Culvertown. If Kenton was hiding, he might be in some old miner's cabin out in the mountains somewhere.

After fifteen minutes of striding around the town, Connery located a livery and shopped for a rental horse. He encountered an unpleasant surprise: the proprietor of the livery apparently had no use for Irishmen, and Connery had enough of a brogue to mark him as one. When the man refused to lower the price to anything approaching reasonable, Connery stormed off in a huff and spent another thirty minutes looking for another livery.

This time he put on his best flat American accent and quickly took possession of a fine roan at a reasonable cost. The horse came with assurances that it was a horse accustomed to the thin air of the mountains and would serve him well as he headed up to the higher altitudes around Culvertown. The saddle was old but comfortable to both horse and rider and for a little extra came equipped with a rifle sleeve. Connery strapped his bag on the back of the saddle, thanked and tipped the liveryman, and rode out onto the sunny street.

One more stop awaited before he began the last leg of his journey. He rode to the nearest gun shop and purchased a used Winchester rifle and a new Colt pistol, with a shoulder holster for the latter and ammunition for both weapons. He felt very extravagant, spending so much in one day, but Gunnison had given him clear instructions to do all these things and not worry about the cost. The *Illustrated American* could afford it, and it was important that Connery be well armed and well mounted.

There were two other men in the gun shop when Connery made his purchases. They were examining rifles in a glass case, seemingly paying little heed to Connery, but when he pulled out his roll of bills he did get the feeling that they noticed it. He promised himself to be more careful in the future about showing the amount of money he had on him.

He left the gun shop and slid his Winchester into the saddle boot. A perfect fit. Connery swung into the saddle and rode to the next corner, pausing long enough to inspect a pole on which various slabs had been nailed, with arrows pointing in the directions of other towns in the vicinity. He found the indicator for Culvertown and rode off in that direction.

He did not notice that the pair in the gun shop had emerged and watched his departure. After he rounded the corner and was out of sight, they glanced at each other, speaking quickly and low, and trotted off to a nearby hitching post where their own mounts waited.

CHAPTER

9

ON THE ROAD WITH BRADY KENTON, ALEX GUNNI-son had spent many days freezing in blizzards or roasting in the sun and many nights sleeping in barns, on the ground, in tepees, shepherd's wagons, line camp cabins, and every other kind of rough shelter imaginable. Now that his professional life was more settled, it was difficult to adjust to the trappings of his family's wealth. The money and mansions had been there a long time.... Alex Gunnison simply hadn't been situated to take much advantage of them until Kenton's "death" substantially ended his wandering life.

He was seated now in a passenger car on an eastbound train, Roxanne at his side. Surrounding them were common passengers—cowboys, sodbusters, traveling salesmen, all sorts. Babies cried and men smoked smelly cigars that made Roxanne cough.

"Alex," she said to him, "how long are we going to sit here?"

"Oh, I don't know. However long we want."

"But we've got a car of our own to go to. There's no crowds, no noise, no cigar smoke. There are padded chairs instead of these benches. Why can't we go there?"

"I don't feel right there. It's too fancy, too uppity."

"Then the *Illustrated American* has paid to have your father's own private car joined to this train for no reason."

"The *Illustrated American* can afford it. And it hasn't been wasted. We slept in it last night, didn't we?" He paused. "Frankly, Roxanne, that car is my father's domain, not mine. I just don't feel right being in it. I'm used to more rugged modes of travel."

"Only because Brady Kenton always insisted on roughing it."

"Not always. At times Kenton loved his luxury. But he always said that to practice good journalism, he had to be among the people, not cut off from them. So he looked for the cheap hotels and the cheap railroad tickets and the roughest barrooms. That's where he found his best stories."

Roxanne took a fresh faceful of cigar smoke and hacked for half a minute. "Alex, I think I should note that we're not looking for stories. We're simply traveling to New York. There's no particular reason to be 'among the people' this trip . . . especially when they smoke cigars as smelly as the one that man over there is afflicting us with."

He smiled at her. "I'm sorry, Roxanne. Old habits die hard, and I've not been thoughtful. Tell you what:

why don't you go on back to our private car? I'll join you shortly."

"Come with me now! How can you abide the smell of that cigar?"

"Actually, I'm thinking of smoking one myself."

She frowned. Gunnison had recently taken up the habit of smoking a cigar a day, and she didn't like it. Nor would she accept his explanation that his father had actually suggested he smoke more often, because it made him seem more professional, more one of the upper crust of the magazine world. In the publishing world, anyone who was anyone smoked cigars.

"If you're going to sit here and add to the foulness in the air, then indeed I will go back alone," she said. "Perhaps you will join me later . . . after the smell has had time to fade off your clothing."

She leaned over and kissed him on the cheek. "Enjoy your cigar . . . in that you evidently prefer the company of tobacco to that of your devoted wife."

"You're very unfair, you know."

"Yes, indeed." She patted his knee, rose, and was gone.

He was halfway through his cigar when she was back again.

"Roxanne? You look pale. . . . Is something wrong?"

"Alex, we're not alone on this train."

"Of course we're not alone."

"No! What I mean is, someone is on this train because of us. Someone is following us."

"Why do you think so?"

"Because when I went back to our car, I saw some-one trying to enter. I stopped and watched long enough to be sure. . . . I sat down in one of the empty seats in the passenger car and watched him at least two minutes. It was only when the conductor walked through that he stopped. He pretended to be looking for something he'd dropped at our door. He came walking back through the passenger car, but he didn't see me. There was a newspaper there and I lifted it and pretended to read, and hid my face as he went by."

Gunnison's heart was pounding faster. He dropped the cigar onto the dirty floor and crushed it out. The car swayed and rumbled.

"Maybe it was just a common thief, trying to break into the nearest private railroad car."

"I don't think so. I saw the same man in St. Louis, as we were getting aboard."

"It's not that surprising. . . . He's on the same train as we are, and he had to get on somewhere."

"He was looking at you before we boarded. . . . I noticed it at the time but didn't think much of it. You are becoming better known in the city."

"Where is this man now?"

"Not in here . . . but he must have passed through."

"Several people have passed through here; I paid no heed to them."

"Let's go back to our car. I don't feel safe here."

"I'd like to get a look at this fellow you saw. Maybe have a word with him."

"No! No, don't do it. I'm too scared for you to do that right now. But why would anyone be following us?" she asked.

"Who knows? Perhaps he is just a common thief after all, and thought I looked wealthy enough to be worth robbing."

"Could it have anything to do with Kenton?"

"Surely not. I can't see how. I mean, nobody knows what we're up to except ourselves and Billy."

"Maybe somebody else is trying to find Kenton, somebody bad. Maybe Kenton is in hiding because of that. And maybe whoever it is decided that Kenton might get in touch with you because you are his publisher and his old partner."

"This is an awful lot to surmise just from somebody trying to break into our car. I'm sure that robbery in private railroad cars is nothing all that unusual."

"Let's go back to our car. Let's stay there. I'm scared, Alex."

CHAPTER

10

THE ROAD UP THE MOUNTAIN TOOK A BEND, AND AS soon as he was around it Billy Connery suddenly veered his horse into the woods and down into a ravine. He followed it a hundred yards, then dismounted and tethered the horse to some brush. Here it was well out of sight from the road. He gave it oats from the feed bag he'd brought from the livery, then cut a straight path toward the road, not the angled path by which he'd reached this point.

He lay in the brush by the roadside and waited. He was there hardly a minute before the approach of two horsemen confirmed the suspicion that had developed about a mile out of town.

This was the pair he'd seen in the gun shop. He shook his head as he watched them pass. He should have never flashed that roll of money so carelessly.

They rode within fifteen feet of where Connery hid, one of them urging the other to hurry because he feared their prey was moving faster than they were.

Ride on, scoundrels, Connery thought. *You're chasing phantoms now.*

They went on and he debated what to do. They probably would figure out before long that he had evaded them and might turn around. So he didn't want to get back on the road and take the chance of meeting them on the return.

Nothing to do but stay out of sight and wait it out, then. That could mean he'd not make Culvertown tonight.

Well, there could be worse fates. Such as being robbed at gunpoint.

He went back to his horse and removed its saddle. He rubbed the horse down as best he could and fed it some more.

Too bad he didn't have a bedroll. He'd not anticipated needing one unless his search for Kenton took him into the mountains beyond Culvertown. In that case he'd planned to buy what he needed in Culvertown.

He'd spent other nights in harder situations. He'd make do, if it came to it.

Maybe he'd get lucky and his followers would come back sooner rather than later and he could ride on and maybe make Culvertown before nightfall.

Connery returned to his hiding place beside the road to keep a hopeful watch.

He dozed off, though he didn't realize it until sound on the road made him wake up. He looked around, then ducked low as he realized that his followers had indeed given up and reversed course.

Connery kept quiet and grinned. Once they were past, he could saddle up again and head on into Culvertown. He'd get there in the middle of the night, but what the devil? At the worst he'd sleep in a barn loft or woodshed, better than the open woods without a bedroll.

The two riders were moving slowly and drinking.

"Too damn bad he give us the slip," one said.

"Hell, yeah. I never seen such a roll of bills. I can't figure how the hell he got away from us."

"Heard us following, betcha. Heard your damn mouth blabbing on. I told you to be quieter."

"Hell, you was making more noise than me. Hey, why you stopping?"

"Gotta wet."

One of the pair slid out of the saddle and headed straight for the woods, only a few yards from where Connery hid. Connery held still as he listened to liquid splattering the ground. Thank heaven the man wasn't any closer than he was.

There was a loud thump out on the road. The other man had fallen out of his saddle.

The first one headed back out to the road, staggering badly. Connery realized just how drunk this pair was.

"What the hell's the matter with you?" the staggering man said.

The other was trying to pick himself up and not doing a good job of it.

"I'm drunk, Wayne. I fell off my horse."

"Ha! You never could hold your whiskey, Hamp. Get up off that ground."

Hamp tried hard but wound up on his rump again.

"Hell, Wayne, I can't go no farther. We got bed-rolls. Let's just lay 'em out and sleep it off here. We'll ride back down in the morning."

Connery winced. If they camped where they were, he was stuck where he was. . . . He dared not move for fear of making noise.

"Come on, Hamp. Get back on your horse. You can make it."

That's right, Hamp, Connery thought. *You can make it.*

"I can't. I can't. Let's stay here and go in come morning."

The debate continued briefly, and in the end Hamp won out. Connery shook his head sadly. An entire night hiding in the brush mere yards away from a couple of drunken thieves! The prospect was miserable.

Maybe they'd pass out and he could sneak off to his horse.

But they didn't pass out. They built a fire right in the midst of the road and sat drinking and talking, their voices growing more slurred. Billy wondered how much they could drink before finally succumbing. Their capacity seemed boundless.

Their conversation was about women, past crimes, and ambitions for future ones that would make them wealthy men. Connery had his doubts about that. These were losers, probably destined to die young and broke and still dreaming of that big crime.

He wished they were dreaming somewhere else to-night.

"Take a look there," Hamp said, pointing in Connery's general direction and giving him a scare. But he realized quickly that Hamp was not pointing at him but somewhere beyond him. "You can see the light of Jack Livingston's place from here."

"Nah. That ain't Livingston's place. It's too far away. Besides, I hear the place is empty. Livingston died last year."

"He ain't dead. I've talked to three men who seen him in Culvertown not three months ago. And six months back, he come into town and walked into a saloon and bought three rounds for everybody in the place. Told them to drink up hearty. Then two of them followed him back toward his mansion and dang if he didn't shoot at them. He's loco as can be, Jack Livingston is."

"Loco, maybe, but rich, too. They say that place has gold hid all through it."

"Just a story. Jack Livingston used to be rich, but he ain't no more."

"Who told you that?"

"Bunch of folks. He made a big strike here at Culvertown and got rich as Beelzebub and married himself off to a woman who had to have herself a fancy big mansion. So he built her one, and filled it all full of tunnels and passages and such."

"That's just another wild tale."

"Hell, no, it ain't. . . . I've talked to folks who say

they've seen 'em. His wife liked book stories with big old houses and secret tunnels and such, and so he built her house that way. Then she up and dies on him, and he goes loco and lives up there alone. Except sometimes he goes off here and there and gambles. So he loses most his money, but every now and then wins him a big hand and gets a lot of it back. That's when he shows up in Culvertown, buying drinks and all."

"I don't believe none of that."

"Well, I'm just telling what I hear."

"Tell you what: if there is money or gold hid up in that mansion, I'd sure like to put my hands on it."

"Amen. That would be a place worth robbing. But you'll not catch me trying it."

"Why?"

"Don't you know? Everyone who's tried to rob Jack Livingston ain't come back from the effort."

"Just more stories, that's all."

"The hell! You go into the Livingston mansion, you don't come out again."

They talked longer, dreaming out loud about the wealth they would someday steal. They drank, too, growing drunker and drunker, until finally they did slide into unconsciousness.

By then Billy Connery was asleep as well. He did not waken until the next morning. He awakened abruptly, though, startled into awareness by something . . . but he couldn't quite remember what it was. Popping sounds. That's what it had been. Like pinewood snapping in a fireplace, but louder. Gunshots? Faraway ones, maybe. The pair on the road were gone, their fire nearly cold. He was glad to see the last of them.

He got up, rubbing the back of his stiff neck, and headed off to where his horse awaited.

CHAPTER

11

CONNERY HAD BEEN CLOSER TO CULVERTOWN THAN he had realized. After only a couple of hours of riding he rounded a bend and saw the town spread out before him.

It was a beautiful and clear morning, but that only served to better define the town's remarkable ugliness. It was a rambling, undefined, mostly unpainted, smoke-stained town, streets muddy, boardwalks uneven. All around the town, rude cabins marked the hills, which were lined by a network of footpaths and wagon trails. To the west, a huge water cannon blasted away at the mountainside, laying bare rock and adding abundant filth to the wide stream that flowed through the center of town.

Welcome to Culvertown. Connery shook his head as he rode in, thinking that Brady Kenton couldn't have picked a less appealing place in which to hide.

He yanked his horse to a halt, however, when his eyes fell on one unexpected exception to the rule of ugliness that governed the town.

On a mountainside stood nothing less than a mansion, looming over the town. Connery let out a low whistle. This had to be the Jack Livingston mansion that the two scoundrels on the road had talked about.

Astonishing. Absolutely astonishing.

He found three hotels and picked the best-looking of the three. The man behind the counter was fleshy and bearded but had eyes that were bright and friendly, at least until Connery asked for a room.

"Ain't got none," the man said coldly.

"Your sign outside says you do."

"Well, what do you know? An Irishman who can read."

Connery understood then, debated mentally whether to fight it or just say the devil with it. The latter. He had better things to do with his time than try to overcome the prejudices of some mountain hotel keeper.

He left the hotel and headed for the second-best one. This time he disguised his brogue, just in case, and got a room with no problem and also arranged for the hotel livery boy to take care of his horse.

Baggage in hand, he headed upstairs to his room.

He was on the street again before long, in his hand the envelope bearing the apparent Kenton sketch. Briefly he admired the technical quality again, then glanced at the front to remind himself of the cafe name. The Buckeye. He set out to find it.

In a town this small he didn't expect it to take long, but Culvertown was cluttered and patternless, and he searched for more than an hour before at last he found the place.

The Buckeye was a nicer place than Connery had anticipated. He walked in and found a vacant table in a corner, from which he had a good view of the entire room. Settling there, he looked around for the waiter depicted in the sketch. But he didn't see him.

A different waiter, bald, short, and plump, approached him. "What can I get for you, sir?"

"Coffee. A piece of apple pie if you've got it."

"We've got custard, sir. That's all the pie we have today."

"Custard it is."

When the coffee and pie came to him on a tray, Connery slid the envelope toward the waiter.

"If you would, sir, take a look at that picture. Is that someone you know?"

The waiter picked it up. "I'll be! That's a picture of Walter Wheelan."

"A waiter here?"

"Not anymore, sir."

This was not good news. "Is he gone from town?"

"Not yet. But in a day or so he'll be moving to Chicago. Walter has gotten married, and his wife doesn't much like small mining towns."

"I see."

"May I ask you if you drew that picture, sir?"

"I didn't draw it. In fact, I'm trying to find the man who did. It was drawn in this very cafe."

"It's quite remarkable. . . . It looks exactly like Walter. Even the way he stands."

Connery took a sip of coffee and picked up his fork. "Have you seen anyone in here doing sketches like this?"

"Indeed I haven't, sir."

"Do you think that Walter Wheelan might know who did this sketch?"

"You'd have to ask him, sir."

"Can you tell me where I can find him?"

For a moment the waiter seemed uncertain, maybe a touch suspicious. "Why do you want to know?"

"I think the artist might be someone I know professionally. I'm an illustrator for *Gunnison's Illustrated American*."

"No! I do love to read that magazine. Though I miss Brady Kenton's touch. It's sad that he passed away."

"Yes. But about Walter Wheelan . . ."

"He lives in a rented room above a hardware store one street over. Unless he's moved away already. I've lost contact with him since he quit working here."

"What's the hardware store?"

"Smith's Hardware and Dry Goods."

"Thank you." Connery took his first bite of pie.

The waiter lingered a moment, looking at the sketch again. "I would half-believe that this sketch was done by Brady Kenton himself!"

"It is remarkably good."

"Who is the artist you believe did this sketch?"

"No one you'd have heard of," Connery said, because he could hardly tell the truth without sounding insane.

"I hope you find him, and hire him for your magazine. It would be wonderful to see this kind of work in it again . . . almost like having Kenton back again."

"There's more truth in that statement than you can know."

"Beg your pardon?"

"Never mind. The pie is good."

"Thank you, sir." The waiter turned to walk away, but a stray thought came to Connery's mind, a possibility that had been playing at the edge of his thoughts ever since he'd entered town, and he called the waiter back.

"What can you tell me about that big mansion on the mountainside?"

"Have you not heard of Jack Livingston, sir?"

"Maybe I've heard the name. But I don't know much about him."

"Not many do. . . . There are more rumors than facts."

"I heard he had died."

"Not that I know of, sir. There's someone living up there now. I've seen lights at night."

"Does Livingston have family?"

"His wife died. I think he had a son by a woman he was married to before . . ." The waiter lowered his voice. "Or maybe not really married to, if you know what I mean."

"How long have you been reading the *Illustrated American*?"

The waiter lifted a brow; Connery knew his stream of shifting questions must seem odd. The waiter would think them worthwhile when he received his sizable tip. "A lot of years, sir."

"Do you ever recall Brady Kenton having done a story about Jack Livingston?"

The other frowned, thinking back. "I don't know that I do."

"Really? Because I have the notion that he did. But I'm not sure." He paused and stared into his coffee cup. "If Brady Kenton knew Jack Livingston, then Jack Livingston might be just the kind of man who could help Kenton hide."

"Hide? But he's dead."

"I know. But if he wasn't, and if he wanted to hide, what better place than a place like that?"

The waiter was looking increasingly uncertain about his customer.

"I'll finish my pie now," Connery said, smiling.

"Very good, sir."

When Connery left the cafe, he paused and looked up at the mansion. Just a feeling . . . and a fragment of something that might be a memory.

The more he thought about it, the more sure he felt that Kenton had once done a story about an eccentric rich man who built a mansion for his wife above a Colorado mining town. It had to be Jack Livingston. How many others like him could there be?

Connery would visit the local telegraph office very soon and send a wire back to the *Illustrated American*. A search of the magazine's morgue would quickly answer the question.

For now, though, there was another visit to make. Connery stepped off the boardwalk and set out to find Smith's Hardware and Dry Goods.

CHAPTER

12

As soon as the door to the room above the hardware store opened, Billy Connery lost any possible doubt that the artist who had done the sketch on the envelope was Brady Kenton. The sketch had perfectly captured not only the image but also the very stance and impression of the man who stood before Connery in the open doorway.

"What can I do for you?" Walter Wheelan asked. He was a little rumpled and weary-looking and surrounded by packed crates and boxes. The arm garters he'd worn in the sketch Kenton had done were not present now. The man had been packing up to move.

"My name's Billy Connery," Connery replied, still suppressing his Irish accent, just in case Wheelan was another one of those who found Irishmen intolerable. "I wanted to meet you, just for a few moments, and ask you some questions about something."

"What kind of questions?"

"Nothing to worry about. Just some personal business I'm conducting. Congratulations on your marriage, by the way."

"Who told you about that?"

"A waiter at the Buckeye. One of your former coworkers."

"What's this all about?"

"Just this." Connery produced the envelope and showed it to Wheelan.

"I'll be!" Wheelan said, looking at the image of himself. "Where'd you get that? Did you draw that?"

"No. It was found in the Buckeye. Not by me, but someone who was there a while back, and who lent it to me. You haven't seen it before?"

"No. Who drew it?"

"That's the question I'm trying to answer. I'm a professional illustrator, and I'd like to find the one who did this. He's quite good, as you can see. Excellent."

"I'd say so. Looks just like me."

"You never noticed a customer sketching you at one time or another in the last few weeks?"

Wheelan thought a few moments. "Well, maybe I did, though I didn't know he was drawing. There was a man with a pencil . . . I thought he was writing."

This didn't necessarily mean anything. Any number of people probably jotted down notes or wrote letters in cafes. But just in case, Connery pressed on. "Do you recall what he looked like?"

"Not really. I think he was a fairly tall fellow. Beard. That's about all."

Maybe they were getting somewhere after all. "How old?"

"Lord, I don't remember. Not young, not old. Just a man."

"Tell me: have you ever seen this man before?" Connery pulled from under his vest a page torn from a magazine. He unfolded it and handed it to Wheelan.

"I've seen this picture," Wheelan said. "This is the picture of Brady Kenton that always ran in the *Illustrated American,* before he died."

"I need to ask you a question that may seem odd. Did the man you saw with the pencil in the café look like Brady Kenton?"

Wheelan laughed. "What kind of joke is this? Brady Kenton's dead!"

"I know. But the man you saw . . . did he look like Kenton?"

"I guess he could have looked like him. But a lot of people could. Kenton is dead. You're not trying to say he isn't, are you? Because . . . hey! Hey, you there! Get out of there!"

Wheelan's attention had suddenly been diverted by someone behind Connery. Connery turned and saw a boy of about ten come running out of a half-opened door of an apartment across from Wheelan's room. The boy darted within a yard of Connery and down the stairs. He had something in his hands—a loaf of bread, Connery thought it was.

"Damned little scoundrel!" Wheelan said. "Sorry thief! You leave a door unlocked around here and that little devil will be through it, taking whatever he can.

I've caught him in here before! It taught me to keep my door locked, I'll tell you."

"So he doesn't live in those rooms?"

"Hell, no!"

"It looked like he'd taken bread."

"He lives on what he can steal half the time. I suppose I should feel sorry for him."

"If he's hungry enough to steal bread, I think there's no choice but to feel sorry for him. Is he an orphan?"

"He'd be better off if he was. He's got no mother, but his father's still alive. But the sorry old devil drinks bad, and beats the boy so bad he has to spend a lot of his time in hiding. I really do suppose I should feel more sorry for him than I do. I just can't abide a thief under any circumstance, that's all. The people who live across the hall there have given that boy food, money, clothes, time and time again. And here he goes stealing from them!"

Connery found this all dismaying and depressing. He'd spent enough time here. Taking back the picture of Kenton, he thanked Wheelan again and turned away.

"Hey, you really weren't trying to say that Kenton is still alive, were you?"

Connery turned and looked at Wheelan a last time. "Why? Do you think he could be?"

"Not if what I read in your magazine is true. He was killed along the railroad near Denver."

"Then I guess you answered your own question. Good day to you, Mr. Wheelan."

"Good day to you, sir. I hope you find your mysterious sketch artist."

"I intend to, sir."

Connery moved on, but Wheelan called to him one more time. "Hey, I think I just remembered something. That man writing with the pencil came back in later on. He looked around the table he'd been at, but wouldn't stay to eat. I remember because I tried to seat him and he wouldn't sit down."

"He was looking for this sketch, then."

"Assuming that man was the one who did it. It could have been somebody else. Like I said, I just figured the man was writing down notes or something. I didn't really specifically notice him drawing."

Connery thought it all over as he walked slowly through town, looking for the telegraph office. If it had been Kenton that Wheelan saw laboring with a pencil and paper and if Kenton had returned to seek the envelope he'd left, then he must have been concerned that the envelope drawing would be found and serve to identify him.

As fate would have it, that very thing had occurred.

Connery found the telegraph office and sent a wire to the *Illustrated American*. After an hour of waiting the reply came back. Kenton had indeed done a story and series of sketches about Jack Livingston.

Connery tucked the telegram into his pocket, beside the envelope bearing the sketch. He was now almost sure why Kenton had come to this unlikely town. He needed a remote, secure place to hide. And what more remote and secure place could there be than the mountainside mansion of Jack Livingston?

Connery walked out of the telegraph office into the midst of excitement in Culvertown: a crowd was gathering around a town marshal who was bringing in two dead bodies draped without dignity across the back of a mule, their arms dangling.

"What happened, Marshal?" someone asked.

"Shot dead," he replied. "Both of them. A traveler coming in early this morning found them on the road, both shot square between the eyes."

"Between the eyes?" someone replied. "Executed?"

"No powder burns on the face," the marshal replied. "Whoever shot them plugged them from some distance away . . . some really accurate shooting, to hit them both like he did." He touched his face directly between the eyebrows. "Hell of a time for it to happen, though. I've got a train to catch to Scallonville this afternoon, and now I've got to deal with this. I'll be lucky to make it on time."

Connery was feeling a little queasy. The men on the back of the mule were the same ones who had followed him and camped on the road the night before.

He remembered the popping sounds that had awakened him. Now he knew what those sounds had been.

He listened to the general conversation around him. Someone noted that the two were a pair of common thieves who had plagued people in those parts for at least a year. Whoever had killed them had done the citizenry a favor, another person noted.

Connery stared for a few moments at the blood dripping from the downturned heads of the dead men and listened to the talk around him. He was a little shaky. Though these men had been a threat to him and he certainly had no trace of affection for them, it was unnerving to see them dead when only last night he'd been hiding from them along the roadside.

He turned away from the crowd and walked off, feeling the need for a change of scenery and a turn around town for some fresh air.

Connery walked briskly, not noticing that another man had also stepped away from the crowd and was following him some distance behind.

CHAPTER

13

"HEY, YOU, MISTER!"

Connery turned. The little bread-stealing boy he'd seen earlier was approaching him. He wore a cocky grin and had a hardened and mature aura about him that belied his years. The face was that of a boy, the glint of the eyes that of a man.

The boy marched up to Connery and thrust his hand out, a gesture that surprised Connery. But he took the offered hand and the boy pumped it firmly.

"You need to be a little more careful, mister," the boy said. "You dropped something back there on the street."

He handed Connery both the return telegram he'd just received minutes before from the *Illustrated American* and the envelope bearing the sketch of Walter Wheelan.

Connery was surprised. Both of these items had been thrust deep into his coat pocket . . . hadn't they? He'd had his hands in his pockets back there while examining the dead men and supposed he could have accidentally dragged these items out when he withdrew his hands from his pockets.

Then again, this little scamp might have picked his pockets while he was distracted. He'd be willing to bet a boy like this had that kind of talent. Well, at least he'd given them back. And a quick feel of Connery's pockets revealed his wallet was still in place.

"Thank you," he said.

"I know that man in the picture," the boy announced. "That's Walter Wheelan."

"That's right. In fact, I was talking to him this morning when you came out of those boarding rooms and he shouted at you. Remember seeing me there?"

"I remember. I remember what you two was talking about, too."

"You listened to our conversation?"

"I listen to every conversation I can. You can learn a lot worth the hell knowing if you just listen to folks."

Cocky, sharp-tongued little street boy, Connery thought. But the thought bore no edge. Connery had been a sharp-tongued street boy himself some years earlier.

"What's your name?"

"I'm Stockton Shelley." The hand came up again for another shake, which Connery found slightly amusing. "Pleased to know you, Mr. Connery."

"I'm impressed. You even know my name."

"I heard you tell it to Walter Wheelan. You came up to his door at just the wrong time, you know. I was just about to sneak out when you came up and brought him to his door. I couldn't sneak out then."

"So why did you make a break for it?"

"Because I looked out the window and saw the man whose apartment I was in coming back home. I had to get out before he got in."

"It's not right to steal, you know."

"It was just a loaf of bread. And Walter Wheelan has stole enough food from the Buckeye during the time he worked there that I'll be damned if I care what he thinks about me getting some food for myself. A man's got to eat, after all."

"Are you hungry?"

"Not no more. I ate a whole loaf of bread. Hey, will you give me some money for bringing you back them papers?"

"To tell you the truth, it'd crossed my mind that maybe I didn't drop those papers at all."

"What? You saying I stole them?"

"If you'll steal bread, you'll pick pockets."

"You're hurting my feelings, mister!"

"Yeah, I imagine you're quite a sensitive young man. But I tell you what: I will give you some money. Not for picking my pockets, but because I'm just a very nice fellow."

Stockton accepted the coin gratefully. After biting it, he bowed to Connery and said, "You're a gentleman and a scholar, sir! A gentleman and a scholar!"

"Kind of you to say so. Good day to you, young man."

"Hold up there, Mr. Irishman. I think you'll be paying me a bit more than this."

"What? Are you going to rob me now?"

"Oh, no. You're going to want to pay me for what I've got to tell you."

"And what might that be?"

"It's who did this drawing of old Wheelan, that's what."

"It may surprise you to learn that I'm already fairly certain who did it. The question is, where can I find him?"

"Maybe I can tell you both things."

"I'm looking for more than maybes."

"I know for a fact who it is, and where he is."

Connery pulled five dollars from his pocket and handed it to Stockton. "Five more if what you tell me proves to be right."

The boy took the money smugly, pinching it between thumb and forefinger and lifting it from Connery's hand. "The man who drew that picture is Brady Kenton. Folks say he's dead, but he ain't, because I've seen him. He combs his hair different than in that picture of him in the magazine, and he's got a longer beard. But it's him."

"All right. You've told me what I already knew. Where is he?"

The boy pointed in the direction of the Jack Livingston mansion.

Connery nodded. "Somehow I had the feeling that might be the place."

"He may as well be on the moon, though, if you want to see him," Stockton said. "Old Livingston ain't going to let you in. He don't let anybody in much."

"He apparently let in Brady Kenton. Or do you really know Kenton is there?"

"I do know. I've seen him."

"Where?"

"Sitting on a rain barrel out behind the saloon, drawing on a busted-off piece of a wooden crate. Then he got up and walked on up to the Livingston house."

Connery frowned. "Was he drinking out behind that saloon?"

"Had him a bottle. I saw him take a swallow or two."

Gunnison would not be glad to learn this. But it was not unexpected, given Kenton's history.

"Was there a woman with him?"

"No. He was alone. Where's the rest of my money?"

"You'll get it when I've met Kenton face-to-face. I have to verify that what you've told me is true." Stockton frowned, chewed on his lip, then said, "If I can bring Kenton to you will you make that other five into twenty-five?"

"Why should I pay you when I can go up and knock on Livingston's door myself?"

"Livingston don't answer his door . . . except with a shotgun, or a pack of biting dogs."

Connery found himself irritated by this manipulative, self-serving boy, even if he did sympathize for his poor situation in life. Stockton had probably overheard enough during the conversation with Wheelan to figure out what he needed to say to gouge money out of Connery.

"I'll take my chances. If I can't get to Kenton, then maybe I'll look you up."

Stockton pocketed his money. "I'll be seeing you later, then."

When Stockton Shelley had gone out of sight, sauntering and swaggering like a miniature gunfighter, Connery looked up at the Livingston mansion and wondered if it really would be as challenging to get to Kenton as had been implied. And what if Livingston was a true lunatic, and dangerous?

Connery stood staring up at the Livingston house, trying to decide exactly what he would say when he got there.

CHAPTER

14

ON THE OTHER SIDE OF A WHITE LINEN CURTAIN that hung over most of one of the upper windows in the Livingston mansion, Brady Kenton gazed down at the lone figure of Billy Connery.

Kenton had not met Connery and had no inkling of who he was looking at. It was not unusual, though, to see someone down below staring up at the house. It was, after all, quite an impressive structure, not typical of mountain mining towns. Long after Jack Livingston was dead and gone, Kenton figured, some canny community leader type would probably persuade the town leaders to make Livingston's house into some sort of museum or historical attraction. Existing legends of the solitary eccentric would be enhanced and new ones created. Livingston would become the fictionalized symbol of a Culvertown of years past.

But probably not much fictionalized. Livingston was enough of a true eccentric not to require much exaggeration. He was a rough man, a hard man, a man easy to come to hate . . . and sometimes a part of Kenton still did, despite himself.

But thank God Livingston was here. Thank God he'd allowed his fortress of a mansion to become a refuge at a time Kenton had never needed a refuge more.

While Kenton watched, the gazing man in the town below reached into a pocket and pulled out a pad. Producing a pencil, he began to write . . . no, to draw. Kenton was startled: it was like watching a reflection of himself at work.

Could the man below be an illustrator, just as Kenton was? If so, why was he here, now, drawing this particular dwelling?

Kenton had cause to be unnerved by this. He stepped away from the window.

The room suddenly made him feel claustrophobic. He went out, into the hall, then down two more doors.

He rapped lightly. "Come in," a soft voice on the other side replied.

Kenton opened the door and entered slowly. He closed the door behind him and smiled at a woman the sight of whom still made his heart hammer like a drum, though they'd now been together for many weeks.

Victoria Kenton smiled back at her husband and lifted her hand, bidding him to come.

Kenton walked across to her and knelt. She was in a wicker chair, a quilt across her legs, and though she looked weak and thin, she was yet beautiful.

He was ever amazed, in fact, that years and the

trials of injury and illness that this woman had suffered had not robbed her of more beauty than they had. Though she was in her fifties now and her hair abundantly touched with gray, her face was still the beautiful vision that Kenton had secretly buried in almost every illustration he had drawn . . . looking out a window, around a corner, sometimes actually embodied in the drawn lines and shadows of trees, buildings, mountains.

She was still his Victoria, and after so many long years of separation, she was his again.

"Did you rest?" he asked, holding her hand as he knelt beside her chair.

"I did. I slept right here in this chair. I feel stronger now."

"I think your color is better. I wish you'd slept longer. Maybe if you'd lie down on the bed . . ." He glanced at the four-poster on the other side of the large room. Victoria's bed, the bed he longed to share with her but which, for now, remained hers alone. They had been separated for too many years for her to welcome him instantly back into her bed. It would take time. They still had to come to know each other again. But it would happen. Every day Brady Kenton felt that Victoria was a little more his again; that little bit of the life and closeness they had lost had come back again.

"The chair is comfortable enough for me. Back in England I spent most of my time in a chair. It was the dream that woke me."

Dear heaven, how good it was to hear her voice!

Kenton drank in the melody of it like a perfect wine. "A good dream, I hope."

"No. It wasn't. I dreamed he found us. I dreamed that he shot you."

"Victoria . . . don't dwell on such things. It's only your fear speaking. He's not going to find us, not this far away. We're a world away from him now."

"No, Brady. You don't know him like I do. He will never abide that you took me away from him. He'll search for us forever, until he finds us."

"He'll not find us here, Victoria. I can think of no safer place for you."

She stroked Kenton's face. "Oh, Brady . . . you're so courageous and devoted and reassuring . . . but if only you knew David like I do! You would understand that in his own way, he is as devoted to me as you are. He loves me, just as you do . . . but his love isn't the love of a normal man. He only knows how to love by possessing and controlling, and he can't stand to lose. And he will especially not stand to lose me. He would rather kill me than lose me."

"He will never kill you. I'll not allow it. I'd die myself before I'd let him near you."

She smiled, a sad smile. "Let me tell you what he will do, what I have no doubt he has already done," she said. "He will not remain in England. He'll follow us here."

"Nonsense, dear. Please don't worry about—"

"Listen to me, Brady! I speak as one who has known this man for many years. He will follow us to the United States. Once here, he'll use his money

freely, hiring the best investigators and the toughest
hired gunmen he can to find our track. He will discover, eventually if not already, that I have a half
brother, and that his name is Livingston, and that he
lives in Culvertown, Colorado, in a strong but remote
and seldom-visited mansion. He'll consider that it
may be a place we would come to take refuge . . .
because he knows that I know he will come after us."

CHAPTER

15

THOUGH HIS HUSBAND'S INSTINCTS MADE KENTON want to tell Victoria that all this was nonsense and all was well, he knew she was right. Of course Dr. David Kevington would come after them! Kenton had known it all along. It was why they had come here, to this obscure, high mountain town, to take up hiding in the house of Jack Livingston, a place Kenton hoped that Dr. Kevington would never find.

Victoria went on. "He'll work as long as he has to, and spend as much as he has to, to make sure we are found. He'll send men to kill you and to take me back to him . . . or maybe he'll kill me as well, to punish me for having gone away with you."

"Don't talk about such things, my dear."

"I have to. Because we have to face this, Brady. Our lives can never be normal lives until the matter of David Kevington has been dealt with. He stalked after me like a wild beast all those years ago and kidnapped me all the way to England and hid me away like his private treasure all these years, telling

me you were dead and gone and that only he loved
me . . . that he was my husband. He took away the
child I bore to you, Brady, and gave her to a servant.
He is an evil and desperate man. He *will not* let us
be! Deny it if you will, but I know that you believe
I'm right. If you didn't believe it, you would have
been in contact by now with your magazine, your
partner, your friends. You know you dare not go to
them because you know that if you do, you might
bring danger upon them."

Kenton could not dispute this. He nodded, heavy
of heart.

Victoria, not used to much speaking, was growing
weary. Despite the years that had passed since the
railroad accident that had been the watershed event of
both her own and Brady Kenton's lives, she was still
an injured woman. She had spent years in a comatose
to semicomatose condition, even given birth to a
daughter without knowing it. Victoria's injuries had
left her brain injured and her mind weakened along
with her body. But she was stronger now, her mind
focused and clear most of the time, the lies that her
obsessed kidnapper had told her now seen for what
they were.

There were periods, though, when her mind would
grow cloudy. She would push Kenton away at those
times, refusing to see him. Three times he had been
so disheartened by her rejections that he had left the
house and gone into Culvertown, where he would
drink and sulk and work on idle and pointless
sketches. It was foolish, he knew, because he ran the

risk of being identified. He worried still about one sketch of a waiter he'd scribbled down for no good reason on an envelope at a local cafe. He'd left the sketch behind by accident and now worried that someone might recognize it as a Brady Kenton work.

But it wasn't likely, he told himself. All America believed Brady Kenton to be dead.

"We can't hide here for long, Brady. He'll come, or he'll send men to deal with us. And it isn't fair to Jack. He's endangered as well, as long as we're here."

Kenton struggled against the sense of despair that so often threatened to overwhelm him these days. He'd not expected despair to be one of the emotions that would remain with him after reuniting with the wife he had loved and missed for so long.

"I don't think Jack worries about any kind of danger," Kenton said, trying to sound brighter than he felt. "Jack rather likes a challenge, I think. He'd probably tell David Kevington to send in his little army, then laugh while he picked them all off through those rifle ports he's built into the walls here."

"Don't take what I say lightly, Brady. We must leave soon, or Jack may pay the price."

In his current state of mind, Kenton might have barked back that he hardly cared about any price Jack Livingston might pay. In his younger days, Livingston had treated his half sister, Victoria, very badly, cheating her out of an inheritance that should have been hers. Victoria had not cared much about the material loss, but the fact that her half brother had taken such advantage of her had hurt her so badly that she'd virtually disavowed his existence. Kenton himself had held a long grudge against Jack Livingston, though a few years back, in a time of personal reflection, he'd chosen to visit Jack and heal over the old wounds. At the same time, Kenton had written and illustrated a well-received story about his eccentric half brother-in-law and made Livingston a relatively famous figure.

Even though the rift had ostensibly been repaired between Kenton and Jack Livingston, ghosts of the old ill feelings remained, and Kenton still believed that Livingston owed Victoria some recompense for the way he'd mistreated her years before.

Maybe, Kenton thought, *he's giving that recompense by allowing us to hide here. I'll try not hold ill will against him. Right now he may be saving our lives.*

"We will leave, then . . . when we can. But your health won't allow it yet, Victoria. Our flight from England, the stress of travel all the way across the country, all our various worries . . . they've left you too weak for us to do anything but stay here for now. Besides, I've seen no indications at all that anyone has followed us." He suddenly thought of the man he'd seen outside, sketching the mansion, and wondered . . . but then he dismissed it. Anyone sent by Dr. Kevington would be up to more nefarious stuff than standing in the open, sketching a mansion.

"I'll be able to travel soon. I don't want to be a danger to anyone."

Kenton leaned over and kissed her cheek, thanking

God deeply that she was alive and here to be kissed at all. He'd lived in a world that for year upon year had told him his wife was dead. Only he had stubbornly refused to accept that "fact," and he had been proven correct.

"We'll find another place," Kenton said. "I know people all over this nation who will be glad to help us."

The truth was, at the moment he couldn't think of anywhere else to go at all.

CHAPTER

16

THE DOOR OPENED. NO KNOCK OR FOREWARNING.

Jack Livingston appeared. He was on the short side but muscular, with silver-gray hair trimmed close to his head and a weathered face with intense dark gray eyes.

"Well, Victoria, how are you feeling?"

"I'm doing quite well, Jack," she said, not quite truthfully. She was beginning to pave the way toward their exit from this place. "I had a good nap."

Jack walked over to them. By now Kenton had come to his feet. Jack gazed down at his half sister. "I still can't believe you're here, Victoria. Can't believe you're alive. All them years that old Brady here spent looking for you, I thought he was crazy. So did a lot of others."

Kenton smiled just a little. "I might note that there are plenty who think you're a little crazy yourself, Jack. You live up here in this big house, run people off who come around, act like a hermit . . . then every now and then you take a notion to go to town and buy everybody a drink."

"It ain't always that. Once I went into the Buckeye and bought everybody in the place a plate of flap-jacks."

"You're an odd man, Jack. Then again, so am I, I suppose."

Jack smiled at his half sister. "Your face is as pretty as ever, Victoria, but I can see the tracks of what you've been through in your eyes. What did this Kevington fellow do to you?"

"He loved me, and he imprisoned me. He saved my life, then took my life away. He delivered my daughter while I lay unconscious, then gave her to a servant family to raise as their own. He declared that I would have all the good things life could offer, but denied me my freedom. He told me I was his wife, but treated me as his slave. In short, he subjected me to a life of contradictions, Jack. That was my life with Dr. David Kevington."

Livingston's left cheek twitched. "I'd like to shoot the bastard myself."

"I'd like to beat you to it," Kenton said. "I almost had the opportunity, you know."

"Did you? I wish you'd done it. Was that while you were spiriting Victoria out of his estate?"

"Yes. I'll tell you all about it sometime."

"Now's as good a time as any, seems to me."

"Later, maybe." Kenton wasn't about to go into details on the spot of what had been a horrifying series of events for Victoria. His removal of her from the Kevington estate near London had been nearly fatal for both of them. When Kenton thought back on the rabid fury that Kevington had displayed when he caught Kenton smuggling away the woman he had in his snare for years, it was easy to realize that Victoria was right when she predicted that Kevington would surely come after them.

"There's things about this I have a right to know," Jack said. "Is Kevington likely to show up here?"

"I don't believe Kevington is likely to find us easily . . . but eventually, yes, I think he will find us. We were just talking about that, Victoria and I, when you came in." Kenton didn't figure this was news to Livingston, who probably had been crouched with his ear to keyhole throughout the couple's conversation.

Kenton despised having to live under the protection of a man he never would really like.

"Let him come," Livingston said icily. "I'll blow his candle out for him."

Kenton realized that Victoria had grown tense in the last few moments, her knuckles whitening as she gripped the armrest of the wicker chair. He felt a surge of mixed emotions. As much as he didn't like to admit it, he knew Victoria still held an affection of a sort for Kevington—who had, after all, nursed her away from the brink of death after her train accident. It was probably difficult for her to listen to him and Livingston talking about killing Kevington as if it would be a privilege.

Victoria had made it clear that she hated Kevington, but Kenton knew that her hatred was not pure.

For her there would always be a measure of affection mixed with her loathing. Kenton could not blame her for this. It was possible, maybe likely, that if not for Kevington's intervention after Victoria's railroad accident many years before she might not be alive.

"Come to think of it, maybe it's time to tell you the full story after all, Jack," Kenton said. "Let's go downstairs, leave Victoria in peace, and get ourselves a glass of that good whiskey of yours. Then we'll talk."

Billy Connery had given up sketching the Livingston mansion only minutes after he started. He wasn't in Culvertown to sketch but to find Brady Kenton . . . and now that he had a likely idea of where Kenton was, his courage was failing him.

Part of it was simple fear over how the eccentric Livingston would react to a visitor at his door. But Connery was almost as worried about how Kenton would receive him. The man wasn't hiding for no reason and surely would not be happy to be ferreted out.

So Connery found himself unable just yet to force himself up to that big house on the hill.

A beer was what he needed. Maybe two. A couple of beers, and he'd have the courage to do what needed doing.

He headed for the nearest saloon and along the way chanced to pass the local undertaking parlor. The door opened as he passed; a man came out. Connery looked through the door before it could swing shut and was just at the right angle to see through a second, interior doorway, back into the rear room where the dirty work of undertaking was done.

For just a moment he caught a glimpse of two bodies laid out, one on a slab, naked, the undertaker leaning over it, hard at work, with a cigar dropping hot ashes on the dead man. The other corpse was still clothed and waiting his turn on the floor. The outer door swung closed, and the vision of mortality was gone.

But Connery was shaken. Maybe he'd have three beers instead of two.

In the saloon with the first beer in hand, he further pondered the two dead highwaymen. Who had killed them? Whoever he was, he was a good shot to have plugged both so neatly, from a distance, with shots between the eyes. That was one man the pair shouldn't have tried to rob.

He wondered if the local law would spend much time investigating the deaths. He would be willing to wager that they would not. No one would be much inclined to punish men who had rid the region of two troublesome highwaymen.

So here's to you, whoever you are, he said mentally as he raised his glass to the unknown marksman. *May you forever eliminate thieves and keep our roadways safe . . . and, just in case, may you forever keep your distance from me.*

CHAPTER

17

HIS NAME WAS BAILEY MCCURDEN, AND HE SAT IN a dark corner of the saloon, nursing a beer and watching Billy Connery.

At least, he was relatively sure it was Billy Connery he was watching. The young man across the room didn't look quite the same as Connery's meager little picture in the rear section of the *Illustrated American*. This fellow looked a bit leaner and had hair a touch longer, and the feeble mustache sported by the young man in the magazine illustration was absent from this fellow.

Despite the differences, the more McCurden studied the young man, the more sure he was that it was Connery. The resemblances outweighed the differences. With any luck, young Connery would lead him straight to the man he really wanted to find.

The English physician who had hired him would be pleased. McCurden was on the verge of finding Brady Kenton. He could all but smell it.

It had been fairly easy so far. After being hired by

one Dr. David Kevington in a very covert manner, McCurden had traveled to St. Louis with several other hired Kevington operatives to keep an eye on the offices and employees of the *Illustrated American*. A talk to a low-level staff member who was smoking his pipe on the doorstep had uncovered the news that one Billy Connery, an illustrator who was a relatively recent hire of the magazine, was making sudden preparations to travel, apparently at the behest of Kenton's old partner, Alex Gunnison. And Connery was saying very little about the details—just enough to let his coworkers know that he was on to something very important.

Sensing a possible lead, McCurden had found Connery's apartment, but without Connery present at the time. But he had found Connery's neighbor, a baker named J. R. Randwick, who had proven to be a rich source of information once plied with a few beers. Connery was going to Culvertown, Colorado, on some secretive venture that would involve "bringing a certain somebody back from the dead."

It was easy to figure out from there: Kenton was in Culvertown, and Connery was being sent to find him.

McCurden made the same journey only a day after Connery. He'd traveled quickly after disembarking the train and would have had a completely unimpeded journey if not for those two troublesome fools who had tried to rob him on the road.

They'd been only an annoyance, a momentary problem. Two quick shots, two slugs between the eyes, and they were out of consideration.

McCurden continued to sip his beer and watch Connery. The young fellow seemed nervous, McCurden thought. Interesting. Nerves implied that he was on to something important.

Maybe Connery had found Kenton. And where Kenton was, there would be the woman Kevington wanted back.

A very valuable woman. Kevington had made that clear, and McCurden hadn't been able to keep his mind off it ever since. *A very valuable woman.*

He'd not let Connery notice him, if he could help it. But he'd also not let him slip out of his sight.

Connery finished his three beers and stared at the empty mug. He felt a little fuzzy but not any more courageous.

Devil with it. It was time to do what he'd come to do. What was there to knocking on a door, after all? If Livingston wasn't hospitable, it wouldn't be the first door slammed in his face.

But Connery had made one slight shift in his plans while drinking his beers. So instead of heading up the hill toward the Livingston mansion, he headed for the telegraph office.

Unnoticed by Connery, a man in the corner of the cafe also rose and left, scooping up a stray newspaper from a table as he did so.

Before they'd gone in their opposite directions, Gunnison and Connery had made communication arrangements. Telegrams would be worded in such a way as to be clear to their intended recipients but not to others who might read them. Brady Kenton, for example, was to be referred to by initials only, but reversed: "KB." And because it was impossible for Gunnison and Connery to know exactly where each other were at any given moment, telegrams were to be sent to several predesignated stations, which would be checked regularly.

Connery rang the bell on the counter of the telegraph station and waited for the operator, a red-haired man with a wide, pale face and many lingering boyhood freckles. This was a different operator from the man who had been here when Connery telegraphed the *Illustrated American* morgue earlier.

"My name is Billy Connery. Have I by chance received any messages?"

"Let me check." He shuffled papers. "No, nothing."

"All right. I want to send some messages of my own. Five of them, all the same, all to different stations in New York."

"Five different recipients?"

"All to the same person, Alexander Gunnison. Just five different stations."

"Odd arrangement. What's the message?"

" 'KB found in Culvertown. Livingston house. Please come.' Sign it off with 'Connery.' That'll be sufficient."

"All righty."

While the operator clicked out the message, Connery paced around the room, humming nervously, glancing out the windows, tapping his heels on the floors. The door leading out to the station porch stood ajar.

There was no one else in the station besides Connery and the key operator. There was, however, a man on the porch, seated by the open door, reading a newspaper. Connery didn't even notice him until he meandered over to the door and happened to look out, and was slightly startled because he knew no one had been on the porch when he entered only two or three minutes earlier.

The man glanced up. Connery said, "Good day, sir," and withdrew back inside.

"That all you need?" the operator asked.

"That's all. I may get a reply to that. I'll check back in with you to see."

"I'll be here."

Connery stepped out onto the porch, walking past the seated man without a glance. He trotted down the steps and onto the dirt street and wondered if he'd just done the right thing. He'd just sent Alex Gunnison a message that would bring him straight to Culvertown . . . and the honest truth was that Connery really didn't know for sure that Kenton was here. He'd yet to verify anything with his own eyes.

But he'd decided over his beers to go ahead and send the message prematurely. By doing so he preempted a difficult situation for himself later on. If he did find Brady Kenton, Kenton might urge him not to contact Gunnison at all. And Connery frankly didn't want to be put into a situation in which he had to choose his duties. Now the issue was predecided. The message was already sent.

The worst that could happen now was that he'd not find Kenton after all and Gunnison would come racing to Colorado all for nothing.

Maybe if Kenton proved not to be here, he'd be able to get a new wire sent out soon enough to counteract the last one. He told himself he'd done the right thing.

Now there were no more excuses. No more beers to be consumed, no more wires to be sent.

Time to go up the hill and do what needed to be done.

CHAPTER

18

"BEG YOUR PARDON, SIR."

Connery turned. The man who'd been reading the newspaper was behind him, smiling in that uncertain way of those who are approaching strangers. It was just the kind of smile Connery would probably have on his face when the door swung open at the Livingston mansion.

"Well, hello. What can I do for you, sir?"

The man laughed, almost a giggle. "You'll have to pardon me, sir, but I was sitting back on the porch at the telegraph office, and I swear I think I heard you say your name is Billy Connery."

"That's right."

"Oh! Oh, my! Well . . . that's something. It is indeed. I wasn't trying to eavesdrop, you understand. It's just that the door was open, and—"

"That's all right. Do I know you, sir?"

"Oh, no. No. But I think I know you. My name is Jim, Jim Grant. And I'm quite a reader, you see, and my favorite reading has always been *Gunnison's Il-*

lustrated American. Me and a million other people, huh? And I have to ask you if you might just happen to be the Billy Connery who works for the *Illustrated American.* And if you're not, I'm going to be as embarrassed as a man can be." The nervous giggle again.

Connery was astonished. Never before had he been recognized by anyone. Among the journalistic stars of the *Illustrated American,* he shone the dimmest.

"I am with the *Illustrated American,* yes." Now it was Connery who wore a silly grin.

"Oh, my. My goodness. I thought it was you. When I heard your name, and heard you say the name of Alex Gunnison, I thought that it really might be you. Oh, my! This is exciting. You're a talented man, Mr. Connery. I've admired your work."

"I'm surprised you've even noticed it."

"Well, I'll tell you, sir—"

"Please, call me Billy."

"Billy, yes. I'll tell you, Billy, I'm not the average reader. When I get interested in something, or someone, I *really* get interested. A bit of a fanatic about things, I'm afraid. Get a little obsessed."

"I see. I'm flattered that you like my work."

"You know, I think I like your work better than Alex Gunnison's. I wouldn't want you to tell him that, though. Was that *the* Alex Gunnison you were sending a wire to?"

"That was the one."

"Oh, my. That's something! Alex Gunnison. I never got the chance to meet him. But I did meet my hero, the greatest one of all. . . ."

"Brady Kenton?"

"Yes. He even signed a copy of the magazine for me. I have it in a frame now."

"When did you see him?"

"It was five years ago, in Chicago."

"Oh."

"I was so sorry to hear when he died." The man paused, licking his lips and frowning strangely. "I . . . I didn't want to say this . . . it sounds very foolish . . . but do you know that I think I've seen Brady Kenton . . . *since* he died? How's that for strange?" The giggle was even more nervous-sounding this time.

"Wait. . . . When did you see him?"

"Well, day before yesterday."

"Up there?" Connery pointed toward the Livingston mansion.

"No, no, not there. In a boardinghouse dining room, across town. I'd gone in to see if they had a room for my brother, who's coming to visit week after next, and there he was, sitting at the table and eating. He looked a little different, and I had the impression he didn't want to be recognized. But I swear it was him! Though I know it couldn't be, because he's dead."

"Can you show me this boardinghouse?"

"Surely . . . but why?"

"I don't want to say just now. Do you mind showing me the way?"

The man grinned widely. "It would be an honor!"

"Thank you, Mr. Grant."

"Please call me Jim." He stuck out his hand for Connery to shake.

And when he did so, his leather coat gapped open a little and Connery saw that he wore a gun belt. Surprised him; Grant just didn't seem the kind to be carrying a hidden weapon. But Connery himself had a pistol, and he probably wouldn't seem the kind to go armed, either. He dismissed the half-second of caution about going off with this stranger.

"What do you do for a living, Jim?" Connery asked as they walked off together.

"I'm a baker," Grant replied. "Here, turn into this alley."

The alley was narrow and shadowed. "What is this, some kind of shortcut?" Connery asked.

"That's right, a shortcut."

They went into the alley.

"A baker, you say. I've got a friend back in St. Louis who's a baker."

"Oh, yes. J. R. Randwick. I met him."

Connery, who was just ahead of Grant, stopped and turned. "You met J. R.?"

"That's right. But he didn't know me as Jim Grant. I told him my real name. McCurden."

"Who the devil are you?" Connery asked, reaching under his jacket for the shoulder-holstered pistol.

McCurden was ahead of him, though. His own pistol came out much more quickly, and he slammed Connery hard on the temple.

Connery collapsed, stunned but not unconscious. McCurden knelt and quickly removed Connery's pistol from its holster and stuck it under his belt.

"Who am I, you ask? Well, starting right now, I'm you. I'm Mr. Billy Connery. Because you're no longer going to be around to play that role in the little stage play we call life. I'm honored to be your understudy. You've never met Kenton, have you? You were hired after his supposed death. Which means Kenton doesn't really know you." He clicked back the hammer of his pistol and aimed it at Connery's forehead.

But he didn't fire. He frowned and shook his head. "Nah. Too loud. We'll do it quietly."

He put away the pistol and pulled out a long-bladed folding knife. It opened with a click and locked into place.

Connery's consciousness faded as the knife went up. He was oblivious to it altogether when it descended swiftly toward his chest.

The telegraph operator was dozing in a chair leaned back against the wall when McCurden entered the station.

"Up at attention, Red!" McCurden bellowed, startling the moon-faced operator out of his chair so fast he knocked it over. "Got a message to send."

The operator ran a hand through his hair and tried to regather his dignity. He picked up the chair, dropped it, picked it up again.

"Yes, sir. A message." He sat down at the key. "What is the name of the recipient?"

"Kevington. Dr. David Kevington. He's in St. Louis at the moment." McCurden grinned. "But when he gets this wire, I can assure you, he'll cut a fast trail to dear old Culvertown."

The operator had no notion of what any of this meant. He picked up his pad of paper and a pencil.

"You can dictate your message now, sir."

The message, broken down into pulses of electricity, made its way across the wires to its destination in St. Louis.

Dr. David Kevington was not there to receive it. He had moved on already, following what had seemed a strong but ultimately proved to be a false lead indicating that Brady Kenton and Victoria were in Denver.

The message, though, was picked up by one of two hired investigators who had been instructed to remain behind in St. Louis and keep a close eye on the offices and personnel of the *Illustrated American,* just in case Brady Kenton decided to come home.

They'd also been instructed to maintain a close vigil on the telegraph wires, in case any other promising information came through from other hired agents such as McCurden, who was following his own leads elsewhere.

The other agents knew that their British employer, virtually a stranger to them, put much stock in McCurden. The man had a record of success as a manhunter and was known to be willing to do whatever it took to achieve his purposes.

McCurden's wire from Culvertown was in the hand of one of the agents an hour after it arrived and for-

warded on to Dr. David Kevington in Denver immediately afterward.

It was delivered to Kevington's hand as soon as it
arrived.

Kevington, a tall, lean, intense man with a thick
and unmoving mass of gray hair atop his head and
eyes that could cut holes through anyone he chose to
glare at, began his preparations for travel as soon as
he'd read the wire.

The arrival of this wire at this time and place was
a sign, surely, an indication that fate was on his side.
Kevington had made a fruitless trip to Denver, following a lead that had petered out to nothing. But now
the journey had proven itself worthwhile after all. Being already in Colorado, Kevington would be able to
reach Culvertown much more quickly than if he were
starting from St. Louis.

And the quicker the better. McCurden's wire said
he had found Brady Kenton and Victoria, too.

· CHAPTER

19

JACK LIVINGSTON POURED ANOTHER SHOT OF WHIS-
key into the cracked mug that Brady Kenton had just
drained. They'd been talking for an hour, and Kenton's voice was tired.

Livingston, never a man to sit silent for long, had
done so while Kenton told his story. It was just too
intriguing to interrupt.

Kenton had just finished describing his harrowing
encounter with the now-dead son of David Kevington,
who had come to the United States in pursuit of Rachel Frye because she was witness to a murder he had
committed in England. Rachel Frye was the daughter
of Brady Kenton, though he did not know of her existence until she tracked him down.

It was from her that Kenton had at last learned that
his missing wife was still alive, living now as the
spouse—and virtual prisoner—of David Kevington.

"Please . . . go on with your story," Livingston
urged when he could stand the waiting no more.

Kenton swished the whiskey around in his mouth,

then swallowed and wiped his lips on the back of his hand. "The circumstances that I found myself in after Rachel and I were finally united allowed me to fake my death with relative ease, and with the cooperation of Alex Gunnison. With me officially dead, Rachel and I were free to travel anonymously to England. Rachel guided me to the Kevington estate, then went into hiding, at my insistence, at the home of some former Kevington servants who agreed to protect her and keep her presence secret . . . and to help her get away if I sent word for her to flee.

"I'll pass over the details and tell you simply that I did manage to get into David Kevington's estate. I found Victoria. . . . She was as overwhelmed at our reunion as I was. She hadn't known whether I was living or dead. She was eager to leave the prison of a home he had given her, and we tried to do it . . . but I was caught. Kevington locked me away, literally threw me in a cellar, and would have killed me right away had not Victoria begged him not to and told him she would take her own life if he killed me.

"A sympathetic servant in the household cooperated with me, and sneaked word from me out to Rachel that she should leave the country at once and come back to the United States. She did that, I was told . . . but now, God help me, I have no idea where she is or what happened to her. There was a boat accident off the coast, right about the time she would have been returning. . . . Dear God, I hope she wasn't on that boat." Kenton paused, poured himself another drink, and took two long sips before continuing.

"Though Victoria's protests might hold him back for a time, Kevington intended to kill me. I knew that. I was his prisoner, the man who had come to take away the woman he perceived as his wife, and even though he dared not do it directly because of Victoria, I knew it would happen. There would be an 'accident' of some sort, or a disappearance. I was doomed, unless I escaped. But I wouldn't leave Victoria.

"It was the same servant who delivered the message to Rachel who proved to be my salvation and Victoria's. At a great risk to himself, he arranged my escape and Victoria's. He even had a wagon and a driver to get us away.

"But it was a nightmare. Kevington pursued us, and with Victoria's condition, it was difficult to travel. Thank God that there are those in the world who will trust people based on their intuitions and give a hand to you even before they know all the answers.

"Through the help of good people and, surely, the hand of God himself, we made it to the coast and took passage to the United States. But we knew that Kevington would follow us. I've tried to deny it at times, but I can't. It was for that reason that I didn't even contact Alex Gunnison, my own partner, when we returned. I know that Kevington will try to get Victoria back, and if he can't succeed, then I believe he'll kill her, and me as well. He'll not be able to bear the thought of Victoria being alive but no longer his possession. And he'll not be able to bear the thought of me being alive at all."

Livingston tapped his fingers on the table. "We're

all in danger, then. Anybody who helps you, anybody who is close to you, anybody who can lead him to you."

"Yes. And I suppose it was wrong of me to put you in that situation, Jack. But I had to find a place to hide that would be remote and not easy to predict. Your place here was the closest I could come."

Livingston looked Kenton in the eye. "You know that Victoria's not fully yours yet."

It stung, but Kenton did not flinch. "Yes. I know."

"She stays in a room away from you. And I know she gets you all angry sometimes."

"Not angry. I could never be angry with her."

"Hell, if it ain't anger, it's something mighty like it. Why, you've sneaked down into town and got drunk two, three times since you've been here. And every time it's been after she shrugged you off."

Jack Livingston's forthrightness was not easy to take, not so much because it was brutally insensitive—which was typical of Livingston—but because it was brutally truthful.

"I know," Kenton said. "I shouldn't have done it."

"Hell, Brady, it was dangerous. You think that because your hair and beard are different people can't recognize you?"

"Look, Jack, I'm not going to defend myself on that one. You're right. I shouldn't have showed myself in town. But this is a hard time for both Victoria and me. There have been times she just can't bear my presence, and when that happens it hurts like a sword run through me. I've had to get out and away, or I couldn't stand it. Do you really think I can stay hidden away in here forever?"

"Brady, don't show yourself in town no more. I don't care how worked up you are. You don't know that you showing yourself in public hasn't already caused word about you to get out. For all we can know, Kevington has ears and eyes everywhere. A rich man can afford to buy all the ears and eyes he wants. And all the trigger fingers."

Kenton didn't mention the sketch on the envelope that he'd accidentally left in the Buckeye Cafe . . . and the fact that it had disappeared. That one worried him a lot. He could take pains to change his own appearance, but his work was as recognizable as ever.

Livingston was right. He'd been overly careless.

"I'll not leave again like that, Jack."

Livingston was thinking. "No. You will leave. We all will."

"What are you talking about?"

"There's another place we can go. Even more hidden than this one. It'll be a place we can hide Victoria a lot better and keep her safe until we know for sure how hard this damned British doctor will try or not try to get her back. My guess is he'll try hard."

"Where is this place?"

"Have you ever heard of a town called Caylee?"

"Yes, but the one I've heard of is abandoned. A ghost town."

"That's the town. It's over the Culver Mountain, about fifteen miles from here. Hard miles, just a mule trail, no good road. But there's a place there we can take Victoria. She'll be as hidden there as anyone can be."

"But a ghost town, Jack? I don't want Victoria to have to live in some run-down abandoned cabin."

"She won't have to." Jack Livingston leaned a little closer and lowered his voice, as if about to say something secretive in a crowded restaurant. "There's one house there that's not run-down at all. You can't tell it much from the outside, though."

"What the devil are you talking about?"

Livingston lowered his voice even more. "Uh, Brady, I might as well tell you, in case you don't know it already: I ain't exactly a saint. I've done some things that wouldn't win me a gold star at church of a Sunday morning."

"Well, all right."

"One of the things I've done is, I had something of an association with a certain woman who wasn't my wife . . . but she was the wife of another man. The mayor of Culvertown for some years, as a matter of fact, up until she died a couple of years ago and he moved off to Colorado Springs."

"What does this confession of yours have to do with a house in Caylee?"

"We would meet there. That's the point. Maude's husband was a fearsome jealous man. We knew we couldn't risk getting together here in Culvertown, not even here in my house. Too many prying eyes."

"Not to mention a wife of your own." Kenton's tone was icy. As a man who had missed his own wife for many years, he had little use for marital infidelity.

A married man should honor his wife, Kenton believed, and give himself to no other.

"My wife was dead before any of this happened, Brady. I was never unfaithful to her."

"Glad to hear it."

"Anyway, Maude and me would meet over in Caylee. She'd claim to be off on a trip to see her sister, who suffered terrible with the gout for many years, but in fact she'd spend a good part of the time with me in Caylee. There was a house there that I fixed up good and pretty on the inside, though I left the outside looking all weathered and run-down. You'd hardly know unless you look hard that it wasn't just another relic. The way it's situated, you can hardly notice the place at all, anyway. But it's there."

"I'll be!"

"Maude's been gone for two years and I ain't had cause to be at that house, but I did go by about six months ago just to take a look at it. It's still in right good shape on the inside. Victoria could be comfortable there, and hidden away where nobody is likely to see her. There's nobody else at all living in Caylee."

Kenton pondered this. The idea was appealing. Certainly not as a permanent arrangement, but as a good one for the moment. In such a place Victoria could grow strong again, and he could care for her like he wanted to.

"What about food and so on?"

"I'd provide it," Livingston said. "I'd haul anything you need in on a pack mule."

Kenton nodded slowly. "Jack, I think maybe that's an offer I'm inclined to accept. If Victoria is willing, that is."

"Then I'll help you. But the truth, Brady, is that I think the wisest thing you could do is go to the law. Just tell them your whole story and ask for protection."

"I've thought the same thing many a time. But there are uncertain things . . . and the fact that Victoria is scared to death to bring the law into the situation. Victoria is afraid that Kevington will somehow be able to use the law to his advantage. And mostly she's afraid . . . blast it, I may as well admit that *I'm* afraid, too . . . that if we show ourselves this early, Kevington will do something extreme. He'd rather have Victoria dead than taken away from him."

"You can't hide forever, Brady."

"I know. I know . . . and it worries me. Because I don't think Kevington will stop until he finds us . . . until either he has stolen Victoria back or both Victoria and I are dead."

At that moment there was a series of loud knocks on the front door.

CHAPTER

20

KENTON CAME TO HIS FEET, GLARING TOWARD THE door, then looking wildly at Jack Livingston.

Livingston got up more slowly, frowning. "It probably ain't nothing," he said. "People come up from time to time, wanting to meet me because I got this reputation of being a strange old hermit."

"Should you answer the door or let it go?"

Livingston gnawed at his lower lip, frowning some more as he thought about it. Another round of knocking rattled the door.

"Hell, I'm answering. I'd rather know it ain't Kevington than think it might be. If there's a problem on the other side of that door, then bring it on and let's deal with it." Livingston reached under his vest and brought out the small revolver he carried there. "I ain't answering it alone, though," he said, shaking the pistol.

Kenton produced a derringer from his own pocket. "I'm of the same mind as you, Jack."

Kenton and Livingston walked together toward the

front of the house, keeping their footsteps light so as not to forewarn whoever was outside of their approach. Kenton positioned himself so that he would be hidden when the door was opened.

"Who the hell is it?" Livingston bellowed through the door.

"My name is Billy Connery," came the reply, in an Irish brogue. "I work for the *Illustrated American,* and I think there may be someone here I need to see."

Kenton felt like going through the floor. The *Illustrated American* had tracked him down! Dear Lord, if they knew he was alive, knew he was here, what else did they know?

He wondered for a moment if this was a ruse. But he knew there was a Billy Connery working for the magazine, an Irish illustrator hired about the time of his own disappearance. Kenton had picked this up through simply reading the magazine itself. Connery worked with Alex Gunnison quite closely. And Alex was probably worried about Kenton because of his lack of communication with him. . . .

It all fell together in Kenton's mind. Alex Gunnison had launched a search for him, had somehow detected his presence in Culvertown, and had sent his new partner to find him. Maybe Gunnison himself was somewhere in town, too.

"Ask him to slide his identification card under the door," Kenton whispered. "The *Illustrated American* issues standard identification cards."

"I want to see some identification!" Livingston hollered through the door. "Prove to me you're with the *Illustrated American*!"

"Just a moment. . . ."

A couple of moments later, the edge of a card appeared under the door. Livingston knelt and picked the card up, glanced at it, and handed it to Kenton.

There were no images on *Illustrated American* credential cards, so Kenton could not match the name on the card, that of William Clive Connery, with the so-far unseen face on the other side of the door. But the card was the authentic item. The accent sounded real enough, too.

He handed the card back to Livingston. "Maybe we should let him in," he whispered. "I think this is all on the up-and-up."

"But how in hell did they track you here?" Livingston whispered back.

"I don't know. I think we're going to have to talk to him, though, and find out. If they could find us, so could Kevington."

Livingston nodded, then put his face close to the door. "Step back. . . . I'm opening this door. You come in slow and easy. I've got a pistol in my hand, and if I so much as don't like the way you look, I'll blow you straight to perdition! You understand me?"

"I do, sir. You have naught to fear from me."

Naught to fear from me. . . . Kenton frowned. It was as Irish-sounding a phrase as he had ever heard, spoken in a distinctly Irish manner.

Too Irish, maybe? Too distinct? Maybe that brogue

didn't sound quite authentic after all. He experienced a moment of doubt. . . .

But Livingston had opened the door by this point and was stepping back to let their visitor enter.

As he entered the house, McCurden tried to come across as nervous, harmless, and even a little scared.

Kenton, behind the door, had a chance to study the new arrival before the new arrival saw him. Something struck Kenton as not right. He'd never met Billy Connery and had heard no descriptions of him, but for some unexplainable reason this man didn't strike him as being authentic. Kenton wished that they hadn't opened the door, or at least that he had hidden himself more completely.

"Mr. Livingston, sir, I've heard much about you," McCurden said.

"Why are you here?"

"I'm looking for Mr. Brady Kenton, sir. I have reason to believe he may be here."

"Ain't you heard? Brady Kenton is dead."

"No, sir. With all due respect, we both know he's not. I was sent here to find him."

There was no point in playing games. Kenton would be seen at any moment anyway. He stepped out from the corner so suddenly that the newcomer drew in his breath sharply.

McCurden looked into the face of one of America's most famous journalists and couldn't suppress a smile and a hungry glitter in his eye.

"Hello, Mr. Kenton." He thrust out his hand. "Billy Connery. It's an honor to meet you."

Kenton did not want to shake hands with this man. Some inner alarm was sounding. But he shook the hand anyway.

"No one was to know I was alive," Kenton said, in no humor for preliminaries and false friendliness. "How did you know?"

"I was informed by Mr. Gunnison. I don't know how he knew."

"Gunnison the father or Gunnison the son?"

Everyone knew that Alex Gunnison was the partner of Brady Kenton, so he seemed the more likely choice. "It was Alex who told me."

"Alex told you . . . after I made him vow not to tell anyone?"

"He's concerned about you."

"How did he know I was here?"

The questions were growing harder. But it wouldn't matter much longer. This pair was about to experience a jolting encounter with the truth. "I don't know," McCurden said. "He didn't tell me."

Kenton stared hard at the newcomer. "Who else knows?"

"Dr. David Kevington knows. That's what has Alex worried. He's afraid Kevington might try to find you and take Victoria back. You do have Victoria, don't you?"

Kenton glanced at Livingston, whose look let him know that Livingston had the same suspicions he did.

"Tell me, Mr. Connery, how is Sarah?"

"Sarah?"

"Alex's wife."

"Oh, of course. Sarah is doing well."

"You've talked to her?"

"Not long ago, as a matter of fact."

"Did she mention to you that her name isn't Sarah, but Roxanne?"

McCurden glared at him. "And my name isn't Connery. It's McCurden."

He pulled a pistol from beneath his coat with unexpected speed and dexterity and aimed it at Livingston's face.

CHAPTER

21

FOR A MOMENT, EVERYTHING WAS FROZEN.

Then Kenton brought up his own derringer, ready to use it, but McCurden swung his pistol and knocked it from Kenton's hand. It clattered across the floor.

Kenton was astonished, also embarrassed. Being outmaneuvered by this younger and swifter man made him feel old and clumsy.

Livingston lunged at McCurden as he whipped the gun at Kenton, but again McCurden was too fast. He swung the pistol back and struck Livingston on the temple, very hard. Livingston let out a grunt and fell to his knees. McCurden brought up his foot and kicked Livingston in the forehead with his heel. The blow was tremendously powerful, knocking Livingston backward.

"No more!" Kenton said. "No more! You'll kill him!"

"Damn right," McCurden answered. And he kicked Livingston again, on the side of the head.

Kenton threw himself at him, but McCurden

dodged, then whipped him with the pistol. Kenton stumbled to the left, fell.

Victoria's voice came from upstairs. "Brady? What's happening?"

McCurden was kicking Livingston yet again. Then he reached under his vest and came out with a knife.

"No!" Kenton shouted. He scrambled to his feet.

McCurden tried to stab Livingston, but Kenton knocked him off balance just in time. The blade missed.

McCurden was limber and quick, however, and managed not to fall. He danced over Livingston's crumpled form and turned.

Kenton did not care at this point what happened to him. He had to stop McCurden at any cost, to keep him from getting to Victoria upstairs.

"Brady?" she called, her voice full of alarm. "Brady, what's happening?"

McCurden took two steps back, steadying himself. He raised the pistol and aimed it at Kenton.

"Freeze! Don't move an inch, you bastard! I'll kill you right here, then go up and kill her!"

Kenton could not find his voice. He stared at McCurden, eyes glaring with hate.

"But first, I kill him." And swiftly he raised the blade again, came down with his full body, and stabbed Livingston in the side. He left the blade where it stuck and was up again in a flash, laughing.

Livingston made a faint sound, moved a little, then was still. Kenton could tell from the sound of Livingston's last exhaled breath that he would not draw in another.

"I'll kill you," Kenton said, hardly able to comprehend what had just happened. "Whatever it takes, I'll kill you."

"No, you won't. You'll never have that opportunity. If anyone else dies here tonight, it will be you. Because I don't really need you, Kenton. It's the woman upstairs that I'm after."

"Kevington sent you."

"He did. But it's not Kevington I'm concerned about. I'm doing this for me."

"What are you talking about?"

"Kevington wants that woman back, Kenton. You don't know how bad he wants her back. He's hired agents, manhunters, a whole spiderweb of people looking everywhere you might be, following everyone you might try to contact . . . but it's me who found you. I'm the lucky one."

"I'll not let Kevington have her back. It won't happen."

"It's not up to you."

"How did you find me?"

"Never mind how I found you. The point is, I did. And as you can see"—he kicked Livingston's body—"there's nothing I won't do to get what I want."

"However much Kevington has paid you, I'll pay more."

"Kevington hasn't paid me yet. And believe me, even he has no idea how high the price is going to be."

Kenton understood. "You're double-crossing him. You're going to hold Victoria hostage!"

"You're a smart man, Kenton. Smart enough to figure that out, smart enough to have faked your own death, smart enough to have found your wife, smart enough to have stolen her away. But you've reached the end of wisdom. This is my game from now on."

Victoria appeared above, walking out of her room slowly, looking down over the balcony railing. She grew pale when she saw Livingston lying unmoving on the floor.

"Well, greetings, my lady!" McCurden called up. "It's indeed a pleasure!"

"Go back in your room, Victoria," Kenton said. "This is a dangerous man. . . . He's killed Jack."

McCurden laughed as Victoria withdrew quickly, the door closing behind her.

McCurden's smile went away. "You and me are going upstairs, Kenton. Your wife is going to tie you up, and then I'll tie her up, and then we'll wait for Dr. Kevington to arrive. He's already been wired."

"You'll not take her away from me. I've gone too far to get her, and waited too long."

"Too bad that none of that matters anymore, Kenton. Now move. Upstairs."

Kenton had to obey. He backed away, eye on the derringer on the floor, but McCurden chuckled and shook his head. "Forget it, Kenton. Keep in mind that I'm not required to keep you alive at all. All I need is Victoria. Though I'm thinking that Kevington might be willing to pay a nice bonus if he got you, alive, thrown into the bargain. I'm sure he'd enjoy disposing of you in his own way, slowly and painfully."

Kenton, fighting a fury that threatened to make him lose control, headed up the stairs. Everything seemed surreal. Only minutes before, Kenton had been seated, talking over plans with Livingston, feeling pleased at the prospect of a safer location for Victoria. Now Livingston was dead, he was hostage, and Victoria was cowering in her room, moments away from being a hostage herself.

Unless she wasn't cowering, but doing what Kenton hoped she was. . . .

They reached the door. Victoria had locked it, which annoyed McCurden. He kept his pistol leveled on Kenton while he stepped back and rammed the door hard with his heel, once, twice. The latch smashed apart, the door swinging open.

"Damn you, woman, I'll tie you all the tighter for that!"

These were his final words. Victoria was standing just inside the door, with the sawed-off shotgun that Livingston had given her for protection, just in case, in her hands.

She had never fired a shotgun before and squeezed down hard on the triggers, setting off both barrels at once. The recoil slammed her backward as the impact of the shot striking his chest sent McCurden flying in the other direction, out against the railing, over which he pitched and plunged to the floor, where he landed in a bloody heap.

Kenton rushed in and gathered up Victoria, who was stunned and bleeding slightly from the forehead. The shotgun had struck her there when it bucked up.

"Are you all right, Victoria? Dear God. . . ."

"Is he . . ."

"Oh, yes. Very much so."

She closed her eyes. He helped her scoot back against the wall, where she sat weakly, breathing hard.

Kenton went out to the railing and looked over at the two bodies below. He hoped against hope to see Livingston move, alive after all, but he did not.

But amazingly, McCurden did move, just a little. And his eyes opened, looking up at Kenton, an expression of disbelief on his face.

"I suppose you aren't quite as smart as you thought you were, Mr. McCurden," Kenton said.

McCurden's lips moved, but nothing passed them except blood. Kenton was looking into McCurden's eyes as they went cold and glazed and life departed.

Kenton went back to his wife and held her.

"What now?" she asked. "Will someone come?"

"I don't know. It depends on whether anyone heard the shotgun go off."

"Who was he?"

"He was hired by David Kevington. And Kevington is on his way here, he said."

"Oh, Brady, we have to leave!"

"We have to go to the law, Victoria."

"No, Brady. I'm too afraid."

"Things have changed now. There are dead men."

"No, Brady. Take me away from here. Don't take me to the law!"

"Victoria . . ."

"Please, I beg you! I've killed a man. . . . What if they don't believe what we tell them? I'm afraid of what the law will do. David always told me that if I left him, the law would be on his side . . . the law would bring me back to him."

"Victoria, I have no choice. We must go to the law. Men are dead here."

She began to cry. "They'll call me a murderer, Brady. They'll take me away from you."

"But if we run, Victoria, it will only make it all the worse."

"But nobody knows we're here, Brady. Nobody knows it but us."

"The man you shot to death tonight knew. And he said that Kevington is coming, so Kevington knows. . . ." Kenton quit talking. *Kevington is coming.*

Kenton would not argue further with her. The law would become involved, now that men had been killed. But perhaps it could happen later, not now. And perhaps he and Victoria could somehow escape detection. When Victoria's "resurrection" was finally known to the world, Kenton didn't want her name associated with a fatal shooting, even one as justified as this.

"What if David is already here, in town?"

"Surely he isn't." But Kenton could not be sure.

"The man was going to have us wait for him. David may be closer than we know. I want to go, Brady. I want to get away from here. But is there a place we can go?"

Kenton could not deny her plea. He would not go to the law. They would gather the meager possessions they had with them, take food from Livingston's pantry, stock up on weapons and ammunition, and wipe out any traces that would indicate Victoria's presence here. They would try to arrange the setting to make it appear that Livingston and McCurden had killed each other. A good investigator would be able to detect otherwise, but it was not likely that a little town like this one would have a good investigator.

"Yes, Victoria. There is a place we can go, if we can find it. A little empty town called Caylee, over the mountain. There is a good place to hide there; Jack told me about it just tonight."

They had to hurry; the sound of the shotgun blast would have been audible outside the house. Kenton hoped the isolation of the house had kept the shot from being heard all the way down in town, but he couldn't assume it had.

Kenton wrapped his arms around his wife, and she all but collapsed in his embrace. He was overwhelmed by a sense of protectiveness and a desire to do what she wished.

"When will we leave, Brady?"

"Tonight. Right now. I'll gather food and supplies and see what kind of horseflesh is in Jack's stable."

"Poor Jack!" she said, voice tightening. "Poor, poor Jack!"

"He was good to us, Victoria. He helped us when few others could have. And I'll be sorry for the rest of my days that us coming to him here brought him such misfortune."

CHAPTER

22

ALEX GUNNISON BENT HIS HEAD LOW AND LET THE brim of his hat deflect the worst of the gritty New York City rain. The day was gray and foggy, the rain penetrating and cold. Gunnison had always loved New York, thought it one of the most visually exciting cities in the nation, but today it was drab and ugly. And ominous.

He and Roxanne had just disembarked from a horse-drawn cab outside a white-painted Catholic-run hospital on a side street close enough to the bay to be bathed in the murky, organic scent of the ocean.

Battling the wind for possession of his hat, Gunnison managed to pay the cabbie, the tip generous enough to bring a smile and a tip of the cap.

"Come back around here in an hour," Gunnison instructed. "We may be waiting for you. If you don't see us, just drive on."

"Very good indeed, sir. I'll do that very thing." He clicked his tongue and gave a little shake of the reins.

The cab rolled on, and Gunnison took Victoria's

arm and raced through the rain and wind for the broad double doors, both of which were marked with the image of the cross. Under the recess that protected the doors, they shook off all the excess water they could.

Roxanne glanced around. "Alex . . . look. But be sly about it."

He followed her subtle gesture and glanced back across the street. A man sat under a shelter built to accommodate those waiting for cabs. He was reading a newspaper and seemingly minding his own business.

"A little wet to be sitting out and reading a newspaper, even under a shelter, don't you think?" she said.

"Maybe. You're thinking he's one of Kevington's agents?"

"He could be. Just like the man on the train."

This was a delicate moment. Despite Roxanne's impassioned claim that she had seen a man trying to peer into their private car during the journey to New York, she had been unable to identify him among any of the male passengers, and no sign of any further intrusions had taken place. Gunnison trusted his wife but was secretly wondering if she had simply misperceived something and set her imagination to running out of control.

"I suppose we can't know. We'll just have to be careful."

"I think we have to assume the worst," she said. "When we leave here, it shouldn't be by this door."

"How would Kevington know that Rachel Frye is

here?" Gunnison asked. "He would have no reason to post a man here unless he knew there was someone here who could attract Kenton."

"Maybe that man is the same one who was on the train. He may have followed us."

Despite his doubts, Gunnison could not rule this out. If Kevington was after Kenton it made sense that he would send men to watch those with whom Kenton had a history of association.

"Well, let's go in," Gunnison said. He reached up and knocked loudly on the door.

A few moments later it was opened by a stoutly built nun, who smiled at them welcomingly while also studying them closely and with no small amount of suspicion. In this part of the city, Gunnison supposed, it was essential to be careful about strangers who appeared on doorsteps. "How may I assist you?" she asked.

"My name is Alexander Gunnison. This is my wife, Roxanne. We've come to see one of your patients, a young woman named Rachel Frye."

"Yes, indeed. Miss Frye is still with us, and much improved now. She will be pleased you have come. She had asked that we contact you."

"Yes . . . I received the letter. She's better, you say?"

"Come and see her for yourself. She is ready to leave us . . . but she has had no place to go."

"She has a place now," Gunnison said.

"Good. I'm Sister Anna. Please come with me."

The hallway was tall and broad, thick with shadows, and cool. Yet it was an unexpectedly pleasant and secure-feeling place, particularly after the soggy coolness outside.

"What happened to her?" Gunnison asked.

"She was injured when the ship she was on sank off the coast. For a long time she was mostly senseless, sometimes awakening but never speaking, not at the beginning. But with time, care, and much praying, she began to improve. She told us who she was and asked that we contact you, Mr. Gunnison, and ask you to come here."

They turned a corner. "Here we are. Wait here in the hall a moment. . . . I'll go in and make sure she is ready to see you."

Gunnison took Roxanne's hand while they waited.

Sister Anna reemerged. "She will see you now."

Gunnison somehow managed to hide his shock when he saw Rachel. She was thin and pale, and if Rachel as she was now was much improved over what she had been when she came to this hospital, she must have been in bad condition indeed.

But she brightened when she saw Gunnison and extended her hand. He took it, squeezed it gently, and smiled at her.

"Rachel, I'm glad to see you, and I'm glad to hear that you're doing better. Please allow me to introduce my wife, Roxanne."

"I'm pleased to meet you, Rachel," Roxanne said, taking the lead. She extended her hand to the seated woman.

"You're very beautiful," Rachel said.

"And so are you," Roxanne replied, even though Rachel at the moment had only a shadow of beauty about her. "We're very sorry that you've been hurt."

"I'm much better now . . . but it was important for me to talk to you. I'm sorry you had to travel so far."

Gunnison turned to Sister Anna, who had followed them back into the room. "Might we talk to her in private?"

"Certainly. Call me if you need anything." She silently glided out of the room.

Gunnison turned to Rachel. "I know there is much to tell, much to talk about, but I want to ask one thing at the beginning: do you know where Kenton is?"

Rachel closed her eyes. "I had hoped you wouldn't ask that question, because it tells me that you don't know where he is, either."

"You've not heard from him?"

"No. Not since I was in England."

Gunnison pulled up a chair for Roxanne, then a footstool upon which he perched himself. "Tell us what happened, Rachel. From the beginning."

She spoke in a soft voice that grew steadily weaker because she was not used to talking for a long time.

She talked at first about the background of the voyage to England that she and Brady Kenton made—how through her Kenton had learned that his wife still lived as the "wife" and prisoner of Dr. David Kevington. Also because of her, Kenton very nearly died because of Kevington's son, Paul, but in the end Paul had been the one to die.

Kenton had taken advantage of his situation and allowed Alex Gunnison to present a story to the world of his "death" and, with the freedom that comes of no longer being believed alive, had gone to England with Rachel to find Victoria again.

Rachel briefly described their voyage, their landing in England, the journey to the estate of Dr. David Kevington.

Though Kenton was her father, she called him Kenton just like everyone else did, because that's the way Kenton liked it.

"Kenton did not allow me to even approach the estate," she said. "He said it would be unsafe and make it more difficult besides, because he would have to worry about getting both Victoria and me out. I stayed, in secret, in the home of a family nearby who had been servants for Dr. Kevington at the same time I was. Kenton disappeared into the estate . . . and seemed to vanish.

"I waited for days for him to reappear, or to send word, but none came. I was sure he was dead, but then a message was sent out of the estate. Kenton sent word that I should flee the country as quickly as possible, and come back to the United States, specifically to St. Louis. I was to contact you, then await his return with Victoria . . . if it was to happen at all.

"There was something about the message that scared me. It didn't seem to me that Kenton was at all sure he would return at all, and clearly he was in some sort of danger. He had been on the estate for days, which could only mean that he had been caught and detained there. But at least his message proved he was still alive. And I knew it was a valid message because I knew his script. It was written by his hand.

"I did what he told me, fled the area, found passage on a ship back to New York. Then there was a storm, and a shipwreck . . . and my next memory was being here. For a time I didn't even know where 'here' was. But my strength, and my memory, came back slowly, and as soon as I could, I had this hospital contact you. And now you've come."

"We've come. But we still know nothing of what happened to Kenton."

Rachel's eyes grew red and moist. "I had hoped you would come telling me that Kenton was home, with Victoria."

"I wish I had news. And perhaps soon I will. We have some indications that Kenton is in Colorado."

"Colorado? Why there?"

"We don't know. It's unexpected, and maybe that's the point. He may be hiding there."

Rachel sat up straighter and looked more vigorous all at once. "Hiding . . . from Kevington?"

"That would seem the likely candidate."

"That would indicate he may have brought Victoria home."

"Yes . . . and also that Kevington has pursued them. Maybe personally, or more likely through hired agents. Or perhaps both."

"He might be *here,* in this country?"

"I don't think he would let Victoria go without a fight, or a chase."

"But if Kenton is back in the country, why hasn't he contacted you? Why hasn't he come looking for me?"

"That's the question we've all asked. And I've got a friend in Colorado right now trying to find the answer."

"Have you heard from him?"

"Not yet . . . not that I know of, anyway. We've made arrangements for me to be telegraphed by him at a certain station here in New York. But so far we've not checked in at the station."

Roxanne spoke. "I think Kenton is not revealing where he is because he's afraid of endangering others around him."

"It seems to me he should feel safer making it all public," Gunnison replied. "Victoria would be safe."

"No," Rachel said with conviction. "If you knew Dr. Kevington, you would understand. He is not a rational man, not a safe man. I can understand why he would hide. And Victoria would know even better. As soon as Kevington knows where she is, she is in danger. And the public will not protect her. If David Kevington believes he has lost her, he will not care what happens to him. He would murder her before the eyes of the entire world and not care what the result was."

"Then Victoria and Kenton will only be safe . . ."

"When David Kevington is dead."

CHAPTER

23

RACHEL STOOD, SLOWLY AND LOOKING WEAK, BUT once upright she did not totter. She walked to the window and looked out into the rain.

"I want to leave here," she said. "They've been good to me here, but I'm tired of being in this room. And I have a feeling that there is danger. . . . I've had dreams in which David Kevington comes here, and appears right in this room. And even though I run, he's always there."

Roxanne rose and joined her at the window. "That will not happen, Rachel. Alex and I are taking you away from here. You'll go home with us."

Rachel smiled. Roxanne smiled back, then looked out the window and lost the smile.

"Alex, he's still there."

"Who?"

"The man with the newspaper. It's raining harder than before, but he's still there."

Gunnison went to the window and looked out. This time it wasn't so easy to dismiss his wife's concerns.

The man did look absurdly out of place, seated in an inadequate shelter in a pouring rain, staring at a newspaper that was growing more sodden by the moment.

"We'll take no chances," Gunnison said. "We'll leave here by a back way. And we'll find a different cab. The question is, though, if Rachel is really strong enough."

"I'm strong enough," she said. "I'll go now. Do you believe that man out there was sent by David Kevington?"

"Maybe so," Gunnison said. "We believe that he might have been on the train that brought us here and followed us from the station. But we'll shake him off. I'll try to get the cooperation of the good sisters as well, should he come inquiring."

Rachel withdrew and seemed to grow smaller and paler as she pondered the idea of being watched and pursued.

"How much do you have to pack?" Roxanne asked Rachel.

"What I have on and two dresses given to me by the hospital."

"The cost of your treatment will be paid by the *Illustrated American*," Gunnison said. "And we'll keep watch over you until we can reunite you with Kenton, and—we hope—Victoria."

The man in the shelter outside was named Morrisey, a name that had once garnered a lot of respect in the Davenport Agency for Detection Services, one of the leading detective agencies in the nation. A certain incident involving the disappearance of a key piece of evidence in a case—a small cache of jewels—had destroyed his career even as it enriched his pocketbook. A poorly played game of cards had made the enrichment short-lived, and from then on he had worked as an independent, contracting for whatever work he could find. It was unlikely that he'd ever again find the opportunity to get his hands on any money to compare to what he'd had so briefly, so he didn't try. The comfort he'd taken in wealth for that one short and glorious period he now found in whiskey.

As he sat on the soaked bench under the leaky shelter, holding a soaked newspaper in his hand, he was looking more forward by the moment to the minute he could leave his position and head for the nearest saloon. Part of him was ready simply to desert his job, which at present was most uncomfortable. But the money the Englishman was paying made this too lucrative a hire. He'd stick it out, no matter how wet he got.

Morrisey, though, had some serious doubts about this assignment. The Englishman just might be loco, with his talk of the legendary Brady Kenton really being alive even though the *Illustrated American* itself had reported his death. Supposedly there was a chance that Alex Gunnison and his wife, whom Morrisey was hired to track, might lead him to Kenton.

It seemed unlikely. Kenton's funeral had been a lavish and highly reported affair, visited by all kinds of dignitaries. Of course, there was the fact that Kenton had been cremated, so there was no body to be seen. And it was always possible that what had really been cremated was a good-sized dog or goat or something, with Kenton himself being alive and snickering while everyone wept over a bunch of animal ashes.

A more likely explanation was that the English doctor was simply crazy and his notion of a still-living Brady Kenton was a madman's figment. What else could it be, considering that Dr. David Kevington also seemed to believe that Brady Kenton's wife—who Kevington also apparently claimed as his own wife—was also still alive and with Kenton. It was absurd; everyone who knew anything about Brady Kenton knew that his wife had died in a train accident many years ago.

Madman or not, Kevington paid well. Morrisey would stick it out as long as he could and milk as big a fee as he could from the obsessive Englishman. And if by some miracle the good doctor's wild notions proved to be correct, maybe he could deliver up Kenton to him as well. Pondering the size of the bonus *that* would generate was enough to make Morrisey's mouth water.

Could it be that Brady Kenton himself was inside that hospital?

Morrisey vowed he wouldn't let this job slip out of his hands. He'd almost gotten himself caught aboard the train when Gunnison's wife saw him looking into their private car. From then on he'd been extremely cautious and somehow managed to evade being seen by them for the rest of the journey.

His newspaper was so soaked now that it looked

foolish to keep pretending to read it. Morrisey tossed it aside and simply sat on the bench, staring at the hospital and trying to look like nothing more than a common pedestrian who'd taken shelter from the rain.

Time dragged by, the rain slowing, then building again, then slowing, but never fully stopping. The cab that had carried the Gunnisons, and which Morrisey had followed, came rolling around again, slowing, but the Gunnisons never came out. Ten minutes later the cabbie made another go-around. Again no Gunnisons.

Morrisey began to grow concerned. But he made himself wait another hour. Still the Gunnisons did not emerge.

The rain stopped and the sun even managed to break through over toward the west. Morrisey could wait no longer. He rose and went to the door.

Sister Anna answered, smiling at him.

"Pardon me," Morrisey said, touching the brim of his hat and nodding a greeting. "I happened to be passing a couple of hours ago and thought I saw an old friend of mine, name of Gunnison, come in here with his wife. I had pressing business and couldn't stop to be sure, but now I'm finished and thought I'd drop in and see if they might be here. It would be good to see old Alex again. He's here visiting a friend or relative maybe?"

"Do come in, sir," Sister Anna said. "I'll go see if this gentleman you are looking for is here."

"All right . . . but if he is, don't tell him I'm out here looking for him. I'd like to surprise him myself, you see." In fact, Morrisey planned to slip out the door again if Gunnison proved to still be in the hospital. The last thing he wanted was to actually run into the man.

"Very well. Do have a seat on our waiting bench. I'll be back around to give you information."

He sat down, picking up a newspaper that chanced to lie beside him. If Gunnison or his wife should appear around the corner, he'd make sure to have his face hidden in the paper, just in case Mrs. Gunnison had caught a clearer glimpse of him on the train than he thought she had.

Ten minutes passed and Sister Anna did not return. It dragged on to twenty minutes, then thirty, and finally Morrisey rose and walked farther into the hospital, where he encountered another nun.

"Pardon me, Sister, but have you seen Sister Anna in the last few minutes?"

"No, sir, but I can find her, if you wish."

"Please do. She was to come give me some information about a man I saw entering the hospital, but it's been some time now and she's not done so."

"Please be seated again. I'll find her."

He didn't sit down but paced, restless and beginning to suspect something was up. Another ten minutes dragged by. He was about to plunge into the depths of the hospital and find Sister Anna on his own when she came around the corner.

She had no apologies for her tardiness. "I'm sorry, sir, but the man you are looking for isn't here," she reported.

"What? Where is he?"

"He and his wife departed, with one of our patients."

"Patients . . . male or female?"

"I'm sorry, sir, but we make it a practice to release no information regarding our patients except through a formal inquiry system."

"They couldn't have left. I'd have seen them coming out the door."

"You told me you were elsewhere on business. How could you see our door? But it doesn't matter; they left by one of our side entrances."

Morrisey swore bitterly, turned, and left the hospital on the run.

CHAPTER

24

THEY'D EVADED HIM. DELIBERATELY OR NOT HE couldn't say, but it didn't matter, because the point was they were gone and the trail was broken.

It would be hard to catch up to them again . . . but wait! That private passenger car of theirs . . . that's where they'd go.

He caught a cab and urged the driver to make the best time he could back to the same railroad station from which he'd departed earlier. The driver made a run fit for a racetrack, and Morrisey overpaid him by a good margin, not so much because he tended toward high gratuities as because he had no time to wait around for making change.

He ran to the rail yard and jumped a fence designed to keep the general public on one side.

There was the *Illustrated American* private car, separated from the train and shunted off onto a side holding track.

"You there, boy!" he shouted at a middle-aged

black fellow carrying a bundle of mail toward a train. "Come here a minute."

The man did so, laying down the bundle at his feet and looking glad to have reason to be rid of the Atlas-like burden for a moment. "What can I do for you, sir?"

"That car over there on the sidetrack was part of a train I rode in on."

"Was it? That's the private passenger car of the *Illustrated American* magazine."

"I know that. Just tell me if someone has come back to that car within the last hour or so! It's important."

"Oh, there ain't nobody on it, I can tell you. Ain't nobody allowed to be on the cars when they're side-tracked like that, except of course for folks working for the railroad. Truth is, sir, you ain't really supposed to be where you is right now, 'less you're a railroad man."

"You let me worry about that, boy. Tell me when that car will be reconnected and pull out again."

"I don't know, sir, but I'll go find out, if you'll watch my mailbag for me."

"I'll watch your damned mailbag! Now hurry! This is important!"

The black fellow nodded, scurried off, then slowed down as soon as he rounded the corner of the building and was out of sight. He plodded along deliberately, not about to hurry up for a man as rude as this one.

He saw a railroad detective and went to him. "There's a man who jumped the fence and took my mailbag from me, sir. He's still around the corner there, I think. I believe he's going to take that mail and go through it for money."

The railroad detective was gone in a shot. The black man pulled a cheap cigar from his pocket, lit it, and moved over to where he could hear the railroad detective giving the intruder some serious attention, threatening a trespassing arrest and maybe worse. The intruder was swearing and furious, denying vehemently any intent to steal the mail, and in the end managed to regain control of his temper and with an apology win the privilege of being allowed to leave without being taken into custody.

When he was gone, the black man finished his cigar, plodded back around the corner, and picked up the mailbag again. Hefting it onto his shoulder, he headed for the waiting car, humming a happy tune to himself.

"Boy," indeed! He was a workingman, and proud of it. It was the fence jumpers of the world, the kind who got themselves run off by railroad detectives, who were the "boys" of the world in his book.

So far this was turning out to be a nice day.

Morrisey was furious, and wishing he could get his hands on that black scoundrel and that railroad detective sometime when they weren't safe on the job! But he had bigger things to worry him now than a wounding of his pride. He had to find Gunnison's trail again or otherwise give up any hope of further gain from his madman employer.

He had the strongest notion that it was Brady Kenton whom the Gunnisons had gone into that hospital to fetch. Kenton himself . . . and if he could only get him and deliver him to Kevington . . .

That private railroad car remained his only potential point of reconnection with his quarry. He found a hidden place on the other side of the rail yard— beyond the fence and out of the domain of the railroad detective—and settled down to watch the car and hope that Gunnison and company showed up at it soon.

Miles away, in a passenger cubicle on a train that had pulled out of New York while Morrisey was still sitting in the leaky shelter outside the hospital, Roxanne Gunnison laid her cloak over a shivering Rachel Frye.

"Thank you, mum," Rachel said. "I don't know why I feel so cold."

"Because it's a wet day and you've gone from being a hospital patient in a chair to running through the rain to catch a train . . . and all the while hoping nobody is watching.

"Did we get away from him?" Roxanne asked Alex.

"I think we did. But we're going to give things one more twist just to make sure. We'll get off at the next station, visit the telegraph station to see if we've heard anything from Billy Connery, then catch another train. Maybe to Philadelphia. From there we'll catch a train to St. Louis. If anybody is following us, him or anyone else, we'll shake him off."

"I'm worried about Kenton," Rachel said.

"So am I," replied Gunnison.

They rode in silence to the next stop, then disembarked. As quickly as possible they entered the station and sat down in a corner, hiding themselves behind the moving crowd in the station. Roxanne sat close to Rachel, occasionally smiling at her reassuringly.

The telegraph station was in the next building. Gunnison walked over. Five minutes later, he was back.

Roxanne knew he had something just from the look on his face.

"There was a wire waiting for me. . . . Billy has found Kenton."

"In Culvertown?" Roxanne asked.

"Yes." He handed Roxanne the wire.

KB FOUND IN CULVERTOWN. LIVINGSTON HOUSE.
PLEASE COME.

"Why 'KB'?" she asked.

"Just to make it a little more unlikely for anyone to think we're talking about Brady Kenton."

"What's the Livingston house?"

"A place Kenton wrote about, occupied by an eccentric fellow named Jack Livingston—a big mansion on a hill he built for his wife. Kenton did an excellent piece of work about him and the house. And I think he may have hinted once that there was some sort of family connection between Livingston and himself, or Livingston and Victoria. I can't remember which . . .

and my memory may be entirely wrong on that score, anyway. It's murky for me."

"If there is a family relationship, it might explain why Kenton chose Culvertown as his hiding place," Roxanne said.

"I've got to get there, as soon as I can," said Gunnison.

"What about me and Rachel?"

Gunnison shook his head. "I don't know. I'd thought of taking you home to St. Louis, but now I'm not sure. If Kevington is having us watched, followed . . . you know he'll have spies observing our house and the *Illustrated American* offices. I don't want to leave you there if I'm gone."

"Take us with you."

"I don't know that Rachel is strong enough."

Rachel said, "I am strong enough . . . and if Kenton is there, I want to join him."

Roxanne looked at the telegram again. "We can't tell from this whether he has Victoria with him."

"My fear is that he doesn't," Gunnison said. "My fear is that he found she was dead, or unwilling to join him, and he came back to the United States alone, and maybe intent on drinking himself to death. I wish Billy had given more information in that telegram."

"Will you take us to Colorado with you?" Roxanne asked.

Gunnison grinned. "I guess there would be no easier way to keep an eye on you . . . and you on me . . . than having you with me."

"I'm glad. That's the way it should be."

"What we find may not be pleasing. Kenton may be in bad shape. Victoria may not be there at all, and may even be dead."

"How delicate do you think I am, Alex? This is something we should do together. And though I've had my share of resentments toward Kenton because of all the times he took you away from me, I want to be there to help him if he needs it. I care about him, too."

CHAPTER

25

Roy Ramsey, underpaid and overburdened town marshal of Culvertown, Colorado, fell back into his chair heavily, making it creak. He threw his hands upward and shook his head.

"Tell me, Jim," he said to James Ramsey, his brother, who held no official capacity but helped fill in for Roy when he was out of town. "How is it that I can go to Scallonville for two days and come back and find the whole town gone to hell?"

"It's amazing, Roy. I'll grant you that."

"Tell me if I've got this straight: there were two dead up in the Livingston house, including Livingston himself."

"That's right."

"Shot to death."

"Yes. It looks to me like they shot each other."

"Who was the other one?"

"Stranger in town. I don't know that we'll ever find out."

"Where are they now?"

"In the undertaker parlor, stinking to high heaven. We got to get them buried fast."

"I'll take a look at them. But I'll probably not be able to figure out anything more than you did."

"We need some big-city police folks looking at this one."

"Well, we ain't got none of them. I'll look at them and we'll bury them. Hell, I never liked old Livingston much anyway."

"Why would anybody shoot him, though?"

"A dozen reasons. Attempted robbery, probably. You know the stories about him stashing money everywhere."

"There was some sign that a woman had been there. I found a hairpin and a woman's brush up in one of the bedrooms."

"Not surprising. It wouldn't be the first time old Jack had a woman. You know he had a big love affair going with the mayor's wife for a long time. But he would see her over in Caylee in an old house he fixed up. He thought nobody else knew about it, but everybody did. Including the mayor, but he didn't care. He had a woman of his own visiting him while his wife was visiting Jack."

"Maybe the woman he had up there lately had a husband who wasn't so go-along about all that kind of thing."

"Maybe."

"Are you going to investigate it?"

"Hell, no. I can't bring 'em back to life, can I? I figure they must have had a reason for shooting each other. That's good enough for me. Besides, if I solve the murder, what good is it? There's nobody left alive for the district attorney to prosecute."

"What about the first two dead men?"

"No witnesses. Two highway robbers . . . nothing there worth looking into, either. Whoever killed them did the world a favor." He shook his head and gave a wry laugh. "Damn, I can't believe this. Two dead men on the road as I leave town, and two more dead men when I come back."

"That ain't all. There could be a third one."

"What? Who?"

"Another stranger. A young man. He was found stabbed in an alley, nearly dead. He should rightly have been dead six times over, given the shape he's in, but he's still alive, or was the last time I checked. Not conscious, though. He's up at Doc Asheman's. The doc swears he's going to make sure this one comes through alive. Sort of a personal mission."

"No clue who stabbed him?"

"Not a one."

"Anybody identified this stranger?"

"Tell you the truth, I ain't tried. What am I going to do? Line up everybody in town and have them file by?"

"Reckon not. Well, if he lives, he can tell us who did it. If not, he's just corpse number five in a week unusually rich with them."

Billy Connery opened his eyes and stared at the ceiling.

Still alive, he thought. *I can't believe it. Still alive.*

Alive, but so weak he could not move, and his throat slashed so that he could not speak.

Billy Connery had no memory of the stabbing beyond its initial moments. The throat cutting in particular was absent from his mind, for which he was thankful. He figured he had been unconscious when it happened.

He said a prayer of gratitude every time a drawn-in breath made his throat burn. It had always been his belief that a slashed throat meant death. Apparently McCurden just hadn't cut quite deep enough.

But his stab wounds had done enough damage to leave Connery incapable of doing anything but lying here, worrying about what McCurden had done.

He'd talked about Kenton, and that was frightening. As best Connery could figure it, McCurden was probably an agent for Kevington.

Connery suffered in a frustration he was too weak even to show on his face. He had to get his strength back, had to get up to the Livingston mansion.

If only he'd done it when he had the chance.

As the sun edged toward the mountaintops to the west, Dr. David Kevington stood in a window on the second floor of the Culvertown Hotel and looked out across a scene of squalor that reconfirmed to him every hatred and prejudice he possessed regarding Americans. In Kevington's view, Victoria was the only worthwhile colonial product. And nothing less than Victoria could have made him visit this miserable nation again.

He scanned the dirty street below, the buildings that seemed even dirtier with their peeling paint and layers of hoof-splashed mud extending more than a yard up their fronts. And most were false fronts, which Kevington found irksome and typically American. The entire American culture was in his mind something of a false front, something pretending to be much bigger and grander than it was.

Damn them all. He wished he could fetch back his Victoria, head back to England, and leave the entire North American continent in flames. He'd never fulfill that fantasy . . . but one he would fulfill. He'd not leave this rubbish heap of a country until Brady Kenton was dead.

And if Victoria refused to come with him willingly, then he would leave her dead as well. Painful as it would be, he would do it. He would not be mocked. He would not be denied.

Kevington lifted his eyes and gazed at the looming Livingston mansion. From his pocket he pulled the copy of the telegram McCurden had sent:

K. AND V. FOUND CULVERTOWN, COLORADO. EN-TER CULVERTOWN HOTEL AND AWAIT WORD.

Well, here he was, but so far there was no visit from McCurden, no word from McCurden. Curse him for the fool he was! His message had been inadequate. He should have given some indication of how to contact him. But if in the end McCurden delivered what his telegram promised, Kevington was prepared to be quite forgiving.

He saw Bartholomew Graham striding across the street toward the hotel. Graham was an interesting man to observe: tall and wide and muscled and bearded, he looked somewhat like a cleaned-up but still unshorn mountain man. Graham's looks were almost stereotypical of the American frontier, and Kevington had found it amusing to watch the reactions of Americans the first time they heard Graham speak in a voice rich with the dialect of his native Essex. Graham might look like an American frontiersman, but he was British to the core and proud of it.

He was also heartless, smart, and willing to do whatever Kevington paid him to do, and those were key reasons Kevington had brought him along from England to help with the great chase. An additional reason was Graham's four years of roaming in the American West, hiring out his gun to whoever paid the highest and had the fewest scruples.

Kevington was awaiting at the door of the room when Graham came lumbering up the stairs.

"Anything?" Kevington asked.

"Not one bloody clue," Graham replied. "Nothing solid, anyway."

"Damn!" Kevington exclaimed, stepping aside as Graham entered the room and threw himself down on a chair. Kevington closed the door. "Where the devil could McCurden be?"

"He may be dead."

"Why do you say that?"

"There's apparently been an epidemic of violent death in this town of late. So go the stories in the pubs, in any case. Two highwaymen shot dead on the road into town and two other dead men in the big mansion up on the hill."

"Who were these men?"

"The two highwaymen were a pair known to plague the region, haunting the roads to' several towns and camps. One of the dead men in the mansion was the man who owned the dwelling . . . quite an eccentric, it seems. The other, though, was a stranger to folks here. It could be our own McCurden."

"Or anyone else. It had better not be McCurden. If he's gone, then it will be hard indeed to learn what he found."

"The dead man could have been Kenton, too."

"He could have been Paul the Apostle for all we know. More than likely he was just a burglar who was confronted by the owner of the house, and both of them wound up dead."

"I'm sorry I've got nothing more to tell you," Graham said, pulling a pipe and pouch from his pocket and beginning to prepare a smoke. "Perhaps the others will do better."

"Perhaps they will," said Kevington, looking out the window again. "They're coming this way now . . . and they've got a boy with them."

CHAPTER

26

WHERE GRAHAM HAD A CERTAIN ENGLISH GRACE about his manner, despite his burly build, George Evaline and Kendall Brown were Americans, products of poverty and violent households, and as rough-edged as men could be. Both were lean, flinty-eyed, and even more unscrupulous than Graham but were loyal to those who paid them. Upon his arrival in the United States, Kevington had hired an underground agent to assemble him a little army of investigators and hired toughs, and Evaline and Brown had come with the highest recommendations.

"Who's this?" Kevington challenged Brown as he threw open the door, gesturing toward the boy with them. The boy wore a smart, disdainful expression and had the butt of a reeking cigar smoldering on his lip. He strode into the room like he owned it, Kevington glaring at him and instantly disliking him.

"That's Stockton Shelley," Brown said. "Local boy . . . he says he knows some things about Brady Kenton."

"What I know I'm glad to tell," Stockton said. "For the right price."

Kevington knelt and looked into the boy's face. Smiling, he reached up and removed the cigar from his lips and handed it to Evaline, who took it to the window and tossed it out.

"Cheap tobacco is rather revolting," Kevington said. "So are little boys with exalted views of themselves."

"You're foreign!" Stockton said, not at all cowed by Kevington's menacing manner. "Where the hell you from? France?"

"England, young man. The mother country of this vast wasteland of yours. Now, tell me what you know about Brady Kenton."

"I know he drawed some might pretty pictures in his day. Anything else I know about him don't come free."

Evaline stepped forward, ready to grab the boy and begin persuading him to change his mind. But Kevington shook his head and waved him back.

"I'm not inclined to pay for that which may prove worthless," Kevington said to Stockton.

"Then I reckon you'll never know," Stockton said, pulling another cigar from his pocket and sticking it in his mouth. It was a cheap saloon cigar, the kind barkeeps sold for a nickel out of jars. Stockton turned to Graham, who was puffing on his pipe. "Got a match, *compadre*?"

Graham laughed as he pulled a match block from

his pocket. He liked this boy. "Here you are, young man."

"Well, well! Another Frenchman!" He fired up the cigar and blew the smoke toward Kevington.

Graham laughed heartily. "You know, young gentleman, I've killed men for lesser insults than that one."

"I don't believe you'll want to kill me. Not if you want to know where to find Brady Kenton."

"You have this information, I take it?"

"Wouldn't be talking about it if I didn't."

"You have a wiseacre attitude about you, young fellow. Do you have any notion how serious a matter we are talking about here?"

With a gesture toward Evaline and Brown, Stockton said, "I know that these two were going around asking whether anybody knew where Brady Kenton was. Most folks laughed and told them to look in the graveyard. But me, I know better. I can tell you where he's been . . . and where he is now."

"A big claim."

"Needs some big money to go with it."

Kevington had never met a boy he disliked more, and he disliked all children. But right now he was short on leads. McCurden had not appeared. Urchins of the street sometimes did know things worth knowing. He'd put up with the boy for now, in case he really did know something.

"If you can lead me to Kenton, my boy, it's worth a hundred dollars to me."

Stockton Shelley's bravado couldn't hold up. His

eyes widened and it was clear at once that he hadn't expected an amount like that. To Stockton, a hundred dollars was a rich man's fortune.

"I'll lead you to him," he said. "And I hope you get somebody to arrest him, because he's a murderer."

"What do you mean?"

"He killed two men up in the Livingston mansion."

"How do you know it was Kenton?"

"Who else could it be? He was up there in that house."

"How do you know?"

"I seen him."

"Was there a woman, too?"

"You're the second man to ask me that. I never saw no woman. But if she was in the house, I wouldn't have seen her."

"Who is in the house now?" Kevington asked.

"Nobody that I know of."

"Who was the second dead man?"

"I don't know. But I know it wasn't Kenton."

"How do you know that?"

"Because I seen Kenton, traveling."

"Alone."

"No. Not alone. There was a woman."

"You told me you never saw a woman with him!"

"I told you I never saw a woman with him the *first* time I saw him." Stockton smirked.

"Damn you, boy, I'll not have you play games with me! I don't know that I believe a word you're telling me."

Graham spoke. "If that big house on the hill is

empty, I think we should go in it. If Kenton and Victoria have been there, maybe there will be some sign of it."

"You said you saw Kenton traveling, boy. Where was he going?"

"All I can say is what he seemed to be going toward."

Kevington reached into a pocket. His hand closed around a derringer that he was ready to pull out and shove into the boy's face. But instead he took a deep breath, put his face closer to Stockton's, and said in an icy tone: "Listen to me, young man. I don't know you, and I don't know whether you are telling me the truth. But I have the strongest sense that you think you are very clever indeed, and that all of this is quite the game. Let me tell you something, my boy. I am not a gentle man. I am not a friendly man. I am not a man who has an abundance of scruples. If I find that you are indeed toying with me, I will personally cut off your ears, one at a time, and send you home to give them to your father and mother for whatever use they may want to make of them. Have I made myself clear?"

Stockton lost his smirk. "Yes, sir."

"Now . . . we will go to this house, and look it over. If we find evidence that Kenton and Victoria have been there, your credibility will rise. But you will tell me—now—where it is you believe Kenton has taken her."

"I'm thinking, sir, that maybe he's taking her to the ghost town across the mountain, a town called Caylee.

There's a house there that Livingston kept up for staying in. I think Kenton killed Livingston and headed for that other house."

"And why would Kenton kill Livingston and some stranger?"

"I don't know. Maybe he was trying to protect the woman or something."

Kenton as a killer. Kevington thought it over and found it perfectly plausible. God knows he himself would gladly kill for Victoria. Kenton would probably do no less.

"Let's go," Kevington said. "I want to look through that mansion. Is it locked up?"

"I know a way in," Stockton said. He was being cooperative now, not nearly so snide and cavalier. Kevington had scared him, almost enough to make him run.

The only thing holding him back was that he didn't have his hundred dollars yet.

CHAPTER

27

THE LIVINGSTON MANSION WAS ALWAYS A DARK AND ominous place but now was all the more uninviting because two men had died bloody deaths there.

Kevington stood looking up at it, with Stockton at his side. The boy's usual cocky attitude was gone now, driven away by a fear of Kevington and his toughs that he tried unsuccessfully not to show.

"How are we going to get inside?" Evaline asked.

"Break out a window," Graham said.

"You don't have to do that," Stockton replied. "I know some secret ways into the house. It was built with secret ways in and out because old Livingston's dead wife liked that kind of thing."

He led them around the rear of the mansion and into a root cellar that was built right into the hillside and nearly hidden in a tangle of foliage and scrubby trees that had been allowed to have their way unmolested for years.

"It's in there."

"What is?"

"The door to the tunnel."

Indeed there was a door hidden inside, on the rear wall. It was designed to blend into the structure in a natural way and had no apparent latch. But Stockton pushed one board, which tilted out and revealed a latch beneath. He tripped it easily.

"Did the man who owned this place know you made yourself such free and easy entrance to his dwelling?" Kevington asked.

"Old Livingston never used this tunnel, and I never went all the way into the house except once, when I knew he was gone. I'd come up here and hide in the end of the tunnel, mostly."

"Hide from what?"

"My father. When he gets drunk, he beats me."

Kevington grunted. He was not a sympathetic man. "Well, I'll be the one to beat you if all this proves unworthy of the effort."

"You wanted in the mansion, I'm getting you in the mansion."

By match light they proceeded into the dank and earthen tunnel, bending low in the claustrophobia-inspiring place. Soon, though, they reached a door similar to the one that had admitted them. Stockton triggered the latch.

They entered a cellar so dark it was distinguishable from the tunnel itself only by the sense of open space around them. Graham struck another match, and by its light they saw and proceeded toward the flight of stairs leading to the main floor.

Stockton still led the way, being familiar with this house.

"There's all kinds of other passages and tunnels and such," he said, much like a tour guide. "Old lady Livingston was crazier than her husband and liked stories about tunnels and towers and passageways and all. That's what everybody says, anyway."

"Honestly, young man, I couldn't give a tinker's damn about the history of this house or the relative sanity of those who built and occupied it," Kevington said. "I want to know only two things: whether Brady Kenton was here alone, or with my Victoria, and where the pair of them are now."

The stairs led them into a rear hallway. Stockton led them to the main room. "There's some lamps and candles around if you want light."

"Candles will suffice," Kevington said. "I don't want much light to draw attention from the outside."

They lit three candles among them and moved through the room, examining the bloody places on the floor where the bodies had lain. Though Stockton found it fascinating, the men weren't much stirred by the sight. They'd drawn enough blood themselves over the years to take little interest in it now.

"Where are the bedrooms?" Kevington asked.

"Upstairs," Stockton replied.

They climbed and began to explore the rooms. It was evident which one had been Livingston's. It was packed and dirty and disordered, the room of a man who had lived for a long time without the organizing influence of a female. They found the room Kenton had been in as well but did not realize it because he had left no identifying traces behind.

In the largest of the bedrooms, however, they found two items of significance: a woman's brush and a ruby-tipped hairpin that Kevington recognized as Victoria's. He held it in his hand and for the first time exhibited visible excitement.

"She was here," he said firmly, then repeated it twice, each time with more emphasis on the final word. "That bastard Kenton took her all the way from England, took her from me, and thought he could hide her here in this damned little mountain mining town . . . but he failed to take into account the determination of his adversary. I've tracked them down! He thought he could hide from me, but I've tracked him down like a hound on the trail of a fox! Ha!"

"Seems to me that some of us had a bit to do with tracking him down, too," muttered Evaline, with a glance at Kendall Brown.

Kevington paced about the room, brows knit and mind racing. "I think I know what has happened here. Kenton is so desperate to hide his trail that he's taken to killing. He's murdered his own host and taken away Victoria to an even more remote hiding place. He's so determined to keep Victoria for himself that he's killing anyone who knows he has her. But I'll track him down. And when I do, it will be Kenton who dies."

"Begging your pardon, Doctor, but Kenton may already be dead," said Graham. "Remember that there were two men killed in this house. I figure the second one was Kenton. Almost nobody knows that Kenton didn't really die last year, so nobody would recognize the dead man as Kenton even if it was Kenton. They'd just assume it was somebody who happened to resemble him. All we've got is this boy's word that he's seen Kenton alive since then. And I figure this boy is saying whatever he thinks will make him a dollar. I've been thinking, and I've got a theory. I believe McCurden tracked down Kenton and your woman, murdered Kenton and the man who owned this place, and took Victoria away somewhere else to hold her for ransom. I expect you'll hear from him before long, making a big demand."

Kevington thought about this, eyes glaring in anger. "If he's done such a thing, I'll see him suffer a good long while before he dies."

Evaline spoke. "Seems to me what we've got to find out is who this second dead man is. If it's Kenton, then we can assume that McCurden's probably got the woman with him somewhere. If it's McCurden, then we can figure the kid here is probably telling us the truth, and Kenton's gone with his woman to the ghost town."

Kevington wheeled and faced him. "Don't ever refer to Victoria as Kenton's woman. Don't ever say that again. Do you understand me?"

"Mighty sorry, sir. I misspoke."

Kevington nodded. "Yes . . . but you have a point. We need to learn who died here besides this Livingston gent."

"They got a morgue in this town, boy?" Brown asked Stockton.

"Just the undertaking parlor."

"Maybe the corpses are still there," Kevington said.

Graham stepped forward. "I'll go see. I've seen Kenton's picture enough to know his face, and I met McCurden when you hired him. I'll go and settle this matter for us . . . if the bodies are still in the morgue."

"A good idea, Graham," Kevington said. "We'll await you."

"At the hotel?"

"Right here."

"What about the boy?" Evaline asked.

"He stays with us, until we're through with him."

This was fine with Stockton, who spent many nights away from home when his father was drinking. It usually took three or four nights away from home before his father came looking for him. If he was lucky, he wouldn't come looking tonight. Stockton right now had one goal: to do whatever it took to see this through to the end and get his hundred dollars.

"I'll be back," Graham said, readying to go.

"Don't rouse too many questions," Kevington said. "Attention is not what we want."

"I'll be careful," Graham replied.

CHAPTER

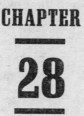

28

GRAHAM WALKED SLOWLY THROUGH THE DARKEN-
ing town, smiling and tipping his hat at the women
he saw and nodding politely to the men. Rough and
rugged as he looked, he was in fact quite smooth in
his manners, even charming when he wanted to be.

His charm vanished, though, when he rounded a
corner and was run into by a staggering drunk who
carried a glass of beer in his hand, taken from a
nearby saloon when the barkeep wasn't looking. The
beer splashed down Graham's front—and the drunk
roundly cursed him, as if it were all Graham's fault.

Graham smiled, but it was a smile to put fear into
the heart of the man on the receiving end of it. The
drunk found himself grabbed by the collar, his face
dragged close to that of Graham.

"My good friend," Graham growled in his English
accent, "I suggest you voice your apologies for your
bad behavior right away, or I'll draw out my knife,
gather a crowd to watch the show, and castrate you

right out there on the street. And my knife is a very dull knife, I might add."

The drunk stared into the Englishman's fierce eyes, slobbered down his chin, and nodded. "All right, mister. All right. I'm mighty sorry."

"Are you now? Sorry, might I ask, for spilling your beer all down me or sorry for making such an ass of yourself immediately thereafter?"

"Uh . . . both."

"Not good enough, sir."

"What?"

"I want you to *show* me you're sorry. See that puddle of beer at my feet?"

The eyes shifted down, then back up. "Yeah."

"Lap it up. Like a dog."

"There's . . . there's folks watching."

"Indeed there are." Graham shoved him away, then drew his pistol. "Would you prefer those folks see you cleaning up your spilled beer or bleeding out your last moments with a bullet in your belly?"

The drunk, trembling, slowly got on his knees. He glanced around, humiliated, then lowered his head and began to lick lightly at the puddle of beer on the boardwalk.

"Oh, come now!" Graham said. "You can do better than that! Lick that boardwalk like you mean business!"

"Folks spit down here," the drunk murmured.

Graham put his foot on the back of the man's neck and shoved his face down so hard onto the walk that it almost broke his nose. "Drink, you cur!"

The drunk licked the boardwalk with full swipes of his tongue while men gathered around and laughed.

Graham was satisfied. "Keep at it until it's all cleaned up," he instructed his victim. Then he turned to the nearest watcher and said, "Might you point out to me where the mortician's establishment is?"

The drunk pulled up and back clumsily, almost rolling over. "Don't kill me!" he begged.

Graham looked at him with disgust. "Get on with you, you miserable sod. I've had all I can stand of looking at you!"

The drunk somehow made it to his feet and headed off down the boardwalk, then cut left into the dark safety of the nearest alley. Catcalls and laughter followed him.

Graham received directions to the undertaking parlor, but the man added, "The place is probably closed right now. But the undertaker lives in rooms up above it."

"Then I'll roust him out if need be. Thank you, sir, for your aid."

Graham walked on, whistling, receiving wide berth from those he passed.

Now that he was alone, the drunk in the alley got his courage back. "Reckon you'll not do that to me again!" he muttered beneath his breath. "Reckon next time I'll know how to deal with you, you damned foreigner!"

But he knew that it would be for the best if there

wasn't a next time. The Englishman had a dangerous manner about him.

As he calmed down, the drunk's anger began to change to maudlin sorrow. He'd been humiliated before the people of his own town! Forced to lap up spilled beer off a filthy boardwalk! He even had a couple of splinters in his tongue.

There was surely no one in the world more miserable than he, no one more despised by man and God. He began to sniff and whimper and wish he had more beer . . . in a glass rather than spilled, preferably.

He began to think back on the times his family had been together and his home was happy. Now his wife was gone, his life was miserable, and most of the time he didn't even know where his son, Stockton, was or what he was doing. The boy would wind up a convict one day with his roaming, stealing ways! Just another reason to feel sorrowful and self-pitying.

He decided to find Stockton. Bring him home. Maybe they could sit and talk or play a game of cards or do something like fathers and sons are supposed to do together. He hoped Stockton never found out that his father had been forced to drink beer off the boardwalk.

Josiah Shelley exited the alley by its rear entrance and vowed that he would not go home again until he'd found Stockton. He and the boy would have a good time together . . . and if Stockton had something cocky to say about it, he'd quick learn the better of it! Sometimes the only way to do good for that boy was to beat it into him.

Josiah wandered through the dark streets, trying to think of the various places Stockton liked to hide.

Graham returned to the mansion an hour later.

"Well? Did you see the bodies?" Kevington asked.

"Both already buried," Graham replied.

Kevington swore.

"But I know who the second dead man is, anyway. I persuaded the undertaker to show me his personal effects . . . including this. Recognize it? I managed to sneak it away unnoticed."

He held out a brass matchbox with initials engraved on its top. Kevington took it and studied it.

"McCurden's. So our agent in Culvertown is dead," he said. "Killed, no doubt, by Brady Kenton, who then fled with Victoria."

"So it would seem."

"Tomorrow morning we travel to this ghost town across the mountain. And before the sun goes down tomorrow, I will have Victoria with me again, and Brady Kenton in his grave."

"What about tonight? Do we return to the hotel?"

"The accommodations here are much more comfortable. We spend the night right here in this house . . . where Victoria has been."

"I left some things at the hotel," Brown said.

"Then go back and get them . . . cautiously. Don't let anyone see you leaving or reentering this house. Bring back everything any of us have left at the hotel, then try to get some rest. I want us all to be at our best tomorrow. Kenton will resist. He'll not surrender Victoria lightly."

"He can resist all he wants. It won't do him any good in the end," Graham said.

"No," Kevington agreed. "It won't. I'll not leave this country without her. Either Victoria is mine . . . or she is no one's."

"And what if she doesn't want to go back with you?" It was a question only Graham was bold enough to ask.

Kevington glared at him. "She will see what she should do when the time comes. She'll come back."

"And if she didn't . . . you'd kill her?"

Kevington had nothing further to say.

CHAPTER

29

Josiah Shelley was growing tired. And for the first time in a long time, he was worried about Stockton. Usually Josiah never bothered to think about him, much less worry about him . . . but never before had he been quite so hard to find.

Over time Josiah had learned most of the places Stockton frequented when he was away from home—at least half the time anymore. Tonight he'd checked all of those places, and no Stockton. Where could the boy be?

He paused, looking up at the Livingston mansion, and realized there was one place he hadn't yet looked. Stockton had been known to hole up sometimes in one or the other of the tunnel entrances to the mansion. Maybe he was there.

If so, Josiah was almost inclined to leave him. He'd always thought the mansion was a dismal and haunted-looking place; he seldom looked at it by night without feeling a chill on the back of his neck. Now that the place had been sullied by two shooting deaths, it seemed even more frightening.

But he screwed up his courage and strode off toward the house anyway. His resolve to find his missing son was high tonight, heightened because of the humiliation he'd experienced earlier. Tonight he needed to do something he could be proud of, even if only finding his straying boy.

He circled around the back of the mansion, heading for the root cellar that was actually the entrance to the tunnel Stockton seemed to favor most as a hiding place.

Stockton Shelley was asleep, curled up on a sofa in the big parlor of the Livingston mansion, and dreaming that his father was calling him.

He cowered deep into the soft sofa. When his father called, it usually meant a beating was soon to come. Stockton murmured in his sleep and actually, through some subconscious awareness that he was dreaming, tried without success to wake up.

"Stockton! Are you here?"

His father's voice was closer now, louder, more vividly imagined than before. Stockton's heart raced.

"Stockton! Boy, are you hiding in this house? I believe you're here! Did you think I wouldn't find you? I know about the tunnels as well as you do, boy! Don't forget it!"

Stockton opened his eyes, then sat up.

Something large and dark passed him, a shadow sweeping past the sofa.

"Stockton, is that you?"

Stockton could not speak. He was terrified, and not of his father. The shadow he'd seen was actually the big Englishman Graham, who had risen from his own bed on another sofa and was moving through the darkness toward the place from which his father's voice came . . .

Stockton's mind surged ahead, putting the pieces together and sensing what was about to happen. It horrified him so much he froze, unable to move or call out.

Pa's come looking for me again. . . . He's come in here 'cause he knows there ain't nobody living here no more . . . but he don't know that there are folks here tonight after all . . . bad folks . . . dangerous folks—

He heard the sound of struggle, a yell of fright from his father, a curse from Graham. A match flared, struck by Graham, and for a second Stockton saw light play across his father's face, looking startled and bewildered by the sight of Graham before him.

"*You* again!" Graham declared.

Josiah Stockton tried to speak, but his voice was cut off suddenly, and Stockton knew Graham had grabbed him by the throat.

A hundred past fantasies of seeing his cruel father die faded away for Stockton Shelley. This was his *father,* and a bad man was hurting him . . .

"What the hell's going on down there?" Evaline called from above.

Stockton leaped up and ran to Graham, whom he

began pounding and kicking as hard as he could. Graham swore but just kept on choking Josiah Shelley.

It registered with Graham that apparently this was the boy's father. But it did not matter. Graham had never been one to abide trouble with the same man twice, no matter what the circumstances. The second time was the last . . . every time.

"Let him go!" Stockton screamed, frantic, still fighting. "He's my pa! Let him go!"

Without even looking, Graham punched a fist backward and struck Stockton right on the mouth, knocking him down, making blood spurt from a cut lip.

Stockton was up again at once, fighting Graham once more. Then strong hands pulled him away— Brown, grabbing him from behind.

"He's killing my pa!" Stockton screamed. "Let me go!"

Brown dragged him backward across the room. Stockton watched in horror as Graham brought out a knife. As dark as the room was, Stockton could make out the shape of Graham's arm rising and the blade gripped in his fist. . . .

It swung down and Josiah Shelley gasped, then moaned. Then he made no more sound at all, and Stockton knew he was gone.

"No!" he screamed. "No, no, no, no. . . ."

Somehow he managed to pull free of Brown. He lunged toward Graham, fists flailing, feet kicking. . . .

Graham cursed and brought up his knife again, then swung it down once, twice. . . .

Bleeding and hurting, Stockton staggered away,

back into a dark hallway. There was the sound of a door opening and closing again.

"Hell, Graham, you stabbed the boy!" Brown exclaimed.

"He was annoying me," Graham replied, very calm. "But confound it all, go bring him back. I'll patch his wounds. I didn't cut him severely."

Swearing, Brown went into the hallway after Stockton.

"Graham, he ain't here."

"What?"

By now Evaline and Kevington were in the room, descended from above. "Where is he?" Kevington demanded.

"I heard a door," Brown said. "Wait. . . ."

He opened a door that seemingly led into a small storage room. But a strike of the match revealed another door on the other side, and blackness beyond it, and a staircase. . . .

"He said there were tunnels and passages all through this house," Kevington said. "The boy's escaping us! Go get him. . . . Bring him back!"

Evaline and Brown obeyed at once, descending the dark staircase swiftly, vanishing into blackness.

Graham did not move. "Let him go, I say," he muttered.

"Let him go? And alert the law to our presence here . . . and to the corpse you've now blessed us with? Why the hell did you kill that man?"

"Because he found us. And because he spilled beer on me on the street tonight."

Kevington swore bitterly. Graham simply sauntered away, through the dark, and lay down on his sofa again.

Brown and Evaline returned soon after.

"He's given us the slip," Evaline reported. "The little bastard must know five or six different ways in and out of this house."

"He may go to the law," Kevington said. "That's trouble and delay we do not need. Come on. Let's gather our goods and leave here."

"In the middle of the night?"

"That's right. We have no time for entanglements with the local constabulary. We're leaving this house tonight, and at first light we'll set out to find that ghost town on our own. There can't be many roads across that mountain . . . only one, if we're fortunate. We don't need that boy to track down Kenton and Victoria. We'll get by without him."

"What if we can't find that ghost town?"

"We'll find it. We'll find it if we have to search to the very edges of hell. Now, move with haste. We must leave this house before that little escapee brings back trouble to us. I have no desire to attempt to justify the killing of an intruder, especially considering that we are intruders here ourselves."

CHAPTER

30

AFTERNOON, TWO DAYS LATER

ROXANNE GUNNISON STOOD BESIDE THE BED, watching Rachel Frye sleep, and tried to remember if she'd ever seen anyone look so pale. She reached down and lightly touched Rachel's forehead, taking care not to disturb her. Rachel was fevered. Roxanne shook her head sadly and left the room.

She walked down the hall a few yards and entered the adjacent room, where Alex was seated by the window, cleaning his pistol and looking quite somber. Outside, beyond the window, the ragged and rugged farrago of Culvertown, Colorado, was visible. Roxanne hadn't liked Culvertown when she visited it recently, and she didn't like it now.

Yet she felt they were supposed to be here. She was not a superstitious woman by nature, but finding that sketched-upon envelope in the Buckeye Cafe just a short distance down this very street had certainly seemed like a stroke of destiny to her. If not for that event, none of this would be transpiring.

"She's worse, I think," Rachel said. "The strain of all this hard travel has been too much for someone who not all that long ago was lying senseless in a hospital bed."

"We shouldn't have brought her," Gunnison said, rubbing the gun barrel gently with a lightly oiled cloth.

"Perhaps not. But it seemed the only possible thing at the time."

They were in the Culvertown Hotel, on the second floor, in the very room, in fact, that Dr. David Kevington had occupied until he and the men with him had simply vanished without paying. But Gunnison knew none of this. They had come here, arriving late the prior evening, simply because they had needed rooms after a long and wearying railroad journey across a big part of the nation, with Rachel Frye growing more weak and sick with each mile.

Now Gunnison was not quite sure what to do. Rachel needed medical care, and he'd already learned from the locals about the violent deaths of Jack Livingston and an unidentified stranger up in the Livingston mansion.

KB FOUND IN CULVERTOWN. LIVINGSTON HOUSE. PLEASE COME.

So had read the telegram Billy Connery had flashed to New York. Well, Gunnison had come, but there was no access to the Livingston house, no Billy Connery, and so far no Kenton.

He was scared out of his wits that the unidentified stranger who had died with Jack Livingston might have been Kenton.

And where the devil was Billy Connery? And why hadn't he sent a more complete and informative telegram? Did Kenton have Victoria with him up in the Livingston house? If so, where was she now?

Too many questions, too few answers, and Gunnison was growing downright irritable about it.

"She's going to need a doctor," Roxanne said.

"I know," Gunnison snapped. "I'll fetch her one, as quickly as I can. Just let me finish cleaning this pistol. Do you mind?"

Roxanne stared at him silently a moment. "No. What I do mind is having my head taken off for a mere comment."

Gunnison softened. "I'm sorry. I'm just on edge . . . and scared. I have this feeling that something has happened to Kenton. Maybe to Billy, too."

"The dead men in the Livingston house?" Gunnison had already told his wife about that bit of grim local news.

"Yes. I'm afraid Kenton might have been one of them."

"Wouldn't he have been identified, though? His face is famous."

"Everyone believes Kenton has been dead for months. They'd just assume this dead man was one who resembled him."

"What are we going to do, Alex?"

Gunnison laid his work aside and stared out the window at the street. "Well, I suppose that we need to make sure Rachel is cared for. I need to find a physician."

"Yes. I think so. She has a fever right now."

Gunnison stood, went to Roxanne, and wrapped his arms around her. "I wish I could say I felt good about all this. But I don't. Since we've gotten here I've had the worst feeling about it all. But I'm glad you're here with me. It makes it better."

She kissed him. "If Kenton is alive, we'll find hiim. And Victoria, too."

"I'm going to go find a physician for Rachel," Gunnison said.

"You're a good man, Alex Gunnison."

"I don't know about that. But I do know I'm a very worried one."

On the far side of Culvertown, a man known to most as Preacher Joe Sammons walked up a rocky hillside toward a church house he had built three years ago almost entirely by himself. It was Friday, and Sammons's habit was to spend an hour or two each Friday getting the church cleaned up for the weekend, stocking the supply of firewood. He would also pray in the empty sanctuary for each of the members of his small congregation, who at the moment were scattered out across Culvertown and its vicinity. Sammons was a big, burly man, rough and leathery, carrying on his body the scars of what had once been a rowdy and violent life. Now he was known as the gentlest, kindest, most tender man in all Culvertown, and even those who declined to set foot in his church respected him.

He never locked the building, believing it should always be open for the sake of those who wished to pray. In Culvertown there were far too few of these, but Sammons was an optimist. Someday the fire of faith would sweep across these mountains, and he intended to be there to see it. Maybe he would even be the one to spark it, if God was kind enough to give him the privilege.

The interior of the church was shadowy and cool. Sammons walked through it, the heels of his boots clumping heavily on the wooden floor. He was proud of this little building, simple as it was. Its interior was spotlessly clean, thanks to his constant attention to it, and painted a clean, oily white.

Sammons went to a closet in the corner and pulled out a broom. He began to sweep between the pews, whistling softly to himself.

Within a couple of minutes he began to get an odd feeling. He stopped sweeping.

"Hello? Is there somebody here?"

He heard the faintest kind of noise in response. Just a whisper of sound, so low that Sammons couldn't tell what it was.

"Hello?" he said again as he began winding between the pews, looking for the source of the sound.

He found it near the front, in the person of young Stockton Shelley. Sammons knew Stockton well; he'd tried many times to bring the poor boy under his influence and lessen the influence of his hard-drinking, abusive father. Sammons worried about Stockton a lot and prayed for him daily.

Stockton was curled up like an unborn child, lying on the pew on his side, staring at the back of the pew before him. His eyes were wide open, hardly blinking, and he was moving very slightly, kind of a childish rocking. There was blood on him, crusted and rusty-colored.

"Stockton, son, what's happened to you?" Sammons said, kneeling between the pews and laying a hand gently on Stockton's shoulder. Stockton flinched at the touch, his eyes still fixed.

"Stockton, it's me: Preacher Joe. It's all right. . . . You can talk to me."

Stockton continued to stare, hardly seeming aware that Sammons was there.

Sammons moved, lowering his head so that his face came into the line of view of Stockton's staring eyes. He looked into the boy's face a few moments and noticed a subtle change. Stockton looked at him, and his lips began to tremble.

Sammons smiled and nodded. "That's right, Stockton. It's just me. I'll help you out, no matter what's wrong."

Stockton began to cry. His lips moved.

"What's that? I didn't hear."

"He's dead," Stockton whispered.

"Who?"

"My pa. He's dead."

Sammons developed a terrible suspicion. This boy, threatened and abused, had killed his own father! That might account for the blood.

"Let's sit you up and take a look at you, Stockton."

Stockton sat up. Sammons saw the cuts in his shirt that told him the dried blood was at least in part Stockton's own. Someone had knifed this boy.

"Did your pa do this to you?"

Stockton shook his head.

"How long have you been hiding here?"

"I don't remember."

"Come on, son. We're going to get you to Doc Asheman. He'll look you over and see what needs fixing, all right?"

Stockton did not reply but did stand. The poor boy was weak and deep in some sort of numbing shock, mind and body, and Sammons wondered what this boy had experienced, and seen, to make him be this way. The Stockton Shelley he had always known was cocksure and sarcastic, hiding fear and loneliness behind a mask of bravado . . . a far cry from the pitiful creature Sammons saw now.

Stockton made it out of the church and down the hill, then slumped to the ground, too weak to continue.

"Don't worry about it, Stockton," Sammons said. "I'll carry you to my house and hitch up the wagon. Then you can lie down and I'll take you in to Dr. Asheman."

CHAPTER

31

ROXANNE SAT ON THE EDGE OF RACHEL'S BED AND wondered how long it would take for her husband to locate a physician in this town. It seemed to her that Rachel's fever was mounting, and she looked worse by the hour.

Hurry, Alex.

Rachel opened her eyes. "I feel like I'm aflame," she said.

"I'll get something to cool you," Roxanne told her. "And Alex will be back soon, with a physician, I hope. He's out looking now."

"You're very kind to me."

"You're our friend, Rachel. It's our pleasure to be kind. Would you like me to bathe your brow with a damp cloth?"

"Yes, mum, if you don't mind."

"Of course I don't mind." Roxanne looked around for a cloth but could not find one. But she recalled that a handkerchief lay on the chest in her and Alex's room next door.

"I'll be right back," she said to Rachel, and went to get the handkerchief.

A minute later, she was seated on the bedside again, the cloth dampened by water from the basin. She dabbed it lightly on Rachel's hot brow.

"Thank you so much," Rachel said. "It's wonderfully cool."

Roxanne smiled and dipped the handkerchief in the basin again. As she did so, she noticed something she had not before.

"Well, that's a surprise," she said. "I didn't realize that Alex had monogrammed handkerchiefs . . . but wait a moment. These aren't Alex's initials."

On the corner of the white handkerchief were the embroidered and highly stylized initials *D. K.*

Rachel turned her head and looked at the handkerchief. "Oh . . . dear God. . . ."

"What is it?"

"The letters . . . they are the same as those on Dr. Kevington's house!"

"Dr. David Kevington? *That* Dr. Kevington?"

"Yes! The shape of the letters, the way they are . . . it's exactly the same! I grew up seeing those letters above the door of his house. . . . I know those letters. The handkerchief has to be his!"

"Rachel, it hardly seems likely. This handkerchief was on the chest of drawers in my room. I assumed it was one Alex had placed there."

"He is here, Roxanne. That is his handkerchief."

"Please, Rachel. Don't say that. You know there

are many people with those initials. If the style is the same, it's only coincidence."

"No . . . he's here. He's come here for the same reason we have, to find Brady Kenton and Victoria! He's here!"

Rachel was drifting toward hysteria . . . and Roxanne was beginning to wonder if she might be right. If Kevington had set an agent to following them all the way to New York, why should it be unlikely that he would come to this town if he, too, had found evidence that Kenton and Victoria were here?

"Rachel, please try not to worry. We don't really know why this handkerchief is here, or whose it is. Alex will be back soon. . . . We'll show it to him. Now, would you like me to bathe your brow some more?"

"Not with that cloth."

Roxanne forced out a smile. "Very well. I'll find another."

Gunnison learned the location of Dr. Asheman's office from a woman sweeping the porch of her cabin. He walked there with a broad and fast stride, not only because of his concern for Rachel but also because of the inexplicable sense of something being amiss.

He climbed the stairs to the office and knocked on the door. No answer. He looked through the window on the door but couldn't see anything through the curtain.

Glancing down, he saw that a little hand-lettered

placard had fallen from the window to his feet. BACK IN FIFTEEN MINUTES.

Well, it would help to know whether the fifteen-minute count started ten minutes ago or one. Either way, he'd wait.

He tried opening the door and found it unlocked. He pushed it open a foot and found himself looking into an outer office, off of which two other doors opened. One of them was ajar. "Hello?" he said, in case the doctor was back in that room and hadn't heard his first knock.

In reply he heard a faint groan. Probably a patient back there.

"Doctor? Is that you?"

The groan was a little louder this time . . . and there was something about it that caught his attention.

Gunnison paused, then said, "Are you all right?"

Not a groan this time, but a word, barely whispered and very hoarse: "Alex?"

Gunnison was stunned. . . . Then he recognized the voice.

He burst into the office and went straight to the back room. "Billy?"

"Alex. . . ."

Sure enough, it was Billy Connery back there. He was thin and weak and bandaged and trying to sit up. His right hand lightly gripped a bandage around his throat.

"Merciful heaven, Billy, what happened to you?"

"Throat . . . my throat was cut. . . ."

Gunnison gaped. "Your throat was cut. . . . Who? Why?"

"Can hardly . . . talk . . . couldn't talk . . . at all until . . . yesterday. . . ."

Gunnison scrambled about until he found a notepad and pencil. "Here, Billy . . . write it down. Take your time. . . . Don't try to talk."

Connery nodded. Gunnison helped him sit up, the exertion of that alone causing Billy to wince and become pale as the blood drained away from his head.

"Billy, tell me one thing: did you actually meet Kenton?"

Connery shook his head.

"But he was here?"

Connery whispered, "Yes. . . ."

"Don't say anything more. Just write."

Gunnison grabbed a chair and pulled it up to Connery's bedside. Forgotten now were Rachel's fever and his promise to Roxanne to hurry back with the doctor.

He sat squirming, as keyed up as a child awaiting a gift, as Billy Connery began to write.

CHAPTER

32

DR. DAVID KEVINGTON, TIRED, DIRTY, SUNBURNED, and angry, swore loudly and sat down on a boulder beside the trail. Or was it a trail or just a path made by the passing of wild game? He and his companions had crossed the mountain in the darkness and lost the road in the process, and now they'd wandered so far and lost themselves so thoroughly in the wilderness that it was easy to imagine that there never had been a human presence in this region at all.

"We're going to have to go back to Culvertown," Evaline said. "This ain't working. We're not going to find that ghost town . . . if there is any such damn place. I think we've been lied to."

"I'm hungrier than a redskin in winter," Brown said. "We've ate up every bit of food we brought, and the last stream I drank out of tasted like a buffalo had pissed in it. I say we go back. If there really is such a town as Caylee, we can find out how to get there and not just wander through all the backside of Pharaoh's Egypt to find it . . . or not find it."

Kevington looked at him bitterly. "I'll not turn back without finding Kenton."

"Begging your almighty pardon, sir, and with all due respect to you for the good wages you're paying us, it seems to me you'll be a damn sight more likely to find Kenton by going back than by going forward."

"And do you know the way back, Mr. Evaline?"

"I know where the mountaintop is. I know how to look for smoke plumes to tell me where the town is. The trouble with Caylee is that it's a ghost town, and you don't see smoke plumes from ghost towns."

"He's right, Dr. Kevington," Brown said. "If there's an abandoned town hereabouts, you'd think we'd find more trails. And if Kenton was holed up there, you'd think he'd build a fire every now and then. There'd be smoke. But there's been no smoke on this side of the mountain."

"We need to go back, sir," Evaline said. "We'll find Kenton a lot faster going back than going forward. If he's here to be found at all. He's had enough time he could have taken her a long distance. We've been looking out here for two days, sir."

"We've got to go back," Brown affirmed again.

"Go back?" Kevington said, chuckling. "So you think we would go back? Might I remind you what we left lying on the floor of that mansion? A dead body. Two days ago. That body surely has been found by now. And keep in mind that the boy got away. He fled, stabbed but alive, and fully able to talk. If we go back to Culvertown, we go back to face arrest."

Brown and Evaline stared at him, frowning, apparently having not thought of this before.

Kevington looked back at them with contempt. "You were supposed to be the best, the most clever, the most persistent, the most heartless when the situation called for it. But now I must wonder. If you are representative of the best that this nation offers, then I stand astounded that the colonies managed to ever win the war." He laughed coldly. "What do you think, Graham?"

"Actually, sir, I'm not thinking of much at all," Graham replied. He'd been sitting in silence on a log nearby, smoking his pipe. "I've been too busy watching that smoke rise yonder."

It took a moment for the significance to sink in. "Smoke?" Kevington stood and turned.

Miles away, a thin line of smoke rose toward the sky where none had been before.

Kevington smiled. "Gentlemen, I believe we just found the town of Caylee."

Kenton knelt by the fireplace, slowly turning the spit upon which he had speared three rabbits. The scent was mouthwateringly good. He'd snared the rabbits during the afternoon, desperate to provide himself and Victoria with meat.

The little bit of food they had brought with them out of Livingston's mansion was almost gone.

Kenton worried about the fire, though. He'd deliberately avoided building one as long as he and Victoria had been here . . . until now, when the necessities of cooking forced it. With any luck he would get the cooking quickly done and the fire out and no one would notice the plume.

In the absence of such evidence as smoke plumes, Kenton actually felt relatively safe here. With much searching and great exertion, he had finally managed to find the house that Jack had used for his illicit romantic dalliances. It was quite a feat of engineering, in its way: a house that looked run-down and barren from the outside but which was actually quite livable inside. It was funny, in its way, Jack having gone to this trouble just to keep his love affair secret. It reflected his eccentricity.

Now the place was protection for Kenton and Victoria. Kenton could only hope it was protection enough.

He was eager to leave here, but Victoria was tired, weak, not ready for travel. And where would they go? Anywhere they went, Kevington would follow.

For now Kenton refused to think further than the next hour or so. At the moment all that mattered was roasting these rabbits and feeding himself and his wife, who slept now on a bed in the other room of this two-room house. Then he would put out the fire and worry about the next hour when it came.

But at some point, this had to end. He would have to deal with Kevington in a final way. There would have to be a showdown.

But how, with Victoria to be protected? She was a woman strong of heart but not of body.

Kenton stared into the flames, watching the rabbits

roast, and prayed for guidance, for help, and for rescue.

And he prayed that if Kevington was out there somewhere, still looking, he would not find this house.

CHAPTER

33

THE FIFTEEN-MINUTE ABSENCE OF DR. ASHEMAN HAD stretched to nearly an hour by the time Billy Connery put down his pen and handed the pad to Alex Gunnison.

His work as an illustrator had given Connery the gift of a nimble pen. Despite his weak condition, he managed with succinctness and celerity to present Gunnison a written account of what had happened to him since his arrival at Culvertown. His account ended with his being stabbed and slashed by the man McCurden, who had initially presented himself to Connery as one Jim Grant.

Gunnison read the account quickly, then again more slowly. "So we really don't know what has become of Kenton," he said. "You never actually saw him yourself."

"No," Connery whispered.

At that point the outer door opened. Someone strode across the room and entered Connery's bedroom. It was a tall, tired-looking man, who was startled to see Gunnison there. He approached him with an outstretched hand and a serious look upon his face.

"My name is Asheman. This is my clinic. I gather you've talked to my patient."

"Yes. . . . I'm Gunnison, Alexander Gunnison. I work with your patient."

"I hope you haven't had him talking much. His throat was slashed and it's too early for him to be using his voice. He's lucky to have a voice at all."

"Yes. Don't worry. I've had him writing rather than speaking."

"How did you know he was here?"

"I didn't. Finding him was a surprise. I actually came looking for you, Doctor."

"You're ill?"

"No. But there is a woman at the hotel, Miss Rachel Frye, who is fevered and in need of your help."

Asheman sighed. It had been a long day already. "Very well. I'll go to her. But tell me, is she—"

The outer door of the office literally burst inward with a crash.

"Asheman! Doc, are you here?"

Asheman headed out the door. "I'm here, Preacher. What's—oh, my goodness."

Sammons carried in his arms the blood-crusted, weakened form of Stockton Shelley.

"The boy's been stabbed, Doc. But not just now. . . . I found him hiding in the church. He says he can't remember how long he's been there."

"Get him on the table there, and help me cut those clothes off him." Asheman turned to Gunnison, who had also come out into the outer office. "Sir, unless that fevered woman is in the most severe condition, I'm afraid I must make a priority of this case."

"Indeed, Doctor. Miss Frye can wait. Perhaps, given the situation you face, I should try to bring her here rather than you go there."

"If you please, sir, I'll go to her. I've got only two beds here, and young Stockton is about to occupy the second one."

Asheman turned his attention to Stockton; Gunnison turned to go back into the room where Connery was . . . but Connery had gotten up and had entered the front room, leaning against the wall to keep from falling.

Asheman noticed what was happening. "Connery! What the devil . . . Get back in that bed before you collapse!"

Connery staggered forward instead. He had heard it all from the back room but had to confirm with his own eyes that it was Stockton Shelley in the room. He went to the table where Stockton had been placed. Asheman continued to protest, but Connery did not even hear him.

Stockton looked up and saw Connery. A spark of life returned to what had been a lusterless gaze.

"It's you. . . . I know you."

"What happened, Stockton?" Connery's voice sounded horrible, hardly audible at all.

Asheman swore and might have physically pushed Connery away had he not been in such bad shape. "What the devil is going on here? My patients are fraternizing now? Get back in that bed before you tear your wounds open again, Connery!"

Connery turned to Gunnison. His words came out riding the crests of his weak gasps of air. "This boy . . . is the one . . . who told me where . . . to find Kenton."

"Quit trying to talk!" the doctor barked, only to be ignored yet again.

Gunnison came closer to the table. Connery had described his encounter with Stockton in the written account he'd given to Gunnison. "Do you know where Kenton is?" he asked Stockton.

"I must insist . . ." Asheworth began, only to be cut off by Stockton.

"He was in the mansion. . . . Now there are men in town who are chasing him. They hurt me. And they murdered my father." Some emotional dam broke inside Stockton, and he began to cry. "They murdered my father!"

Now even Asheman was drawn in. "Your father has been killed, Stockton?"

"Yes. . . . He's in the mansion. . . . They tried to murder me, too."

Stockton's wailed declarations would have sounded hard to believe except for the evidence of the wounds on his small and pale body.

"Where is Kenton now?" Gunnison asked Stockton.

"Who is Kenton?" the doctor asked, only to be ignored.

"In Caylee," Stockton replied. "I think he is in Caylee. The men chasing him were going to go there. . . . They were going to pay me to take them."

Asheman seized control again. "That's enough, all of you!" He barked an order to Gunnison: "Help Connery get back to his bed, and for God's sake don't let him open his own wounds!" He turned to Sammons. "You'd best go fetch the marshal. This boy is talking about a murder having occurred, and if he's right, I don't think it's even been detected yet."

Sammons nodded and headed for the door without a word.

The doctor looked at Gunnison. "You may as well make yourself useful. Get that fool back into bed before he kills himself, then come help me with my patient."

CHAPTER

34

BY THE TIME GUNNISON RETURNED TO THE HOTEL almost three hours after he had left, his wife was over-whelmed with worry.

"Thank God!" she said as she embraced him. "I was afraid that Kevington had gotten you. He was here . . . right in this hotel, in the very room we've rented. At least, Rachel is sure he was. We found a handkerchief with his monogram that had been left on the dresser."

Gunnison, so laden with news of his own, could hardly find room in his mental basket to accommodate yet another item. But he knew there was not an im-mediate need to worry about Kevington, because he knew where Kevington almost certainly was.

"Where's the doctor?" Roxanne asked, only just then noticing that Gunnison had returned alone.

"The doctor is very occupied with two patients he has bedded down in his clinic across town. How is Rachel?"

"Doing better on her own, I'm glad to say. She's

sleeping now, and her fever is down. But tell me why these two patients are so important that the doctor refused to come see a sick woman?"

"Don't judge him harshly. From a medical standpoint he made the right decision, I have no doubt, because these patients are quite injured. One of them is a little street boy named Stockton Shelley, who has—listen to this!—been in contact with Kevington himself. And he is reasonably sure he knows where Kevington has gone . . . and where Kenton is. The other patient is Billy Connery."

"Billy! Why is he being treated?"

"Because somebody—one of Kevington's hired agents—cut his throat. He was left for dead in an alley, but survived, thank God."

"Oh, mercy! He'll live?"

"Amazingly, yes. The doctor said he was fortunate to fall in the way he did. The cut in his throat, maybe not as deep as his attacker thought, was held closed by the angle of his head when he passed out in the alley. Someone found him and got him to the doctor, and he's slowly getting better."

"How did he manage to get into a row with one of Kevington's agents?"

"It's a long story, one built of this piece and that, most of which I've only just learned. Billy has provided me what he knows and experienced, and the little Shelley boy has contributed what he knows—including his witnessing of the murder of his own father by an agent of Kevington."

"Murder! Oh, Alex! This grows worse by the moment."

"Yes. And it may grow worse yet. Kevington may have already found Kenton and Victoria. And he has three hired guns with him. . . . They wouldn't have stood a chance."

"I think I need to sit down."

"Do. Let's both sit down, and I'll tell you what I've learned. This is cobbled together from assorted pieces of information, like I said, and I'll try to order it for you as I go. Forgive me if I backtrack some; it makes it easier to give you the context of what has happened.

"We already know from Rachel how the English side of this affair fell out: Kenton enters the house, finds Victoria but is caught by Kevington and made a prisoner, but still he manages to sneak word out to Rachel that she should flee back to the United States. She does, but her ship goes down off the coast. She is injured and goes into an extended, anonymous hospitalization in New York, unconscious much of that time, and of course is unable for a long time to contact us. When at last she does, you have also returned from your trip to Colorado, and have stumbled across that sketch that makes us realize Kenton is hiding here in Culvertown.

"All right. So I send Billy Connery to Culvertown, and he manages to learn very quickly, mostly from this little Stockton Shelley character, that Kenton really is in Culvertown and hiding out in the mansion of Jack Livingston, who, if I recall, has family ties to

Victoria. Kenton never talked much about that, but I'm sure I'm right. Anyway, Billy doesn't realize that an agent of Kevington's had already been sent to look for clues in St. Louis among Kenton's professional and personal circles, and this agent, named McCurtin or McCurden or something such as that, learns that Billy has run off to Culvertown and figures out that he might be coming because of Kenton. So McCurden follows right on Billy's heels, apparently follows Billy around town in secret, and learns along with Billy that Kenton really is holed up in the Livingston house.

"McCurden intercepts Billy before he can get up to the mansion and leaves him for dead with his throat cut in an alley. My guess is McCurden had come up with the idea of capturing Victoria for himself and holding her hostage, making Kevington pay him high dollar to get her back. But something goes wrong, and McCurden gets himself killed up in the mansion, along with Jack Livingston. My guess is the pair killed each other. Kenton and Victoria disappear, knowing now that Kevington is very seriously pursuing them. They head across the mountain for an abandoned mining town called Caylee. We guess this, anyway, because they happened to be spotted by young Shelley, heading in that direction, and apparently Jack Livingston had a sort of secret second dwelling there, a place they might logically go to hide in.

"Apparently McCurden must have telegraphed Kevington that he'd found Kenton, because Kevington and a couple of agents show up in town and begin going around looking for McCurden and bringing up the name of Brady Kenton, too. Stockton Shelley learns about this and decides he'll go tell Kevington— for a price—where he can find Brady Kenton. Kevington agrees to hire the boy for a guide to get them to Caylee, which apparently is a hard place to find, and the whole gaggle of them sneak up and hide out in the Livingston house, which of course is empty at that point. Stockton told me that one of Kevington's men was sent to find out whether one of the two men killed in the mansion earlier was McCurden. The fellow comes back and says that it was.

"Later on, Stockton's father goes hunting for him, and one of the places he looks is the mansion, because he knows Stockton has hid there in the past. One of Kevington's agents kills the man, before Stockton's eyes. Stockton attacks him, gets knifed up himself, but manages to get away. He's hurt, weak, sick with grief over his father's murder, and he goes to hide in a church, where the preacher found him earlier today. The preacher hauled him to the doctor at the same time I was there, looking for help for Rachel. And of course I'd stumbled across Billy Connery there as well and was getting a lot of this information from him even as they were coming in. After the doctor finished patching up Stockton, I interviewed the boy . . . and that's how all the pieces came together."

"It's astonishing . . . but where is Kevington?"

"Gone. I suspect he and his agents decided to go find Caylee on their own, since they lost Stockton.

And they've had about two days to find the place . . . and Kenton."

She thought about that somberly. "Maybe Kenton and Victoria didn't go there after all. Maybe they just kept moving."

"We can only hope. But I'm going to Caylee to see, Roxanne. I have to know if Kenton and Victoria are there."

"But Kevington is out there. . . . You could be in danger! You mustn't go alone. . . . You have to take an officer of the law with you."

"That option has been explored. All this news was borne to the town marshal before I came here, and he was uninterested in anything except that there is another corpse up in the mansion. As for Kenton, the marshal believes what the rest of the world does: that he's dead. Besides, he said, Caylee isn't in his jurisdiction."

"But you can't go alone!"

"I won't. I'm taking a man with me. He knows where Caylee is, and he's a good man in a fight. Says that when he fights, God fights with him."

"Who is this man?"

"His name is Sammons. He's the preacher who found the boy hiding in his church. And he tells me that when he has to be, he can be mean as the devil for the sake of righteousness."

"Can you trust him? And can a preacher really be a fighter?"

"This one can, I believe. You'll know what I mean when you see him."

"Will he come here?"

"Yes. Before dawn tomorrow. He's bringing me a horse and saddle and rifle. At first light, he and I will ride out for Caylee."

Kenton opened his eyes and sat up in the bed, drawing in a gasp of air. He stared into the darkness, unsure what had awakened him.

Beside him, Victoria stirred a little but did not wake up. He looked at her, barely able to see her outline in the dark room, and said a quiet prayer of thanks that, since they had come to Caylee, she had allowed him to sleep in her bed.

Kenton remained quiet, unmoving, trying to figure out what had made him wake up. And he wondered, too, why he felt so afraid right now.

He'd spent a lifetime trusting his instincts, so he didn't dismiss the alarm sounding in his mind. He quietly slipped out of bed and crept to the door. He opened it and passed through.

He was not outside. Jack Livingston's clever interior construction involved what was essentially a house within a house, walls erected a few feet back from the actual exterior walls, creating a box that hid everything inside, including most light.

Kenton was outside that box now and moved carefully. He slipped toward the nearest window and looked out into the night. He saw nothing. He went to the other side of the house and looked out a window there.

Quickly he ducked again, his heart rising in his chest.

He crept back to the door to the inner part of the dwelling and reentered. He went to Victoria's side.

"Victoria, dear, wake up . . . quietly. They've come. They're here . . . and we must do nothing to alert them as to where we are."

It took a couple of moments for her to comprehend.

"David is here?"

"Yes. With others. And they're looking for us right now."

CHAPTER

35

SAMMONS WAS THERE EVEN EARLIER THAN PROMISED, bringing good horses, rifles, and the news that he'd just spent an hour praying for their mission. He was confident God would give them the victory . . . but he wasn't sure it would be a bloodless one.

"I can assure you it probably will not be, if we actually encounter Kevington," Gunnison said, out of earshot of his wife. "He will fight to the death before he'll let Kenton take away the woman he sees as his."

"She was a stolen woman, you said?" Sammons had been filled in by Gunnison the day before, but it had been a lot to absorb and he still didn't seem fully cognizant of it all.

"She was stolen, and hidden away in England for years, with Kenton believing she was dead."

"That's a great sin indeed. And this is a righteous battle."

"I can only hope it isn't a battle already completed. If Kevington found them . . ."

"Have faith, my friend. I believe we'll find them safe and sound."

"Why are you doing this?" Gunnison asked the preacher.

"Because I'm able to. I'm a good fighter, Mr. Gunnison. There was a time when I used that fighting skill in the wrong ways. I hurt people, hurt them bad. I've even killed men, sir. It was always what folks called 'fair fights,' but I can tell you that I'd have killed them all the same, fair fight or not. I regret all that. So now, I'm going to fight the good fight."

"Even for a stranger?"

"Brady Kenton a stranger? Everybody in the land knows and loves Brady Kenton."

Gunnison said good-bye to his wife and to Rachel, who without the help of a physician now seemed to be mending fast. They did not linger on their farewell or allow themselves to discuss the darker possibilities that lay ahead.

As Gunnison and Sammons rode out of town, Roxanne felt bitterly guilty for the thought that flashed without bidding through her mind: *If it is destined for Kevington to find Kenton and Victoria, I hope it's already happened. I want my husband to come back safe.*

She watched them ride away, their shadows stretching long in the light of the rising sun.

When the rising of the sun was a fading memory of an expired morning, Dr. David Kevington, exhausted, hungry, and frustrated, plopped down on the edge of a rotting boardwalk and shook his head. Graham was near, probably as hungry and perhaps as frustrated, but he seldom let his feelings show.

On down the street, Evaline and Brown were searching through empty buildings. They'd been complaining for the last hour, declaring that Kenton obviously was not in this town. Time to move on. The man had escaped and taken his woman with him, and Kevington would just have to accept it.

Kevington was not about to accept it. He would search this ghost town until every possible hiding place was ferreted out. If Brown and Evaline wished to be relieved of their duty, he'd be glad to oblige them with two quick shots to their heads. Right now it would be cathartic to do it.

Graham brought out his pipe and loaded it slowly. "Let me ask you something, Doc," he said. "Just to make sure I have my facts straight. You and Brady Kenton's wife were on a train together, and it crashed. Many years ago."

"I was on the same train. We were not together."

"Coincidence?"

"Not coincidence. I was following her."

"I see." He lit the pipe. "Following the wife of another man."

"She was his wife in the legal sense. But in the eyes of heaven she has always been my wife. She was meant for me."

"But she married another."

"She said words before a clergyman. I attach no significance to it."

"But Kenton obviously did. When he found out she was alive, he came all the way across the ocean to get her."

"What is your point, Graham?"

"I must say I admire Kenton for what he did. He showed a husband's true devotion, just as my father showed to my mother, may God rest them."

"A husband's true devotion, Mr. Graham, is what you see being carried out before your eyes at this moment. Do you think what Kenton did was remarkable? Look at what I've done! It was I who dared to claim the woman who was intended for me! It was I who saved her life and gave her a home, and love, and care, for so many years. Now I've followed her across an ocean again, and hired an army of men to find her and rescue her from her kidnapper."

"So it's Kenton who is the kidnapper."

Kevington studied Graham a few moments, then said, "This conversation will end. Now."

At that moment, three shots blasted from down the street, and they heard Brown scream in a remarkably high-pitched voice.

Kevington came to his feet and Graham knocked the ashes from his pipe. They picked up their rifles and trotted down the street in the direction from which the gunfire had come.

Unseen by them and at the far edge of Caylee, Alex Gunnison and Joe Sammons reined their tired horses to a halt and looked at each other.

"Gunfire, three shots," Gunnison said.

Two more shots rang out; it seemed they could hear a man screaming.

"Ride in or on foot?" Gunnison asked.

Sammons thought for a moment. "Ride into that barn there and leave the horses. On foot the rest of the way. We don't know what we're getting into."

CHAPTER

36

BRADY KENTON WAS TRYING HARD TO FEEL BAD FOR the man he'd just shot through the gut, but he just didn't have it in him. The man had been about to shoot him. It was a true case of self-defense.

More than that, it was defense of Victoria. She was hidden on the upper floor of what once had been a saloon. She and Kenton had slipped out of Jack Livingston's well-disguised house an hour ago, when Kevington and his searchers drew near and Kenton had been sure they were about to be detected.

Livingston had built himself a sort of trapdoor that opened onto a stone-floored area beneath the house upon which firewood was stored. The trapdoor, intended as a convenient way to bring wood in on cold days, had proved just as convenient as an escape route for a pursued man and woman.

Kenton had lodged Victoria in the upstairs of the former saloon, then had taken the role of the killdeer bird, allowing himself to be seen so that he could draw his pursuers away from where Victoria was hidden.

If Kevington got his hands on Victoria, it would be over. Kenton would be killed forthwith and Victoria hauled away, this time never to escape.

"Brown!" the second of the two gunmen yelled. "Brown, how bad you hit?"

"I'm gut-shot, Evaline! Help me, please . . ."

Kenton actually did feel sorry for the man now. He was writhing about in the dirt. He'd been emerging from an alley when he'd spotted Kenton trying to take cover behind a rusted piece of old mining equipment. Brown had prepared to take a shot at Kenton but had taken a slug through the gut instead. He was doomed. Wounds of this sort a man did not recover from.

With a new round levered into the chamber of the Winchester he'd taken from Jack Livingston's mansion, Kenton watched Brown slow in his writhing and go quiet and still. He felt an odd sensation. It had been many years since he had been forced to kill a man, and it was not a pleasant feeling, even though the man he'd killed would have gladly killed him.

Now Kenton turned his attention to the other man, the one named Evaline. He'd heard him but not seen him, and there were plenty of places about in which a man could hide. Evaline might be sneaking up on him right now, even taking a bead.

Kenton was too edgy to stay put, and he was still too close to the saloon where Victoria hid. He'd hurriedly instructed her to keep deathly quiet, no matter what happened to him. If he died, she was to remain hidden until Kevington and his men were gone, then make her way back across to Culvertown, being sure to avoid Kevington, and wire Alex Gunnison at the *Illustrated American.*

But Kenton didn't intend to die here. He would fight his way out of this, no matter what it took. He'd not spent more than two decades searching out his stolen wife only to have Kevington rob him of her again by killing him.

Kenton rose and scrambled toward an old woodshed that was overgrown with ivy. A shot fired, the bullet singing past him. He caught a glimpse of the powderburst from the corner of his left eye.

Kenton dropped, rolled behind the woodshed, then scrambled back up and fired off a quick shot at the place he'd seen the powderburst. He saw Evaline dodge back behind a tree.

No sign of Kevington and the other man with him. Good in one way, bad in another. What if they had found Victoria?

Evaline popped off another shot at Kenton. The corner of the shed shuddered and splinters blasted off in all directions, stinging Kenton's face.

Victoria huddled in the corner of the old saloon loft, wincing every time she heard a shot. She was terrified for Kenton and full of hatred for David Kevington. She vowed that if her husband died, she would personally see that Kevington died as well, no matter what it took to bring it about.

She heard another round of shots, then the sound of feet pounding up the street outside.

Victoria pulled herself into an even smaller, tighter human ball, wishing she could simply vanish, and take her husband with her.

She prayed hard . . . and then heard something that caused her to cease to breathe for several seconds straight.

Somebody was downstairs, just below. A thumping sound . . . feet on the stairs?

She had to look, and did. With great relief she saw that the thumping was simply a loose hanging board, swinging in a breeze.

Encouraged, she moved to a window and carefully looked out. The street below was empty . . . but then she saw movement.

Her breath failed her again. David Kevington was down there, along with a man she did not recognize. They were both armed and heading up the street to the place where Kenton was still fighting.

Victoria wanted to weep. Kenton was one man, fighting impossible odds.

All because of her.

Kenton had left her with a pistol, to defend herself in case she was found.

She looked out the window, watching Kevington advance, and the man with him. The gunfight up the street was continuing . . . and now she saw even more men, two more, moving in on foot through an alley, coming from the other side of town.

How many men had Kevington brought? How

could Kenton be expected to single-handedly fight away four, five men?

Victoria said another fast prayer, checked her pistol, and turned to descend the stairs.

Kenton was lifting the rifle to fire at Evaline when he got a shot off first. The bullet struck Kenton's rifle in the stock, shattering it and inflicting a cut on his jaw. The rifle shivered out of Kenton's hands and fell, useless, to the ground.

Evaline laughed and emerged, coming in for the kill.

Kenton drew his pistol, stepped out, crouched, aimed, and shot Evaline through the forehead, two fast shots.

Even as Evaline fell dead, another shot blasted from up the street. Kenton's leg kicked out from beneath him, and he fell with a grunt. It was as if someone had just driven a hot metal stake through his calf.

Kenton saw him then: David Kevington, rifle in hand, coming toward him. Beside him was another man, also armed, this rifle smoking. Kenton knew who had shot him.

He lifted his pistol and fired at the man, narrowly missing him. A second shot did better.

Graham let out a yell as Kenton's bullet passed through his middle. He looked down, watching blood gout from the bullet hole, and shook his head. "I think you're on your own now, Doctor," he said to Kevington, and then pitched down on his face.

Kevington, seeing Kenton raising his pistol again,

headed for the nearest alley. Kenton fired at him, once, twice, missing both times.

The next click of the trigger fell on an empty cylinder. Kevington heard it and stopped in his tracks. He turned, facing Kenton, and laughed. "Well, my old nemesis!" he said. "It seems that the worm has suddenly turned!" Kevington advanced toward Kenton, working the lever of his rifle. "Where should I put the first bullet, my friend? Your leg? Your shoulder? Your gut?"

Kevington came right up to Kenton, who was about to make it onto his feet again. At the last moment, though, Kevington kicked Kenton's injured leg and made him fall again.

Kevington leaned over and glared down at the man he hated above all others. "I should have dealt with you in England when I had the chance. Too merciful, that's my problem. It always has been. Well, Kenton . . . it's time to say good-bye. I don't know where you've stashed Victoria, but I'll find her. For now, seeing you die is enough."

Kevington aimed his rifle at Kenton's forehead, squinting down the barrel.

Kenton shoved the rifle to the side just as it fired and wrenched it away, so hard he took some of the hide off Kevington's fingers. Kevington roared in anger and tried to grab the rifle again, but Kenton pounded him back with it, then flipped the rifle in the air. He levered it. . . .

Before Kenton could fire, Victoria did. Her bullet caught Kevington between the shoulder blades. He grunted loudly, turned, and sank to his knees.

"Victoria . . . dear God, Victoria . . ." He gaped at her, unable to believe the woman he had come this far to find had just shot him.

Victoria, trembling now, dropped the pistol. Kevington stared at it, then reached into his pocket and pulled out a small hideout gun. He lifted it, aimed it at Victoria . . .

From a kneeling posture, Preacher Joe Sammons fired three shots in succession, each of them striking in the area of David Kevington's heart.

Kevington fell straight back, dead well before his head bounced on the earth. Victoria fainted, and Kenton managed to rise.

Sammons stood slowly, bowed his head, and prayed for the soul of the man he had just killed.

Alex Gunnison was running up the street toward Kenton. "Kenton!" he shouted. "Kenton!" There was no need to say anything else.

Kenton's calf was bleeding, but he managed to stand upon it, even stagger forward. He was headed for Victoria.

Gunnison met him, threw his arms around him.

"Alex, where did you come from?"

"It's a long story . . . but there will be plenty of time to tell it. Thank God you're all right. Thank God!"

Kenton sat on the ground beside Victoria, who was reviving. She looked at him. "It's over?"

"Yes," he said. "It's over."

She smiled.

Gunnison touched Kenton on the shoulder and smiled at him and Victoria. "Come on," he said. "It's time for us all to go home."